BRIDES
of the
GAUNTLET

BRIDES
of the
GAUNTLET
·SONS OF THE NEW WORLD·

·JAMES SHORT·

For my mother
June Marcy Short

PART I—1744

THE RAG AND BONE POOR OF LONDON

"'Tis a miracle again, Mistress Kate!" Mrs. Pinnock, the tenement's self-appointed bringer of bad news and authority on neighborhood oddities, trumpeted as she barged through the door of the small apartment. The candle brightened momentarily in the rush of fresh air. A rat nibbling a flake of rotting plaster fallen from the ceiling was displaced and scurried into a gap between the floorboard and the wall.

Julian tried to disappear into the bedclothes as his mother—Mistress Kate—instinctively shielded his narrow truckle bed. After a nudging by the formidable Mrs. Pinnock who had brought what appeared to be a bowl of two-day-old porridge as an offering to their sparse larder, she stepped aside to reveal the pale wispy miracle.

"Yes, Mistress Pinnock, my poor darling's fever broke at last." His mother sighed the familiar sigh which comes after a wakeful night of tears. "The blisters is burst and already scabbed over, and it don't seem he'll be too badly pitted. Dear me, I think I wore out God's ear praying for my little Julian. I doubt he has passed altogether two of his fourteen years free of contagion or distemper."

"What a brave child!" Mrs. Pinnock bent down, bringing her large red face within inches of Julian's. "Don't he get them all—lung fever, grippe, typhus, shakes, fits, agues, fluxes, vomitings, and now smallpox?" She enumerated, not suppressing her morbid glee. "Whole blocks of humanity wiped clean by pestilence, and your Julian sweats and coughs, loses flesh until the skin covering his bones is mere parchment, yet he lives. As I say, 'tis a miracle. Would it were his father been such a hardy weed."

Mistress Kate briefly hung her head. Although his father was carried away by spotted fever before Julian reached the age of understanding, his presence still hovered in their shabby tenement rooms. At odd moments, out of loneliness perhaps, his mother addressed Julian as if he were her husband, her dear Mr. Stephen Asher. She would explain that although life had not turned out as they hoped, she was raising their Julian to be a good man. She was teaching him to read and do sums as her dear scholar had taught her. She feared that his long illnesses made him a solitary dreamy boy, but wasn't it better that the London ragamuffins, ignorant of letters or morals, didn't lure him into their unwholesome company? She prayed daily to God and to her Stephen who must be nearby in heaven for Julian's welfare, often imploring: "Most Merciful Lord, give me wisdom to raise this boy. I am well acquainted with the needs of a man, as you from who nothing can be hidden well know, but the needs of a son are a different thing altogether."

Instead of learning to pickpocket, steal apples, or

torment cats, Julian made his own amusement fighting heroic battles in his bedclothes using sticks, pebbles, rusty buckles, and cracked buttons to serve as soldiers, and two pewter spoons to take command as generals. When he explained to his mother what he was doing, she seemed appalled, but then she said that it must be something boys did for her dear Stephen had once confided that he mastered Latin so early because his father forbade him to read about war except in the language of the Caesars.

While Mrs. Pinnock expatiated on a niece's lip abscess, Julian turned his head away and tried futilely to lose himself in his daydreams of brave deeds. His imaginary valor, however, had lately ceased to divert him. Julian was tired of being the helpless sickly child, the over-loved burden. His uselessness was borne in on him the previous summer when a lady left for the West Indies still owing Julian's mother the equivalent of a month's rent for an expensive gown. After weeping tears of rage, his mother put on a bright red dress Julian had never seen before, which exposed the upper part of her breasts, and donned a cap with a peacock feather. She stood awhile trembling either from anger or from the biting cold, then declared, "Fie! Stephen's son will not witness this. Come, dear. I'll present you to your Aunt Clarissa. As she loved your father, so she will love you."

His mother then changed into her usual black dress and a gray bonnet, and an hour later they were squeezed into a crowded coach trundling underneath the wooden arches of London Bridge, constructed to hold the houses that lined the bridge on either side from falling into the river. The coachman drove the horses on through the center of the city, which left Julian squashed against the window with a confused impression of broad avenues, mud-splattered gilt, a jumble of smoky chimneys, and a thousand voices hawking wares. Finally, they left the city and passed along the empty fields and woods of the countryside in the sinister gloom of twilight.

"Madam, or if you permit me to say, dear sister," his mother addressed the pale woman in a loose satin gown seated in front of a platter of tiny fat fried songbirds. The room was the largest that Julian had ever been in except for the church sanctuary and, despite a fire in the hearth and wall hangings, the coldest. Aunt Clarissa, now a widow, had been their father's childhood confidante and closest friend.

Aunt Clarissa frowned and adjusted her wig at the word "sister," but otherwise did not acknowledge their presence.

Blushing, Mistress Kate forged on with her little speech pushing Julian forward. "Madam, I come in the hope that you'll condescend to make the acquaintance of Julian, your nephew, the son of your late brother. Despite having only a poor teacher such as myself, he is accomplished with his letters and his sums. He speaks like a little gentleman. With the right encouragement and the right advantages, I'm certain he will make a fine scholar like his father."

Julian stared fascinated as his aunt speared one of the small brown creatures with a fork then, behind the privacy of a napkin, softly crunched it. Lowering the napkin, she speared another.

"You claim this boy is a great scholar," Aunt Clarissa said abruptly, turning her keen gaze on Julian. "I see very little of my brother Stephen in him."

His mother's blush deepened. "He has dear Stephen's blue eyes and…"

"Stephen read Latin fluently by his seventh year," Aunt Clarissa interrupted. She gestured to the tall stout bracket-faced footman. "Gunter, fetch a book from the Latin shelves of the library so we can try this young man's ability in the language of Cicero and Virgil."

"Madam, I never learned him Latin," Julian's mother said flustered.

His aunt contemplated the songbird impaled on her fork, ignoring her.

Gunter returned and set a great book before Julian.

"Read to us, dear boy, so we may be astonished at your scholarship," his aunt said from behind her napkin.

Bending over, Julian opened the book, determined to prove himself. He took in a deep breath, and with all the will in the world to make his mother proud, started to speak: "Ah… ah… ah…" Strange words swam meaninglessly across the page. He tried sounding them out in the hope his tongue made sense of what his mind could not. "*A mas reglases…*" Realizing that he was failing his mother, Julian shouted his mangling of what seemed already mangled words. "*A mas reglases…*"

"Enough of this farce!" his aunt barked, dropping her napkin and exposing the half-chewed songbird in her mouth. "Indeed, as I suspected, you're a slovenly stupid deceitful child. Our dear father taught us that to be charitable towards sin is to be in league with sin. Furthermore,

I don't intend to encourage this unfortunately modern trend of bastardy with patronage."

"Please, madam. Julian is not a natural child. Stephen and I was wed in a church under the eyes of God, as properly done as any marriage in England."

The aunt's eyes widened with outrage. "A proper marriage? Fie! How could a woman like you pretend to a proper marriage? You snare my unworldly brother with your harlot's wiles, then dare call it proper? Stephen would surely be alive today and a great man of learning if he had took our late father's admonition and cast you off instead of shaming our family's name and breaking my heart with his repugnant union to… to…the word has such a nasty taste… a whore."

Julian's mother bowed her head.

Julian, comprehending now that his aunt had played a trick on them, thrust the book in front of her and commanded in his high firm voice, "You read the text, madam."

The footman Gunter spun Julian around, tweaked his nose and cuffed him on the side of the head knocking him to the floor. "Dare you show disrespect to the lady. You be bleeding brains unless you beg forgiveness." The shadow of a large boot hovered over Julian's head.

"Please, spare him." His mother fell to her knees. "Julian never was a troublesome boy. He sits still at church and knows not how to say a naughty word."

"No, Gunter, don't trouble yourself. Violence upsets my digestion." Aunt Clarissa stabbed the last songbird viciously and held it up with her trembling fork.

"As you wish, madam," Gunter replied, pulling Julian

up and dragging him out by the ear. His mother followed weeping.

When Gunter locked the gate behind them, Julian realized that they had made no provision for failure. Their last pennies had been spent on the coach. They were stranded in an unfamiliar country, at least twelve miles outside of London, and evening was approaching fast.

Luckily, after traipsing the first cold mile, a farmer driving a cart of cabbages took pity on them and offered a ride. Their rescuer, having liberally taken refreshment at various inns along the way started to converse with himself in different voices, claiming that by making it sound like there were more people in the cart, highwaymen would keep away. He promised to share his pot of ale with Julian and the "fancy lady" if they contributed two or three new voices to the conversation. The ale and the silliness of the exercise put them in better spirits. When the cart clattered to a stop in the vegetable market at Covent Garden, the hour was nearing midnight, and the streetlamps on the broader boulevards were mere pale blurs in the soupy mixture of smoke and fog.

After profusely thanking the farmer, Julian and his mother started out on the furtive dangerous labyrinthine journey to their fourth-story rooms in the East End. Avoiding watchmen and rakers of night-soil, they traversed thoroughfares and dark squirrelly alleys, crossed London Bridge, then delved into the muddy unpaved ways of the East End. Julian wanted to complain about his wet numb face, the loose sole of his right shoe and the aches in his calves and ankles pleading with him to rest. He knew his mother's moods, however, and her stony demeanor signified that along with bodily discomforts, she was heartsick, and he was the cause.

Church bells struck one. Julian began to fear they were lost. Finally, the slightly fecal whiff of the tanneries indicated they were approaching the Southwark district and the tenements known generally as the rookeries and to Julian as home.

"Don't cry, Mama. We're almost there," Julian whispered when he heard her gasp, not yet discerning the three men, two masked and with one disguised by a scarf, materializing out of the gloom.

"We are Mohawks," announced a voice behind a grinning mask. "And you are a French maiden we captured and who we will use according to our savage nature."

Julian shrank back. For sport, young gentlemen often adopted the name of that fierce New World tribe and roamed in gangs terrorizing the citizens unfortunate to be out so late.

"Come now, mademoiselle, the nicer you are with us, the gentler we'll be with your cunny," a frowning mask explained as he pushed Julian's mother against a wall.

"'Tis a shame to hide such fine bubbies," a third man said underneath his scarf, then growled and advanced with open hands and wriggling fingers at the level of her bodice.

Julian, who had disappointed his mother once this day, wasn't about to let it happen again. He hurled himself at the grinning mask, fists windmilling. Unfortunately, Julian was a thin wheezy child with stick-like arms and a sunken chest. The grinning-mask Mohawk laughed as the fists fell furiously and ineffectively on his buckskin waistcoat. He pushed Julian toward the frowning mask who batted him to his comrade disguised by the scarf. The Mohawks indulged in this game a minute calling him their shuttlecock. The frowning mask then lifted Julian and tossed him to the grinning mask who dropped him into a rancid puddle. Rising from the muck, Julian lowered his head to charge. A soft restraining hand fell on his shoulder.

"Loves, dearies," a sweet voice sang out. "Why do you pester a boy and his aged mother when you might entertain yourselves with an eighteen-pence girl like me? Surely you are men of discernment. My custom house is open, and I am as fresh and clean as a rose after an April shower."

"I see no apparent reason why the three of us don't chive the pair of you," the grinning mask replied in the amused tone of playful banter.

"No reason dearie, except I'll not allow it. I have a cozy nest around the corner, and you're all invited to share it; that is apart from the ancient crone and her little boy. La! You think you might oblige me by force? A lady like me always got her bully boys and bruisers to do her bidding lest she encounters mistreatment, don't you know. Two of you is old friends already. Isn't that so, Gerald and Hal? And by the morning, I expect the amusing gent with the scarf around his mug must also be. …" With great skill, she drew them in, and the fierce Mohawks were even agreeing to pay as Julian and his mother crept away.

The farmer had given them two cabbages, providing sustenance for two days, which was just enough time for his mother to find work as a seamstress in a fashionable millinery. As for Julian, he learned that day that he was neither clever nor strong. He did not see how these defects could be remedied even if he lived three lifetimes. He was fated to be insignificant; pitied and loved only by his mother, and would spend his life among the thousands of the insignificant poor of London.

Every child in London, poor or middling, worked—selling small coal or candles, black booting, pickpocketing, running errands, cleaning jakes, sweeping chimneys, collecting rags, and dozens of different apprenticeships from the common ones like smithing and coopering and tailoring to the richer sort like watchmaking and silversmithing. The poorest might even skin the carcass of a dead dog to sell its pelt, and in Julian's tenement, two French girls earned their living chewing paper to make papier-mâché. Then there was the mysterious occupation of the prettily dressed children that involved catching the eyes of strangers, taking them by the hand and asking them if they were lonely.

Every child worked, it seemed, except for Julian. Born feverish and coughing, Julian had spent most of his life on one side or the other of a close call with death. Eleven weeks, by his mother's reckoning, was the longest he had gone without at least an ague. Then in his thirteenth year a miracle happened: Julian managed to stay in good health through the entire winter and spring. A pale rose bloomed on his cheeks. He had grown so that his mother no longer called him, "my little twig." The other day, after watching bull-baiting in which a terrier was tossed twenty feet into the air and caught by the alert owner, and then two women in shifts fight with wooden swords until blood was drawn from the cheek of one, he ran the whole length of Hyde Park just for the joy of running. Today, he might run it twice. At least that would give me something to do and make the day different.

Now that her dream of her son becoming a scholar was quashed, Julian's mother, with a note of disappointment in her voice, began to suggest other suitable vocations. If he became a servant in an elegant house, he might acquire fine manners and rise to the level of footman or even valet. Glovers always made respectable livings. Much good could be said about the vocation of tanners once you became accustomed to the stench.

When Julian declared that he wanted to become a captain of a great ship, maybe even a famous pirate, or highwayman, her reaction was furious—she actually slapped him and cried, "La! That's a foolish profession."

"Why should I not be a great sea captain?" Julian protested, rubbing his cheek. "I want to do something brave."

"Brave men always take another heart with them when they die, and they always die," his mother replied bitterly. Then, caressing his stinging cheek, she told him she had made the resolution that he would become a printer's apprentice. He could read unlike many boys of his station. His father had loved books, and she believed that Julian, if given the chance, would develop the same abiding love. With the determination of a devoted mother, she dragged him around to a dozen shops. The printers reinforced Julian's estimation of himself.

"Such a wee pale thing, my customers might think I'm a terrible master who abuses his apprentices," one explained. "Pray, consider Miss, that with his slender shoulders and skinny rump, your lad might be better suited to sweeping chimneys," another suggested. After a dozen such refusals, his mother decided to wait a few months until Julian could make a healthier impression. When Julian contracted smallpox, worse to endure than the boils and the fever was the resignation in his mother's eyes. Her darling could never be more than what he was now: the child who would always need her care.

And in his heart of hearts, to become more than the sick child seemed to Julian beyond the reach of any miracle.

THE BOY WAYFARER

JULIAN DID NOT remember his father, which was fortunate because if he had, he was certain he would have detested Mr. Skylar more. Mr. Skylar was definitely not what a boy with an adventurous spirit would want in a stepfather. The good man owned a haberdashery squeezed between a staymaker's shop and a millinery where his mother had just obtained employment. He had taken to shyly walking his mother home. But a haberdasher should wear a wig big enough for his head—at least that was Julian's opinion. Also, a man who aspired to be his father should be able to speak about other things than notions, threads, buttons, baubles, and ribbons, and he definitely shouldn't be bowing and scraping in front of every lady or gentleman who happened to enter his shop. Furthermore, a father shouldn't be so round that he couldn't see his feet over his frock coat without bending.

However, Mr. Skylar was kind to Mistress Kate. He was always giving her little gifts—ribbons and fruits, once a goose to roast, and once very especially a half-finished bottle of sherry. Yesterday, to Julian's amazement, his mother spilled four oranges from her kerchief onto their table. When he asked her whether she could marry such a man as Mr. Skylar, she protested, "He's just a nice gentleman." Her blush told a different story.

These were the thoughts niggling Julian as he wandered the streets of London with the objective of getting lost. For the sake of adventure, he had tried many times to lose himself in London's backways and alleyways. Even while riding in a cart with closed eyes, he could identify by smell whether he was passing through the neighborhood of the tanneries, or the breweries, or the timber yards, or the coffee houses. Earlier that day, eager to be in the proximity of adventure, he had climbed atop a hackney-coach for a clear view of a hanging. The highwayman, who had preyed on the stagecoach travelers between London and Bristol for a half dozen years—robbing, killing, ravishing—stood on the cart before the crowd grinning unrepentantly.

"Chaplain, get down," the highwayman loudly ordered the black-coated minister who was feebly reading psalms. The chaplain tottered, then stumbled off. "Save your prayers for them who deserve them." The condemned criminal's rapacious eyes then slowly surveyed the silent expectant throng. "I intend to die hard, and I give not a pig's fart for repentance."

A fat man in front of the crowd guffawed, then belched. This was followed by several other guffaws and sympathetic belches from the onlookers.

The highwayman nodded to the crowd as if he had expected no less from them. "You think I'm going to hell, well, what of it? Given a choice between heaven and hell, I opt for the warmer real estate. Tell me, why would the

Devil punish his faithful disciple? Arrah, no, he'll give me a whole county of damned souls for my pleasure to torment. I lived a better life than all you poor sods, well worth this airy dance that no doubt will amuse you in a nonce, and when you arrive in hell—most of you is too ugly and too poor to be wanted in t'other place—I'll be greeting you with a pitchfork, a pail of hot coals, and my peter straight as an arrow."

Then the highwayman knelt and stretched his hand toward a group of three women holding babies. The caress of a dead murderer's hand had special curative properties for wens and boils; and these caring mothers wanted to make sure that their suffering children received the benefits as soon as the corpse stopped twitching. The mothers squirmed and cringed in terror. The crowd hissed its disapproval.

The highwayman rocked back and forth roaring with laughter, then stood. "Bah, let's end this. I won't waste the little breath I have left on you poor sods; and we mustn't keep these ladies and their brats waiting."

After the execution, Julian set off in a new direction and found himself sauntering down a crowded narrow lane lined with shops and coffee houses. Thanks to Mr. Skylar's unceasing commentary on his business, Julian could tell by the ribbons and buttons the women wore that the people were mostly of the middling sort—prosperous enough to imitate wealth but not so much as to fool a keen eye. Confirming this opinion, he spotted Mrs. Pinnock exiting a confectionery, clutching three paper bundles to her bodice like her last hope. She, of course, did not want to be put into the position of acknowledging her acquaintance with such a ragged specimen of humanity as Julian and looked through him, then turned in the opposite direction.

Suddenly, a loud clatter and several screams interrupted these observations. Two racing phaetons swerved around the corner. People pressed back against the shop windows and covered their faces as the phaetons tore down the cobblestones, wheel to wheel, splattering mud, the drivers red-faced and furiously whipping their horses. A hat was torn off a lady. An occupant of a sedan chair was spilled into the doorway of a Foreign Spiritous Liquor Shop. A chicken was caught by the spokes of a wheel and flung against a lamp. Dogs chased the carriages barking wildly.

Julian squeezed up against the window of a glazier's shop between two tall young men. Julian had the youths pegged as cutpurses because their sallow complexions didn't match their elegant attire, which helped them mingle with the crowd without suspicion. They also kept their lips tight when importuned by a proprietor of a clock shop to look closer at his wares, likely because the cutpurses feared their speech would betray their low station. They had been following an old gentleman with a fat pocket peeking out from beneath his frock coat and his servant—a giant African in bright green livery. The old gentleman and the servant were now pressed with them in the recess of a glazier shop. Julian had wondered how the cutpurses were going to get past the gentleman's formidable guard.

Julian didn't know which cutpurse insinuated a hand behind the small of his back and pushed. He slipped as he tried to scramble out of the way of the careening phaeton. He heard a crunch and wondered what unlucky person had fallen beneath its wheels, that is until he attempted to stand and saw the bloody strangely twisted appendage dangling on the end of his leg. He didn't feel pain yet, but he screamed just the same. Julian then saw the look of concern on the face of the old gentleman as he bent over, his pocket now absent, and behind the kind face, craning forward, Mrs. Pinnock, her eyes wide in admiration.

When Julian woke, he found himself laid out and tied down on the rickety table in his tenement apartment. A screw-like object with bands was attached to his left calf. Further down, where his foot should have been, this red splayed thing stuck out. His mother sat on one side, all tears and caresses. A barber-surgeon squatted on a stool on the other, whistling a tune and sharpening the inside edge of a large curved knife on a whetstone. Julian attempted to speak, but in the flood of pain that came with consciousness, he only emitted pathetic whelps.

"Payment in advance, Mistress Asher. That'll be ten shillings and a sixpence," the barber-surgeon demanded. He had a long red nose, a great belly, and the air of a man who appreciated himself.

"I only got the five shillings saved for rent," Mistress Kate pleaded tearfully.

The barber-surgeon slowly shook his head. "That's enough for me to saw, but not to stanch the blood or cauterize the stump. You'll have to perform those operations yourself, madam."

"Only I am not knowing how," Mistress Kate protested helplessly.

The surgeon stopped sharpening the knife. "I do not relinquish my expertise for naught for then it will be worth naught. To be honest with you, madam, if you don't cut off the foot, your son will die a hellish death within the week from blood poisoning. If you don't stanch the blood, then he'll drain dry within the quarter-hour. Some opine stopping blood is easy, but give no credence to those fools. Even for accomplished surgeons like me, 'tis touch and go, although I never lost a patient yet from bleeding out. I'm as skilled as any barber in London in the cauterization of the stump, which is where an unpracticed hand oftentimes loses the game."

Julian's mother began another round of weeping.

Oblivious to her tears, the surgeon continued: "The trick is to apply the boiling tar immediately to the fresh cut. Another four shillings, but well worth the expense because it makes for a smooth surface afterward. Then, there is the tuppence for the gin—mind you, superior gin from the distilleries on the river above the city, not the rag-water from the distilleries below. I might give you a break there. If after a few strokes the boy don't faint, I'll provide the gin at a penny a pint."

"I promise to pay you before next Sunday." Julian's mother sniffled and wept.

"Aye, and I promise to perform the operation before next Monday."

"The gentleman who will certainly lend me the money is not in town at the present, but…" Mistress Kate fell to her knees.

The barber-surgeon held up his hand indicating he had heard it all before. "I suggest Mistress Asher that you make your pleas and promises to your neighbors. If your gentleman is so trustworthy, they will have a greater acquaintance with that fact."

"Do me the favor of waiting here a moment," his mother said and hurried out the door. Julian wanted to tell her not to bother because he was going to die very soon, but to his shame the words wouldn't leave his mouth.

Surprisingly, Mistress Kate quickly returned with a large woman whose presence made their room shrink and the barber-surgeon cringe. The woman's unfamiliar face, although ugly with deep folds, was kind.

"I am Mrs. Gunn from Pennsylvania. I am visiting my sister who lives across the way. What be thy name, friend?" She addressed the barber-surgeon.

"Robert Eagleton, surgeon, ma'am."

Mrs. Gunn smiled a warm smile. "Friend Eagleton, wouldst thou be so kind as to fetch water and clean rags. I want to examine the foot before I lend money to have it amputated."

Eagleton hesitated. "With all due respects, Mrs. Gunn, I doubt you possess sufficient experience in these matters to render a judgment."

Mrs. Gunn's smile hardened. "With all due respects, friend, I have ministered to the illnesses and injuries of my family, servants, and neighbors these twenty-five years. I sewed back the hair of a scalped girl; I set the broken leg of a twenty-stone man, and coaxed breeched twins out of the belly with harm to neither mother nor babes. Thou earnest more if thou cuttest, and I do take thee for the sort that enjoys the labor of cutting."

"It is no sin for a man to find pleasure in his profession." Eagleton started running the whetstone down the blade again.

Julian's mother brought a large rag and a pail of water. The folds in Mrs. Gunn's face deepened as she contemplated Julian's foot, which bent out sideways. Before he turned his head away, he saw her lift a loose fold of skin on the top of his foot revealing bones enmeshed in the red muscle. She took a very long time studying the mangled appendage.

"The bones broke cleanly," she said finally. "I see all of them, and with the help of this ingenious device preventing the blood flow, I will set them. With the grace of God, dear boy, thy foot will heal. Thou will have to hobble about with a cane or crutch, but thou will have thy foot until the end of thy days. I cannot set thy ankle for 'twill further displace the small bones, which must heal first."

There was a clatter as Eagleton dropped his knife and started to protest that a proper lady should know her place and refrain from interfering in a man's profession. Julian shook his head attempting to convey to the kind Quaker woman that he wanted to die.

"Open thy mouth, dear child," Mrs. Gunn instructed, ignoring both.

When Julian finally obeyed, a wooden spoon was thrust lengthwise between his teeth.

"Now, bite down, dear."

The last thing Julian remembered after his teeth clamped down was Mrs. Gunn bending over his foot holding a darning needle in one hand and pliers for pulling teeth in the other.

Over the following weeks, Mrs. Gunn visited daily to inspect the progress of what she called "the mending." Julian wasn't certain that not chopping off his foot was the right decision. He doubted that the purplish, swollen thing at the end of his left leg could ever be serviceable, and in any event, the outward twist of his ankle meant that throughout his life he would have to shuffle sideways with the foot. Mrs. Gunn made him a gift of a crutch before she left for Pennsylvania.

"Thy foot won't please the eye, but 'twill serve thee better than a peg," she smoothing his hair. "I do so miss my sons. They would make good brothers to thee, and thou, I dare say, would also make a good brother. Come visit us when thou comest to the age of manhood. Come, I will give thee a wagon and thou will carry goods from farm to market."

When Mr. Skylar returned, he demanded that his Katy and Julian move to better accommodations. He declared that he'd bet his haberdashery their tenement like two others owned by the same landlord would collapse before the year was out. With only one flight of stairs to climb to the second-story apartment and a window that opened out onto a courtyard, the new accommodations were vastly superior to the old. Julian had never experienced the luxury of a window before, nor a courtyard that was swept daily, and a week could pass without spying a rat in the hallway.

Julian's foot healed slowly unlike his broken dreams

which seemed beyond repair. Perhaps it had been childish to want to be a pirate, but it wasn't childish to desire to cut a figure in the world, become a man admired, not pitied as a cripple. Making matters worse, Mr. Skylar started advocating apprenticeship in his shop. "Every lad's head is filled with notions, Kate, and little Julian's head got more than most for he spends so much time with nothing to do but think about what's in his head. 'Tis well known too much cogitation unbalances the humors and causes melancholia. As you no doubt can conclude from my example, there are few better enterprises in the world than that of being a proprietor of a haberdashery. A woman will pay her last sixpence on a spool of gold thread."

Mr. Skylar visited his Katy every day now. Katy cooked for him, brushed his breeches, polished his shoes, and stood approvingly beside him when he admired himself in the mirror, and if he sneezed, inquired after his health with genuine concern. She even prevailed on him to buy a wig that fit his head.

Unlike his many illnesses where his body rebounded with no effort of will, Julian had to force himself to walk again. For a month, he hobbled around the room with the crutch, then afterward with a cane—the rap of the wood tip, the soft step of the injured foot, and the firmer resonance of his good foot making a clip-clunk-clop sound. Thus, he tottered back and forth, weeping and biting his knuckles. A group of boys threw pebbles at him when he first appeared outside hobbling with the cane, saying it was pennies for the cripple. Julian threw the cane at them vowing never to pick it up again and, choking with pain, lurched back inside and up the staircase to their tenement

apartment, his stride becoming an uneven step, slide...
step, slide...

A week later, he stepped, slid... stepped down the
stairs to the street and then to the end of the block where
a little girl sold apples from a wheelbarrow in front of
a dram shop. When he returned, his face sheathed with
sweat and tears, he took two bites out of the hard-won
apple and promptly vomited. Repeating the trip the next
morning, Julian walked five paces beyond the apple girl—
step, oh-God-have-mercy-on-my-foot slide... step—and
then turned around. Every evening, Julian resolved to go
easier on himself the following day, but each morning,
he repeated the ordeal lured by the belief that if he just
dragged himself far enough, he might encounter something new and interesting. Julian tried to explain this
restlessness to his mother and Mr. Skylar, but it didn't
make sense to them. Mr. Skylar kept reminding him that
as a haberdasher he could sit on a stool between the times
attending to customers.

"Every boy dreams," Mr. Skylar lectured, "only dreams
are just airy fables that put not a penny in the purse nor a
morsel in the stomach."

While Mr. Skylar delivered such homilies, Julian
either glared at the smug prig until he shut up or he stared
at the door abstractedly, imagining running the length
of Hyde Park as he had once done. When Julian finally
proclaimed that he'd rather be a beggar than haberdasher,
for the second time in his life his mother slapped him.
After that, Julian forced himself on longer walks, gimping along the most dangerous streets on dark evenings,

daring—maybe even hoping for—a footpad to rob him or stab him. *Better than becoming Mr. Skylar*, he told himself.

Being a naturally timid man, Mr. Skylar's courtship of Julian's mother progressed slowly. Two years after the accident, Julian woke up in the middle of the night to the sound of two people snoring. He lit a candle and walked into their front room. His mother and Mr. Skylar had fallen asleep side by side on a small divan. Julian was certain Mr. Skylar had never done anything improper with his Katy. The haberdasher was a fool and pompous, but he was also kind and considerate to a rare degree. He never treated his Katy less than a lady. Julian suddenly realized that his disdain for Mr. Skylar was in truth jealousy. He had always owned the entirety of his mother's affection. Julian was certain he could still reclaim it. By becoming the whiny sick little boy again, he could drive Mr. Skylar forever out of his mother's life.

He fought off an impulse to go back to his room and cry out, pretending his foot was causing unbearable pain. He fought off the desire to wake them and amuse himself with their embarrassment. Instead, he took a scrap of purple-stained sugar paper and wrote with a dull pencil:

"Dearest Mother,

Remember the Quaker woman who was so kind to us and offered me a wagon so I might carry goods from her farm to the market in Pennsylvania. I decided to accept her offer. I am not suited to be a haberdasher although it's an admirable profession. I will write to you as often as I can. I hold the greatest respect for Mr. Skylar. May he continue to treat you with the goodness and kindness you so deserve.

Your Loving Son,

Julian"

Julian kissed his mother on the forehead and put the note in her lap.

It was late October, and the chill sank deep into his bones as he stepped slid down the dark streets toward the docks. Julian realized that he had forgotten his overcoat. Returning to the apartment where his mother and Mr. Skylar leaned companionably against each other asleep on the divan, however, seemed as impossible as going back to yesterday.

PASSAGE

A BOY IN his tenement nicknamed The Governor explained how it was done. The Governor boasted he could out-drink, out-whore, and out-swear any sailor, and had never lost a game of chance, and at the age of sixteen had acquired all the knowledge necessary for getting ahead in the world. When Julian confessed that he wanted a life of adventure, The Governor explained, "'Tis simple, lad." He called all those younger than him 'lad.' "Go down to them docks 'n carry yerself aboard one of them great ships, 'n exercise yer knuckles on this or that captain's door 'n say you wants passage to them colonies. The captain shake yer 'and you puts yer mark on paper, 'n that's that. You 'ave a contract in the eyes of God 'n King 'n off to them colonies, off to the land of milk 'n 'oney 'n bloodthirsty savages you goes. I might done it myself, 'cept an old gypsy told me I be fortune's pet, 'n I no want to upset 'er by not being around when she come fer me."

Near the docks, Julian asked a dozen different sailors in various stages of inebriation where he could sign on as an indentured servant to the colonies. Several different boats were pointed out, but Julian always lost his nerve as soon as he set foot on the gangplank. He had given this enterprise up as another failure and was wondering whether he had time to creep back to his apartment and steal the note off his mother's lap, when a large hand clamped down on his shoulder and a hollow voice intoned, "Come with me, lad. I'll serve as your agent."

This self-proclaimed agent—an old sailor with long arms, short legs, and one good eye—dragged Julian to a squat tub with two masts, pulled him up a gangplank, and banged on the door below the quarterdeck. The reply wasn't recognizable, but his "agent" apparently took it as an invitation to enter and propelled Julian forward. Julian stumbled into a desk behind which sat a scowling man with whiskers that stood straight out and eyes that might have belonged to a demon. Julian supposed, correctly as it turned out, that this was the captain.

The old tar began humbly, "Captain Broom, sir, my son here desires passage to the colonies to make his own way in the world. He is a hard worker, and I am regretting the loss of him, only there's no holding back young blood when it gets a mind to do a thing."

"Is this man your father, lad?" Captain Broom asked Julian after the merest disdainful glance.

Julian moved his head in a circle, not wanting to lie, but catching on that a lie was necessary.

"I take it your wobbling noggin means he can sign for you." Broom studied Julian like an insect in his soup. "What's your name, lad?"

"Julian, good sir."

The captain shook his head. "What sort of work can you do, Julian?"

"Farm work," his agent interjected.

Julian nodded slightly thinking that the less he nodded the less of a lie he would be telling.

"Balderdash! Show me your hands," Broom demanded.

Julian stretched out his hands.

The captain snorted in disbelief. "Your hands are softer than the hands of my five-year-old niece. You never have done a day of hard labor in your life, boy. On the docks in Philadelphia the first sold off are strong-backed stout-hearted lads who think nothing of pulling out a dozen tree stumps before noon, then taking in harness the plow the balance of the day. Have you ever seen a tree stump, boy?"

"I wish to try my fortune in the colonies, sir," Julian quaveringly asserted.

"You wish?" The captain's eyes drilled into Julian. "Fie on wishes, lad. I wish I weren't obliged to sail this spongy bark through stormy seas with a crew of disgruntled Yorkshiremen to the damn colonies so miserable souls can condemn themselves to further misery. The question is, boy, if this rascally impostor signs for you and I take you, how much with your narrow shoulders, sunken chest, blotched complexion, and broomstick arms you fetch on the docks in Philadelphia? And what's wrong with that foot that you dragged in after you like 'twas an unwanted relation? It sticks out oddly."

"I broke it, sir." Julian tried to hide his bad foot behind his good.

"Call me Captain," Broom corrected and grimaced.

"Captain, sir. I broke it in a farming accident. A tree stump fell on it."

His agent pinched him hard in the ribs and said, "He meant to say a horse trod on it, captain."

"How old are you, boy?" Broom asked.

"I reached fifteen last April, captain," Julian replied with relief that for once he was speaking the truth.

The captain shook his head. "No one will buy your indenture to work their land. I doubt I could give you away. Have you special skills? Don't include lying. You're as poor a liar as ever arose out of the riffraff of London."

"I can read and make my letters and have a fair head for my sums, sir, captain, I mean," Julian replied hopefully.

"I'm overjoyed to find out you're not a total disgrace to the English nation. So why do you think anybody will give you bed and board for seven years, even if you have your sums and letters?"

"A Quaker lady promised she will supply me with a wagon to drive her goods to the market if I visit her," Julian answered, again glad to muster more than a figment of truth. "She said I won't be required to walk much if I am driving my wagon all the time."

"Hmm," the captain said and wrinkled his brow, seeming interested. "What is the name of the Quaker woman?"

"I cannot recall her name," Julian answered. "Only she said she lived in Pennsylvania."

"Then how am I to contact her? Pennsylvania can swallow England whole and still have room leftover to digest Wales, Scotland, and Ireland. And Quakers there are as thick as fleas on an old dog." The captain now addressed the man who claimed Julian's paternity. "If we mark his age down as twelve, which by his looks nobody would question, a buyer might see an advantage to a nine-year indenture instead of seven. How old is your son?"

"Aye, captain, my son tends to exaggerate his age. He is twelve this March," The old tar replied promptly.

"Fair enough," The captain replied.

Julian opened his mouth to protest.

The captain didn't let him speak. "Don't tell me this red-nosed baboon isn't your father after you swore he was. I'm captain, which is to say king, judge, and executioner on this boat, and the punishment for lying to a captain is a hundred lashes, and there's not enough flesh on your bones for fifty. I'm not promising aught. We might squeeze one more below. Get your arse on deck in the meantime. We sail tomorrow morning. If better prospects fail to show before then, you got a berth." The captain paid the agent a thruppence, muttering as an afterthought: "Usually, I lose a fifth of the human cargo—maybe he dies instead of a more promising prospect."

Julian spent the first hour pacing the deck, wishing mightily for his overcoat. When the ache in his foot became unbearable, he curled up next to a coil of rope. He didn't believe sleep possible with the chill, his throbbing foot, and all the new sounds and the unfamiliar shapes surrounding him. Worse, regret began to gnaw at him. Why not resign himself to the respectable trade of haberdashery? Mr. Skylar would treat him like a son. Mr. Skylar earned a good living, and more than a few of his mother's friends had complimented her on how lucky she was to have snagged such a fine suitor. Julian couldn't see anything particularly fine about the man, except, perhaps, his appreciation for his Katy.

Julian began to feel ashamed that he was already yearning for his mother and miffed he had not anticipated this engulfing sadness. For near sixteen years, he had slept under the same roof as her. She had the kindest face imaginable, broad and handsome. Until Mr. Skylar intruded into their life, she had often spoken about her Stephen, his real father, with reverence. "A great scholar who read and wrote in Latin and Greek, a good virtuous man who never suffered a door closed in his face." Then she would weep and admonish Julian, "He was a foolish fearless man. Julian, I beg you, never be a foolish fearless man."

Julian failed to understand how a schoolmaster for the children of artisans, merchants, and others of the middling sort could be foolish and fearless. Whenever his mother shared a recollection of her dear Stephen, his father appeared as an exceptionally kind and mild-mannered man. His students loved him and never played tricks on him although they might have easily because of his weak eyesight. She claimed that he had never caned a child. He died of a fever caught from one of his pupils. The boy's parents were too frightened of the contagion to tend to their son. Not Stephen. He spoon-fed the child hot broth, changed the soiled linen, cleaned him, read to him. The boy recovered.

Eventually, fatigue won out over the discomfort and the vast feeling of regret, and Julian fell asleep, his head resting uneasily on the coiled rope.

It must have been several hours later when an oath and a kick woke Julian. Rough hands pulled him up, and he groggily followed the shadowy sailor down three ladders into a low, dank, and gloomy space that his guide called steerage.

"This way, this way," voices beckoned and hands reached out, directing Julian forward until he stumbled against a curving barrier.

"There you be. Yer the lucky soul getting the coffin berth," his guide gruffly remarked.

"Where?" Julian asked, glancing around. The oil lamp swinging from a low ceiling dimly illuminated a long row of double-stacked pallets. Each pallet accommodated three to five people—strangers or families. Buckets were tied to each upright post, their fetid odor making it plain that this was where the steerage passengers relieved themselves. It seemed doubtful the occupants of the berths would be inclined to divide their meager pallet space yet again to welcome him.

"That be your place." The sailor directed Julian to a plank slightly larger than a tray, attenuated at one end because of the curve of the ship's bow. "You piss in their bucket. If they not approve, piss on them. You're just the right size—not a hair's width to spare. The captain sure has a good eye for packing them in."

With difficulty, Julian fitted himself onto the plank. The wood oozed rot. The sea sloshed eight oaken inches away from his ear. He tried turning, but the space was so cramped that he couldn't do so without falling out. A cheery voice in the gloom answered his question: "Make yerself comfy, lad, that be your home and hearth for the next nine weeks if winds blow fair, fifteen, if foul."

This was simply too much. Julian rolled off the berth, stood, straightened, and steadying himself against the upright beams dividing the pallets, started toward the hatchway.

"Where do you think you're going?" inquired an unidentifiable woman from the shadowy depths of steerage.

"Back," Julian proclaimed. "I changed my mind."

"Back where?" The voice gurgled with suppressed hilarity.

"To my mother." Julian didn't care how childish he sounded.

Several laughed. "Sprouted fins and a tail, have you?" His interlocutor continued.

"What?"

"Or wings? They might serve. What a chuckleheaded darling you are. Can't you feel the ship moving? Swimming or flying be the only way home." The speaker obviously relished Julian's mortification.

Julian crawled back onto his small plank. He fell asleep before he could decide whether to rage or grieve.

A hundred and fifty people—a third of them women and children—were stuffed into the steerage of the forward hull, like bodies in catacombs. Two hundred occupied another compartment in the steerage aft. Dimly lit by swinging lanterns, the steerage was a cold, swampy, lice-infested, wooden cave. On the second day the rolling seas caused general seasickness, Julian and a few others excepted. The odors of human waste, vomit, and unwashed sick bodies thickened the air. There was never not a child crying, a consumptive coughing his lungs inside out, a man cursing, a nauseated individual groaning or voiding the contents of his gut. Julian decided that any description of hell that left out vomit wasn't wholly accurate. The pregnant women and the newborns fared worse. One of each died the fourth day; and after the vulnerable were culled from the emigrants, the loss of healthier passengers unerringly maintained a high mortality rate for the rest of the voyage.

On the eighth day, Julian made enemies of the Lyle brothers, two sharp shrew-like boys whose greatest pleasure was the torment of weaker creatures. Like Julian, they were immune to seasickness. The second day out, the brothers caught a rat and cut off its legs on one side. They giggled as the rat struggled to escape, but kept going in circles because its brain wasn't able to comprehend the missing limbs. Not quite satisfied with the diversion this cruelty provided, they tortured the creature for a whole day with a penny knife until they lay on their pallet shaking with laughter. Several passengers protested, but the brothers had this odd stare, their tiny eyes glinting on either side of a deep furrow that conveyed the message that they didn't see much difference between you and a rat.

The brothers dearly missed their gin. By the sixth day, they had exhausted their farthings purchasing grog from the sailors. After trying various wheedling scams with indifferent results, they concocted a plan to replenish their funds by selling the sexual favors of a girl in steerage. From the brothers' conversation, Julian gathered that Abigail was pretty, unaccompanied, and innocent. She had been a dressmaker's apprentice, but the dressmaker died, and so she had indentured herself to a dressmaker in Phila-delphia. She shared a pallet with a Palatine couple and their baby. To avoid the frequent scoldings of the jealous frau, Abigail took to sitting on the floor near the hatch hoping for a breath of fresh sea air. The brothers planned to lure her to the bottom deck to see newborn kittens. For a discount on Abigail's sexual favors, the sailmaker provided a piece of canvas that would serve as the bed amid the barrels and casks that made up the ballast. The brothers debated whether to pay the girl a halfpenny for her trouble but eventually decided that would be immoral because, "She might take on the unwholesome habit of charging for pricks."

Julian only had the blurriest notion of the facts of life and didn't quite catch on to what the brothers intended. With his cramped berth and throbbing foot, he had enough misery himself to be overly concerned about a girl who had no thought for him. However, as the brothers became more explicit in their whispered fantasies of Abigail's deflowering, Julian's conscience began to nudge at him. With an effort, he resigned himself to suffer his troublesome conscience and leave Abigail to her fate, which couldn't be so bad—after all, she wasn't a rat.

After the brothers commiserated with Julian when the hour of the deflowering had come because the lack of a sixpence kept him from joining the fun, they sidled over to Abigail's pallet. A moment later, Julian heard them whispering to her about kittens in the cargo hold. The poor girl issued a mew of assent. Two dead bodies in gunny sacks temporarily blocked the short passageway to the hold, so the three of them passed by Julian. This was the first time Julian had more than glimpsed Abigail. He had somehow imagined the shadowy figure by the hatchway as a hale and hearty girl, well able to endure the handling of rough men. The person clutching a dirty blanket to her gown as she was led to her deflowering, now seemed more child than woman. Her large slightly rheumy blue eyes were clouded with uncertainty, and her trembling lips were as vulnerable as an open wound. Five minutes later, four sailors discreetly slipped down the hatchway into the hold.

In the mental wrestling match, conscience bested Julian's resolve to not interfere. Hobbling over to Abigail's berth, he blurted out the brothers' intentions. The Palatine family stared at him blankly. The rest within earshot were too oppressed by their own miseries to be much interested in Abigail's plight with one exception.

Mary Winn was a washerwoman in her late twenties. She had bright red hair, the forearms of a pugilist, and shoulders as broad as any hauler and hewer of wood.

"Just as I suspicioned," Mary Winn muttered as she extracted her square frame from her berth. She flexed her hands and growled, "Poor lads." Julian feared that Mary didn't comprehend the situation and began to explain again how many men might be involved. Mary Winn brushed him aside. He followed her to the hatch leading to the cargo hold and stared hopelessly as she descended, grasping in her teeth a marlinspike she had somehow acquired along the way.

In no time, Mary Winn located the lair. The battle was unseen, although not unheard. "The filthy bitch punctured my bum!" "Let go! Let go! Oh, bloody Lord, I'll never piss again!"

Mary Winn's husky contralto rose above the commotion. "I'll unman ye all!" The sailors came scrambling up from the hold, clutching their gashes and bruises and spitting out broken teeth.

"Run, run, run for your lives, she's bedlam in skirts!" yelled another to Julian through a bloodied mouth as he emerged. Mary Winn reappeared supporting the quivering Abigail who now wore a sailor's shirt in-between the blanket and the gown. The male part of the steerage gave the pair plenty of space. Unfortunately, the Lyle brothers were agile enough to escape disabling injury. When Julian returned to his plank, the brothers, with an infallible instinct for the informer, fastened their malicious, unforgiving eyes on him.

The seas rose. The brothers succumbed to the violent rolling with olive faces and pea-green vomit while Julian was still spared the general seasickness. Nature continued to keep them at bay for several days, but eventually, they adjusted, and again they directed their villainous stares at Julian. Aside from an occasional kick as he lay in his berth and nasty snarls, the Lyle brothers continued to leave him alone. Then, ominously, several sailors who had suffered Mary Winn's wrath visited the steerage and mutely gave Julian the evil eye. Sensing that he had become a pariah, the rest of the steerage kept their distance.

Mary Winn meanwhile was occupied with the job of protecting Abigail and herself, which required the utmost vigilance. Two days after the initial engagement, the stout washerwoman was called on deck where eight of the crew ambushed her as much for the sake of redeeming their manly honor as exacting vengeance. When they threw her against the capstan, Mary drew out of her voluminous bodice a pistol she had confiscated from the chest of a dead passenger and reminded her attackers she always aimed below the waist. The small army retreated, viewing the possible loss not worth the redemption of their honor.

As the ship struggled across the Atlantic and November passed into December, the weather turned bitterly cold. The passengers huddled sharing body heat, sometimes seven or eight in a pallet shivering under their combined blankets. Julian's only covering aside from the clothes on his back was a threadbare blanket bestowed on him the twelfth day out of port when a cooper's apprentice died. The rag couldn't quite cover his head and feet at the same time, but it was better than nothing. Julian always kept the blanket with him for fear that the Lyle brothers would filch it.

Julian wasn't welcomed into the communal sharing of warmth. After making the best he could out of his meager covering and dirty straw, he would lay down, hug himself and chatter loudly. On the coldest night yet, a brother hit him on the head with an empty slop bucket and ordered him to shut up.

"Leave him to his death rattle," an ungenerous voice down the passageway commented.

"He'll be stiff as dried cod, tomorrow," another added. The conversation then turned on the theme of bemoaning Julian's lack of property to divvy up.

The next day, failing to oblige the predictions and freeze to death, the brothers and the wounded sailors conspired to hasten his end.

On a night so cold the urine froze in the buckets, Julian was shaken awake and told that there were new blankets waiting for him in the captain's stores. Groggy, teeth chattering, Julian stumbled to his feet, draped the thin rag around his shoulders and followed the sailor up two hatchways to the deck of the ship.

There he found himself in an incredible frozen world. The sails, the sheets, the spars were encrusted with ice.

"Here's your blanket." His guide smeared Julian's face with the fresh bloody side of a rat's skin. Cackling, he fled.

When Julian tried to return to his berth, he found the hatchway closed and barred. He pounded on the other hatchways to no avail. Then he pummeled the door of the captain's cabin. The vulturine sailor who opened it informed Julian that if he wanted better blankets, they cost two pence in warm weather and five in cold, and then before slamming the door, advised, "Do us and the world a favor and heave thy carcass overboard. Davy Jones will give thee a minute of rough handling, then cast thee up into the lap of the Almighty, where thou be as warm as thy good deeds if thou hast any."

Julian then approached the tarpaulin-shrouded steersman standing at the wheel like the grim reaper without the scythe. "Pray, sir, I entreat you to tell me where I may shelter from the cold."

The sailor pulled back his hood momentarily, showing in the dull binnacle light a savage grin and a gash in the cheek caused by Mary Winn's marlinspike. "Say thy prayers, kinchin, another ice storm anon. Freezing be a kinder death than thou deserves. Half this crew desires thee kingdom come, and with thy crippled foot and pasty pallor thou be no great loss to the captain."

Hobbling toward the bow, Julian found a residue of

warmth in the galley chimney. He hugged it, but fireless below, the chimney soon cooled and sucked more heat out of him than it had given. He returned to the grim reaper and asked when the cook would light up his oven. The steersman scratched his scabby wound and informed him not until the morning watch—eight hours hence. Julian covered himself with his now ice-stiffened rag and curled up between two coils of rope. He closed his eyes hoping that the steersman was telling the truth about freezing being a kind death.

A numbness not too different from warmth crept over him. Death wasn't that bad, Julian mused, and heaven would most likely be warm. There would be plenty of food, and all the people would be nice. This serene acceptance of fate was interrupted by a rude kick. An old tar with a foul toothless mouth bent over him.

"Get up and start pacing, lad." He kicked again. "To your feet lest you want to give satisfaction to those who is wagering on whether you die before or die after the last dog watch."

"I can't feel my legs," Julian protested as he staggered to his feet to stop the kicks.

A mug of hot grog was thrust into his hands. "Lucky for you, the cook can't refuse heating up grog for his old pap." The sailor draped a blanket over Julian, then kneed him in the rear to start him off. Julian limped painfully—step, drag…step.

"Keep them stumps moving. Keep them moving," the tar commanded as Julian staggered around mindlessly. "I nearly put all the money I have in the world—two crowns—that you give up the ghost afore the first dog watch, then I say to meself, 'Josiah 'tisn't right,' and I took my two crowns back. They're all sons of mongrel bitches. I'll steal you more grog in a bit, and I'll pass the word to the captain when he wakes. He won't like cheated out of a passage, even on such poor cargo as you. Keep them stumps moving."

His savior brought three more mugs of grog, which made Julian dizzy, and a plate of cold peas which had to be thawed in his mouth. After the peas, the tar did not appear again. Julian thought he heard the tar engaged in an argument below decks, a losing argument as the shouting overwhelmed the old sailor's irritable hectoring voice. For the next three hours, Julian crept and crawled around the creaking deck of that lumbering vessel, every so often begging the steersman to tell his mates to unbar a hatch. Julian thought it couldn't be worse, but then he had never experienced an ice storm at sea.

First, the wind began to hiss as the deck tilted. The hissing grew as the boat laid into the water bucking and leaping, finally turning into a yowling like giant cats fighting in the rigging. The captain emerged from his cabin, eyes wild, tarpaulin askew, and shrieked orders in a hoarse voice. The sailors rushed on deck, pushing and trampling Julian, and yelling, "Out of my way, you stinking turd!"

Julian grappled unsuccessfully for a line not in use and was kicked frequently as he slid back and forth. After fifteen minutes of furious activity, the sails were reefed, the storm sail set, and the sailors retreated below, leaving Julian fumbling for a handhold in a wild world where now two steersmen, both tarpaulin-cloaked grim reapers, leaned into the wheel. Julian finally clutched a mainmast shroud with all his passion for life, his feet slipping on the slanted deck, his head turned away from the hard pellets of frozen rain. His hands froze to the rope. With ship tossed to and fro like a tennis ball, Julian feared being shaken loose and leaving most of his skin on the hemp.

Time passed. Vaguely aware that the frozen howling was diminishing, Julian's mind began to wander. Then, abruptly, he was jerked into the present by scalding pain as boiling water was poured over his hands. He yelped, then cried as the scarred steersman unbent his fingers. "If thou had died quick, like a good lad, then I might lull my conscience, but here thou stands as right as the true gospel, and either I murder thee or I succor thee."

He guided Julian toward the hatch, which miraculously opened. As Julian climbed down, blankets were laid over his shoulders and a pound loaf of warm bread was thrust into his embrace. On reaching his berth, a sailor ordered the Lyle brothers to vacate their pallet, adding sarcastically, "This lad owns this berth. Go beg a bed from those here who may love thee." He assured Julian there would be no more trouble from the brothers.

Julian slept for three days, vaguely conscious of Captain Broom examining his feet and hands for signs of frostbite and the murmur of amazement when none were found. The punishment of the brothers wasn't over. They were hauled onto the deck to experience for themselves an ice storm. The eldest lost a finger to frostbite, lopped off compliments of the captain. Neither would glance Julian's way for fear of incurring the wrath of the sailors who now considered Julian a marvel. Abigail knitted one mitten for him—which was too small for his hand. When she presented it, she stared down at her feet. Abigail could not look at him or any man without blushing and lowering her eyes.

Mary Winn was the opposite. She bullied the cook into fixing a special chowder for him. "If I was ten years younger, I'd make you into a husband, club foot and all. You'd have no choice in the matter, my pretty lad."

"You do me too much credit, Miss Winn," Julian protested. Even in theory, being the husband of Mary Winn was a daunting prospect.

"'Tis to their shame you was the only man among them," she insisted.

"I haven't vanquished six stout sailors like you." Julian backed away from her bright blue gaze.

Mary smiled fondly. "I done what I wished done for me in my maidenhood. No man since has gotten another chance, although truthfully few dared. A husband like you suits me just fine. You're so meagerly I'd swear a puff of breath could knock you over, yet you stood three watches in a mortal cold and hurricane and still have all your fingers, toes, ears, and nose. If the captain don't think I'll suffer loss in value, I'll ask him to marry us on the morrow."

Mary Winn harped on this theme for several days and seemed to be honing in on how they could tie the knot despite the difference in age and years of indentured servitude—hers being seven. Julian was relieved when before she had perfected her plans, they came within sight of Philadelphia. He desperately hoped they would be indentured in different cities.

THE INDENTURE

DESPITE THE STORMS, or maybe helped by them, the passage took only 52 days. This was fortunate because the last week nobody could keep in their stomachs the fare of weevily biscuits and cold-pea gruel. The passengers weren't allowed on deck during the final hours of the approach to Philadelphia, so the first view Julian had of the new land was when they had anchored. Then all 279 of the immigrants crowded against the rails, silent except for a few whimpering children. The gray sky was thick with gulls and terns. A breeze ruffled the flags of the other anchored ships and spit winter at them. The city stretched along the river, clean, orderly, with just a few steeples piercing the sky. The hour must have turned because the sound of pealing bells echoed across the water. The former grim reaper sidled up to Julian, gazed down on him affectionately, a smile creasing his eyes as he said, "Most who come hither like thee perish. Hard master, sickness, savages. May the Lord protect thee, lad, and the devil forget thee or leastwise consider thee not worth his effort."

There were two types of indentured servants: those who already had their contract with employers and those whose contracts the captain sold to pay for the passage. For the latter group, advertisements were promptly printed. By the afternoon of the second day at anchor, boats began to arrive with interested parties. Julian stood in line on deck to be questioned and examined with the other not-yet-redeemed souls. This process left no doubt in his mind of his legal status as property. Teeth were inspected; muscles palpated; eyes peered into; chests thumped. Behind a screen set up on the quarterdeck future servants could prove they weren't infected with the pox. Wives generally inspected the women and girls, husbands the boys and men. With a good spyglass, sailors on other vessels could follow the proceedings.

The partings were heartrending. Five passengers, three men, and two women, lost spouses during the last half of the voyage. These grieving souls were therefore obliged to double the years of their contract to pay for the passage of their deceased loved ones. Consumed by despair and grief, they stood numbly while the captain promoted their salable attributes to potential purchasers. Then there were the families torn apart—wife, husband, children sold to different buyers and unlikely to see each other ever again. Some told lies to ease the pain: "'Twill just be a little while, my loves, ere we all sit together at the table again." Some prayed: "God keep you, dear. Be good." Some advised: "Work hard. Do us proud." And some screamed as if their limbs were being torn from them.

Despite the extra years tacked on to his indenture, Julian fully expected to be the last chosen. Standing in his thin shirt on the frozen deck between a joiner and a cooper, skinny arms wrapped around his skinny chest, he felt keenly his lack of useful skills. Tradesmen and farmers sniffed at him doubtfully and shook their heads when they saw his deformed foot. "The captain's a fool to think you're worth more than a pot of p..." the grim farmer glanced at his frowning wife and continued, "watered rum." A well-dressed woman who vaguely resembled Mrs. Gunn commented, "Poor boy, if I hadn't six mouths to feed, I might take thee out of pity, only sometimes 'tis best to leave pity to the Lord." Yet out of the hundred plus passengers unengaged, Julian's contract was the twenty-fourth to find a buyer.

His new master caused a fright when he swaggered onto the deck and bellowed, "Blood and thunder, I be not sailing this wormy log across a washbasin!"

Most of the farmers, merchants, and tradesmen possessed an air of civility and curiosity. Their dress showed sober prosperity, and Julian could imagine that some might be generous and kind. The rocking boat made more than a few of these worthy souls swallow hard and frequently look longingly toward the shore. There was no such awkwardness when Julian's purchaser, a short, broad man, with a wild grizzled beard, small gleaming black eyes, and hawk's bells woven into his hair, stumped up and down the line of the hapless aspirants to servitude. A stained red blanket half-covered his buckskin shirt and filthy leggings.

With an Irish lilt he replied to Captain Broom's question, "Bragg is me name. Bartholomew Bragg, your servant, sir."

The other interested parties backed away, unwilling to

interfere with the half-savage apparition. Julian was certain he wasn't alone in praying that this particular party would pass him over. Bragg pinched the plump arm of a girl, making her squeal. The captain informed him that if he were a serious buyer, he could examine her for pox. A matron squawked a protest against this indecency, saying she would conduct the examination to preserve the maiden's modesty. Master Bragg appeared amused. "Arrah now, captain, there's only one thing I am knowing how to do with such a wench, and she's a bit over-fine for the likes of me, don't you think? Nay, I'm after a boy who can assist in me trade. I had poor luck with the last three. Morgan, the mooncalf, succumbed to the pox, which there was no pleasure in the getting; a savage shaved bran-faced Isiah's head a little too close, and a bear ate Thomas." Bragg thumped the chest of a muscular young farmhand, who paled and flinched.

"What sort of trade are you engaged in, Mister Bragg?" Broom asked.

"Trading with the heathen, the Sons of Ham," he muttered, continuing his inspection. He stopped in front of Julian, who slumped and limped a step forward and raised his leg to show off the strange angle of his shoe on the end of his deformed foot. "I require a boy who is knowing how to keep his head on his body and his hair on his head. That be the main thing, sure. Everything else can be learned." Master Bragg lifted Julian's arm, felt up its bony length and snorted. He ordered Julian to open his mouth, and he snorted again. He again paraded down the row of the passengers without indentures, thumping and looking at teeth, then paused in front of Julian. "Have you no covering beside your shirt and breeches, lad?"

"No, sir," Julian replied weakly.

"Nothing?" He tapped a sturdy forefinger on Julian's chest.

"Only what you see on my person, sir."

"Might you feel a bit frostbitten?" Bragg grasped Julian's chin and twisted his head to one side, then the other.

"Cold don't bother him," Captain Broom added. "He spent the voyage in his shirt on deck so happy as a naked savage in the tropics, even when we sailed into a blizzard. I never saw the likes of it."

"The captain claims you be not sensible to cold, lad?" Bragg inquired.

"That is not true, sir. 'Tis just I had no choice in the matter," Julian said with difficulty because Bragg was inspecting his teeth.

Bragg made a skeptical grunt. "I encountered savages, time to time, dancing naked in the snow, but nary an Englishman. Tell me about yourself, boy? Have you any useful abilities?"

"I'm afraid I possess none, sir," Julian answered hopefully.

"He knows his letters, Master Bragg," the captain interjected. "And he's not yet twelve, so he'll provide you ten years good service."

Julian bridled at this lie.

"Knows his letters." Bragg mused. "That only gives a lad pettifogging airs. The boy has mouth rot and is the color of a half-digested oyster. I doubt he'd survive a fortnight in the backwoods, much less a decade. The pox will carry him off the next time it sweeps through, to be sure."

"I had the pox, sir." Julian would soon regret his honesty.

Bragg peered closely. "Hard to see with your other blotches whether you be cribbage-pated or no. You wasn't talking about t'other pox, was you?"

"What other pox are you referring to, sir?"

Bragg laughed heartily. "An innocent babe. Well, then the grippe will take you and I'll lose me investment."

"I had that more than once, sir," Julian persevered in trying to portray himself as a sickly prospect that would die soon.

"What other distempers have you acquired, lad?"

"I can't remember them all," Julian replied, wishing he could.

"Let me help you. Was you ever ill with spotted fever?" Bragg scratched his grizzled chin.

"I was ill once with spots."

"And the bloody flux?" Bragg asked,

"Yes, master, if you mean I bled down below."

"Bled out your arse and living to tell about it. How about the plague? Have you caught that also, lad, you know with them stinking pustules over your face and in your armpits?" Bragg laughed as if he had caught Julian on that one.

Julian nodded meekly. "I believe so, sir. When I was eight, they nailed shut the door of our room calling my illness the black pestilence, but later they said 'twas probably a mistake for no one else came down with it."

Bragg walked around Julian reciting a catalog of illnesses and symptoms—agues, fluxes, boils, blisters, fevers—and asking what was his experience with them.

Except for dock fever and barrel sickness, Julian was able to confirm that he had either contracted the disease or had suffered the symptoms of the disease but was too young to remember its name. Julian believed that such a history of infirmity reflected poorly on him. Master Bragg, however, seemed to hold a contrary opinion. "Well, I've found me a lad. We'll be signing the papers."

"But what about my foot?" Julian shook off his shoe to display the twisted appendage.

Master Bragg contemplated the object. "Aye, 'twasn't put together right after you broke it, sure, so we just break it again and do the job properly."

Twenty minutes after the contract was signed and the sum of three pounds passed hands—down from the asking price of five because of his lameness—Julian found himself climbing out of the bumboat and trailing after his master into the streets of Philadelphia. As his left sideways foot desperately tried to keep up with the right, Julian hoped futilely that they might stop at one of the taverns with warmly lighted windows and happy drunken voices. For several blocks, they continued along a broad cobblestone thoroughfare lined with large plain brick houses, the windows shuttered tightly, smoke swirling out of the several chimneys of each residence.

Just beyond a park, Bragg turned down a narrower gravel street. Dim lights shone in the windows of the ground-floor shops. The evening was settling in fast, and the wind began to pelt his face with hard bits of snow. The few people about hurried to their destinations with cloaks pulled over their heads and hunched shoulders. A carriage passed with hissing wheels. A little girl ran out of a baker's shop, handed Julian a warm roll, babbled a few words in German, and then ran back in. On a street corner, an old Indian, bundled in a filthy cloak, waved back and forth two brooms that he was selling. With his face harsh and gaunt as if chipped out of stone, one elongated earlobe split and dangling on his shoulders, the other bowing with a gap big enough to fit a child's fist, and a bone thrust through the septum of his nose, he appeared to Julian doom and death personified. A watchman yelled threats at the Indian and even raised a cudgel, but the ancient demon stood his ground unflinching.

Three blocks further, Bragg entered a livery stable. Julian waited outside, his foot burning, the rest of him shivering and doubting the possibility of ever becoming warm again. Bragg finally emerged leading a horse with large empty panniers. He threw a greasy blanket to Julian saying. "I suspicioned the captain were trying to inflate your value when he was claiming you took no notice of cold."

Julian followed Bragg and the horse on a rough cart trail beyond the outskirts of Philadelphia. His left leg buckled with every other step, his teeth chattered, his nose dripped. The chimney smoke from isolated farmhouses merged into the sky; the barking of dogs echoed in the vast spaces. There remained a smudge of light in the west, but hell could not be darker than the woods that seemed to extend limitlessly beyond the fields. As the squat form of his new master and the rear of the horse faded into the darkness and the cold fire consumed his entire leg, Julian began to suspect that he might be what people called unlucky.

Finally, a tiny dot of light hovered in the distance.

Master Bragg stopped, walked back to where Julian stood, balancing on his good foot. Kneeling down, Bragg grasped the other appendage that hovered an inch above the ground and with inexplicable cruelty twisted it violently. Julian fell backward screaming. Firmly bracing Julian's twisted foot against his chest, Master Bragg jerked his whole body clockwise several times resulting in a series of small cracking noises.

"Arrah now, 'twill not do. For making the thing you claim is a foot render decent service, I am having to truss you up and finish the job. Stop sniveling. 'Twas more Christian to try me hand at straightening your thing before it thawed." Bragg pointed to the dully lighted oil-paper window. "By the time you crawl there, I'll have gathered the tools to do the job properly."

Julian crawled the last hundred yards in complete darkness. Twice, he blacked out, and twice a booming voice roused him back into agonizing consciousness: "Make haste, lad, make haste for if you overly abuse me patience, I might just be chopping the damn thing off!"

At last, Julian arrived at the rude log house. A woman who, except for the beard, could have been Master Bragg's twin, opened the door and helped him onto a pallet. Flickering between consciousness and pain-induced delirium, Julian was bound and completely immobilized with a series of complicated knots. Bragg then lashed the twisted foot to a wooden plank.

"Minerva, bring whiskey," Bragg commanded. The squat woman handed him a wooden bowl.

Bragg pinched Julian's nose and poured the liquid fire down his throat. Julian began to spit and gag.

"Waste good whiskey, will you? No more of that. Now, lad, time to set your foot in its proper mooring. Bite down on this broomstick and pray for the Lord's mercy." The thick fingers twisted the board. Julian screamed through the broom handle. "Bloody shit," Bragg muttered. "I'll be needing to use the ax."

"Let me die," Julian begged and spat out the handle and splinters as Bragg took a long-handled ax from the corner. He watched horrified as Bragg hefted the ax, then closed his eyes to avoid witnessing the severing of his ankle. Strangely, nothing happened. He peeked just as the ax's flat end had begun to head swiftly and purposefully toward his bound foot.

When Julian awoke to his own weeping, his still attached foot was tightly wrapped in rags.

Master Bragg loomed over him. "You see the difficulty, lad, is you can't be going out into the wilderness walking sideways. 'Twas one bone that not set right so I had to break and set it again so more of your foot plants itself on the ground and fits into a stirrup. In a half dozen fortnights, you'll be striding like a Christian, though never will you be fleet of foot. That isn't altogether a disadvantage. On encountering savages you might take fright and get the notion to run away, which never ends well. You either have to make peace with those savages you meet or be fighting where you stand."

"Half a dozen fortnights, sir? Am I to reside here that long?" Julian asked.

"You be needing the time to mend, and mid-March is when I am accustomed to begin me business with the heathen. 'Twill be rough going at first, but I like to visit the western villages in the early thaw. Having all winter to dream on their hearts' desires—a new musket, a tin whistle, or a coat with ruffles—the savages welcome us like long lost brothers, and we strike deals more to our advantage. In the meantime, I am still after purchasing eight packhorses, sufficient trading goods to load them down, and three violins."

"Violins?" Julian latched onto this word which didn't quite make sense.

"Aye, violins. I traded one to an Oneida sachem last season making three other sachems envious and desiring of their own fiddles. Can't say much for the caterwauling they make on them."

"How am I to occupy myself while you do your business, sir?" Julian asked.

"I am not supposing I paid enough to expect to have good use from you at the start." Bragg contemplated Julian appraisingly. "I'll instruct you in usefulness. The time you take learning and mending, I add on to your contract along with any other day you're choosing to be ill."

"But the contract has a date on it." Julian's heart had sunk when he saw the nine-year eight-month contract.

"As I stated, I'm having no tolerance for pettifoggery." Bragg scowled. "I paid for nine years eight months of labor, not nine years eight months of idling about. I mean to get every day of the nine years, eight months out of you, and if you're sick a day, you haven't held to your side of the contract for that day."

Thus, began a strange interlude in Julian's fifteenth year. Minerva and Bragg shared a pallet in the sleeping loft above him. They went at each other lustily and noisily two or three times a day causing a moderate downpour of straw. They both drank vast quantities of rum, and they both snored robustly. Ignored, Julian whiled away the hours in his dim corner, futilely trying to shift his bound foot into less painful positions. Twice a day Minerva spooned corn mash out of a pot over the hearth fire into a bowl and presented it to Julian. Sometimes there were dried berries or pumpkin mixed in, sometimes scraps of meat. He also found canine teeth and once his spoon uncovered a small pointed rodent face. Minerva gave him a stout stick to use as a crutch for whenever he needed to go outside to relieve himself. Sitting on that cold board across the trench and using the snow to clean himself at least gave his eyes and lungs a few minutes respite from the smoke.

Julian made friends with a lugubrious hound who occupied the other corner. He conversed with the beast, mostly about his mother. Running away could only be seen as a vile betrayal now—cowards and scapegraces stole away in the middle of the night. Julian plotted ways to return such as sneaking aboard a ship and offering to work for his passage. Murdering Bragg seemed too risky, but maybe the next bear would choose to eat his master. Julian also considered writing his mother begging her to beg Mr. Skylar to pay off Bragg. He would be a haberdashery slave for the rest of his life. Better that than huddling in this corner friendless except for a flea-bitten hound and having to relieve himself witnessed by the immense sky and the endless forest of this cold empty world.

MOHAWKS

BRAGG NEVER INVITED his occasional visitors inside. Instead, no matter the weather, they would converse while strolling around the house or into the woods. When Julian inquired about this, Bragg replied, "Keeping Minerva in rum is costly enough without having goddamn friends drinking away me capital." Once, after relieving himself, Julian found Bragg in front of the cabin consulting with a small dark man whose intense black eyes and the nervous alertness of his pinched features showed a general wariness of the world. With a start, he realized that Bragg and his companion were speaking the language of the paper-chewing girls who had lived above him in London.

On spotting Julian, Bragg called out, "Boy, I'd like to present you to Mr. Grayson who buys furs for a tuppence and sells them for a guinea."

Grayson smiled tightly. He wore no hat or overcoat despite the razor edge to the icy air. With a hint of Irish brogue in his voice, Grayson remarked, "You sell dear, Bragg. You always have. You're lucky I don't take up trading with the savages myself and give my tuppences to them instead of you."

"Would you fancy a dram of rum, James?"

Grayson shook his head. "Nay, nay, I must be off." When he turned, Julian noticed a large brownish stain on the back of his shirt.

"Did you see that Mr. Grayson was bleeding, master?" Julian asked once the visitor was out of earshot.

Bragg scratched his chin. "To be sure, strange man, James Grayson. 'Tis always safe to offer him a drink. He has been mortifying his flesh ever since I made his acquaintance and that be twenty years. I'm surprised he is having any flesh left to mortify."

"Why does he do that?" Julian asked, watching as Grayson turned down the road leading away from Phila-delphia and wondering where else would he be going on such an inhospitable afternoon.

"I suspect to shorten his spell in purgatory. A wise thing for those of us who sinned our youth away. As for me, a century of mortification wouldn't dent me purga-torial half of eternity."

Julian watched the speck of a man disappear over a rise. "'Tis not my place to question, only why were you speaking French to him?"

Bragg clapped Julian on his back. "Is that what you heard us speaking lad, French?"

"I don't understand the language, sir, but I know the sound of it."

"No, 'tis not your place," Bragg agreed. "Despite that I'll answer you all the same. I speak French to those who are understanding the tongue for 'twas in that tongue me mother sang to me over the cradle. She was an innocent French maid, seduced by an Irish wastrel who carried her to Limerick, then abandoned her to misery and poverty and a nasty imp of a son."

If Bragg received word of a ship docking, he would leave for the day in search of violins and other interesting cargo. "I like bringing me savage friends doodads and gewgaws to tickle their fancy. Makes them welcoming, and I never forget little gifts for the squaws—colored thread or brass buttons."

Minerva would take advantage of these absences to show interest in Julian. "You have a sweet face, lad," she might say, caressing his cheek. "When you grow into manhood, you'll make the ladies swoon at the mere sight of you."

Once, after she boldly plunged her hand into his breeches and fondled what she found there, Julian excused himself and spent a cold hour outside sitting over the trench. When he returned, Minerva met him at the door stark naked. She was a woman of nearly overwhelming proportions—Julian doubted he could get his arms around half of her body with its immense breasts and hips that brushed each side of the door jambs. The odor emanating from her was a fermenting mix of sweat, old straw, and rum. Julian must not have hidden his discomfiture because she said, "Well, fie on you boy, if 'tis not to be, then 'tis not to be." She donned her gown matter-of-factly, and the rest of the day acted as if nothing unusual had occurred. Master Bragg returned leading two horses loaded with Jew's harps, wampum beads, gunpowder, vermilion, rum, several yards of silk, red cloth, ten old muskets, mirrors, ruffled collars, a dozen knives, a waistcoat, flutes, and one violin. He also presented to Minerva a sack of rice and a yard of cambric.

That evening Bragg ordered Julian, "Show me your foot." Without waiting for assent, Bragg then unwrapped the stiff canvas rags swaddling it. Holding the swollen purple but straighter appendage up admiringly, he commented, "Not a thing of beauty, to be sure, but in another fort-night or two, you'll be going about without your stick. Good thing too, for we'll not detain ourselves if winter breaks early."

Three evenings later, as Julian was settling into a long sleep, the sad hound gave a half-hearted woof which was followed by a rap at the door. Bragg climbed down the ladder bare-assed and picked up a primed pistol.

"Stranger, you better have a damn good reason for broaching me dreams," he growled, lifting the latch and leveling the barrel. On seeing the visitors, however, Bragg dropped the gun. "Why, Chief Nickus? What sainted miracle brings you to me poor abode? Minerva, throw down me breeches." He then kicked Julian. "Make space for these gentlemen, you lazy jackanapes."

Julian slid to the corner and comforted the hound as three figures with the grave bearing of bishops entered the room. Uneasy and fascinated, he stared while the visitors removed their woolen caps, revealing bristling patches of hair that ran down the middle of their heads and ended in scalp locks. Blue geometrical tattoos covered the lower half of their faces, and silver nose rings hung so low that their tongues could have licked the dangling appendages.

They then doffed their dreadnought coats, shaking off the snow and revealing on their persons a bristling collection of weapons. Minerva cowered in the loft above, weeping softly. Julian wished he could join her, although the visitors hadn't deigned to acknowledge him.

The three guests seated themselves on the floor cross-legged, as did Bragg. The youngest scanned the cabin restlessly, his dangerous eyes passing over Julian as if he were not there. A bright pink scar ran from his right ear to his chin, and he was missing entirely the left ear. The second brave didn't turn his head, although his dark eyes gave the impression of taking in everything. His skin shone like polished mahogany and his flaring nostrils seemed about to exhale fire. The oldest, whom Bragg had addressed as Chief Nickus, possessed perhaps a gentler countenance. A gold gorget hung around his neck. His scalp lock was gathered through a gold band at the nape. Gold rings encircled his thumbs, and long silver earrings brushed his shoulders. At first, Nickus maintained a forbidding silence. Julian was starting to doubt whether the regal savage would speak at all when he began in a strange resonant formal English: "Brother Bragg, Mr. William Johnson out of respect and affection for your friendship put into my mouth a warning that he implores you to heed."

"So Chief Nickus Brant, what be this warning from William Johnson?" Bragg's reply possessed the same solemn tone but sounded slightly mocking.

"Brother," Nickus continued, "Mr. William Johnson forbids you to trade neither with the nations of the Iroquois nor the nations that are their sons and daughters—the Mingos, the Lenape, the Wyandot, the Shawnee."

Bragg bared his teeth in a gargoyle grimace. "That be Willy all over, claiming friendship on one hand, while denying a fellow his livelihood on t'other."

After an uncomfortably long pause, Nickus responded, giving equal emphasis to each word. "You may pursue trade with the Cherokee, Creeks, and Choctaw, if the commissioner of the southern colonies gives you leave." Nickus unloosed a heavy purse from his belt and dropped it jangling in front of Bragg. "Because he fears he may be interrupting your plans, Mr. William Johnson has instructed me to purchase your trade goods at a fair price."

Bragg weighed the bag. "That's exceeding generous of Willy, so I am starving next year instead of this. Why is Willy wanting to shut me out?"

"There are many little birds whispering news about you in Mr. William Johnson's ear. They all sing the same song, so he has no choice but to listen," Nickus replied slowly.

"Aye, there always be those little rumormongering birds," Bragg grumbled.

Nickus continued: "The little birds say you acted for the French in King George's War, telling the Abenaki and our French Mohawk brothers where the settlements were weak and where strong. Three towns in Maine were raided and burned after you passed through last year."

"And how many villages in Maine I had not passed through was raided and burned." Bragg took a coin out of the bag, bit it, then put it back in. "Shush woman!" he yelled to the whimpering Minerva above him.

"Now that the French and English smoke the peace pipe, you find new ways to make discord. You tell the young braves of the Onondaga, Oneida, and Seneca that their land is barren like an old squaw. You tell them to leave their villages and go to King Louie's land, which is fertile and full of game."

Bragg snorted. The brave missing an ear unsheathed his knife, and Julian's vision in his panic briefly went out of focus. When he recovered, the brave was picking his teeth with the knife's point.

Nickus went on: "You tell them that if they stay, they are King George's women. You tell the Irish, the Palatine, the Swedish settlers they are fools to pay for land when they can have without payment as much land as a man wants to work. William Johnson has no desire to see you suffer the fate of a traitor. I saw such a man hanged, drawn, and quartered in London. I, a Mohawk, was speechless in admiration."

"Me fate is me fate, Nickus." Bragg dropped the bag of coins. "The French are having eyes and ears and mouths in every village from the Mississippi to the Hudson. They are not needing an old man to tell them where to strike. If anyone is to blame, 'tis the poor foolish settlers who plant their miserable homes on the hunting grounds of the savage nations. And as for land, I am doubting I told any brave, young or old, aught about what lies beyond the Ohio that he isn't already knowing. Only that isn't all, is it Nickus? I can see by your scowl you are not finished with me transgressions. Of what other great crimes am I accused?"

"Last spring at Johnson's fort, a tenant recognized

you as the pirate who boarded his ship and gouged out his eye when he was sailing in the Caribbean twenty-five winters ago. You are the pirate, Johnny Duggan or Jacques Dugard, who took many ships, murdered many men, and who has a bounty of five hundred pounds on his head."

Bragg gave a wild laugh. The hound followed with a low woof. Minerva howled in despair. "So, being a treacherous French spy isn't enough for Willy? I am also an infamous pirate. Next, I suppose he'll accuse me of being an infidel Turk just to complete me villainy. So, tell me Nickus, if I flaunt Willy's wishes, what are his intentions?"

"You have lived too long to be so unwise as to ignore the warning," Nickus replied.

"Willy makes the danger and can unmake the danger as he sees fit," Bragg asserted angrily.

Nickus suddenly drew out his tomahawk and buried the blade with a reverberating thwonk in the wooden floor of the cabin. Minerva wailed again, and fear shivered up Julian's spine. "I make the danger, Master Bragg. You may sing your lies to the Irish, Palatines, and Swedes, but not to us. The Mohawk are one end of the longhouse, the Seneca, the other. Our brothers, the Onondagas, Oneida, Cayuga, and Tuscarora, live between."

The brave who was picking his teeth put the knife back into its sheath causing Julian to emit a sigh of relief. He then felt Nickus's eyes on him but was unable to tell whether the old chief's stare was amused or contemptuous.

"When brothers in the longhouse fight, the earth is sick," Nickus continued. "When you tell the Cayuga or the Oneida they should not listen to the Mohawks because we are Johnson's women, you are trying to make brothers fight. This tomahawk would be planted in your skull were it not for the affection Mr. William Johnson bears you."

Bragg picked up the purse, dislodged the tomahawk and handed both back to Nickus. "I can't help with your family quarrels, Chief Nickus. Tell Johnson I give not a widow's mite for his warning. The country is free to all traders with good will, which I be, so I am going where I bloody well please. Nor can Johnson be bribing me to do what I no intend to do. I always deal squarely with friend or enemy. You know that. Now, unless you're after scalping me, you may leave. Your servant, Chief Nickus."

Nickus nodded, and the three Indians stood, donned caps and coats, and gravely and proudly filed out the door.

After they had left, Julian asked, "Sir, 'tis not my place to question, only will it not be dangerous for you to take the violins to the sachems?"

Bragg laughed. "Of the thousand ways to lose your life trading with savages, the danger of William Johnson's displeasure rates rather low. But I think I will be giving Fort Johnson a visit and having a little tête-à-tête with me friend—Irishman to Irishman."

"Won't he arrest you, sir?"

"Nay, Willy always presumes more authority than he possesses. Likelier, those three jolly fellows who were enjoying our hospitality will waylay me and you, scalp us, spit us and slowly roast us over a fire whilst they dance, sing, and tell jokes. Don't be giving me that hang-gallows' look, lad. You can't be whistling danger away—you either stare it in the eye or show it your heels."

FORT JOHNSON

THE NEXT AFTERNOON, Bragg returned from an outing with two large sturdy horses he claimed were good snow-plowers. The following morning before even a suggestion of dawn, Bragg kicked Julian awake, threw him a blanket, boots, and a pile of clothes, saying, "Look lively! 'Tis colder than a witch's teat outside. Put these on over what you is wearing unless you want the blood freezing in your veins."

"Master, will there be inns along the way?" Julian asked, shivering as he struggled into a second pair of breeches.

"Don't be worrying yourself with vain hopes of warm hearths and feather beds. If we are finding a public house, I'll save meself a penny or two stabling you with the cattle."

Julian balked when he confronted the great shaggy beast he was to mount. Sensing his fear, the horse snorted and shifted uneasily.

"You better introduce yourself to Frida," Bragg advised. "Else she be throwing and trampling you. She's Mennonite, in case you can't tell by her name, so you can soothe her by reciting scripture in German."

Julian approached the huge animal, placed his hands on either side of the great head and looked into the large brown equine eyes. "We'll get along fine," Julian whispered, somewhat surprised at his own certainty that he could handle this new mode of transportation. The horse lifted its head as if nodding. Julian patted its nose, his hand easily fitting in the space between the nostrils. Then Frida patiently stood while he clumsily scaled her back.

For three weeks, they traveled through a world so white that earth and sky and frozen water merged together and so cold that breathing burned deep into the throat and lungs. Most of the time, Julian kept a blanket draped over his head like a cloak and a rag wrapped up to his eyes around his face. Through a sliver between the folds of the blanket, he was only able to see Frida's broad neck and ears, the swirling mist of snow, and a bit of white ground. Despite his aching inner thighs caused by straddling her wide back, Frida was a marvelous animal that provided body heat along with saving him the painful effort of walking.

Bragg usually managed to find nightly lodging in a farmer's rude cabin or barn. These farmers seemed the loneliest people on earth. Miles of wilderness separated the homesteads. Even the poorest turned out their best provender which often merely consisted of cornmeal sweetened with molasses and dried pumpkin. Bragg encouraged their efforts by mentioning how generously a neighbor down the road had shown them hospitality. What their hosts expected in payment was news—they listened hungrily to any news, all news from the condition of a neighbor's barn to the rumors of the return of the Jacobite Pretender to England.

A few times, the night caught them in the open far from any homestead. Julian would then spend dark miserable hours dragging his numb foot through the undergrowth breaking off frozen branches and pulling decayed logs out of the snow. Bragg would huddle over a small pile of oily birch bark and with what could be described as magic strike a few sparks off a flint creating a tiny flame which he would nurture with the concentration of a crystal-gazing fortuneteller. Taking a burning twig from that fire, he would ignite another pile six feet away, and they would lay down between the two fires. Most of the wood was too wet to burn immediately, so it was set nearby to dry out and later fed into the flames. No matter how much wood was collected, the fuel was exhausted and fires burnt out before morning.

Bragg showed little indication that the cold bothered him. Then again, he wore several more layers of clothing than Julian, who had to make do, aside from the rag and blanket, with a woolen undershirt, a leather jacket, and two leather breeches that could freeze so stiff that they could stand up on their own and made walking nearly impossible whenever he dismounted from Frida. Bragg did allow Julian an extra pair of boots which were stuffed with raw wool. Twice, they stayed at inns, sleeping in the dark chilly rooms. Bragg paid for Julian's lodging. At both inns, they were fortunate in only sharing a bed with one fellow traveler: their first bedfellow was a snoring woman whose disreputable smell protected her virtue and the second was an old man who argued with himself about the price of barley in his sleep.

Unable to see much beyond Frida's neck and a narrow slice of white ground for three weeks, Julian had no idea why they had stopped. It was too early to ask for lodging, and Bragg had just relieved himself a mile back. The sharp raps of metal on metal came as a surprise. A knocker? What farmhouse in this wilderness would ornament its door with a brass knocker? The raps grew louder and more insistent. Julian wouldn't have blamed the poor farmer if he answered Bragg with a blast from a loaded musket.

"Master William Johnson!" Bragg shouted. Julian lifted his head and made a bigger opening in the blanket to peer out. Yes, Bragg was vigorously exercising a brass knocker on the door of a large sturdy brick house that had suddenly sprung up in front of them out of this white desolation. "Willy Johnson!" Bragg boomed loud enough to shake the snow from the eaves.

The door opened.

"Boy," Bragg called to Julian, "If your arse isn't frozen stuck to Frida, get down and come on in."

Julian dismounted. Unseen hands took away Frida. He stumbled forward three-quarters blind as he tried to readjust the blanket and collided into the thigh of what seemed a giant—and who, in fact, turned out to be a giant. Huge hands lifted the blanket off and straightened Julian. When he gathered the courage to look up, Julian saw a blond liveried servant gazing benevolently down at him from an altitude of seven feet. Behind the giant stood the regal Nickus in fine European dress, his uncov-

ered head showing the bristling strip of hair and a ring
still adorning his nose, and from behind Nickus peeked
an Mohawk girl of about Julian's age whose smooth face
would have been pleasing had it not contained a smirk and
maliciously twinkling eyes. Wearing a pale gold gown with
a pale green petticoat, she was as properly dressed as any
well-to-do girl in London, but unlike such a girl, instead
of a modest cap, she wore a band around her head sprout-
ing several large feathers.

"I am after making peace with me friend and fellow
countryman, William Johnson," Bragg proclaimed as he
unwound his scarf, doffed his hat and matchcoat, handing
them to the giant.

Nickus's expression hardened. "Brother Warraghiyagey
is smoking the pipe and conferring with a delegation of
Onondaga sachems in the blockhouse. He is giving them
costly gifts to undo your treachery. You will not find him
in a well-disposed humor toward you."

"Bah, Chief Nickus, ever wonder why the more your
brother Warraghiyagey—who I be calling Willy—gives,
the richer he becomes. Warraghiyagey knows the price
of a man's heart, which is always less than its worth. As
for me supposed treachery, the Onondaga chief, Yellow
Turtle, will confirm I never uttered a traitorous word in
his hearing."

"You whisper your treachery to the young braves
who are impatient of the wisdom of their elders," Nickus
replied coldly.

Bragg snorted. "Who be saying that lies, to be sure.
I come to justify meself to Willy. If I was a French spy,

I wouldn't bloody well come all the way to his demesne, risking me mortal flesh to make things right."

"Fifteen years I know you, Master Bragg," Nickus replied. "Lies fall as readily from your mouth as truth, and the bigger the lie, the easier it slides off your tongue. Johannes will lead you to the study where you can wait. In a few hours, Brother Warraghiyagey will attend to you. Your frozen servant can stay here until Brother Warraghiyagey decides what to do with both of you. Molly will bring the young man tea and buns."

Nickus, Bragg and the giant servant left. The girl frowned, obviously displeased with her task, and disappeared. Julian sat down on an elegant chair with a red velvet pillow cushioning his bony thighs and little carved faces snarling at the ends of the armrests. He slowly began to peel the rag from his face and take in his surroundings. On the wall, a painting showed a singularly intense young gentleman pursuing a young shepherdess with pink rounded breasts. Abutting that idyll, a horrifyingly thin and reddened visage returned Julian's gaze. For a moment, he didn't realize that it was his own ravaged image regarding him from the gilt-framed looking glass. He glanced down at his shoddy breeches and jacket stained from three weeks of having nowhere else to wipe his hands after meals. He cringed at the smudges of dirty snow his feet were leaving on a rug embroidered with cavorting peacocks and unicorns. He returned to the frightening face in the looking glass and decided it might be wiser to absent himself and hide in the stables before he was booted out of this elegant setting. The girl returned with the tray. His resolution surrendered to hunger. The tea was scalding deliciousness. The buns softly dissolved in the mouth.

"Thank you, Miss Molly," he said.

"I am a Mohawk princess," the girl announced with princess-like authority. "You may address me as such."

Julian didn't know how seriously to take this girl.

"In London do princesses have to serve beggar boys tea and buns?" She continued.

"No, I don't think so, although 'tis different there," Julian replied.

She sniffed contemptuously. "Are you saying the princesses in London are better than me?"

"They live in mansions and palaces, which are bigger than houses."

"Do their stepfathers order them to serve beggar boys tea and buns?" She demanded.

"They must obey their fathers like all well-behaved girls. If you're a princess, your stepfather must be a king."

"Yes, he is king of the Mohawks. My brother Joseph is a prince, and one day he will also be king. I think after you finish your bun, I'll take your scalp." She drew out a wicked looking knife that she had secreted in the sash behind her back, smiled at him, spat on the blade, and wiped it on her dress.

"Princesses in London don't scalp boys." Julian watched uneasily as she swished the curved blade near his hairline.

"They must be different like you said. I am an obedient Mohawk daughter, so I bring you tea and buns because my stepfather tells me to bring you tea and buns, yet I am also a Mohawk princess, so I take your scalp."

"How did you learn to speak English so well?" Julian hoped to change the subject.

This question did appear to flatter her. "My stepfather insists his children are well bred and educated like children of a king should be. He said that I must be an English princess as well as a Mohawk princess. I am learning to speak French, and I have a dance master, or I had one, but he resigned after I told him I would scalp him if he spoke mean to me again. Do beggar boys learn to dance?"

"No, I have a bad foot," Julian explained.

"Let me see, let me see," Molly insisted excitedly.

Julian took off his boot and carefully brushed away the wool threads which still clung to his foot. Molly stared in fascination.

"'Tis as ugly as a hoof. Can I touch it?" She poked at the foot gently.

"A carriage ran over it in London." Julian tried to keep his foot from twitching as she poked it.

"It should be cut off. No foot is better than that horrible thing," she declared and looked at Jonathan as if daring him to contradict her.

"I do not want to hobble around on a peg for the rest of my life," Julian protested.

"Why not? At least you are able to polish a peg so 'tis not ugly. I see you are finished with your bun. Do you want more buns or may I take your scalp now?"

"I'm not permitting you to take my scalp."

"I am aware I have to stab you a couple of times first, but that shan't be hard for you can't run away on that hoof." She sliced the air underneath his chin.

"I believe I need more buns," Julian said.

She pranced off and soon came back with another platter of steaming rolls. When she bent to put down the platter, Julian pulled the knife from her sash.

"That's not fair. Give me my knife back." Molly circled around to get at her weapon.

"So you can scalp me." Julian held the knife as far away from her as he could.

"Yes!" She stamped her foot. "So I can scalp you."

"Well, I don't want to be scalped."

"Well, I didn't want to bring you your buns. Now give it back to me, or I'll call Johannes to take it from you. Remember, I'm a princess and if you lay a hand on me, my stepfather, the king of the Mohawks will cut you into little pieces and put you in his stew." Molly caught his arm with both of her hands. Julian kept his grip on the handle. She tried to bite his wrist.

"Princesses don't bite." He placed his other hand on her forehead to push her away.

"When Mohawk princesses can't scalp, they bite," she said struggling.

Julian succeeded in making her fall back. Plucking a feather out of her band she renewed the attack, dodging in and out, tickling his exposed foot and then his ears, all the while trying to grab the knife. Julian was fully occupied keeping the knife away from Princess Molly without cutting himself or her.

Suddenly, winter gusted in through an open door.

"Molly!" A large broad-shouldered man wrapped from head to toe in a red blanket exclaimed, shutting out the snow and wind as he closed the door. When he threw off his covering and revealed a brightly painted face, leggings, breechcloth, and buckskin beaded shirt, Julian's first thought was that the savage must be Molly's brother Joseph. The trace of brogue in his voice, however, betrayed his origin. "Molly, stop tormenting the boy!"

"He started it, Master Johnson." Molly's demeanor suddenly turned meek. Her large eyes brimmed with innocence.

"Miss Molly, you always start it." William Johnson scowled menacingly at her.

"He wouldn't believe I am a princess."

"Are you acting like one now?" Johnson inquired.

"Yes, I most definitely am." Molly folded her arms.

Johnson turned to Julian. "What is your name, lad?"

"Julian, sir."

"Did Miss Brant threaten to scalp you?"

"Yes, sir."

"Julian, give Princess Molly her knife back," Johnson ordered.

Julian reluctantly did what William Johnson requested, thinking fate was fate.

"Now, Molly, go ahead."

She stood before Julian, momentarily put off. She lifted the knife. Julian winced, and she sighed. "I don't want to now."

"Julian, Miss Brant is an overly-indulged child," Johnson declared.

"How dare you call me a child," Molly interrupted.

William Johnson continued in a schoolmaster's tone: "An overly-indulged child who is amusing herself at your expense, which she does to everybody she encounters. If she fails to redress her behavior, I'll prevail on Nickus to send her to a proper school in England where they will cane her morning, noon, and night to teach her manners and respect."

"I'll scalp any old hag who canes me." Molly's eyes spit fire.

"I do half believe you, Miss Molly, so to save a schoolmistress's life or at least her coiffure, I'll not make that suggestion just yet."

Molly stuck out her tongue and pranced out of the room. Johnson's eyes narrowed, he chuckled, then turned a wry gaze on Julian. "Who are you, lad?"

"I'm Julian Asher, Master Bragg's bondservant, sir," Julian replied.

"Bragg's servant? Where's the old pirate?"

"I believe he's waiting in the study, sir."

Wrinkling his brow, William Johnson regarded Julian without showing any sign of revulsion at his sorry condition. He then remarked: "I imagine he brings you here to fatten you up."

"I believe I need fattening, sir," Julian replied.

William Johnson had a big laugh, which filled the room for a minute, then he went on: "'Tis not that your master has an aversion to the truth that is so difficult to stomach, 'tis that he won't quit disputing until you agree with him. For the next hour the rogue will swear on the Bible, the Koran, and his mother's grave he's not a French spy."

"I haven't observed him spying, sir."

"Since when are you employed by your master?" Johnson asked.

"Since December."

"With all this talk of peace, spying recently stopped being profitable. Yet as soon as peace is coming, it will be broke, and Bragg will be in the business again. Now so far as what I see in front of me, Julian, you had a hard time of it. Face and hands covered by chilblains—lucky you didn't lose any fingers—and what happened to that foot and why is it uncovered?"

Julian tried to hide the naked appendage. "A carriage ran over it, sir, in London. Miss Molly wanted to see it."

William Johnson studied Julian doubtfully. "Why in the world has Bragg chose you as a servant?"

Happily, Julian could satisfy Johnson with an answer to this question. "He said he chose me because I've survived every affliction known to mankind."

Johnson exploded with laughter again. "Well, Julian, did your mother teach you the manners that a gentleman must display at a fine table?"

"I believe she did her best," Julian replied uncertainly.

"As did my mother. I invite you to my table. Do not be overly concerned about manners. Yours won't be no worse than the Onondaga sachem's manners. At the very least, you'll keep Molly occupied so she won't pester the rest of us. Your master also may be present, or he may be a prisoner in the icehouse—an appropriate place for the traitor—or if I convene a court quick enough, the rogue may be hanging from the oak tree out front, it being too cold to erect a gibbet. In the meantime, Madam McGregor will take you to your quarters and provide you with decent attire. Is there anything you're wearing you don't want burned?"

"I believe my jacket will be necessary for when I

travel back, sir," Julian mumbled ashamed of the greasy stained object.

"I'm certain we can find a coat and cloak that will do better service. Now, if you excuse me, I have to wait upon your Master Bragg, my friend, and condemn him to death."

McGregor was a stout, platter-faced, gimlet-eyed woman. She conducted Julian up a staircase to a bedroom with a large bed, a fire in the stove, a bearskin sprawled on the floor, damask curtains, a writing desk with a chair and three books. To his mortification, McGregor insisted that he strip off everything, including the undershirt and drawers which, having seen him across the Atlantic Ocean and up the colony of New York, seemed to be glued to his skin. She exited, ostentatiously averting her nose from her burden. It was a small consolation that in his naked-ness Julian was warmer than he had been for the last four months. However, Julian couldn't suppress the fear Molly would all of a sudden show up wanting to scalp him. From another part of the house, the raised voices of Bragg and Johnson reached him. Julian couldn't distinguish the words, but the vigorous dispute seemed to consist largely of oaths and fists slamming on wooden surfaces.

McGregor returned with three sets of clothing—woolen breeches, stockings, quilted shirt, and a thick green cloak for the bitter cold; a brocaded waistcoat, linen breeches, lace-trimmed shirt and accompanying fineries for the dinner; and plainer garments for general wear. While Julian gazed astounded at his sudden wealth of wardrobe, McGregor, brandishing a washrag and a comb, assaulted him. Julian had no idea that his face could hold as much dirt as he saw on the blackened cloth. As for the comb sorties, the housekeeper pulled out more hair than she straightened. She then queued his hair, helped him dress, and informed him that he was expected at supper within the hour. If he couldn't tell time, he should listen for the gong.

Yearning to go to bed, but afraid he wouldn't wake for several days, Julian sat down at the desk and picked up a book titled *The Polite Lady*. It didn't contain the hoped-for advice that he could pass on to Molly, so he laid the book aside and started to peruse a compilation of sermons and divinely inspired homilies, which seemed likelier to reinforce his spirits in his present circumstances.

Molly peered through the door. "Beggar boy pretending to read?"

"London beggar boys read very well," Julian answered in the same mocking tone. "'Thus, sayeth the Lord in our time of troubles...'" He continued for several minutes enjoying the deepening frown on Molly's face.

"You are to come to supper, beggar boy," she blurted out before prancing away.

In a room brilliantly lit by four chandeliers, William Johnson presided at the head of a long table with thirty guests. Attired in a blue velvet frock coat, leather breeches, and silk stockings, and the paint now washed from his face, their host appeared as proper as any English gentleman. A dozen servants pressed themselves against the wainscoted walls. A fire roared in the hearth. Nickus and another regal red-coated Mohawk introduced as Heinrick occupied the chairs on either side of Johnson. Although Heinrick's face carried a pleasant expression, its left side bore a vicious scar starting at the corner of his mouth and extending between eye and ear to his hairline. Wearing the scowl of a man about to make trouble, Bragg brooded next to Heinrick.

Further down the table, two ladies were situated across from each other—one black-haired, ample breasted, rosy complected, the other sloe-eyed with dark cherrywood skin. By their solicitude of the guests and the tone of mistress they took with the servants, either might be taken for the lady of the house, although they seemed careful not to contradict each other. Eight children with various combinations of the two women and Johnson's features were dispersed among the guests, which also included a Lutheran pastor, a Dutch alderman, a frontiersman in buckskins, a Mr. Skell who called himself a botanist, and an astonished Irish family unable to do nothing else but gape at their fellow invitees and nudge each other. In a corner, a small hunchbacked singer sang in Gaelic accompanied by a fiddler and a blind girl playing a harp.

Julian wasn't quite finished taking in this scene when he felt a tap on his shoulder. He turned to see a dwarf holding a jug. "Would you enjoy a sip of Madeira, master?"

Put off because no one had ever referred to him with the title 'master,' Julian managed to nod, and the deep purple liquid streamed into a crystal goblet that, for some reason, he never imagined was meant for him. That began an endless train of dishes starting with nuts and sweetmeats and continuing on to turtle soup, soused oysters, beef, venison, a sturgeon four feet long, a ham, hot rolls, custards, meat pies, larded partridges, puddings, whipped syllabubs,

and strange nutted white mounds that Molly called floating islands. Julian had only tasted wine on rare occasions,
usually, a few drops measured carefully into a cup by Mr.
Skylar. Although he was never aware of the dwarf filling the
goblet, Julian's glass never came close to empty.

After gravely introducing her brother, Prince Joseph,
who was a six-year-old with a runny nose, Molly thankfully ignored Julian. Instead, she quizzed the dancing
master of Johnson's children, a man who took himself with
great seriousness, on why he had pursued the profession of
dancing master instead of soldiering. Not accustomed to
such impertinence, the dancing master was slowly turning
red under his façade of indulgent good humor as he tried
to explain the importance of refinement in young gentlemen and ladies.

Bragg's voice suddenly rose above the din, silencing
the table. "What advantage am I gaining from spying for
the French when me heathen friends only want English
goods? I'm not so dull a trader as to work against meself."

"A man's heart isn't always in his purse. Besides the
French pay well, especially to English traitors," Johnson
parried at the same volume. "Do you deny, Bartholomew,
you were meeting one Master Grayson who combines the
insidious occupations of Catholic priest and French spy?"

"Grayson may or may not be what you say. He's an old
acquaintance of me mother's family, and out of respect to
the decent side of me lineage, I welcome him as a friend."
Bragg bared his teeth.

Johnson shook his head. "We just hanged the damned
papist Ury for inciting the slave insurrection. Grayson is
cut from the same cloth."

"An addle-headed maid spouts nonsense, and a score of hapless Africans and an old gentleman with a fondness for Latin is gibbeted in consequence, and you call that an insurrection?" Bragg stood, red-faced and swaying. "I am demanding you retract your accusations."

"If you're after a duel, Bragg," Johnson replied, "I'm not obliging. If I win, you die quickly. If you win, Nickus will draw out your death until you regret having ever been born. What's the longest you took to kill a captive, Nickus?"

Nickus considered. "My father, a patient man, took a fortnight to kill a Cherokee who murdered his brother. We lost our skill in lengthening our enemy's suffering because you discouraged us in what you call our barbaric excesses."

Johnson nodded. "True; as an Englishman, I don't want to deal with an enemy more barbaric than me, but I give you permission to make an exception with my friend, Bartholomew."

Bragg ignored the threat. "And this be the gratitude you show me for saving your life? God's love! You're sure a hard rogue."

Johnson slammed his just emptied goblet of wine on the table. "Saving my life was the best investment you ever made in the six decades you've plagued this earth. Seven times I saved your life since. Right now, if I send a communication to Sir Peter, my uncle and the king's favorite admiral, who happens to be residing now at his estate downriver, I'm certain he will spare a few men to retrieve you."

"I just can't be a spy and traitor in your book, which get me as good a death as any, but also a pirate." Unfortunately, Bragg in his anger did resemble a murderous pirate at that moment.

"Yes," Johnson continued. "You're Jacques Dugard, or rather the second Jacques Dugard, who plundered and terrorized the Caribbean for eight years."

"Dugard was French. From the side of me bastardizing father, I'm as Irish as you are, or more so for I don't have an uncle who turned King's admiral. You don't even speak like an Irishman but like a damn Church of England vicar. I won't be denying I spent part of me youth as a common tar, but then I became heartily sick of the profession. And from what I hear, I in no way resemble Jacques who was a dapper man and fancy dresser. In my life I was never flattered thus."

"Take away several stones and add a suit of fancy clothes and I would wager that you're so like Dugard as the spit out of his mouth. Yes, you were born in Ireland. Nevertheless, when the French pirate, the first Jacques Dugard, boarded the vessel in which you were a common sailor, you joined his company. When Dugard was halved by an English—or was it a Spanish—cannonball, you assumed command of the ship and escaped into a fog bank. You carried on in his business and adopted his name on account of the fear it inspired."

Little Joseph Brant burst into giggles because Molly was contorting her face, making a fair imitation of the dead top half of Jacques Dugard. Johnson's stern eye quickly put a stop to her antics.

"You prospered, preying on small traders between the islands. You went too far when you kidnapped the fifteen-year-old daughter of a governor. The governor refused to pay the ransom, so you sent him her little finger with the message that if he didn't want his young flower toothless, earless, and her belly swelling with your brat, he should reconsider. He paid, but not before you so enraged sensibilities that the bounty for your capture was put to five hundred pounds. The Caribbean then got too hot for your comfort, so you fled to New Orleans and took up your present profession."

"Stuff and nonsense, Willy!" Bragg exclaimed. "I was never so bold a fool. If you be certain that I am Dugard, then arrest me and collect the bounty yourself."

"'Tis hard to find witnesses to events that occurred more than two decades past, but I just happen to have a tenant who crewed on a ship you boarded. He, in fact, claims that Jacques Dugard, who he recognized as a fellow Irishman, gouged out his eye. Bring in Jacob."

There was a shuffling and an old man with a ruddy complexion, a sailor's swaying gait and a large red malmsey nose entered. His drooping left eyelid didn't completely hide the vacant socket.

"Now Jacob, am I right in saying you claim you can identify Jacques Dugard, who boarded your ship and gouged out your left eye?" Johnson asked.

"Aye, sir," Jacob replied. "He ordered me to stop it from twitching, only I was so afeared I couldn't, so he dug it out to teach me a lesson."

"Do you not see Dugard in this room?" Johnson asked.

Jacob walked the length of the table, carefully scrutinizing each guest, including the Mohawk and Onondaga guests and Julian. He stopped in front of Bragg who sat with his finger rubbing his right eyelid.

Jacob started to speak, but then Bragg interrupted, "Pray, tell us Jacob, was that infernal rascal Jacques Dugard imparting to you any other lesson he might teach you if you displeased him further?"

"Jacob, don't let Bragg intimidate you," Johnson said. "This isn't a boat. Bragg cannot harm you. As justice of the peace I have authority to try, condemn, and hang the scoundrel, here and now, and I assure you such an event would cheer my day."

"What were that scurvy dog who deserves to be roasted forever in the fiery pits of hell saying to you?" Bragg asked as he lifted his finger.

Jacob hesitated, his whole face twitching. " 'Tis so hard to remember a face. So hard, only… I do not think now you is Jacques Dugard."

Bragg slammed his fist down on the table. "Bloody damn right you are. I'm not that villain!"

Johnson heaved a long sigh. "That was quite a demonstration of the fear Jacques Dugard still inspires in men. You're a thorough knave, Bragg, and could bluster your way past Saint Peter. I loved you once for you saved my life and you were a fellow Irishman. Your being the notorious pirate Dugard wouldn't make a difference. I've always found it advantageous to take a man as he stands now. Otherwise, we are all beyond redemption. I no longer love you for you're an agent of the French and many widows can thank you for their cold beds and meager fare. Ply your trade and your sedition to the Creeks or Cherokees, nations whose people don't half reside in the French colony. Do not trade with the tribes of the six-nation confederacy, nor the Shawnees, nor the Delawares, nor any of their subject tribes."

"You're not having one witness as to these unfounded accusations. You're just after squeezing me out of me livelihood." Bragg glared and downed his cup of wine.

"Yes, I want to squeeze you into a new profession. This is the last time I do you the favor of preserving your life. Maybe, 'tis not much of a favor. I can't imagine the Cherokees or the Creeks suffering you for long." Johnson glanced at Julian, then continued. "You can lodge here a week. Your boy needs time to thaw the frost out of his bones. As a matter of fact, so do you. But do not petition me again about trading in the northern colonies. You can dine at my table; you can keep your horses in my stable; you can even seduce any maid over fifty, only confine your conversation to jests and your fabulous fictions."

Bragg threw his napkin down and stood to leave, but at that moment, the dwarves arrived carrying a huge platter of cornpone with glistening chunks of meat and six fresh decanters of wine, so muttering, he took his chair again.

As Julian ate and drank, a fog enveloped his mind, his thinking and speaking slowed and thickened. He remembered Molly making a side comment that she had never seen a boy before consume his weight in meat and drink. He vaguely remembered his plate being replaced by the dwarf servants four or five times because they were filled with bones. He remembered thinking that the quantity of wine he had imbibed was ten times greater than his entire previous consumption of that marvelous beverage. He remembered being shown a small closet where he could relieve himself and contemplating amazed the china chamber pot trimmed with gold and painted with cavorting couples. He retained the vaguest recollection of Nickus and the giant blond servant carrying him upstairs and depositing him in a bed next to his snoring master. Julian's last thought was that if it weren't for his aching belly, he would have been persuaded that he had died and gone to heaven.

Julian wasn't certain it was still morning when he woke. Bragg was gone. The feeble daylight gave no clue. He dressed and cautiously peeked into the hallway. McGregor spotted him. "Well, if 'tisn't the little glutton. If you think I'm serving you a gentleman's breakfast, you is greatly mistaken. Follow your nose to the kitchen. They might have a few trifling scraps for you there."

Julian descended the stairs on tiptoes, not wanting to be noticed and told he didn't belong in such a house. Passing a parlor, he recognized from the night before several young daughters of Johnson doing needlework while their mother read out of a book of devotions. In another room, two boys, also familiar, argued over a game of draughts.

On arriving at the kitchen Julian discovered that his reputation for gluttony had preceded him. The cook, two black scullery maids, and a dwarf pulled up chairs to watch while Julian consumed the porridge, eggs, bacon, and sweet cakes placed before him. Tankards of tea were provided to wash the food down. Molly peeked in near the end of the meal and proclaimed, "Are you ready to serve me today?"

Julian saw no reason to try her goodwill. "Yes, Princess Molly, so long as you don't scalp me and so long as Master Bragg doesn't require me for an errand. Why aren't you doing needlework with the other girls?"

Molly shook her head disdainfully. "I detest needlework and I only pray once a day because I think God tires of my prattle. Besides, Mr. Johnson's children dislike me. His daughters are of the opinion I'm not genteel enough, and his sons prefer I not remind them they'll never measure up to their father. Although I may attend their dancing classes today. The dancing master told me he uses a switch to teach his pupils refinement. I'll bring my tomahawk to show him how Mohawks teach refinement."

This novelty of pretending to be Molly's servant didn't last. She ran out of errands and really was more interested in conversation. She listened attentively to Julian's life and trials in London. When he expressed a wish to write his mother, Molly produced paper and quill and promised to lend him a shilling to send it. They spent the next hour arguing over exactly what to say. After a while, Nickus called her away to her French lessons, which Molly said she didn't mind. Julian returned to the kitchen and had his first taste of salted and buttered potatoes. While he was eating, Bragg wandered into the kitchen, held out a tankard, which the cook filled with rum. "Nobody here thinks I'm fit company," Bragg grumbled and staggered away, caroming off a table, chair, and door jamb.

Julian returned to his room, read two sentences of a sermon before dozing off. He soon awoke with a surprising appetite. The kitchen obliged again, and giving the audience of maids no little amusement, he consumed three bowls of soup, two beefsteaks, and four rolls doused in honey. Molly reclaimed him as a servant since Bragg didn't need him, stating the opinion he shouldn't become lazy from lack of use. This, of course, meant more conversation.

"My stepfather wants to return tomorrow because he agreed to be Johnson's emissary to the Ottawa and Mingo," Molly confided. "But I told him I couldn't possibly leave the beggar boy. I despair of you surviving a fortnight, Julian, unless I teach you what you need to learn."

"What's wrong with me?" Julian asked, still surprised at Molly's effrontery.

Molly cleared her throat. "To begin with, Julian, you're so skinny I practically see through you. You don't know how to prime and fire a musket much less hunt for your supper; you never stabbed and scalped an enemy, skinned a raccoon, cut bark off a tree, or done anything else with a knife except maybe pick your teeth; you never threw a tomahawk; I would wager you can't start a fire; you consume a bear's weight in meat every week; you're unable to flee from danger with that thing on the end of your leg you call a foot; you are as guileless as a kitten; and you owe your contract to a master who's a French spy and who, if he could chop you into little pieces and sell each piece at a profit, would. I never met a person so ill-fitted for his circumstances. Go back to London so when I visit there, you can tell everybody that I'm truly a princess. Failing that, you'll need my advice…"

Julian tried to think of the words to refute Molly's contentions, but she would not be deterred. Addressing his lack of guile, she opined on the characters of her acquaintances who, aside from her stepfather, mother, brother and William Johnson, were greatly defective in many particulars.

The following morning, when Julian yawned and blinked awake, he found himself confronted by Molly's moist accusing eyes six inches from his. Bragg, of whom he had a vague memory snoring beside him, was gone.

"I have important news to impart," she announced.

"Do you think the kitchen might mind…?" His thoughts drifted toward hot porridge with maple syrup.

She pinched his arm. He yelped. "I said I have important news to tell you."

"If you pinch me again I'm going to pinch you back." Julian was awake and angry now.

"You stupid boy. You think this is all a game. Everybody thinks I'm playing games, amusing myself. Mr. Johnson even had the temerity to call me a child. That makes me want to…" She didn't complete the sentence. "Well, foolish beggar boy, your master will be killed as soon as he leaves here, and if you accompany him, you'll be scalped and left in the snow to rot in the spring thaw."

"Who's planning to murder Master Bragg?" Julian tried to sound as if he believed her.

"My stepfather caught Bragg creeping along the hallway towards Mr. Johnson's room with a knife. When your master realized he was discovered, he pretended to be sleepwalking. He also saw Bragg watering his rum so as to keep his wits whilst pretending to be drunk. My stepfather assigned two boys to sleep in front of Mr. Johnson's bedroom. He also made plans with other braves.

When you and Master Bragg depart, you will be followed and murdered."

"Did your stepfather inform Mr. Johnson about my master creeping down the hallway?" Julian asked.

"The most gracious foolish William Johnson refused to give it any importance, even though the French have not retracted their offer of a thousand pounds for his scalp. Why else would your master come here? As if he could persuade Mr. Johnson into changing his mind. No, his intent was to assassinate his host and depend on darkness and blowing snow to cover his escape." Molly began to pull him out of bed.

"A thousand pounds is a lot of money." Julian doubted anyone's head of hair was worth that much.

"'Tis a pittance compared to what Mohawks earn from being the preferred traders by the English, and that all rests on Master Johnson's arrangements. But I have worse news: Mr. Johnson won't save you."

"Did I request that Mr. Johnson save me?" Julian asked.

She pinched him again painfully. "This isn't a game. I asked Mr. Johnson if he would buy your indenture from Master Bragg. He asked me if I was in love with you. I said that if you were the best I could do, I'd die of grief. He said he had no employment for you, which was true for who could have use for a boy with your foot thing and all your other disadvantages. I thought of some new defects I haven't told you about yet. Don't frown; I didn't tell Mr. Johnson either. In fact, I said that you were clever for a beggar boy, but he said he didn't value cleverness in servants and furthermore since you were my friend, his children would not take kindly to you."

"I thank you for asking," Julian said, not sure that he was. "What should I do?"

"What you must not do is leave with your master. Or if he obliges you to go with him, run away as soon as you can. I'll tell my stepfather to spare you, only the braves may not think Bragg's one scalp enough for their troubles."

"Are you certain about my master?"

"Yes, of course I am, beggar boy. But even if your master means no harm, what do we Mohawks lose by murdering him and his bondservant? Bragg has no family to mourn him, no tribe to take revenge; no friends to come to his aid except other French spies, and they'll be too frightened. Don't worry. I help you escape. Maybe we find a place to hide you and when Bragg tires of looking, he leaves you behind."

Molly had more ideas on how to save his skin. Julian was skeptical, but whenever he expressed his doubts, she would call him names and enumerate his inadequacies. He felt relieved when Molly joined Johnson's daughters for a sleigh ride. He visited the kitchen then took a nap. On the way to the bedroom, he discovered Bragg apparently dead drunk under the billiard table. Julian sniffed the bottle of rum still clutched in his hands, and couldn't help but notice a small knife hilt peeking out from underneath the coat. On finishing his nap, Julian made a third detour to the kitchen. After ordering him to sit, the cook presented him with three baked apples. Julian was self-conscious now about the amount of food he was consuming, but if Molly were correct, it didn't matter really because he didn't have many days left to live anyway. He attended another supper, a lengthy affair during which it was commented that Julian must be dieting for he only ate as much as an English hog drover instead of a Dutch alderman. Johnson was in high spirits. Bragg was glum and hardly spoke, although he did partake generously of the wine.

"I witnessed a whole village of Cayugas get soused on what you drink in an afternoon, Bartholomew," Johnson commented.

Bragg looked up blearily from his cup. "You be taking away a man's livelihood and what's left for him but the consolation of spirits. I aim to square me losses by drinking up your rum and making meself as drunk as a Lord. You know I never touch the stuff when I am plying me trade, preferring wit to courage."

When Julian retired to his room, Bragg was lying on the bed snoring, mouth agape, eyes open. Julian had been debating with himself all day whether to pass on to Bragg what Molly had told him. Except for straightening out his foot, the occasional painful kicks to make him pay attention, and calling him "imp of Satan," "beetle-headed gollumpus," and other abusive names whenever he made a mistake, Bragg wasn't a cruel master. Back in London, Julian had known apprentices who were never without bruises and black eyes. And indentured servants frequently fared worse than slaves, especially when their indentures were nearing the end. They were flogged on the slightest pretext or no pretext if their master or mistress needed to vent anger on a person who couldn't strike back. In one of the farmhouses, they had met a sad girl of sixteen named Piety, impregnated by her master, hated by her mistress, and because of her immorality condemned to an additional seven years of servitude. Bragg had taken pity on her and slipped her a shilling. Piety said she would save half the shilling to give to her sister Deliverance also in a bad situation. "Me mother was an innocent girl such as her," Bragg explained later. Many masters would never consider sharing bed and board equally with a servant. Bragg showed no such qualms.

"Master Bragg, Master Bragg." Julian nudged Bragg's shoulder, feeling traitorous. The snoring stopped, the eyelids flickered, and a strange voice intoned, "Is that you, Imelda?"

"'Tis me, Julian, your bondservant."

"Thank you, thank you, thank you, Imelda. Oh, oh, naked Madonna come to me." He flung out an arm, which Julian dodged.

"Wake up, Master Bragg," Julian continued, but the rum and the conviction that he was the naked Imelda made the task difficult. Finally, Julian exclaimed: "They plan on murdering us when we leave here. You must wake up and hear me. I'm not your Imelda, and they intend to follow…" A long snore interrupted Julian, and he gave up for the moment.

In the morning, Bragg was gone and Molly was once again at his bedside staring at him with her bright dark eyes. Her plan for the day was to explore the stone and brick outbuildings in spite of the cold and wind to search for hiding places.

Three families from three different Iroquoian tribes—Mohawk, Onondaga, and Cayuga—occupied the first building. They had no business with Johnson but had decided to winter at Johnson's fort nevertheless. Occasionally, their emissary appeared at the table to pick up food—a leg of mutton, a calf's head, a four-foot pike—and carry their acquisition back to their quarters. Several dozen now sat on bearskins in front of a fireplace with a roaring fire. Molly saluted the families using the Six Nations' common political and trading patois. Seemingly, as put off by her effrontery as everybody else, they ignored her.

"The only reason they're here is for the pint of rum a day Mr. Johnson gives them," Molly said in a voice loud enough to be overheard as they left.

The slave quarters in the next outbuilding were cold and gloomy, slaves having only a small allowance for firewood. A child in a dirty shirt turned this way and that trying to get warm and cried in front of a meager fire. A woman, whose lined face seemed much older than her smooth breast, suckled a baby and half mumbled half sang "*Hush Little Baby, don't you cry, angels will come by and by.*" A man shivered with fever on a pile of rotting straw. The water in a pail was partly frozen. The smoky air started Julian coughing. Molly shook her head with disdain. "Some peoples are meant to be beasts of burden. I thank God in my prayers that he made me a Mohawk."

"I do not think they were beasts of burden in their own country," Julian replied.

"How would you know?" Molly retorted.

They explored the stables, the curing shed, and several unfinished outbuildings without finding a hiding place. Even Molly realized that he would freeze to death without a fire. They last visited a round structure used as a council and meeting house when it was too cold to construct one out of willows and bark. Inside, high narrow windows let in the graying light. Although carpeted with bear, beaver, and other pelts, it lacked a fire and therefore was bitterly cold. "Maybe I'll roll up in a bearskin and pretend to be part of the floor," Julian said half-jokingly.

"Pish!" Molly replied, showing her displeasure.

They were just about to leave when William Johnson flung open the door and entered followed by an old red-bonneted Indian wrapped in a red blanket and so bent that he appeared to be walking on all fours. Johnson was carrying an armful of furs from a long-haired animal. He gave a quick glance at Molly and Julian, which would be a signal to anybody with the exception of Molly to depart but said nothing. He led the trembling ancient to the middle of the room. One by one, Johnson handed the furs to him speaking in a low voice. With a shock, Julian realized that what he thought had been furs were scalps—five altogether—including two from women and one from a child. The old Indian nodded, pleased, then tottered out with his precious armful. Johnson walked up to Julian and Molly. His face was grim. His eyes were narrowed and hard. He lacked only war paint to complete the impression of savagery.

Speaking in a low voice, Johnson said, "Black Wolf was a great warrior in his time, feared from Saint Lawrence to Albany. Now, he barely sees and barely walks. In the war, a band of Abenakis led by the French attacked his village. Instead of torturing the great warrior, they decided to inflict more grief by torturing his old wife, his daughter, and his three sons in front of him. Then they continued on with his grandchildren. They turned him out, fully expecting him to die from the cold. A daughter who lives in Canajoharie and a son who was away hunting survived. I gave him scalps also taken in the war from a French family like his family for the deaths of his wife, daughter, and three sons. He will cherish the scalps, and when he sees them and touches them, he will be satisfied with knowing a French family suffered as his family suffered, and he will remember his wife and children fondly."

Julian felt a mortal chill. Johnson's features briefly displayed pain, then hardened again as he continued speaking: "Providence has a preference for balancing out the humors in his beings. Those who hate greatly, love greatly, those who grieve greatly, experience joy profoundly. I pay bounties for French scalps, and the French pay bounties for English scalps. The more scalps I pay bounties for, the less grief comes to my people. I like this not. I have no wish that children pay for the sins of their fathers, only 'twill take a better man than me to remake this world."

"When my stepfather brings you Julian's scalp, will you pay him a bounty?" Molly asked, her eyes flashing.

"Molly, you're always brimming with plots and conspiracies."

"Well, will you?" She demanded.

"No, I won't. But I'm not going to purchase this young man's contract just because he's polite enough to agree that you're a princess."

Molly stamped her foot. "There's not a man you've met that you haven't turned to your advantage. You can do the same with Julian."

Johnson hesitated, then said, "Molly, I'm going to impart to your friend advice in private. I do not want you to question him about my advice for you'll contradict what I say and confuse him."

Molly gave Johnson an unnaturally sweet smile. "Sir, your confidence in my judgement overwhelms me."

"Would you were a daughter or a maid, you wouldn't be able to sit for a month."

"Your humblest most obedient servant, sir," Molly held on to her syrupy smile, made a bow, turned around and made another low bow to the door, then ran out.

William Johnson seemed distracted for a moment then turned to Julian. "Miss Brant has a point, lad. You might make a living as a clerk or a scrivener in a town, but the back country is hardly the place for you. You get few second chances to learn a lesson there. I will ask around and see if a merchant in Albany will purchase your indenture, that is if Bragg will let you go. I wouldn't depend on the success of my applications, although your usefulness to him has declined."

"Why might that be so, sir?" Julian asked.

Johnson leveled on Julian a pitying gaze. "You see, he required a helper who wouldn't catch on to his machinations. Now that you have learned of his agency for the French, he won't have much freedom to further his conspiracies until he rids himself of you or turns you into a French agent and traitor to the king. I have the impression Bragg is fond of you, at least fonder than the last boy who he let the bear eat. In your circumstance, the only counsel I can offer is to befriend as many and offend as few as possible. Most traders are no better than drunken thieves, and they abuse and cheat the savages and each other as frequently as the opportunity arises. Mark my word, three years hence, if you live so long, a third of your backwoods acquaintances will have lost their lives at the hand of the savages or their brethren, and another third killed through the cruel mischances of nature. Come to mention it, if you last so long, I'll buy your indenture. I will make you either a servant or front you trading merchandise, which you can repay from your profits. In return, I ask a favor."

"Yes, sir."

"Your master may or may not be the pirate Dugard, but he's certainly a French agent. Since you are aware of this accusation against him, Bragg will not act openly. In each village you visit, he will take a few braves off to the side and speak to them. Keep a log in your head of those he speaks to, discover whether he is talking to sachems, or restless young men, or a war chief who wants to make a name. No need to listen to the conversations. He'll be pricking old wounds and disaffections and making unkeepable promises. Note his demeanor afterward. When Bragg is disappointed, he prattles on and on to distract himself. If he's pleased, he looks like the maid who hid her mistress's gold ring by swallowing it. Don't put on such a glum face, lad. I will inform important men about the great service that you're doing for king and country."

"How am I to convey this information to you?" Julian asked.

"An Indian, maybe even Chief Nickus, or trader will approach you when you're alone and ask you if you remember William Johnson's gift to Black Wolf. Then you tell him all you have found out."

FLIGHT

Two NIGHTS LATER, after a day so fiercely cold and stormy that Molly and Johnson's daughters were forbidden to sleigh, Julian was jarred awake by the words, "Get up, you loutish slugabed. We're on our way." Bragg then pulled him upright by the hair. To prevent further assaults, Julian staggered out of the bed.

"Hurry up, lad. Our horses are saddled and packed."

"Why do we leave now, sir?"

"Because even for bloody old Nickus, our scalps aren't worth freezing his arse off," Bragg replied, lowering his voice.

"Maybe they aren't, sir, but maybe they are."

"Maybe," Bragg muttered. "But at least with a numb noggin, scalping won't hurt half so much."

Julian trembled as he dressed—he couldn't tell whether from cold or fear. Seven days of warmth and luxury left him feeling ill-equipped to face the hostile frozen world again. Bragg didn't allow much time for regret, however. Within minutes, they were creeping through the front parlor. When Julian gazed longingly in the direction of the kitchen, Bragg whispered, "The cook is asleep. The larder is locked. You ate enough breakfasts for a month. Let's get on with it."

Unexpectedly, a light wavered in a side entryway giving Julian a rush of panic. Molly stepped out, holding a lamp with a small flame and a bundle. She blocked them.

"Julian is my subject," she proclaimed with her natural authority. "I am his princess. I expect you to value and protect him."

"Putting on airs don't make you a princess, Miss Molly," Bragg snarled. "And even if you was, I purchased his indenture, and 'tis biblical the lad cannot serve two masters."

"You will endeavor no harm comes to him because I command it," Molly persisted uncowed. "Master Johnson owns a good heart, and so he does not hang you. Keep in mind, I don't have a good heart."

"Arrah now, Miss Molly you speak as if..." Bragg wrinkled his brow, then nodded gravely. "I wouldn't be doubting it. I be doing me best protecting your subject, little princess, sure."

Molly then walked up to Julian and handed him the bundle. "'Tis a blanket made of woven rabbit skins so you never feel cold again."

"Thank you, Princess Molly," Julian said. "I am your obedient servant."

Before they got out the front door, Molly had run down into the cellar and emerged carrying a huge wheel of cheese. "Don't eat it all at once, my faithful Julian. And only share it with your master if he is kind to you."

They left in a blizzard, which soon passed, leaving air so sharp with the cold that it bruised the lips and nostrils. After covering twenty-five miles, they sheltered in a farmer's small barn. Julian thought Molly had been exaggerating the attributes of the blanket as she was wont to do with anything she favored, but when he laid down and pulled the woven rabbit skins over his head, he discovered himself inside an impenetrable cocoon of warmth.

After two hours of sleep, Bragg prodded him awake. Outside, a blizzard was howling again, and Julian considered offering his soul to the devil in exchange for a few hours more of rest in his divinely warm refuge.

"I don't relish playing the part of an Irish fox chased by savage hinds," Bragg explained as they mounted their horses and bent their heads into the dark blowing snow. "Only if I am to be a fox, the hinds will be panting hard for their kill."

Near dawn, when the winds had abated enough to allow conversation, Julian decided to clear up several questions concerning his master. "'Tis not my place to inquire, but did you save Mr. Johnson's life, sir?"

"A plague on your inquiries," Bragg growled. "Yet so true as the Gospel, that I did, and like most good deeds, 'twas paid with ingratitude. Willy was a callow jingle-brained youth new come from Ireland to manage his uncle's property. Wanting to make a name for himself as a trader, he took himself off into the wilds with a couple of packhorses. He wasn't out a week when a band of Abenakis ambushed him. They shot his horses and chased him into the forest. They might have caught and scalped him except one of their number being greatly fond of rum started in on the keg that Willy had planned to trade, and the others didn't want their companion drinking up their share whilst they chased this green Irish fool who they could be tracking and scalping in the morning. Willy had the good sense to keep on running. He had lost his coat along with his gun, his trade goods, and his provender. Shirt, britches and dirk—that was all he had on him."

Bragg looked around as if he were afraid someone was listening. Julian found himself doing the same but only saw snow-encrusted trees.

"By the grace of God and me misfortune, I found Willy half frozen and so hungry he was gnawing bark off trees. No grand gentleman in flimflam and finery then. I gave him victuals. I lent him a blanket. I took him back to his cabin—a rude place that even an old blind squaw would despise. I told him that in this country a fool is only lucky once. To be sure, he took me words to heart, learned, and now he's considered a wise sachem by the Mohawks, a trusted diplomat to the savages by the King, a cunning trader by the Dutch, and a thorough ingrate by me."

"He said you were behind the raids on the frontier." Julian wanted Bragg to deny this accusation so he wouldn't suffer the guilt of aiding a traitor to the king.

"Raids on the frontier?" Bragg sighed in exaspera-tion. "There be always raids on the frontier, lad. You got three score savage nations whose restless young men like nothing better than puffing out their chests and boasting about their prowess in plundering and scalping. You got the English and the French stabbing each other in the back so they can corner the trade. You got countless barrels of rum and whiskey which rile up the heathens. And you got settlers who hold the opinion that savages shan't be owning the land where their grandsires fished, hunted, and raised their families. Why wouldn't there be raids?"

"Is the reason Master Johnson accuses you of being a French spy because you're friends with the priest Grayson?" Julian asked timidly.

"Aye, Grayson is a priest, which I should have mentioned, but didn't want to alarm you so early in our acquaintance. Grayson might be a spy, at least he's good at spying out Catholics that miss their mass, but we don't do spying together. He possesses the feet of a spy, to be sure. He is traveling up and down this continent more times than pastors tour their parishes. Yet his heart belongs to the true Church. He never carries above three days provision, claiming God will provide, and God appears appreciative of his trust and always does. The reason we seek each other out is we have a commercial arrangement. He tells me where I might be finding furs, I tell him where he might be finding Romish believers."

The problem of speed was solved the next morning when Bragg purchased a sleigh and double harness from a suspicious, narrow-eyed farmer whose tight lips let out no more than three words at a time. They hitched up their horses, who after trying to shake off the unaccustomed harnesses, resigned themselves to this additional human imposition. Julian ensconced himself underneath his rabbit skin blanket. Sitting red-cheeked and erect, Bragg flicked a whip over the backs of the horses, and they slid off the road onto the broad ribbon of the frozen Hudson River.

The snow had stopped, and underneath a sky of the purest distilled blue, they slipped through the crystal and lace countryside. They weren't alone. As the sleigh's metal runners scraped over the ice, a vigorous postman skated alongside them for an hour, keeping up a conversation that Bragg mostly ignored. Out of a farmhouse with dark smoke billowing from its chimney, a woman appeared and skated up to them carrying a platter of steaming squirrel-and-possum pies to sell. Children hallooed as they played on the ice or sledded in the snow in front of their homesteads. Later that afternoon, they glided past a team of twelve horses dragging eighty-foot sections of white pines for masts of His Majesty's Navy, and soon after they came upon an army of oxen pulling a huge sled loaded with heaps of granite. In the early twilight, a young man and a young woman who must have spent much of the year gazing at each other from opposite shores skated onto the ice and met in the middle, laughing as they made circles holding hands.

Few demands were made on Julian during the sleigh ride, and he had time to wonder whether in his mother's eyes he was being foolish and fearless like his father. His present circumstances proved him undeniably foolish, but he was as far from fearless as any human being could be. According to Molly, she had never met a person so ill fitted for his vocation. On mentioning this to Bragg, the echo of his master's hallooing laughter likely was heard miles down the frozen Hudson.

"That is what the impudent little savage maiden said? By god, who be fit. Arrah now, let me tell you how to survive. You need to think of the frontier like you think of the Lord in heaven. She is supremely jealous. That means you don't love anything overmuch including your own skin, for if you do, she be taking it away."

This reassured Julian who could honestly say that there was nothing he valued overmuch including his own life.

After six days of chilly pleasure and ease, they left the Hudson. Bragg sold the sleigh for its purchase price, and the dream was over.

When they arrived at Minerva's cabin, Bragg barely paused to bed her before setting off to purchase more trading goods. Despite the constant drizzly slushy rain alternating with fits of wet snow, Bragg and Julian rode into the city every day. The variety of items amazed Julian—scissors, files, hoes, tea, chocolate, packets of vermilion, flutes, reams of fabrics, fifty brightly dyed blankets, a hundred Jew's harps, gunpowder, lead, brandy, whiskey and rum by five-gallon kegs, dresses, lace handkerchiefs, muskets, thousands of beads of different colors. Bragg also combed the docks, inquiring of the captains if they carried anything out of the ordinary. One very profane captain sold him six music boxes. Another, a sick marmoset. Bragg purchased a third violin, making Julian fear that they were going to defy William Johnson and visit the Oneida. By the end of a fortnight, Bragg had also acquired nine packhorses. Julian's first New World skill was loading up the packhorses, which Bragg made him redo a dozen times, either to gain practice or because he kept changing his mind on how he wanted the goods arranged.

Bragg announced that they would depart the beginning of March, but early one February morning, Grayson rapped on their door. Dressed perversely in a thin shirt and breeches, face splotched with red patches, Grayson's communication consisted of three words: "*Scorpion* docks tomorrow." Then barely acknowledging Julian's presence with a shift of his eyes, he turned and as swift and silent as a leaf driven by the wind disappeared into the forest. Bragg immediately set Julian to work loading the pack-horses while he galloped into town to finish up business. By early afternoon they were underway, passing fields, half mud and half ice, surrounding the forlorn farmhouses and gray barns. Bragg, thankfully, left the irritable marmoset with Minerva, instructing her, "Be nursing the poor creature like 'twere your own babe."

NATIONS OF THE WILDERNESS

BRAGG PUSHED HARD, stopping only when the horses couldn't hold up their heads and began to stumble. They found an inn on the second day—a filthy heatless sty of a place owned by a surly wall-eyed mistress. After three hours in a cornhusk bed stuck between the snores of Bragg and a young man pleasuring himself, Julian found himself again riding off into the impenetrable darkness. Bragg explained when he handed Julian in the way of breakfast a strip of dried venison as tough as a roof shingle, "Don't have your heart set on idling anywhere, lad. We must persevere like our packhorses who make up for their lack of swiftness by lengthening the day they travel."

"Master, who's after us?" Julian asked, sucking on the dried venison in a vain effort to soften it.

"I am not knowing for sure," Bragg said, casting a glance beyond Julian down the path. "Only in me experience not expecting the worst is the surest way of inviting it. Besides, this is a good time to trade. The savages have sorely missed getting liquored up and will not bargain too hard. With their hollering and drinking, it might become a little wild, but they'll scalp you afore they scalp me for no matter how soused they pretend to be, they be wanting to see me and my spiritous liquors the next trading season."

In the frosty light-grudging dawn, they found themselves riding along an almost invisible trail separated by the nine packhorses. The patchy ice and snow underfoot gave way in sunnier parts to mud that sucked down the horses' hooves. Julian's thoughts kept on returning to the child's scalp that William Johnson had handed to Black Wolf. If the Almighty didn't protect such innocents, what chance had he? Near midday, deciding that the packhorses knew their business, Julian rode up to Bragg. "Master, I have another question."

Bragg glanced back at the horses who were behaving themselves. "What inquiry be so pressing as to make you shirk your responsibilities?"

Julian blushed. "Master, if you're not the pirate, why were we in so much a hurry to leave Philadelphia before the warship docked?"

"If I was a pirate, I'd be skewering you right now for your plague of questions." Bragg gave a crooked-tooth grin and then continued: "'Tis like this, lad. If William Johnson suspects I be this Jacques Dugard, and if his savage friends or other associates go to New York or Boston and inform certain people about his suspicioning, the Royal Navy will be coming after me, and because they are putting so much effort into getting me, 'twill no be very convenient that I'm not Jacques Dugard, so they'll apply the thumbscrews and crush me stones until I am swearing on me mother's grave I am him, then they'll employ the confession to convict me, hang me up in a cage naked at the entrance of the harbor 'til I starve to death so me rattling bones warn other would-be pirates. Arrah, I prefer to make the Royal Navy chase after me where they can't sail their ships."

For seven nights they camped in the snow or mud, which required the tasks of unloading the horses, then feeding, hobbling, and brushing them, then collecting the firewood, building a fire, boiling water for raspberry leaf tea with perhaps a small dram of rum. Dinner usually consisted of pemmican. The bear grease and cranberry mixture initially tasted vile to Julian, but hunger compelled, and admittedly, it was preferable to the gristly strips of dried meat that Bragg handed him while they were on the trail. If they were lucky, Bragg might shoot a squirrel or raccoon. If Bragg was in a querulous mood, he might confine their meal to nookick, a parched corn powder that when mixed with saliva became cement. Julian's foot still ached constantly, but it fitted in the stirrup and solidly supported him.

Bragg had told Julian not to expect much from the first village, which he called New Babel. "You won't be encountering a sorrier lot of heathens," he explained. "'Tis a mishmash of nations—savages who lost their families and families who lost their tribe and have nowhere else to go. Lenape, Creek, Shawnee, Cherokee, Pequot, Tuscarora, Congeries, Mahicans, all squashed together, not comprehending each other properly, not knowing which dance or prayer or ceremony to be worshiping their gods, not wanting to stretch their understanding beyond getting enough rum to make the day pass. The neighborhood is hunted nearly clean of valuable pelts. They might have a few deerskins, maybe they try to pass a dog pelt off as something else. I'll trade them a keg of weak grog for whatever they got, which is their preferred way of filling their empty bellies. Generally, traders are paying no heed to New Babel as not worth the effort. That is a mistake. Their young bloods being great travelers visit kin all the way to the Ohio and the Mississippi, and the rest of them are shameless gossips once you water their thirst, so they impart the latest news from the frontier."

They arrived in New Babel on a misty morning. A squaw emerging from a wigwam spotted Bragg and squealed a greeting. Heads peeked out of other wigwams, and soon dozens were swarming toward them. Women and children crowded around as Bragg dismounted, their poor ravaged faces smiling, their hands invading his person. Master Bragg had evidently prepared for this game because the hands pulled out various small gifts from his sleeves and leggings—a few inches of ribbon, a bent nail, a dried fig. Two bold maidens reached deep into the front of his breeches and giggled. He winked at Julian and said, "That present don't come out 'til nightfall."

Julian stood back, guarding the packhorses. A little naked child toddled up to him, gave a toothless grin, then buried a bone awl into his thigh. Julian's yelp brought gales of laughter from the other children and sealed his fate. Making him squeal became their favorite pastime. The children were inventive and relentless. Aside from sneaking up and poking him with sharp objects, they mixed an herb into his cornmeal that made his lips swell, shoved a red-hot ember underneath his blanket while he slept, and later that night tied a wet leather thong around his large toe which tightened as it dried. When he threatened them, they waved a decaying scalp in his face, pointed to his forehead, mimed cutting motions with their hands, and gave blood-curdling screams. Julian began to hate these children as much as he was supposed to hate the devil and sin.

Their departure was abrupt. One moment Bragg was chasing a giggling squaw around a wigwam, the next, after a young brave arrived in the village shouting a message, he was ordering Julian to pack the horses. Within an hour they were on the road. Bragg commented: "For the near future we be only halting to piss and shit."

"Do they still pursue us?" Julian asked.

"Damn Johnson," Bragg muttered, then asked in a false jocular tone, "Whatever put that into your head, lad?"

Over the next fortnight, while they traveled along the trail of churned mud and stony inclines, Bragg behaved like a man unable to resist the need to constantly look over his shoulder. Spring had arrived with fits of rain, fits of wind, and occasional hours of soft sunshine. The branches of the hardwood and softwood trees were flecked with green. Quail and partridge sometimes complemented their meals. They spent only a few hours of a morning or an afternoon trading at the villages.

An influenza epidemic preceded them. Deaths were minimal, however as one Lenape sachem put it, "When my father died in the first sickness, I mourned for him, but he was an old man who had lived well. When my wife died in the one that followed, I wept for her. She was my companion since youth. Her smile and laughter were the medicines that healed my heart. When my eldest son died in another, I tore out my hair and wailed because the sickness had stolen so much life. When my second son became ill, I begged the Great Spirit to take me instead. Three more of my children and five of my grandchildren are now dead from all the sicknesses. I don't weep anymore because no riverbed can hold my tears."

The resident traders in the larger villages universally complained that the surrounding forest and streams had been hunted and trapped clean. "If you're looking for old squaws and cornhusks, this is the place," one said. "For anything else, go west." Bragg dealt solely with the traders, grumbling at the poor takings as gunpowder and raw whiskey were exchanged for pelts and deer hides.

The smaller villages appeared temporary affairs, the fields of maize, squash, and beans overrun with weeds, the wigwams poorly constructed. The squaws and old braves would present their meager haul of pelts, their eyes shining with desire as they examined the colored beads, iron hoes, red and blue matchcoats, yet they almost always settled for the rum. When they came across a deserted village. Bragg always searched the wigwams for plunder. He once discovered wampum clutched in the hand of a skeleton—the last valuable possession of a squaw too feeble to accompany her people on the trek to the Ohio. When they came across a homesteader tilling the same fields the Indians had harvested the previous fall, Bragg commented, "Him and his devouring kin like wolves always be nipping at the heels of the poor savages."

In an isolated half-settled valley, Bragg and Julian came upon a man in front of a blockhouse hammering a blade into a plow. Bragg hailed him "How be faring me favorite Old Testament prophet, Micah?"

Micah and a pregnant squaw who was pounding maize a few feet away looked up.

"Well, if 'tisn't the original Hibernian devil," Micah replied, straining at jocularity. He was skinny-ish, fortyish with deep-set eyes peering out of the cavern of his brow, a remarkable beak of a nose, and scraggly hunks of gray-blond hair. He brightened when Bragg dismounted and unpacked a bottle of rum. They repaired to the blockhouse.

The squaw continued pounding maize while Julian tended the horses. Apparently desiring company, she motioned to Julian to come with her into the blockhouse saying as her pleasant round face smiled, "Come. We eat." She served Julian a steaming plate of venison mixed in cornpone. She held her hand above her mouth miming downing a drink, giggled, and pointed to the second story where an animated conversation was taking place. "I go friend," she then stated and abruptly left. Julian edged closer to the ladder so he could hear the conversation.

"I ken three problems with your offer, Bragg," Micah was saying. "One: you no have title to the land. Two: savage nations hold a curious belief that 'tis their land, and they are no very obliging when a body disagrees. Three: the French claim the land for King Louie who is even less obliging than the savages as to giving it up."

Bragg cut in: "You might as well be claiming the ocean waves as claiming that land, Micah. I crisscrossed that country for weeks on end without encountering a soul. To be sure, every tenant farmer in England could be having his own lordly estate so fertile that it must be made out of left-over dirt from the Garden of Eden. You can be plowing in a straight line sunrise to sunset for a fortnight. And even with a million such tillers of the soil, there would still remain plenty space for all the savage nations. If farming is not to your liking, there's game enough to be keeping London in meat for a century and enough furs to be giving every Chinaman ten suits of clothes."

Taken in by Bragg's description, Julian forgot that his master might not look kindly on him eavesdropping on his private conversation.

Bragg raised his voice as if he wanted to aid Julian's hearing. "The land can't be bought or sold for 'tis like buying and selling water or air, there being so much of it. I'm not requiring you to pay hard coin. I know you're as straight as the day is long, Micah. I'm just asking you to peek. Next year, come with me, bring Sparrow Song if she wishes and your brat too. See for yourself whether I am speaking the truth. I'm telling this to you as a friend, Micah. 'Tis a waste of a life to spend it guarding property that isn't yours. Fortune is holding out what is better than a pot of gold to you, which unlike land can be spent in a day. All you need to do is to stretch out your hand and grasp it."

Julian realized that he had made a fist.

"I'm not blaming those weak-hearted souls afeared of losing their scalp," Bragg went on in a pitying tone. "In truth, I didn't figure you that sort. Mind you, I'm talking about the very property which God made for us to steward and populate with our progeny. Why should plantation owners and rich merchants who never leave their counting houses have it? As if a surveyor drawing lines on a map makes them entitled. Why should the French keep you out of a land that is meant to be farmed like a healthy young wench is meant to be wedded and bedded?"

Micah protested, "Aye, you always was a prodigious good talker Bragg, only what will happen to your paradise when the kings decide to war again?"

"Christ's blood!" Bragg exclaimed. "Are you telling me the war is ended? Whilst the kings, politicians, and generals are believing they're signing a treaty, making peace, giving back what they gained like 'twere a game of draughts to be started over, the real war goes on as ever—farms burned, men's hearts teared out, women and children scalped, savages drove from their villages into the wilderness to starve in the winter. In the new land, we will be out of it."

Bragg's voice now boomed so loud that it would have made an outdoor evangelist envious.

"We'll be no one's enemy and no one's friend. We will be Virginia men, Carolina men, Pennsylvanian men with Shawnee wives, and Seneca wives, and Miami wives, so whoever attacks us will be attacking all other nations. Even Frenchmen will be joining us when they see the advantages. I tell you there's no better place for wandering souls like you and me who are neither here nor there in the world. Are you going to throw out Sparrow Song and disown your brats? When was the last time you were invited to cider making or even a funeral? Or are you after becoming savage, dancing naked to their gods, digging up your ancestors once a year to have a meal and a conversation with their bones? You're not fitted here nor nowhere, Micah. You must make your own place where you fit. That's what I'm offering."

Sparrow Song returned, rolled her eyes when she heard the conversation still going on and said, "I sleep now." Julian excused himself. He had a difficult time settling down as he thought about Bragg's new country for the new breed of mixed people. He recalled a Tutelo girl near his age in an impoverished village where they traded for a morning, pretty, shy as a fawn, yet wanting to make his acquaintance. Their brief stay prevented any understanding beyond an exchange of glances. Julian now glimpsed the possibility of making a life with such a companion. A country for him with the sweet doe-like girl by his side seemed a fine idea.

For the first time since dreaming of becoming a highwayman or sea captain, Julian envisioned a place for himself in the world. His merit and his fortune rather than station would determine what he became. Julian doubted he possessed much merit, but good fortune often overlooked the inadequacies of its recipients.

REDCOATS

No MATTER HOW rapidly they traveled, Julian's reputation with the Indian children as an amusing object for their torments preceded him. When he couldn't hover near Bragg, Julian armed himself with a quirt, and he would flick it in the face of any child coming within striking distance. Still, he couldn't always be on guard. While unpacking the horses in front of a trader's log cabin in a large Munsee village, a little boy with a tiny closed woven basket sneaked up behind him. Shaking it vigorously, the boy opened the basket, letting out a dozen angry wasps, then fled avoiding the swishing lash. An audience of children watching at a safe distance roared with laughter as Julian dodged the agitated insects. The resident trader, Abinadab Smith, emerged from his cabin with Bragg and chased the children away. He and Master Bragg were long-time acquaintances, fierce competitors and, depending on how you looked on it, confidantes to an unfortunate degree. While Julian trembled with rage, they continued their argument.

"I can't allow you to trade here, Bragg. Croghan takes

ill your association with the French." Abinadab was a beanpole of a man with sloping shoulders, a head that seemed to peak and the scrapings of a beard. His Choctaw wife was as round as he was thin.

Bragg squared off like a fighting cock. "It passes understanding that Croghan pays heed to Johnson. Besides, the fact of the matter is the you may bluster all you want, Abinadab, but I'll do what I be pleasing until God or some villain is pleased to stop me breathing."

"Mighty tempting to become that villain," Abinadab replied. "My stores sunk pretty low, and your packhorses will greatly replenish my supplies."

Bragg emitted a skeptical hiss. "Going after knocking me on the head whilst I sleep? That be a pretty way to treat a friend."

"Friend or not, I work for George Croghan who's as close to Johnson as a brother."

"Croghan is his own man like all Irishmen and less a loyal subject to the crown than I am. I saw him raise a cup more than once to the health of Bonnie Prince Charlie."

"And I witnessed you drunk, Bragg, cursing in French."

"Sometimes English don't answer the occasion, especially when I'm quenching me thirst with French brandy. When I'm drinking Madeira, sure, I be swearing in Portuguese."

"As I said, you can't do business here," Abinadab insisted.

"Arrah now," Bragg replied grinning. "I'll be laying out me goods, and we can let your savages decide. I wager you're low on powder and rum. Spare your threats. You're not a murdering man, Abinadab, and you're not starting with me. Besides, your savages harbor an affection for their dear old friend Bragg. Sure, I drove hard bargains, but I cheated nary a one. I never told them less than the truth. I never started a quarrel. I never took a heathen's wife, sister, or daughter which wasn't offered. I never bought or sold a savage slave. I never watered the rum. I never tricked them out of land, even when they were drowning in their cups. I killed a few, to be sure, but even when the savage was after me scalp, I always made good with gifts to his family. Now is you inviting us to supper or is you afraid that I might start a war by swearing in French?"

Abinadab stuck out his lower jaw frowning. "You only trade with me at the prices I set. If you don't like the price, then no trade."

"Aye, we'd be negotiating about those things over supper."

Abinadab sighed, thoughtfully stroked his chin, then turned to Julian and said: "You're going about this all wrong, lad. Savage children are taught from the cradle to despise weakness. The weak are poor hunters, and poor fighters, and bring shame to the clan. Better they die young. You must prove you're not weak."

"Pray, sir, how can I do that?" Julian asked.

"These people are great wrestlers. Challenge the boy, Night Fox, who's the strongest, to a match."

"And lose my scalp when I lose the contest," Julian protested.

"Who's to say you lose?" Abinadab asked.

"How can I win, sir?"

Abinadab glanced from side to side, then lowered his voice. "This is what happens, lad. In such contests 'tis considered fair to trick your foe. Night Fox will do so, not because he needs to but for the fun of it and to give a good show. So, you only have to be more cunning."

"And what sort of cunning helps me out-wrestle a boy who is superior to me in strength?"

Abinadab's smile revealed that he enjoyed being a conniving man. "You will fight in a sandy area…"

Julian resisted the suggestion, but the situation became intolerable over the course of the next day. It was a tribal feast day, and while the adults engaged in their marathon eating, drinking, singing, and dancing, the younger children were free for mischief. After being pinched, jabbed, and bitten for a good part of the afternoon, Julian found himself humiliatingly hiding in the cabin behind the Abinadab's fifteen-year-old daughter who although treated him with scorn, at least didn't torment him. Abinadab's wild scheme would likely result in his death, however, Julian suspected his persecutors were plotting to kill him in any event, and Bragg hinted that he was contemplating a long stay, which would give them plenty of opportunity to successfully do so.

Accordingly, the following morning, while Night Fox was strutting back and forth recounting an adventure, Julian walked up to him and pushed him. Surprised, the young brave drew a heavy-bladed knife. Julian held out his hands showing he had no weapon and pointed to the patch of ground where the young men usually wrestled. Night Fox laughed, threw down the knife and walked over to the sandy spot. All the children and a few adults followed. Ominously, a friend of Night Fox retrieved the knife and wiped it on his leggings as if expecting it to be used soon.

After vainly searching the onlookers for Abinadab, Julian squared off with Night Fox. He harbored no delusion he could outwrestle this savage Adonis who was taking off a loosely hanging necklace of bear claws, seemingly to divest himself of an encumbrance. Julian began to wonder how the match might begin when without warning Night Fox charged and wrapped the necklace around his neck.

Julian tried to protest as Night Fox used the twisted necklace as a leash to drag him this way and that. Julian flailed at Night Fox, his fists making as much impression as they would on the bark of an oak. Fox pinched his nose, poked his eyes, and pulled his ears at will while amusing the crowd with his taunts. Bleeding and half choking, Julian passed from rage to resignation, then back to rage. Suddenly, Abinadab called out to Fox, ostensibly requesting him to pull Julian over to where he was standing so he could taunt him. Fox complied. Through his tears, Julian discerned his salvation, which was Abinadab's foot. He concentrated all his mental energy on that large splayed beaded moccasin. Abinadab uttered a mocking comment in Lenape and then whispered to Julian, "'Tis up to you, lad."

Taking advantage of a sudden loosening of the strangling clawing necklace while Fox laughed, Julian managed to entwine his fingers between the leather cord and his neck and fall forward. The young brave tumbled with him. Slipping a hand away as Fox twisted and jerked the necklace, Julian dug his fingers deep into the sandy soil where Abinadab's foot had indicated until he felt a scrap of folded buckskin. Grasping the buckskin, Julian swung his hand back over his shoulder, pressing a hot coal wrapped between the folds to the young brave's shaved head. Fox screamed and let go. Julian lurched forward, quickly unwrapped the necklace and slipped it around Fox's neck. Julian then twisted. Fox started to choke and fell to his knees. Bracing a knee against Fox's chest, Julian furiously wrenched the crossed strands of the necklace in opposite directions. At that moment, Abinadab laid a hand on his shoulder. "That's enough, lad. Compose yourself."

"I'm just returning to him what he gave to me." Julian relaxed the tension on the necklace in preparation for wrenching again.

"Nay," Abinadab whispered. "You're trying to kill him, and that wasn't his intent."

"How can you say so when he almost did kill me?" Julian cried angrily.

"Let go, lad."

Julian obeyed. He stood panting, while Fox unwrapped the bear-tooth necklace. Smiling, he addressed Julian in Lenape, which Abinadab interpreted: "Night Fox invites Crooked Foot, that's you, to his family house to share a meal. He promises that if you sleep there, no one will dare molest you, and perhaps one of his sisters will warm your bed."

"It passes understanding how he can befriend me after I nearly murdered him," Julian commented, still recovering his breath.

"You gained his respect with your cunning." Abinadab smiled wryly. "That's not to say he won't look for an opportunity to even accounts, only not while you're his guest."

Abinadab initially acted as an interpreter during the meal. Night Fox loved to talk about his hunting exploits and looked forward to the day when he could take his first scalp. Regretfully regarding Julian, he added that he had hoped this day might be that, but now, since Julian was a guest, scalping him wasn't possible. In between Night Fox's stories and boasts, Julian expressed his gratitude to Abinadab.

"Least I could do. Although I think you would prefer Mr. Fox lifting your scalp to what might befall you," Abinadab replied.

"What do you mean, sir?" Julian sensed bad news.

"Do you not know how Bragg's last boy met his end?" Abinadab paused, holding his breath.

"Thomas was eaten by a bear."

"Bear, you say, lad? Bragg has a humorous way with the truth. His Senecan name is Roaring Bear, and 'twas Roaring Bear who ate poor Thomas."

"What are you saying?" Julian stared hard at Abinadab for signs he was jesting.

"'Twas probably not what he set out to do when the blizzard first trapped them. Then food ran low, and the canny old pirate saw little choice." Abinadab patted his stomach.

"Really ate him, sir?"

"Down to the knuckle bones." Abinadab was enjoying the revelation, but Julian didn't doubt he was serious. "Now to be fair, the choice was either two starving, or one surviving and t'other becoming his provender. Don't be alarmed. If you aren't stuck in a blizzard and run out of food, Bragg prefers venison or even dog to human flesh, although he maintains that human meat savors better than polecat."

Unfortunately, Julian had no trouble imagining Bragg eating him. "So, what am I to do when the next blizzard comes? Will you purchase my indenture? I could help you in your store."

"What would I do with you? I've plenty of help with my wife and daughter, and I don't find you appetizing in the least."

"In case of a blizzard then I have no choice other than to kill him before he eats me," Julian asserted.

"Do you believe you could survive alone two days in the wilds, surrounded by hostile savages? Besides, it might have come to your notice Bragg sleeps with an eye open and his hand on a primed pistol. Nay, lad, you're caught as surely as a fly stuck in tree sap. Your best bet is to pray for mild winters. Pray earnestly. When I was born, my father opened up the Bible and gave me the first name—Abinadab—his eyes first fell upon. He said if God chose my name, He might take care in looking out for me. Until I was twelve, I sat with my family in the front pew of the church before a great eye painted on the pulpit. Every Sunday, that big yellow eye stared at me whilst I was sermonized. It made me nervous, that eye, yet when I set out for the frontier how I missed that peeling yellow orb watching over me. It was then I began to pray daily, hoping the eye still kept me in its sight because of my godly name, and here I am twenty-eight years later with nary a scratch on me."

The next morning, just to prove the point, Abinadab started to joke with Bragg: "Julian is too scrawny for more than a snack, and the way you let the savages abuse him, he'll never fatten up."

Bragg seemed mildly embarrassed by the implication that he planned to eat his bondservant. "I won't say 'twasn't a stroke of luck Thomas stumbled into that bear's den. I would not have survived the winter without both of their contributions to me larder, and it would have broke me heart to kill the lad meself. Was I to be dying first, I'd not have held it against Thomas if he carved steak or two out of me. Same for Julian here. If I die and he finds himself in a bad way, he's welcomed to whatever of me parts he deems most savory."

"I'd never eat you, Master Bragg," Julian declared.

Bragg frowned. "You disappoint me, lad. You won't be surviving long with such a tender regard for your stomach."

The next afternoon, while Julian was brushing the horses and feeding them dried corncobs, a long train of pack-horses and mules began filing through the palisade's gate. Leading the caravan was a well-formed man with a narrow face, a strong prow of a nose, and eyes that smiled in amusement. Skinners and drovers with lashes and curses kept the pack animals moving. Bragg appeared at Julian's side and watched these new arrivals, arms folded. The leader stopped in front of Bragg, eyed him up and down, shaking his head. At that moment, at the tail end of the caravan, five men in the white breeches, red coats, and tricorn hats of British marines came into view.

"Good day, Mr. Bragg. I believe those men are wanting you," the leader said.

Bragg's eyes shifted right and left as if looking for escape, then his face settled into a grin. "Good day, Mr. Croghan. I would have appreciated a fair warning."

"The life you led up to this moment was your fair warning, Bartholomew," Croghan replied.

The captain of the marines approached. His face was pinched and scowling as if his upper lip had a stench his nose couldn't escape. "Tell your heathens to unpack our horses. We stay over there," he said to Croghan, pointing to a longhouse. "The savages inside will find other lodgings. Inform them also that we'll endure none of their pagan ruckuses tonight. It has been a wearying trip, and we require restful quiet. I also desire you to advertise the bounty for Bragg—fifty pounds—and I must insist they don't attempt to pass off any old scalp as his to collect the bounty."

"Only fifty pounds, captain? I thought Bragg, being a ferocious pirate and a cannibal, might be worth more," Bragg said conversationally.

"The bounty is five hundred pounds," the captain explained. "But my men soon will disband to Nova Scotia and need their ten pounds each to buy cattle and farm tools to settle themselves, and, of course, I require a fair remuneration for my services."

Bragg lowered his voice confidentially. "Well, if you're looking for Bartholomew Bragg who's rumored to be the notorious pirate Jacques Dugard in disguise, I could be leading you to him, but I require two hundred pounds for me services."

"You value yourself overmuch, sir. I offer you twenty pounds because my men surely will think poorly of me if I remunerate them less than five."

Bragg shrugged his shoulders. "I am supposing they will."

"But, no," the captain said, reconsidering. "I cannot cheat my men out of their fair share of the reward. You, on t'other hand, as a loyal crown subject, are obliged to guide me to him. If you refuse, then I believe the sting of the lash might change the color of your opinion pretty quickly, sir."

Bragg turned to Croghan who appeared to be enjoying this interchange. "What man who values honor wouldn't choose to go a-pirating over serving under such a bacon-faced, slab-headed toad?"

"You insult me, sir," the captain asserted, beginning to draw his sword.

Bragg suddenly heaved his shoulder into the captain, knocking him to the ground. Croghan drew his pistol. "This be your man, Captain Gorse."

Bragg bowed. "Bartholomew Bragg, your humble servant."

The captain got up slowly, red-faced and fighting for breath. "I would hang, draw, and quarter you here and now for insolence, however I want not to deny the people in Philadelphia the spectacle."

"Very considerate of you," Bragg commented.

The captain pushed in his sword and looked around. The backwoodsmen, drovers, skinners, and even marines were smiling, enjoying the joke. Julian must have been smiling also because abruptly the captain drew out the sword and hit him hard on the side of the cheek with the hilt, knocking him to the ground. Blood welled up inside Julian's mouth, which he spat out along with a tooth. He spat again and again and thought he might faint with the pain. A flustered Abinadab helped Julian up and offered him a rag to bite down on. Julian wished it were a sword to strike back.

The captain went on as if the blow given Julian was no more than swat at a fly. "We start back tomorrow at the first light. Mr. Croghan. Tell your men to be ready to break camp at five."

Croghan's lips formed several different words silently before answering, "I'm not at your beck and call, Captain Gorse. Now that you have your man, me business with you is ended. You can hire a guide from the village or find your way back yourself."

"Keep in mind," Gorse continued in his harsh nasal voice, "I could compel you in the name of His Majesty's government. Why any man of any degree prefers the company of these heathen to even such a disagreeable village as Philadelphia is beyond comprehension. I'm also taking the boy back. He'll be charged with abetting the flight of a criminal, which is a hanging crime."

Julian didn't quite comprehend the words Captain Gorse was saying until Abinadab interposed. "That boy had no choice. He was purchased as a servant by Bragg on the docks."

"Yes, I imagine that the courts in Philadelphia might be inclined to see it your way," Gorse replied coldly. "Yet since Bragg's crimes were on the seas, the boy will be tried in a maritime court. They might mercifully decide to only give him two hundred lashes. 'Tis unlikely he'll be much more than a bloody stain on the whipping post after the first hundred."

Bragg and Julian were both tied to a pole in the center of the village. Eventually, the bleeding in Julian's mouth stopped, but outraged by the injustice of Gorse's accusation, he couldn't put together any words to speak. Bragg uttered a stream of curses in French under his breath, but whenever an Englishman came within hailing distance, he'd call out cheerfully. "Have you letters for Philadelphia? I'm bound for that brotherly village." His comments to the Munsee, on the other hand, incited threats and frowns. A young brave even rushed them with a raised tomahawk and a war cry causing Bragg to laughingly exclaim, "Aye, do me the mercy of a swift death."

Croghan avoided them. Gorse kept Abinadab busy translating his orders to the Indians who scurried to and fro until late at night with tasks that had little apparent purpose or sense although an armed marine accompanied the recipients of these commands to provide encouragement. Gorse approached once, smugly regarding Bragg and Julian as he adjusted his hat, then ordered the rawhide cords tightened.

"You be a Barbados man," Bragg observed.

"You know me?" Gorse asked.

"I know your kind, sure. Barbados men are so accustomed to play the master that they treat all beneath their station like they was their slaves."

"True enough." Gorse nodded and walked away.

When night came and the village quieted, Bragg spoke directly to Julian for the first time. "Fortune be not after smiling on you, boy. Your best chance is getting word to William Johnson. He'll vouch that you're spying for him. His uncle is the famous admiral, Sir Peter Warren, who took Louisburg, and King Georgie can't do enough to please him."

"How do you know Mr. Johnson asked me to spy?" Julian was surprised to find his voice.

Bragg chuckled. "Arrah, I didn't hitherto, only I had a fair inkling for I'd be doing likewise. 'Tis hardly a matter for concern. To slacken me curiosity, since both of us will adorn a gibbet ere long, can you be telling me how Johnson planned to contact you?"

"I saw Master Johnson giving scalps to Black Wolf. When a person asked me if I remembered Black Wolf's gift, I was to tell him what I had learned about your plots," Julian answered.

"Aye, Johnson's a deep file, to be sure."

At four o'clock in the morning, they were untied from the pole. Bragg was given a mount and Julian, hands secured behind him, was attached to Frida by a long rope noosed around his neck. Frida was also burdened with furs and other items appropriated from the Munsee village. Patting Julian on his sore cheek, Captain Gorse commented, "Don't worry about keeping up, boy. The dragging and choking saves the king the expense of an executioner." Gorse also confiscated their packhorses claiming the merchandise belonged to the crown. He refused a guide stating it was an aspersion on his character to suggest he was capable of getting lost.

A horse walks at roughly double the pace of a man, so Julian had to run to keep up, which with his bad foot and bound hands was an ungainly and laborious effort. Skipping favoring his left foot helped; still Julian was unable to see how he could last the morning, much less, weeks of such travel. Several times he tripped and was dragged until one of the marines, defying the reprimands of Gorse, took pity and halted Frida.

"It matters little if he chokes now or in a fortnight," Gorse snarled and pricked Frida with the point of his sword to make her lurch forward.

What saved Julian were the frequent dead-ends. Upon arriving at one, Gorse's eyes would cross and his bottom lip protrude. Julian then could sit and catch his breath while the captain digested this proof of his incompetence. With a thinning air of authority, Gorse would order the convoy around, but, inevitably, after a brief spell, they would confront another dead-end.

Finally, Bragg spoke up: "Free the boy and give him a horse. That's me price for leading you back to the trail."

"I would be court-martialed for letting a criminal escape," Gorse insisted in a high irritating voice.

"Or you could be going around in circles 'til we go mad. The boy is as much of a criminal for helping me as me horse is a criminal for carrying me."

Captain Gorse flushed with anger. "I know a better way to handle the likes of you. Take him off the horse," he called to the marines. "Tie the felon to that tree. Make a fire. In my experience the brand and lash unfailing make the unwilling speak the truth."

The attack that occurred at that moment was swift beyond imagining. Four shots rang out. Two marines fell dead. Spooked, Frida jerked Julian off his feet and dragged him into a meadow where she was distracted by a clump of clover. As Julian sat up, a marine with a tomahawk stuck halfway into his forehead staggered by him and collapsed. The scalpless head of the fourth was booted high into the air. A moment later, Bragg was untying Julian. "We will tender our thanks and leave this party early afore they decide they are needing extra scalps."

Julian shakily rose to his feet and walked with Bragg toward the horses. Nearby, Captain Gorse stood between two braves, trembling and holding an iron pot in his hands. Blood streamed down from a deep slash on his jaw mixing with the red of his coat. Four other Indians were rummaging the packhorses. Night Fox paced excitedly around the bloody meadow. Seeing Julian, he grinned and waved a fresh scalp. A brave with a grizzled queue and blackened face except for circles of vermilion around his eyes blocked their way and asked in English. "And how shall we punish you, Roaring Bear, who insults us by calling us women and dogs?"

"You should never be punishing a man for stating the truth as he sees it, Wolf Eyes," Bragg answered. "I be not calling you women and dogs now."

Wolf Eyes nodded, then ordered the braves to stop rifling the packhorses. "Go, quickly," he advised them. "I only take the life and property of enemies. You're not an enemy like this man for which we have a special punishment." There followed an exchange in Lenape, which ended with Bragg shaking his head.

"Why do they insist I carry this pot?" Gorse asked.

Bragg sighed. "Since you ask, I be telling. 'Tis not me doing. I was suggesting they just cut your throat and lift your scalp, only they want to repay your insults to their pride in kind. They are cutting off a piece of you—nose, finger, ear—and tossing it. You must fetch it and put it in the pot. Then they cut off another piece and you fetch it again. When you're too weak to play their game, they boil your parts in the pot and be making you eat them. You're a cruel overbearing thickheaded ass, Captain Gorse, but you aren't deserving this."

Gorse squeezed his eyes shut and said, "Please deliver this message to my wife."

"With a bounty on me head, I won't be delivering no message, yet I will render you one favor," Bragg whispered into the captain's ear.

"Thank you," Gorse said.

While the Indians stoked their fire. Bragg and Julian separated the packhorses, leaving one as a gift for their rescuers, and left.

"Why did the captain thank you?" Julian asked as soon as they were out of sight.

"I told him the bark of the willow stimulates blood flow. There was several willow trees at the edge of the meadow. If the poor captain gets a chance, he will gnaw into one, swallow as much bark as he can and be dying sooner."

CAROLINAS

FOR THE NEXT several weeks, they made their way south into a bleak countryside of swamps and rugged brush-tangled hills and ravines. The villages where they stopped, mostly Creek, mostly dismally poor, preferred stealing to trading. Often, they didn't light a campfire after leaving a village and would take turns guarding the packhorses through the night.

Julian had a difficult time reconciling himself to the brutal massacre of the marines. He had witnessed hangings in London, but there was nothing unexpected in a hanging. He had seen carts loaded with corpses after epidemics, however those people weren't acquaintances. To see a man show you a small kindness and curse the flies one moment and then his scalpless head laying in the weeds the next—that was different. It seemed unjust that death could be so sudden. Julian comprehended now why Molly and Johnson held out little hope for his survival.

Julian's list of questions for Bragg had grown, yet he was afraid to approach his master. Bragg appeared similarly grimly preoccupied with his own meditations. In any event, eight packhorses separated them and not conversing was easy. Finally, at a cold camp, after a long futile day of travel to an abandoned Creek village, Julian gathered up the courage to break the silence: "Sir, we might wander here ten years and not trade a tenth of our goods."

Bragg riveted a harsh stare on Julian, then his expression softened. "We be aiming to intersect the Great Warriors Trail, thence head southward to the country of the Choctaw. If the Choctaw don't murder us and boil us for supper, the trading will be brisker there, to be sure. Prices are higher for buckskins, and that's what they have aplenty. Only you're after another question, lad. No beating around the bush. Your face does the asking before your tongue."

"Will we ever return to Philadelphia?" Julian ventured.

"Why are you after going back to Philadelphia? We weren't there long enough for you to form attachments unless you and Minerva took a liking to each other behind me back. Nay, we'll not be paying visits to any port that also welcomes the British Navy—New York, Charleston, Boston. I'm not saying we won't ever find our way back. After wintering in New Orleans, I intend to meander up the Mississippi to the Ohio, up the Ohio as far as it will take us. When I make the delivery of the violins to the Seneca. I'll inquire if Johnson is open to interceding on your behalf. He'll be of a different temper towards you than that ill-fated buffoon Captain Gorse. After all, you was his spy, and Miss Molly will work in your favor, sure."

Julian was doubtful whether Molly had any influence with Johnson, but he let that pass. Falling silent for a minute, he gathered the courage to ask the real question festering in his craw: "Master, I heard what you told Micah about a new country you're making in the west. I'm sorry for listening, only Singing Sparrow invited me in and served me cornpone and venison, and I couldn't help but hear."

Bragg whistled tunelessly, then asked, "Me nation be of interest to you?"

"How could it not, sir?" Julian responded earnestly. "I don't want to stay on the bottom my whole life because I had the misfortune to be born there. If I start out fresh, I have an opportunity to make of myself what I can. Even though I might not possess the talents to rise above my station, at least I won't be kept there because somebody on the top is pushing me down."

Bragg spat into where the campfire would have been. "To be loyal to a new country, you might find yourself disloyal to the old."

"Sir, I don't believe a man ought to be called a traitor for trying to better his position in the world."

Bragg nodded. "What do you see yourself doing in me new country to earn your daily bread?"

Julian had unsuccessfully given this thought. "I have yet to learn where my talents lie, sir. I must possess some ability, I mean there is always something one man does better than other men. I doubt farming is for me. I wasn't born to it. Maybe, like you, I'll trade with the savages. I know my letters and sums. A new land must need scriveners."

"Scrivener?" Bragg screwed up his eyes. "I spent a good part of me life avoiding dealings with scriveners, and I end up taking on one of that scurrilous profession as a servant."

"I was just thinking about my abilities."

"Some men are never finding out what they do best. Truthfully, I can't claim gifts superior to other men. However, this I've learned: always be after a beginning. If you do that, when death strikes you down, you hardly notice." Bragg retreated momentarily into his thoughts. "And you must love the land, to be sure. Loving her is the only way to make peace with the jealous bitch."

"What's the land like?" Julian asked.

"Beautiful and sad like a young widow. 'Twas filled with savages not too long ago. The sicknesses came, and now only bones are populating the villages. We would be marrying the young widow like the savages once did. We would be making farms and villages. It will be our time until our time passes, and we'll be leaving and dying, and the land will become again the beautiful young widow waiting to be courted." Bragg paused, considering. "That's it—a-marrying. That's how you can further me enterprise. You be marrying a Lakota or Mandan girl or some dusky maiden from a nation rubbing elbows with us. Heathen girls fancy you. So marry a pretty dark-skinned bright-eyed lass with a war-sachem father, knit yourself into their bosoms, make them into our friends. That way, when trouble starts, they stand with us."

"Will I be obliged to live like them?" Julian asked.

"After a fortnight of living savage, you might be finding their way more to your liking."

"I guess I'll do what is necessary," Julian conceded.

Bragg roared with laughter. "I'm offering you a hot-blooded maid who will be pumping you dry of pleasure day and night, and you glumly say you will do whatever is necessary as if I was telling you to spend the rest of your precious life yoked to a plow and given as your only sustenance vinegar and bitter herbs."

The next day they passed a mule ambling along at a leisurely pace carrying a dozing grandmotherly lady. A quarter mile further, they came upon the main party—three or four families who were taking themselves and their worldly possessions into the wilderness. The road was too narrow for wagons, so anything that couldn't walk, ride, or be herded was carried by horse—the panniers were not only stuffed full of supplies but also carried chickens, geese, and young children. The strain of the trek showed on the settlers' burnt gaunt faces and the hobbling gait of the horses. At Julian and Bragg's approach, a loud voice commanded, "Hold to! Give the gentlemen room to pass." The group slowly pulled off the trail.

"We thank you, good sirs and madams," Bragg called out. The people showed various degrees of interest or disapproval as they rode by.

A young girl with an open freckled face and blond hair that spilled out from beneath her cap regarded Julian curiously. On the same horse, her pretty sister with a single brunette curl hanging below her bonnet observed tartly to a boy riding beside her, "Look what the ill wind hath blown us."

When Julian and Bragg reached the head of the party, a man pulled his large black horse into the path blocking their progress. Deep-set eyes bored out of a flat granite visage. Gray hair trimmed his temples. Lips were set in a hard line. His air of command indicated he was the leader of the settlers. Four other reddened hard-bitten men closed in behind them, cutting off their retreat.

The leader's eyes locked with Bragg's. "We was told in Charleston to keep a lookout for a man and boy of your descriptions. We was told if we took you captive, we'd receive the full bounty. A thousand pounds for the old pirate and fifty for his young mate."

"Fifty for me?" Julian blurted out before he realized this constituted a confession. He had the impression that the blue eyes of the blond girl just doubled in size.

"Who be telling such tales?" Bragg put on a grin as if the leader were jesting.

"A captain of the marines was found wandering in the woods crazily babbling for a woman named Anne. He had headed a detail escorting you and the boy back to stand trial for piracy when your savage friends ambushed him."

"Is that what the captain was saying?"

"Just so. Those were his words. The savages left him his tongue, but little else which would identify him as human. He made his report then died."

"Well, part be true," Bragg said. "And part not. When this captain was escorting us back, we was attacked by savages who he had offended. Having no quarrel with us, the savages allowed us to go."

"I might believe you," the leader said. "What was done to the captain wasn't the work of any Christian."

"Well, we certainly be Christians," Bragg replied nodding. "A thousand fifty pounds is a lot of money. You might be buying a plantation, purchasing a dozen sturdy slaves, and setting yourselves up as gentlefolk with so much. I'd not be blaming you for taking the bounty. Why, any man would. We be hanged if you do, yet some say a pocketful of silver is a great salve for the conscience, although Judas learnt otherwise."

"They say you was a pirate," the leader said, his forehead wrinkling.

Julian heard behind him pistols drawn and cocked.

Bragg shook his head regretfully. "That I was, to be sure, and for that me skeleton should be rattling in the cage at Sullivan's Island in Charleston harbor."

"Did you murder men in your pirating?"

Bragg shook his head again. "Aye, I killed men striving to do the same to me. I never took pleasure in killing, yet, on occasion, a man can't avoid it."

"And you plundered and stole," the leader pressed.

"Aye, I've broken the seventh commandment along with the tenth enough times so the devil will need to stock up on extra firewood before I'm allowed into hell."

"We all covet, but it don't make it less a sin," the leader stated. "Why are you giving me reasons to take you back to Charleston and collect the bounties?"

"One purpose, and one purpose only, to be sure," Bragg replied. "When I tell you we was nowise having a hand in the death of the marines, you believe me. The savages were neither friend nor enemy. They was only holding a grudge against Captain Gorse, a Barbados man."

"That's only one crime you failed to commit among the many you just confessed to." the leader's voice lowered threateningly.

Bragg lowered his voice also. "Those many was committed thirty years ago. I believe you're a man who's lived enough years to know how little say we have in our destinies. If the die had fallen differently, I might be leading me family into a fine new country, and you carrying the bounty on your head. There don't exist a soul out here whose life, one time or another, depended not on the mercy of another. Savage, French, English, and all the breeds in-between. Now, are you after showing us mercy or are you after turning us in, collecting the bounties, and living off the sweat and misfortunes of others?"

The leader gave a bare nod. "At the age of sixteen, I was impressed. Five years the Royal Navy robbed from me. My brother got the farm, my cousin married my sweetheart, my mother and father died not knowing whether I was alive or dead. I can't take my life back. Whether you is telling the truth or no, I neither will aid nor abet the Admiralty's justice. You're free to go." Addressing the other men, he declared, "We never saw them!"

"Not yet, Horace," A freckled heavy woman rode forward on a mule. "This gentleman should do us a favor in turn. We lost not only the plates and piglets when our horse missed its footing by the falls but our salt too. If we don't find a lick, we'll have a hard time of it."

Without a word, Bragg rummaged in a satchel of a packhorse, lifted out a canvas bag, and handed it to the woman.

She took the bag with salt, held it as if she were unwilling to accept the gift, then asked, "We was told the savages were glad to give up the land because it was hunted out and they was paid more than what it was worth to them. Is that true?"

"Hunted out? One might say the land was hunted out," Bragg replied.

"Is it true they are glad to sell the land?" She pressed. "The savages killed the marines because they took offense at how they was treated; might they take offense with us?"

"In thirty years of trading with savages, I never had a disagreement with them that wasn't remedied with an apology and gifts."

The woman frowned doubtfully. "We have a son not yet weaned and two daughters thirteen and seventeen."

"This be a fine country for youngsters," Bragg proclaimed. "Plenty of room for them to grow, sure."

"Then you do not fear for us?" She asked in almost a whisper, her lips slightly trembling.

"I am fearing for no soul in this fine country." Bragg spurred his horse on.

"Thank you, sir, for putting my mind at rest," she called out hollowly.

"Because fearing never saved a damned soul," Bragg muttered when they were far enough away to not be heard.

Once out of sight, Bragg picked up the pace. They diverged from the main trail, taking a path nearly obliterated by the overgrown brush. They stopped a few hours later and made camp without a fire in the waning daylight.

"Are you afraid they'll change their minds about the bounties?" Julian asked, breaking the silence after their cold meal.

"Nay," Bragg replied. "Yet those good folks give me an uneasy feeling." He directed at Julian a hard stare, "Go ahead, lad, I hear another question rattling in your noggin."

Julian inhaled deeply. "You told the man you were a pirate, sir."

"That's what he wanted to hear."

"You told me you weren't."

"That's what you wanted to hear, was it not?" Bragg yawned.

"Are you, or aren't you?"

"What difference will it make? The end be the same." Bragg spat at where the fire would have been.

"If I'm to be hanged because I'm your servant, I want to know whether I truly am helping a pirate or you are unjustly accused," Julian insisted.

Bragg closed his eyes and leaned his head back. "Being Johnson's spy, you'll condemn me if I say yes and not believe me if I say no."

Julian didn't want to try his master's good humor so changed the subject, "Their leader was no common man."

"Aye, 'tis a rare gentleman whose heart is large enough for both justice and mercy."

"Are they justified in their hopes, sir?"

Bragg yawned again. "Depends on the mood of the Creeks. They are the touchy sort of savage. They may embrace you, share with you their last morsel, and send their daughters to warm your bed, then on the morrow change their opinion and cut your throat. I'd not be settling in their country. When I saw those fine people, me heart was already grieving. Nay, lad, we be moving through here swift as ghosts blown on the wind."

MASSACRE

WHEN THEY CAME upon the site of the massacre, thousands of birds rose from the bodies like the lifting of a huge blanket and scattered. The carnage was horrifying. Most had been scalped, many burned at stakes, a few showed signs of having been eaten. Julian recognized the wife of the leader, partially burned curled around her son. Suddenly nauseous, he spurred Frida down the trail, leaned forward and vomited. When he returned, Master Bragg was carefully picking through the bloody scene searching for items of value.

"Aha!" he exclaimed and extracted the sack of salt. After contemplating the body of a scalped young woman, he tugged at her dress as if he wanted to strip her, then grunted reconsidering the project. Julian left the clearing again. Dismounting, he sat on the ground, rocked back and forth and shuddered uncontrollably. Then, suddenly, his mind went blank and he keeled forward in a faint. On recovering, Julian steadied himself, made camp, and settled down to wait until Bragg finished scavenging.

Bragg showed up in the late afternoon with several

large bundles added to the packhorses. "You should have stayed with the horses, lad, but I won't be holding your tender stomach against you. Not bad takings. Two sacks of flour, a keg of rum the savages missed, some fine combs, pewterware."

"And fabric?" Julian asked coldly.

"'Twould be a shame letting good dresses go to waste. The savages must have gotten pretty darn drunk to overlook so much."

"So you rob the dead, sir," Julian observed scornfully.

"'Tisn't possible to rob the dead," Bragg replied, eying Julian coolly. "You need be alive to own a thing."

"These people were kind to us. They deserve respect," Julian protested angrily.

"Arrah now. What use respect be for them?"

"Did you bury them, at least?"

"Bury them?" Bragg half laughed, half sneered. "What's gotten into you, boy? They are with the Lord, to be sure. They are past caring about their mortal flesh. But since you're after criticizing your master for not providing them a Christian burial, take a shovel, dig a pit six feet down and twelve feet across and bury the poor souls yourself so the next time you be thinking twice about catechizing your betters. I say, go to it. I was counting twenty-four bodies. Of course, if you are believing each deserves its own grave that might take a bit longer."

The company of mangled corpses being more endurable to that of Bragg, Julian went to work. He found soft soil just beyond the massacre, measured out the area, and started to dig. Evening came on fast, but a halfmoon peeking over the pines provided sufficient light. It was past midnight when he started to fill the grave. He had to drag the bodies of the men, however the grandmother was as light as a bird, and the children rested in his arms like feathers. Thankfully, he couldn't discern the nature of their mutilations in the darkness. He tried to summon a prayer as he laid the children in the hole. The Almighty, unfortunately, wasn't giving any clues on what to say. With grim satisfaction, Julian realized that two months ago he wouldn't have had the strength to finish this task.

After stamping down the dirt over the grave, Julian started back to the camp. In the outer limit of the firelight, he was surprised to see two huddling shadows. Julian approached cautiously and made out the faces of the sisters that had belonged to the massacred families. The younger girl looked directly at him, her wild blond hair without a cap, her thin face scratched, her wide eyes reflecting the flames. The older one stared down and held a bloody cloth to her mouth. Looking toward the campfire, Julian received a second surprise. A young African man was lounging in front of the flames, sucking a corncob pipe.

Julian accommodated himself on the other side of the fire and addressed the visitor, "You belong to them?"

The visitor took out his pipe and slowly digested Julian with his gaze. His features were thick, almost dull, but his eyes were something altogether different—intelligent, probing, and menacing. "Nope," he answered.

"Who do you belong to?" Julian insisted.

"I needing belong to a body, suh?" The words rumbled from deep in his chest.

Julian was stymied.

"Resurrection Peter lives roundabouts," Bragg added.

"Roundabouts? I haven't seen village nor cabin this last fortnight." Julian glanced from Bragg to the visitor. "Don't the girls want to come closer to the fire?"

"Best leave them be, suh," Resurrection Peter said.

"Why? Look, they're shivering," Julian argued.

"Best leave them alone." Resurrection Peter emptied his pipe. "The misses not wanting our sort of company. They off in the forest when the bad men come. Two of them rascals smell out the misses. The rascals jigger the sister with the brown hair." His eyes shifted briefly toward the girl with the bloody cloth in her mouth. "And she bite her tongue near clean through. They forget about the young'un, and afore they finish, she brain the scoundrel jiggering her sister with a rock as big as a melon, then she take his pistol and shoot dead t'other kneeling on the poor girl's arms. I find the brained man crawling into the swamp. His companions been too drunk to remember him or his dead friend. I think to kill him, then I think he not deserve the mercy of a quick death. Better he taking his time to die. The misses seen the worst of menfolk this day, and want no more of our kind, so best let them alone." Peter stroked his chin and slowly smiled. "You the boy with bounty of fifty pound for murdering five Royal Navy marines. Right promising start to profession of outlawry."

"My hands were bound and a rope around my neck was tied to a horse," Julian replied angrily. "I was unable to even scratch my nose, much less murder five marines."

"Whether that true or no, when the lie worth fifty pounds it not signify. I doubt you not, suh. You bury the bodies even after your master strip them of their garments. Outlaws no showing respect to the dead like you."

"You be speaking as if you think dead people feel cold," Bragg objected.

"I think dead needing respect," Resurrection Peter answered.

"Us living is who be needing respect," Bragg asserted. "The dead require only God's mercy."

"If you live roundabouts, aren't you afraid of the savages who did this?" Julian asked Peter.

"Who saying savages murder these folks?" Resurrection Peter sucked on his pipe.

"Who else?" Julian squirmed uneasily sensing unwelcomed news.

"Nay, boy, this no work of savages. Nay, this work of backcountry boys that show the governor of Georgia or Carolina their passel of scalps, claiming they defeat a Choctaw war party and demanding the governor pay them bounty. You take note the color of the hair of the two girls untouched by the scalping knife? No savage overlooking those fine yellow and red tresses and no governor paying no bounties for such. Brown hair pass for they blackening and smoothing the hair with grease and soot, then half curing it so the scalp stinky and maggoty. Holding his nose, the governor handing over the guineas. You take note of the clothing the women wear afore Bartholomew rob the dead souls' modesty? No savage passing up such finery to make a present to his squaw, and no Christian trading a bloody dress or hat, excepting Bartholomew who no Christian."

"English and Christian men don't torture women and children," Julian declared indignantly.

"You finding few men of my hue agreeing with you, suh. What been done to these folks, been done so governors laying blame on savages. When word of the massacre coming to the settlements, the governor increasing bounty on scalps, meaning more profit for them."

Julian called out to the girls, "What are your names?"

The blond girl stood, walked to the campfire, holding her dress together at the thigh where it had been ripped, hesitated, went back and took her sister by the hand and led her forward.

"Rebecca," she whispered, answering his question. Gently forcing her sister who still kept her head lowered to sit, she pointed, "This is Meg."

"Tell us who attacked you, Miss Rebecca?" Julian asked.

"The man on Meg was painted all over so I thought he was a savage, only he cried out, 'Bloody stinking hell,' like a common rogue when I cracked his head with the rock," Rebecca explained calmly. "T'other might be half-half. Hard to tell because I shot him in the face. He's there by the creek if you care to look."

Peter continued: "The rogue Miss Rebecca brain carry T burnt into his cheek. Any brave cutting out that T and wearing scar rather than the brand of thief." Resurrection Peter made this last point with an air of finality indicating that the topic was beyond debate.

"That still doesn't explain what you're doing out here alone?" Julian challenged Peter, suspicious that he had some involvement with the massacre.

"Why I here? Visiting my old friend, Master Bragg. That why I here."

"Resurrection Peter isn't traveling alone," Bragg explained. "Why don't you be inviting your boys to the fire? They are cold and tired, to be sure, hanging back there in the shadows." "I post them to warn us in case the rascals remembering their friends and coming back to find them."

"You see, lad, Resurrection Peter is a wise sachem and the most feared war chief hereabouts," Bragg asserted.

"But he's African," Julian protested. "What sort of savages can he lead?"

The question tickled Bragg's humor. "A nation of black savages, lad, black savages," he bellowed and laughed.

"Are there tribes of Africans here?" Julian was certain he was being played for the fool.

"And why wouldn't there be?" Bragg grinned. "Tell the lad about your village, Peter?"

"Nothing I saying 'bout it," Peter replied.

"Are you afraid I might ken where it be?" Bragg asked. "This country isn't like fastness of the Great Dismal where nobody wants to live anyway. You be rooted out by and by, sure. You might then be after taking up me offer."

Peter shook his head. "You talking about your big country with free land. No such thing as free land, Bragg. Coin or blood buying land."

Bragg nodded. "Coin or blood—to be sure. There are settlers already west of you. Soon, they be knocking on the door of your vale and asking the price in blood. And the thing about blood is the more you pay, the more you have to pay."

Peter exhaled a long stream of smoke. "Who paying blood for our poor patch? We making no trouble."

"Don't be foolishly blind, Peter," Bragg exclaimed, suddenly roused into anger. "Most of your people have bounties on their heads and will end up back in the slave quarters whipped at every opportunity to keep them in their place, and the rest will have their final view of the world from a gibbet in Charlestown. That is if you stay where you are."

"Your lad knowing about you?" Peter asked changing the subject.

Bragg seethed for a minute then let go of his anger. "William Johnson planted the idea in his head of me acting as an agent for the French so he's spying on me."

"Well, that true," Peter said.

"Aye. I am an agent for whoever's interest be coinciding with mine—French, Spanish, English. 'Tis easy for an Irishman to do. That's why we're so good at surviving in the wilderness where you have to be flexible in your allegiances. The boy is understanding this. He is seeing a man should only be loyal to King George insofar King George is loyal to him. King George is after hanging him for his association with me. King Louie is not wanting to hang him yet, only that's because King Louie isn't knowing him like King George. Him being English, King Phillip would hang him on principle. The only person out for his welfare is me."

"Fie!" Peter snorted disbelievingly. "Nary a lad surviving two winters in your company."

"That's a falsehood, sure. Thomas survived three years, four months and six days. As for my enterprise, the truth be that England, France, and Spain are lecherously eyeing the land I intend for meself. They all are agreeing to let me promote their claims, only they're not knowing it yet. I am commissioned by the King of France to settle the empty portions of the Ohio Valley with such who would trade loyalty to an English king who thinks nothing of them for land they can plow, sew, and reap. I'm also commissioned to survey choice parcels all the way to the Mississippi by a speculating English gentleman who is trading his pretty wife to be his sovereign's mistress for a million-acre grant. The governor of New Mexico is promising me a silver mine if I stir up trouble between the French and English, which I do by merely existing."

"You forgetting the nations of savages," Peter remarked.

"I'm not forgetting them." Bragg shook his head. "The land be as empty as a churchyard at midnight. The few bands of heathens left will be grateful for the company."

Resurrection Peter stared dully at the fire. A long silence followed.

Bragg broke the silence: "This is not the sort of business you're after, Peter. We've never met without you despoiling me of a portion of me goods."

"I enough furs to burden two packhorses—beaver, bear, otter, deer. I needing all powder and lead you can trade." Peter emptied the ashes out of his pipe.

"What about disappointing me other customers also needing powder and lead."

"Three years nobody see you in these parts. Nary a soul expecting nothing so nary a soul disappointed."

"And if I refuse?" Bragg paused.

"You making a jest, Bragg?"

"That's what I am liking about you, Peter. You offer an unprofitable trade, then be threatening to rob or kill me if I'm not in accord. Where are your furs?"

"The boy coming with me. Seven days from now, he bringing back furs." Resurrection Peter delivered this last statement as more a demand than a request.

"And what shall be done with the misses?" Bragg gave a sideways glance at Rebecca and Meg. "Likely festering in the new grave be all the kin in the world having a care for them. I can't take them back to a settlement without surrendering meself. And it shames me to say I am distrusting meself with those pretty wenches. Even now, one part of me head is trying to convince t'other that those tender things might come to fancy this shaggy old pirate."

"The misses also coming with us," Peter said. "I saying they the boy's sisters. Then I sending them on to the Moravians."

"I suppose I'm having no say in this transaction?" Bragg asked.

"Nope." Peter gave a loud whistle. Presently, a huge Indian with a withered arm and an African coal-black with scarified cheeks emerged from the shadows. The lead and powder were transferred to one packhorse, the two sisters shared another. Julian mounted Frida.

PETER'S VILLAGE

THEY TRAVELED THROUGH a desolate broken-up country until the early afternoon. Peter rode next to the Rebecca and Meg, conversing with them in a low voice. Suspecting that he was angling to take advantage of the sisters, Julian also kept close. When they stopped so the sisters could relieve themselves behind the bushes, Julian positioned Frida between the girls and Peter.

Shaking his head and smiling, Peter remarked, "Brother, no need fearing for the misses. I just telling them we have best doctor in Carolinas and other kind and hopeful things to ease their heartsickness. My overseer, Francis Hayes, been hard man crazy in his head. You knowing you nearing Boss Hayes' plantation by smell of piss and blood. He force Uncle Marcus eat raw oats 'til belly burst. He whip young Cassie to death for laughing when he fall off horse. Little bit of kindness all Cassie want when she dying. She been so grateful for little bit of kindness. So, I kind to suffering souls like her."

"Why are you called Resurrection Peter?" Julian asked,

coming to the conclusion it might be worthwhile to know this man better.

"I young boy when they capture me, dress me in chains and put me on the ship to journey across the big water. Having no words folk understand, first day Boss Hayes making me fetch water for the men and women working in the rice fields. I see Boss Hayes taking apple from tree and eating it so I taking apple from tree and eating it for I hungry. I just swallowing the stem and core, when Hayes hit me in the back of the head with his whip. To learn us nigger folk to not steal, Hayes nail my hand and my foot to the apple tree. From midday to midday, I partway standing partway hanging there afore they take out nails. See, here the scar." Peter showed a small whirl of raised white skin on the palm of his hand.

"When you ran away, weren't you afraid Hayes would do worse to you?" Julian asked.

"After white folk put down the Stono rising, Boss Hayes want us chattel to learn another lesson. He take us all in five big wagons to a road. He make us walk down the road where we seeing a hundred black heads atop a hundred poles. I so afeared my knees shivering, but then it come to me like lightning at night showing what hides in the dark Boss Hayes doing this 'cause he afeared also. He afeared of black folk like we afeared of him. This strange thought worry away at me day and night, telling me I must act. I must use his fear for my gain.

"Every night Hayes playing the cards and drinking rum at Jackson plantation with other overseers. Every night, he taking same road back. So, I sit up in a tree he pass under. I sit and wait 'til he come along drunk as a skunk. I fall on him hard, knock him off horse, take his knife and gun, tie his hands. I always strong lad. I walk him to the turpentine shed in the hills while he curse me and threaten me with his big voice. No matter—I master now. Boss Hayes ignorant of name of boy he nail to tree, only he learning my name now: Boss Resurrection Peter. I gag him. In the shed, I light two lanterns. I bind him to chair and pull down his pants. I stretch out his little tallywag with its two little nuts. I so wanting to nail it to the chair, but that not enough. I slice the wrinkly skin open, separate out one little nut and snip it off. He watching wild-eyed when I show him his little pigeon egg, then step outside and throw it so the birds eating it. Then I sew his little sack up and tell him I know if he finding me, he skinning me alive, but if I finding him first, then I taking t'other nut. My bounty only fifteen pounds, for Hayes tell plantation owners I worthless nigger boy anyway. A year later I back for Harriet."

"Who is Harriet?"

"Harriet wife." Peter engaged in the soft laughter of people who have told themselves a joke. "Harriet house slave. Smile pretty as sunshine, speaking so fine like a real lady. She having no eyes for rough field hand like me."

"She must have been better treated. Why did she run away?" Julian asked.

"Boss Hayes come to fancy Harriet. Every night, after returning from Jackson plantation, he calling for her. She always hiding in the woods 'til he finding another girl or falling asleep. When the owner of the plantation, Master Aldridge and his family visit from Charlestown, Harriet pick up and eat grape that fall off plate to floor. Hayes stitch her lips shut for a day learning her manners. He say to her, 'No more hiding, dearie lest you want more of the sewing needle.' I hear rumors of this, living close by in the swamp. I go to her and make my offer. The next night, when Boss Hayes desiring her, he find pigeon egg on his bed and no Harriet. If I a leper with one eye and no teeth, Harriet still running away with me. By and by, I thinking she coming to hold a bit of affection for her field hand."

Then the conversation turned to Julian's history. Peter listened to the narration carefully and, if his questions were an indication, sympathetically.

Near nightfall, they descended down into a narrow valley where a mishmash of lodgings—wigwams and split log cabins—straggled along a creek. When they rode into the settlement, the inhabitants of the maroon village—even the children who were playing a game of tag in-between the dwellings—ceased their activities and followed them. The crowd appeared to be made up in equal portions of escaped slaves, runaway indentured servants, and dispossessed Indians.

Midway through the village, they came to an open space where a large dirty man was tied to a stout pole. His only covering was a long shirt ripped halfway down his chest. Graying-blond hair hung over his shoulders in clumps. One eye stared off at an angle while the other was fixed straight-ahead, glowering. A puddle had formed at his feet.

Peter dismounted, helped Meg down and spotting in the crowd a tall fleshy black man and an old bent Indian squaw with a flattened head called out, "Mussulman Billiam! Owl Woman!" He took them off to the side, and after a brief explanation, they led Meg into a crude log cabin. Rebecca followed.

Returning to Julian, Peter said, "No better healers in these parts than Mussulman Billiam and Owl Woman. Billiam saying he have three masters: Egyptian barber-surgeon, a fellow named Anubis, who cut his stones to sell him to harem, then decide Mussulman bright boy so keep him and teach him his profession; next Doctor Umberto from Milan who rather look underneath the skin of a dead pretty girl than the naked outside skin of a live pretty girl; then Scot graverobber, Angus Barclay, transported for stealing and butchering his mother's corpse for he been of the same curious mind as Doctor Umberto. Billiam claiming dead flesh and bones telling secrets of live flesh and bone. Owl Woman been Choctaw medicine woman who run away from her people when they come to believe she witch of the Horned Owl who kill a soul for every soul she cure." Peter then turned to a pinkish grayish man in front of the crowd. "Why Ivan tied up, Henry?"

"He got thoroughly liquored and tried to choke Fernando." Henry wore a scraggly beard on the left half of his chin, strangely balanced by only having teeth on the right half of his mouth.

"That all?" Peter asked.

"Then Jimmy Black Throat jumped on Ivan's back, and Ivan threw him breaking his neck. Jimmy Black Throat is dead."

"No one grieving Jimmy Black Throat. Fernando start the fight?"

Henry spat out of the toothless side of his mouth.

"Fernando said 'twas a shame Ivan's woman Maria was taken by the pox for she was the best whore hereabouts."

Resurrection Peter walked up to the man tied to the post. "'Tis terrible what Fernando say about Maria." He poked Ivan in the ribs with his pipe. "But you must pay for Jimmy Black Throat's death."

Ivan's good eye fixed on Peter. "You're a bloody damn nigger slave, not a vucking magistrate."

Peter addressed the crowd: "Anyone saying word why Ivan not paying for Jimmy Black Throat's death with his own?"

"Fernando should also pay the same price," Henry stated.

A small dark grinning man with spidery limbs pushed himself forward. "Why?" He asked, not hiding his sarcastic tone. "Alive, Maria would have took my words as compliment."

Ivan strained forward trying to tear the post out of the ground. "His savage bitch is vucking whore, not Maria."

Peter spoke calmly. "Maria been good woman, and we grieving her mightily. Fernando time to time good, time to time bad. Ivan, you never good."

"Vucking hang me before I piss myself again or vucking let me go."

"No word to say for yourself, Ivan?" Peter asked.

"Maybe I deserve to be vucking hanged, maybe I don't, but one thing you all vucking know in your hearts." He scanned the crowd menacingly. "If this bloody little nigger chooses when I die, he chooses when all you vucking damned shits die too."

"We all voting," Peter said unperturbed. "One last chance to speak for yourself, Ivan."

Ivan thrust his head forward and smirked. "I'd murder him again, more slowly the next time."

"I'll speak for Ivan." A young black woman squared off in front of Peter. Her face was open with softly luminous eyes, a contrast with Peter's closed inscrutable features and narrow gaze. She had a child at her breast, another hugged her knee. "Dearest, you must consider Ivan never harmed no one here before and didn't mean to kill Jimmy Black Throat."

"That true. Also, true when Ivan liquored up, he boasting about sticking this man, carving that man. He always warning us watch out, watch out, for one night he sticking all us for joy it giving him. That true, Ivan?"

"It took ten of you to wrestle me here. You're all white-livered shits. Vote or just vucking hang me, shoot me, or stick me." Ivan stamped his foot.

Peter drew a long line in the dirt in front of Ivan. "Those for saving Ivan, stand here. Those for hanging him, stand there." The crowd divided into two groups. Mostly, the blacks stood with Peter—Harriet the exception. The Indians divided evenly. The indentured servants predominated for clemency. A mixed band of surly men glared at those who wanted Ivan executed, intimidating several into changing sides.

"You're two votes short," Henry said to Peter.

"Mussulman Billiam and Owl Woman voting with me." Peter turned to Julian. "Looks like you deciding."

Julian was taken aback. "How can I? I don't live here."

"Good. Then it matter not which half these folks hating you."

"'Tis not my place," Julian insisted. "I refuse to decide."

Peter seemed to think his answer amusing. "Then we all hating you."

"You ask me to condemn a man I have no acquaintance with."

"Bless your good fortune having no acquaintance with Ivan. If you no vote, brother, then we fighting it out with fist and knife, which making a big bloody mess."

Julian couldn't find it in himself to condemn a defenseless man. "Well, a plague on both your houses. Let him go, but so he wreaks no further havoc, turn him out."

"Turn me out, turn me vucking out," Ivan repeated snorting, stamping his feet and grinning like a madman as he was untied.

Harriet insisted on inviting Julian and Rebecca to eat in their cabin. She was soft-spoken and modest. After putting the baby into the cradle and humming it to sleep, she showed herself fully as curious as her husband about Julian's world. The other children were at least as well-mannered as William Johnson's children and definitely politer than Molly. Billiam interrupted them halfway through the meal. He and Peter had a whispered conversation outside.

When Billiam left, Peter beckoned to Julian to join him. "Child keeping most her tongue," Peter explained. "Nothing else Billiam can do. Tomorrow, brother, you must leave."

"Why do you call me, brother?" Julian asked. "I voted against you?"

"Harriet stand against me and I still calling her wife," Peter observed. "Four men I give the name brother— Shawnee chief Mist-on-the-hills, Mussulman Billiam, priest Son-of-gray-wolf, and the trader Corinth Avalon who trade with us year in and year out and tell nobody secret of our village. Scarlet fever take Brother Corinth last spring. When I see you showing kindness to the lasses, I say to myself, this lad like me: we both cast our fortunes out into the world as boys, both know servitude, both protect those too weak to protect themselves. I feeling our lives twining together, so I asking you to take place of Brother Corinth, if you of the same mind." Peter took out a knife.

Conscious that he could have refused and maybe should have, Julian stretched out his hand, flinching. "Well, I'll call you brother for those reasons and because I am convinced I need a family to survive and yours is as good as any."

Peter nodded and quickly sliced Julian's palm, then did the same to his. They clasped their wounded hands together. They returned to the cabin. Neither the women nor the children commented on the hands bound with handkerchiefs.

"The girls also have no family. Can they remain here instead of escorted by me to the Moravian mission?" Julian suggested as he sat down glancing at Rebecca who was nervously biting her fingernails.

"You don't speak for us," Rebecca protested. "We're not staying here."

"Moravian mission the place for them," Resurrection Peter stated, meeting Rebecca's frown. "These misses too much like wives, sisters, and daughters of the masters who hurt folk here. The Moravian brothers, they making a place for them."

"How can I protect the girls on the way to the mission? I don't have a gun nor never fired one," Julian admitted ashamed.

"A gun no saving you from savages on the warpath nor from those scoundrels who murder the lasses' kin. The Moravians welcoming the lasses, to be sure, for they innocents. Not you, brother. You moving on. Traders, the Moravians hating and damning to hell. If you carrying rum or firewater, they paying penny a gallon, then pouring it out."

The following morning as their small party stood shivering in front of the horses, Peter shook Julian's hand, presented him with an ancient flintlock pistol, and explained, "Riding this trail three days and three ridges west, you coming to Moravian praying town. Take care, brother. We seeing each other again. Whether the roll of the die bringing you back in a year or ten, we seeing each other again." Then the three of them set off, Julian on Frida leading the packhorses loaded with furs, Meg and Rebecca trailing, sharing a large mare.

PRAYING TOWN

WHILE THEY WERE descending a steep trail down a ridge an hour later, Ivan stepped out in front of them holding a curved Indian war club. The horses shied, having no wish to pass the giant.

"Get off them vucking horses." Ivan waved the weapon slowly making the animals skitter back. "Off them vucking horses."

"Don't," Julian cried to the girls, not wanting them to lose the advantage of the horses' height and weight, and shakily aiming the ancient pistol.

Ivan laughed. "What are you vucking doing with that."

He grabbed at the barrel. Julian jerked it away. The gun went off, blowing the club out of Ivan's hand. Frida reared. Ivan grabbed the reins and with incredible strength wrestled her head down. Meanwhile Julian primed the pistol, spilled powder into the barrel, fumbled at the little bag that had two more balls, tamped down one of them forgetting the patch and aimed. Ivan swatted at the gun. It went off again, and blood immediately welled out of a groove beneath Ivan's ear. Turning the pistol around,

Julian pounded Ivan's head with the handle. Roaring, Ivan grabbed his hand and started to pull him off the horse. Frida surged forward, knocking Ivan off-balance. Julian was wrenched from the saddle and fell on top of him. Ivan easily flipped him over, pinioned Julian's arms with his knees, raised up a rock the size and shape of a small cannon barrel, then hesitated, and teetered. The rock suddenly dropped backwards, and his arm dangled. Julian realized he had just heard a gunshot a few feet away. Resurrection Peter stepped in front of Rebecca and Meg, one of his two pistols smoking.

Ivan slowly staggered to his feet and faced Peter. "I know you'd vucking come to kill me. So vucking do it. Do it, I beg you." He closed his eyes and spoke in a calmer voice, "I think maybe, maybe I think I see Maria now. When I got feverish, she put my head in her lap like I was her child, her precious child. Maybe, I think she do that again."

Peter approached and fired the second pistol. The massive chest shuddered as it received the bullet, blood began to drench the front of the shirt, and Ivan smiled as he slumped to the ground.

"I owe you thanks, brother, and an apology for my vote," Julian said.

"Nay, brother," Peter replied. "Best this way. Ivan no longer want this life since Maria pass on. As for the folk against me, they see too many kith and kin executed to vote with an executioner."

"We bury him?"

"Yes, for Maria's sake," Peter said. "She been good woman."

Although the girls now rode closer to Julian, Rebecca rebuffed his attempts at conversation with silence or curt cold replies. On the first evening, Julian netted and roasted two trout. Rebecca refused the fish, preferring to share Meg's cornmeal gruel that Billiam had made. The rest of the evening Rebecca hovered protectively near her older sister who seemed still overwhelmed by grief and the mutilation she had suffered. Julian offered his rabbit fur blanket to the girls shivering under deerskins when they bedded down. Rebecca shook her head, apparently loathe to accept any kindness that might obligate them in return. In the early morning cold, however, Julian was awoken by the deerskins falling on him and the two sisters pressing in on either side. Meg wept softly.

"We're cold," Rebecca whispered. The rest of the night they shared their warmth. The next two days Julian and the sisters barely exchanged four words, but those were followed by nights where they desperately sought out each other's warmth. Julian was questioning how long he could maintain the role of a gentleman when he saw the smoke rising from the chimneys of the Moravian mission.

They entered the Indian praying village on a wide gravel road that divided two rows of neat split-log cabins. The squaws tending the gardens in front of the houses wore European clothes or fringed buckskin dresses and the braves, leggings and loin cloths. They stopped their work to stare at the visitors but didn't formally greet them. In the center of the town, a man in a black frock coat clasping a German bible to his chest and a younger companion with rolled-up sleeves and a hammer in one hand strode forward to meet them.

Julian cleared his throat. "Sirs, I am Julian Asher, the bondservant of Master Bartholomew Bragg. This is Meg and Rebecca. They lost all their family in a massacre. Meg hurt her tongue and cannot talk. Peter said you could help them."

"Resurrection Peter?" the older man asked in a German-accented English. He was a stumpy individual with a short neck, arms and legs, and a good-natured face, which contrasted with his lanky hammer-toting companion who to all appearances seemed divinely designed for height and reach.

"Yes, he said you could help," Julian tried not to plead.

"I am Georg," the older man continued, "the pastor of this flock. This is Albert. Excuse him for not making talk. He arrived recently. He speaks only German and Lenape."

"Are you able to take in Meg and Rebecca?" Julian asked. "They have no kin now."

Georg nodded. "Ja, ja, we take care of the girls. Do you carry spirituous liquors?"

"No, only furs," Julian replied.

After an exchange with Albert in German, Georg said, "The bondservant of the pirate Bragg is welcome to remain with us until the morning after Sunday. We discuss later what we do with the sisters, Miss Meg and Miss Rebecca."

Julian was allowed to sleep on a pew in the church. No demands were made on him, social or otherwise. At loose ends for a few days, Julian attended the morning and evening church services. He perhaps understood one word out of ten of the sermons preached energetically in Lenape, but he enjoyed immensely the hymns, the congregants transforming the staid German tunes into something mad and unearthly and pleasurable with Lenape rhythmic intensity. Outside the church, the resident Indians kept their distance. When Julian mentioned this to Georg, the pastor recounted what his flock had endured thus far—forced expulsions, murders, and rapes—at the hands of militia, settlers, and other tribes.

"'Tis difficult to trust in this world when so many do not love God," Georg said when he finished.

On the second day, Julian discovered that Rebecca was shadowing his wanderings. He stopped, sat on a log and watched while she hesitated a hundred paces away. Finally, coming to a decision, she marched forward and seated herself on the same log. At first, Rebecca was quiet. She wore a clean dress and had brushed her hair in such a way as to cover the spot where it had been torn out. With her narrow, freckled face, pleasing features, pale hair, it was hard to determine whether she would grow into a beauty or remain plain. Her blue eyes, which could draw you in or push you away, was her most arresting feature.

"I want to tell you the rapscallions took me afore they went after Meg," Rebecca announced abruptly.

This didn't seem a promising start to a conversation. "I'm sorry," Julian said.

"Oh, 'twasn't as bad as a bee sting or a horse's kick, and when I cracked open the head of the scoundrel who was taking Meg and shot the other in the face who was holding her, I got even. I just wish I done it sooner. I had my courses so I'm not carrying a dead man's baby. You need to know for I decided I'm leaving with you."

"I'm a bondservant." Julian meant this statement as an argument.

"That don't mean you can't run away. When you do, I go with you."

"And you won't brain me with a rock?" Julian realized too late that this humor was ill-advised.

Rebecca wasn't bothered. "What good would that do me if I'm running away with you?"

"What about Meg?" Julian asked.

"What about Meg? What about Meg?" Rebecca cried. "Everybody is talking about poor Meg. My whole life they've talked about her—how pretty she is, how good she is, how clever she is. I save her life, and still nobody talks about me."

"It's a terrible injury," Julian reminded her.

"You don't know Meg. That young German man, he's fallen for her. She can't speak, may never speak, and she can't understand a word he says, yet every chance he gets, he's right next to her trying to figure out a way to help her. And I can tell the things he say to her are mighty nice."

"The Moravians are kind to you," Julian said.

"Bah, I have to deal with Matilda—Georg's wife." Matilda was a buxom young woman with twice the energy of any human being Julian had ever encountered and an exuberant sense of humor. You usually heard her laugh before you saw her coming. The Indians found her quite amusing. Matilda also possessed a dead certainty as to what everybody else should be doing. She had taken charge of Rebecca, giving her a multitude of chores and frequently lecturing her not unkindly in German. Before Julian could articulate further his protest, Georg and Matilda appeared walking hurriedly down the path obviously bent on intercepting them.

"Bloody hell," Rebecca whispered, giving Julian a sideways glance, then blushed.

Georg and Matilda blocked them. "I know what plans you make," Georg said.

"I'm not making any plans," Julian declared.

"She is still too much childlike." Georg pointed to Rebecca.

"I am not!" Rebecca stamped her foot and glared at them.

"And you are a bonded servant." Georg directed his finger at Julian.

"As I told you," Julian replied.

"You don't know aught because we're not planning aught." Rebecca smirked.

"Just because my wife Matilda cannot make English speech, it does not mean she cannot understand English speech," Georg stated.

"You played a trick on me." Rebecca now glanced around like a cornered animal looking for an escape. Seeing none, she began to cry.

"Yes, she understand all insults you make at her like barrel-bottom Palatine witch, curse of …"

"No, I didn't mean…"

Matilda broke out into laughter.

"Why is she laughing at me?" Rebecca flushed bright red with anger.

Georg grinned. "Because you never understood the names she was calling you back."

"How dare she…" Then Rebecca to her credit began to laugh also.

After they had recovered, Matilda and Rebecca forged ahead, engaging in parallel discussion in German and English. Julian said, "I wasn't going to take her away."

"Ja, ja, I believe you. Matilda is the person to handle Rebecca if there is a woman to handle such a girl with spirit."

"Rebecca told me that the man who tried to take Meg violated her first."

Georg nodded. "Matilda suspected Rebecca was hiding a wound she was too proud to admit. There is no better place for Rebecca now than with Matilda. The girl needs a strong character to put the reins on her strong character. Look at how they go at it now—like sisters—and they don't even speak the same language. She's not the girl for you."

"I never believed she was."

"When you marry your squaw, come back to us. We make problems like other villages, only we make more peace and love here than," Georg spread his arms out wide, "the other world. Murders, drunkenness, debauchery, how much you see already in this new land. Come hither with your squaw wife."

"I haven't met any squaw girls who want me."

"You will. As God is my witness, you will."

Julian wondered at Georg's certainty.

URIAH

JULIAN DEPARTED MONDAY morning. Georg, Meg, and Matilda along with a dozen Indians saw him off. Conspicuously absent was Rebecca, although he had heard another English-German argument earlier that morning. He left richer than he came. Georg gave him an old firelock musket with the warning that it would only be useful for scaring off wild beasts, not killing them, also three hard cornbread loaves with dried huckleberries, and luxury of luxuries, a half-pound of tea. Georg refused to consider payment. "Our savior was generous even unto his life, so we can make generosity with a small amount of tea."

A young Indian, clad only in a breechcloth and with just a few hickory nuts as sustenance, guided Julian the first day. He walked or ran instead of riding, quite sure of the way, although at times the trail seemed indistinguishable from its surroundings. When his guide turned back, Julian realized that for the first time not only in this country but in his life, he was truly alone, with nothing but two ancient firearms and a worn knife for protection.

"Better than being a haberdasher," he reminded himself, unpersuasively.

That night, the dark form insinuated itself in front of his campfire before Julian realized it was there. On looking up and seeing Grayson, he was so astonished he couldn't find the words to greet him. Grayson put down his satchel, squatted by the fire, and turned to Julian. "Where's your master, lad?"

"I don't know, sir. I am to meet him somewhere on this trail."

Grayson shook his head and gazed at the fire.

"You're a priest" Julian tried to keep the accusatory tone out of this statement.

"To be sure," Grayson replied evenly.

"And a spy for the French."

Grayson's mouth formed into a smile, yet the rest of his face remained hard and sharp as if grimly cast out of iron. "Nay, not for the French, only for our Lord. I spy out the lost souls, the wandering sheep who belong to the true church. I believe I have a gift for discovering them. When I hear a Catholic family lives isolated somewhere in this sea of heresy, I visit them, hear their confessions, and say mass with them, so they do not forget their mother church or their God. In many places, the letter of the law prescribes death to papists, but usually, I'm not bothered except the occasional whipping and branding, a thousand times compensated by the look of awe and joy when I administer communion to a hungry soul. Here, these are the tools of my trade." He took out of his satchel a robe trimmed with ermine and then a white cloth. "Blessed by

His Holiness," he said fondly as he laid the cloth on the robe. On top of the cloth, he put a chalice and a bowl. "You are not Catholic?" He inquired shyly.

Julian shook his head.

"'Tis a pity." Grayson rubbed an eye. "I would have heard your confession and said mass with you. I have baptized in the Floridas, given last rites on the shores of Hudson Bay. I have brought the church to a thousand camps and villages."

"Why did you visit my master?" Julian asked, wanting to see if he gave the same answer as Bragg.

"I came to inquire of him what Catholics he may have encountered in his travels. 'Twasn't necessary to shrive him. Philadelphia is not so evil as to disallow the true church."

Desiring to change the subject, Julian offered, "I have dried venison I could share and tea."

Grayson put the robe, chalice, and bowl back into his satchel, then stood. "No thankee, lad. I've come here to advise you to sleep little, rise early, and push hard. These parts are dangerous."

"What is the nature of the danger?"

"If you see it, 'twill already be too late." Then after the slightest of nods as a farewell, he turned and melted into the darkening forest.

Death paid Julian a visit on the third evening. Just as he had scraped the wooden plate clean from supper, twenty plus mounted men with an equal number of packhorses swarmed into the small clearing where he had camped. Dressed Indian style in breechcloths, buckskin blouses, moccasins, they surrounded Julian, some staring with dull dead eyes as they unsheathed knives, a few showing embarrassed grins, a few looking away shamefaced. Despite their dress and mix of skin colors, they would not be mistaken for a band of Indians. From their packhorses came the sickening odor of rotting human flesh.

"Looks like somebody has gone to the trouble of making our fire," a tall scraggly man said as he swung his long legs off his horse. Obviously the leader, he approached the campfire and squatted while the others also dismounted and went about the tasks of tending the horses and unloading provisions. Three scalps hung from a ring on his belt. His thin face was painted black like an Indian, a stubbly beard breaking through the paint. His eyes, disconcertingly one brown and one blue, regarded Julian coldly.

"Them your furs?" he asked in a low slurring voice. The smell of rum nearly knocked Julian over.

"I'm a bondservant, sir. The furs are the property of my master," Julian replied, striving to keep his voice steady.

"You might say that. You might also say you and your master have a bounty on your heads for murder. Maybe you even murdered for them furs, so they don't rightly belong to you." The man spat, the string of saliva landing close to Julian.

"Maybe I'm not the person you believe I am." Julian absurdly wanted to claim that he was a haberdasher's apprentice.

The man spat again. "Don't think we harbor a prejudice against murderers, and we surely will treat you kindlier than the magistrate at Charleston. Let me tender another question. What will your master do when you show up without the furs he thinks belongs to him?"

"I don't know."

"I am acquainted with Bragg. Two winters ago, I come across him finishing his supper in front of a fire. We get talking, and I ask him whatever happened to the young 'un who was helping him. He don't answer, but gives me a strip of jerked meat. A while later I get around to asking him again, and he tells me that I just swallowed the last of the young 'un. You see what I'm getting at is if you don't want to become Bragg's shit, you better ride with us. We lost two men recently. Even though you're not much of a replacement, we'll give you a hundredth share on account of them furs you're bringing along with you. I hear there's a village of praying savages just two whoops and two hollers away. After we acquaint ourselves with them, a hundredth share will make you a man of substance."

"And afterward you won't turn me in for the bounty?" Julian asked, desperate for a way to survive the night.

"Fifty pounds out of your stake in the enterprise will compensate us for not collecting on your pickled head." The leader's broad smile wasn't comforting.

"I never took a life nor scalped nobody," Julian said, experiencing a tingling at the back of his neck. "I never learned how."

"There's nothing to killing a man. After a bit of practice, one picks up the knack of scalping. My boys will vouch I'm so clean and smooth I don't even have to put my foot to the face when I pull the hairpiece off. Not dying is the hard part. That requires luck and cunning in equal measure. So, what do you say? Come with us, lad? Or not?" The man spat a third time, took out his tomahawk, weighed it in one hand, tossed it up and caught it with the other.

Suddenly, a familiar voice broke the tension. "Uriah be toying with you, lad." Bragg walked into the clearing. The men doing their various tasks froze. "He be only wanting to boast that he talked you out of the furs afore adding your scalp to the bunch."

Uriah jerked his head up and grinned. "Well, fortune smiles on me today. I'll be the hero of the Tidewater and a rich man to boot when I bring back the pirate and his mate and collect my bounties."

"You must be killing me first, and you might not have the stomach for that." Bragg's hands rested on a brace of pistols as he calmly surveyed the group. "The question of the moment being who will die when you all rush me. Maybe, some of you be not wanting to take the risk. Two of you, at least, maybe three or four will regret the attempt. On the other hand, I'll let Uriah fight me outright, just me and him. He can prove his mettle, give substance to his boasts that no one ever got the better of him."

A smile snaked across Uriah's face. "I was pulling your leg, Bartholomew. You have naught to fear from me. I'll even save you the trouble of visiting the Shawnee across the two rivers. I doubt they are in the temper to trade."

"I suppose not if you just paid them a visit, Uriah."

Uriah nodded. "The menfolk will be hopping mad when they come home from their hunt. Careless of them leaving their wenches and kinchins guarded by grandfathers and boys. We got ourselves a passel of scalps worth ten Spanish dollars apiece to the governor of Carolina."

"What will the governor be saying when he sees so many women and children's hairpieces?" Bragg matched Uriah's frightening smile with one of his own.

"His man that deals with us says not a word," Uriah replied. "A savage is a savage, young or old, squaw or brave. I keep them from breeding, and I keep them from reaching manhood and scalping me and other civilized folk."

Bragg eyed Uriah coolly. "Well, you got your fur trade and I got mine. Still, you shouldn't scalp our friends, the Shawnee."

"Why not? The Shawnee were our enemies not two years past, and they'll be our enemies two years hence. Besides, the governor's men never took the trouble to learn the difference between a Yamasee scalp and a Shawnee scalp for it don't signify to them. I hear tell instead of burying or burning them hairpieces, the governor sends them to the ladies in London who use them to decorate their parlors or wear to their fancy balls." Uriah hawked up another mouthful of spit without depositing it.

"Well, I'm never of a mind to meddle in another man's business unless he be meddling in mine," Bragg observed, catching the eye of and stopping with a hard stare a brigand who was trying to back away into the trees. He continued: "I always admired your profile, Uriah. It resembles a hatchet, the tool of your trade. Not many men so fortunate to be resembling their tools."

"Now, Bragg, you really are itching for a fight." Uriah shook his head pityingly.

"Nay, I'm just commenting on your profile. Tell me, Uriah, are you liking your trade?"

"I was born to it. Killing a bear or a cougar is as easy

as picking my nose. Savage game is something else. To outsmart, out-sneak, and outfight a Creek or Cherokee makes me feel like I'm using my God-given talents."

"Would you be having any bone of contention against those nations, Uriah?"

"I'm not a man of sentiments, one way or another, but I do honestly say I approve of the redskins, just like the fox approves of the hare because it provides sustenance. Some of my men who lost kin to the savages have an ax to grind. I never had kin to lose. I make it harder for those grinding their axes. The rule is you don't get a cut until you've evened accounts. If you lose six brothers, then you get no part on the first six scalps you take. I want men with me for the profit; men out for revenge make mistakes."

"I met the man who was wearing that head of hair two weeks past." Bragg pointed to a grizzled scalp hanging from Uriah's belt. With a shock, Julian realized that it belonged to Horace, the leader of the massacred settlers. "He was a good man."

"The good man got mixed up with the wrong savages, which was his misfortune and not my concern, Bragg."

"After slaughtering those lambs, you did a poor job of plundering. I salvaged a keg of rum and two bags of flour. Resurrection Peter saw your handiwork. He said he be killing you the next time you cross his path."

"Expect me to be afeared of that black coon?" Uriah sneered.

Bragg continued: "I bet you was starting out real friendly with the settlers. You was mingling and smiling and then on cue, you drew out your tomahawks and knives and made short work of the lambs. There be a real subtle art to your cowardice, Uriah."

"I'm doing my best to keep my temper even, but I won't allow no one to call me a coward, Bragg."

"Arrah now, I'm only fiddling with you," Bragg replied. "But if you are after traveling up into the northern frontier and scalping one of Johnson's Indians, he will set his Mohawk friends on you. Now, I hear a Mohawk can start at the soles of your feet and spend a leisurely week carving his way up to the crown of your head."

Uriah shifted uneasily. "The governor of New York pays shit for bounties even when there's war, so I'm down here reaping my harvest. Now, I insist, Bragg, that you take back the word, 'coward.'"

"Well, Uriah, I am not retracting the word until I look at your scalps and judge whether there be any of real braves."

"There are plenty of brave scalps. And why is you so persnickety about women and children? A child of an enemy is an enemy. Rumor has it when you were a pirate you made no such distinctions. You ravished a sixteen-year-old girl, murdered her, then sent her parts back to her father in a bag."

"Rumor be an evil lying thing that never stops growing, sure," Bragg responded.

"Take back calling me a liar and a coward," Uriah insisted and rose, his face now a furious red.

Master Bragg laughed. "Is that how you're planning to get me—by starting a fight?"

"You're a pig's arse, Bragg, and you're the one after a fight."

"That's the best you can do, Uriah? You be a regular fiend when it comes to butchering women and children, but in cursing you're hopeless oaf maybe because you are never spitting out all the excess phlegm in your mouth."

"You called me a coward in front of my men." Uriah's voice trembled. "Take it back!"

"Your men know what you are by now. Why should they care whether I recant like a wayward Christian or not? If you're after fighting me, Uriah, we'll do it square, so you can boast you killed Bragg in a fair fight. Killing an old pirate shouldn't be any more trouble than knifing a Choctaw baby."

"Take the word back!" Uriah screamed.

Bragg cocked the pistols and gave them to Julian. "Be aiming for the belly, when they come at you, lad. The death is slow but sure." He faced Uriah. "'Tis easier to raise the devil than put him to rest, and as you know I may be him."

Uriah spluttered incoherently.

"I tell you what, Uriah," Bragg continued. "Prove you can beat me and I come meekly along like a lamb to slaughter. Me bondservant too. You collect the bounty on both of us. I win, and your men let us depart in peace."

Several of the band nodded in agreement.

"Then 'tis settled," Uriah hissed. "Draw your knife, Bragg. Mine is still warm with savage blood."

Bragg ran his hand around his belt with a look of concern. "'Tis seeming I forgot to bring it."

"That is your poor luck." Grinning, Uriah drew his blade and lunged. Bragg danced away from the wild slashes until Uriah tottered off-balance. Bragg then sprang at the exposed flank, knocking Uriah to the ground, bit the knife-hand, retrieved the weapon and sliced off an ear. Uriah staggered to his feet, holding his hand to where his ear had been, the blood running through his fingers. "Dammit to hell, Bragg, why did you do that?"

"So there be no doubting who won, Uriah." Bragg tossed the ear into the fire while Julian aimed the brace of pistols in the general direction of Uriah's men. "Feeling a bit lighter on that side of the head? Don't worry. 'Tisn't possible to make you uglier. Be laying off scalping Shawnee babies. It makes me savage friends indisposed for business. Now are any other of your brawlers willing to risk their parts—a nose or an eye?"

"He's worth a thousand pounds," Uriah yelled. "Take him and you're rich."

Suddenly, the knife flashed out of Bragg's hand and buried itself in the shoulder of a man who had raised a musket. The musket dropped; the man sat down astonished as color drained from his face. Julian stood beside Bragg, pistols quivering slightly, attempting to glare formidably at the frozen band.

"Go on your way," Bragg calmly advised the brigands. "The Shawnee hunting party be coming home anon and picking up your trail. I am suggesting you divide your spoils and scatter. At least a few of you might escape." He turned to Julian "We'll also hurry along, lad. The braves who lost their kin won't be too discriminating as to which Christian scalp they hang in their lodge."

CHINA

THREE MORNINGS LATER while fording a shallow stream, six braves, faces painted with red and black stripes, and bristling with tomahawks, feathered lances, and muskets, confronted them on the opposite bank. Behind them, another six, also in warrior regalia, blocked their retreat.

"Bloody shit," Bragg muttered before calling out in a friendly manner, "Good day to you, White Bear." They finished crossing the stream. Bragg had a brief exchange in Shawnee with the leader, a brave with a white streak in his scalp lock and the muscular proportions more akin to a wrestler than to the Indian's usual perfectly balanced physique of a hunter. Bragg then turned to Julian and announced in a cheerful voice, "We are invited to their festivities."

They followed the stream a few miles, Bragg keeping up a one-sided conversation with White Bear who barely acknowledged his presence. Once, Bragg drew back alongside Julian and whispered, "Well, boy, was you ever believing you'd visit China?" And in reply to his bewildered look, he added, "The village is called Chinoota, the guarded place, however, we traders call it China. We're damn lucky China be not the village Uriah raided, but they captured ten of Uriah's band and are enforcing their justice for the murder of innocents. The Satan, Old Nick, visiting afflictions on the sinners in hell could not do a better job than a Shawnee grandmother with her little knife. Stare straight ahead. Turn your phiz into stone. Close your ears and your mind to the sense of things."

It wasn't enough to look straight ahead. In front of the village, a red-bearded man was affixed to the ground on a lance that ran the length of his body and protruded out one side of his neck. He made a garbled sound, too pathetic to be a cry. Just inside the palisades, a squaw with tongs was trying to force a red-hot coal into the mouth of another of Uriah's band staked to the ground; and a third unfortunate soul tied to a post watched dogs fight over the entrails spilling out of his split belly. Wild screams indicated other tortures were going on elsewhere. The village itself was in a state of high excitement. Children ran back and forth to see the progress of each torture. Squaws were laughing, gossiping, and cooking.

Distracted, Julian almost rode over a girl with honey-colored hair who staggered in front of him carrying a heavy basket of corn. He pulled up just in time. Her eyes caught his, and he briefly glimpsed her universe of despair. A squaw hurled a stone at her which missed. She lowered her head and staggered on.

They dismounted in the center of the village and followed White Bear into the council house, a fifty-foot-square log structure with carved masks decorating its posts, high slits in the walls letting in a flaccid light, and a linden branch ceiling. At first not deigning to notice them, the braves inside continued taking their ease with their pipes. Bragg sat down cross-legged, placing a large satchel in front of him. Julian followed suit. A middle-aged woman with green eyes, plaited gray-auburn hair, and wearing the buckskin shift of a squaw entered, followed by a swarthy man with a thin high-bridged nose, black protuberant eyes, and a pugnacious jutting jaw.

"Good day, Hilda," Bragg greeted the woman. "Good day, Girard. Girard is the war sachem," Bragg explained to Julian.

"Goot day to you, Master Bragg," Hilda replied with a heavy Palatine accent. Apparently, she was going to serve as interpreter. Girard, the war sachem, did not acknowledge the greeting.

"How be your children, Hilda?" Bragg inquired.

"Very vell. Victor took his first scalp so now calls himself a man."

"That must be making you proud, Hilda."

She hesitated, her face hardening, then replied, "'Tis a good day when a son kills an enemy." She then translated the conversation for those around her.

Other braves including White Bear arrived and accommodated themselves, the last to enter being a small wizened man, his bright red robe of cardinal feathers bestowing on him an air of authority.

"Greetings to you, Red Eagle," Bragg addressed the wizened man, "and to White Bear, Girard, and all the brave Shawnees who so ably avenged their brethren..." Bragg launched into an interminable speech, stating that he had come in peace, reminding them of their long friendship and his honest dealing, enumerating the trade goods that he had brought, congratulating the chief on the just punishment of men who had not only murdered Shawnee women and children, but also Christian women and children. Hilda translated, although Bragg was conversant enough to interject phrases in Shawnee. Bragg claimed he had a special gift for Red Eagle. He took a bundle out of the satchel, slowly unwrapped it, held up the violin to the assembly, then plucking a string, handed it to Red Eagle. While the violin was being admired by the chief, Bragg commented, "I do not see Uriah among your captives. Was he vanquished in the battle?"

Red Eagle spoke with the usual Indian unhurried drum-like cadence: "The devil Uriah led his friends to an island. There he abandoned half of them, taking the canoes so while we fought them, he escaped east with the plunder and scalps. When we captured his friends, we mocked them for being such fools."

"That's pure Uriah. I should have been cutting his throat instead of just his ear."

Red Eagle handed the violin to White Bear. Grimacing, the warrior tossed it on the ground, then began to speak. Hilda translated: "You pretend to be a friend, Bartholomew Bragg, only a little bird tells us otherwise. You scheme to steal our land for your people. Many little birds tell us this so we doubt not what they say. When I was a boy, settlers came on the great path into our land where we hunted since memory, came with their wagons, and their cattle that eat all our corn, and their pigs that leave nothing for the animals of the forest to eat. They said the land belonged to them and waved a paper in our faces. They told us a chief whose name we knew not sold it to them. They said it was their law."

Bragg nodded sympathetically.

White Bear spat and went on, Hilda translating: "When we protested that 'tis our law to protect our land, they sent the Mohawks and evil men like Uriah to drive us away. The chiefs who desire peace more than honor told us to move whither there is still land for us. We go west. No more than six winters pass, and I am still a boy when they come again with a paper and claim this is their land. A chief whose name we know not sold it to them. He sold what he didn't own for rum to forget his shame. Do not talk of friendship, Bartholomew Bragg, when you are planning to steal our land. Here I stand—here I die. No Englishman, no Frenchman, no Mohawk, no Cherokee will move me from this spot."

Girard now stood and spoke. "'Tis well known that Bragg is a great friend of William Johnson who is a Mohawk sachem and officer of the King of England. The English brandish the Mohawk like a war club to strike those who don't do their bidding. The Mohawks who insult us to our faces, call us women, who insist on a tribute of furs. The Mohawks are no longer great. The English are nothing without their war club. Bragg is an English spy. I say add two more to those suffering tonight. When the Mohawk come, we'll give them their bones instead of tribute."

Bragg picked up the satchel and rose, shaking his head. "Call an Irishman an English spy—you certainly be knowing how to wound a man to the bone, Girard. Wherever I go I am accused of spying for t'other side, sure. I never met me father, and me mother is a shadow in memory. The only English part of me be the price on me gray hairs. 'Tis plain, Girard, your French blood is poisoning your judgment towards me."

Bragg then slowly opened a satchel. "'Tis God's truth I'm after land—not your land, which isn't worth the spit in me mouth for you will lose it, sooner or later. Nay, 'tis other land I'm after. White Bear claims that he will die where he stands rather than retreat from this place. Mark me word, he will be dying where he stands. Girard wants to roast me over your fires as an English spy, please his French heart with me screams while the flames consume me flesh. I might be saying 'tis diverting for once to be accused of spying for the English rather than for the French. Yet, I might be having proof I am an English spy so Girard may begin to stoke the fires. Let me show you." He put his hand into the satchel. "You know the mark of the king of England, Red Eagle?"

Red Eagle nodded.

Bragg extracted a wampum belt with the design of the cross of Saint George and threw it down. Molly had explained wampum to Julian as more valuable than gold and no more valuable than the character of the man who possessed it. She then said it was the Indian book, which memory enriched at each reading. Julian had witnessed a Canadian Mohawk declaim in front of William Johnson, pause and angrily hurl down a belt of black wampum. Everyone present shuddered. He had also seen an Indian, thin and trembling, trade a belt of wampum for a cup of rum.

"White Bear also speaks the truth to a point. Remember me island was conquered by the English a hundred winters past. When the English are calling you children of the king and claiming their armies will preserve your land, you already lost it. Does not a father give and take away from his child as he sees fit? Does not a father change his mind when other children make a claim to whatever bauble that child is holding?"

The council room was dead silent

"Be the French father different from the English father?" Bragg seemed to magically produce a wampum belt with the fleur de lis out of thin air. He threw it down. "I am telling you the French father only cares for the furs you bring him. The muskets he trades are poor, his tools break, and when you have no furs, he tells you to starve until you bring him some. Who is better, the thief who steals the meat from your larder or the guest who eats it all leaving you none?"

Bragg gathered up the wampum belts. "Nay. This you also know to be true. If you find a ladder up to the sky and discover a land above as big as the sky, the French and English will follow you up to the sky and claim the land for their king who they declare is your father and therefore can be stealing from you."

Giving a hard stare to Girard and White Bear, then a friendlier one to Red Eagle, Bragg continued: "Aye, I'm after land and more than land. A few years back, I was traveling west of the great river and passed through the villages of bones. The earth was rich. Game abounded. Yet not a soul. One night in this land of bone villages, I fell into a fever and in the feverish dream, I saw me life as it was. I am walking down a stream all me years, the water running around me, making ripples, then leaving no trace. The men who called me brother are dead. The women owning me heart gone, me children have disappeared with the winds. I have no family, no people, no nation. I call meself Irish, but forty winters have passed since I've looked on the emerald shore of me home.

"I took as the message of the dream that I must do a thing of worth. Like many foolish old men, I dream the biggest dream I can, thinking 'tis better to die for a big dream than a small one. I dream to make a nation—me own nation, me own people. All I be needing is families with good men who are not afeared to die for the land, for their sons and daughters, and each other. Simple, aye. Near impossible, aye. 'Tis a foolish dream, yet your possible dreams are more foolish because they bring war."

Bragg took out a small black wampum belt and threw it down. "War is pleasing to young braves but leaves their squaws cold and alone in their wigwams and the children unborn who would make your nation great. You think differently?"

Bragg now took out a handful of beads from the satchel and scattered them on the ground, then another handful and another. "I am not alone," Bragg went on. "I am one of these beads and there are thousands more—families, clans, tribes broken up, spread across the land. You are also like this little bead that I can grind into the earth. What I propose doing is to take up one." Bragg knotted a thread, held it out and slid a bead onto it. "Then another and another." He threaded more. "Foolish dream, eh, but not so foolish as yours. You may one day come to the nation I make, me foolish dream, and I will welcome you as brothers. Or you can be using your friend Bragg and this lad as kindling for your fires."

Red Eagle rose and gave a short speech saying he would consider all that had been said. Julian had a difficult time preserving his composure because one of the captives had started a wild barking screaming that seemed to perturb even those in the council house.

Just outside the council house, Girard confronted them. An exchange followed in French. When Girard stalked away, Bragg said to Julian, "I now must parlay further with Red Eagle. Beyond the fields lies a glen where you can be setting up camp like we always do. Make a fire, hobble the horses, lay out a few matchcoats and tools, but don't unpack much. A few squaws will be coming to trade. They aren't the ones after murdering you. Press not overmuch in the matter of prices. Nearing eveningtide, young braves will show. These are friends of Girard. They will pretend to want everything and offer to pay well in furs, putting you in a good mood, making you hopeful, before taking your life."

"Wouldn't it be easier for them to murder us outright without all this play-acting, master?" Julian asked, not seeing the point in delaying death if death was inevitable.

"It might seem so," Bragg said. "Only the Shawnee think it a great joke to toy with their victims, promising friendship and the companionship of their maidens before planting the tomahawk in the skull. So you be playing your own game. Set aside a bottle of good rum and put in it all the brown powder you find in the pack with the silk scarves. Offer them a drink. They will accept because they are a wee bit afraid. They will soon be stumbling around and falling asleep. Pray none quit breathing. You must pack up then and leave. Do not stop for aught. I'll catch up with you anon, that is if I'm still in the land of the living."

"Wouldn't be wise to flee now?" Julian asked.

"Fleeing is proving our guilt. We must abide cheerfully in this hell until dark."

Julian regretted that he could still hear the screams of the tortured men as he set out matchcoats, blankets, ribbons, pots of vermilion, a spool of fabric, several hoes, and axes, and then waited. An old squaw with bloody fingernails was the first customer. Others followed. None haggled much as if they expected soon to get back what they had traded. Julian packed up the furs and pelts as the day progressed. Near twilight, there were a few moments when Julian was alone, and he took the opportunity to pour the powder which smelled of cloves and cinnamon into the bottle of rum. Soon after that, like Bragg had predicted, four wolfishly smiling young braves arrived. One offered Julian a piece of raw whitish meat. Julian suspected that it was cut from a prisoner.

"I must give you a gift in return." Julian bit into the raw meat and swallowed quickly suppressing the urge to vomit. He uncorked the bottle of rum, raised it to his lips, pretended to swallow and passed it around. The young braves drank greedily all the while pressing on Julian more raw pieces of meat, which he refused. Initially, Julian suspected the powder wasn't working and became very worried because the young braves had formed a circle hemming him in. Abruptly, one sat down. The rest followed a minute later. The bottle went around a third, fourth, fifth time. Julian finally noticed their eyes were beginning to wander and their expressions slacken. The first brave to have seated himself lapsed into incoherence and stupor and slumped forward. The others quickly did the same.

"I must depart, but this is a gift for our friendship." Julian gave an unopened bottle of rum to the last conscious brave who blearily regarded him as he packed up the remaining trade goods and unhobbled the horses.

Julian was preparing to mount Frida when a voice stopped him cold. "You do not stay for the dance, monsieur? A pretty dusky maiden is anxious to show you hospitality." Girard stepped into the clearing. His flushed face showed that he had been drinking.

"No, I must be leaving." Julian noticed a bloody scalping knife dangling from his belt.

"With Master Bragg's goods, yet not with Master Bragg?" Girard's protuberant eyes regarded Julian unblinking.

Julian wrested the bottle with the powder away from a comatose brave clutching it to his chest. A mouthful remained. He pretended to drink, then held it out to Girard. "We wait for my master, then?"

Girard looked with disgust at the four braves sprawled around the clearing. He took the proffered bottle and threw it, shattering it on the rock. "I will not deprive those warriors of the chance to avenge their shame on the boy who outwitted them." At this point, Bragg's voice rose in the distance followed by a gunshot. Julian took the opportunity to extract a pistol from Bragg's horse.

"And how far would you get after shooting me, boy?

Go. If these fools fail to capture you after they wake up, I'll catch you myself and skin you alive." Girard stalked away.

As the sounds of the celebrating drums and the screams of the last remaining victim faded, Julian led the pack-horses down a trail illuminated half by twilight and half by moonlight. Bragg had instructed him to follow the river adding, "'Twill appear impassable where the current narrows between two cliffs, only at this season, there be a knee-deep passage in a rivulet that runs along the side of the churning water."

As he was approaching the narrow channel, Julian suddenly sensed movement and went cold with fear. Large eyes were fixed on him as the girl with honey-colored hair seemingly materialized out of the river. She carried a basket filled with roots and berries. She wrinkled her nose as if deciding what to do. Would she betray him? Foolishly, he felt compelled to say, "Come with me, miss."

She continued staring with her fathomless child's eyes.

"Come with me." He reached out to take her hand, unable to resist the overwhelming desire to protect her. "Do you understand? Come."

She backed away, quivering.

Julian realized the absurdity of what he was asking. "Yes, 'tis dangerous."

She spoke. At first, he thought he couldn't understand because her voice was so soft, but then after trying to take her hand again, she raised her voice and he realized she was speaking French and pointing to herself. *"Je suis une…"*

"I won't let anyone harm you." Julian uttered these words before reflecting on how much a lie they might be.

Still, feeling an intense desire to protect her, he repeated, "I promise, I won't allow nobody to harm you."

The girl shook her head, put down the basket, placed her two hands on the long shirt—the only garment she wore. "*Revenir...*"

Julian was at a loss to understand, but when she pulled the fabric back over her belly, he realized she was pregnant.

WESTWARD

JULIAN DROVE THE packhorses for two days along a trail heading north, resting little, weaving through rough hilly terrain, fording dozens of creeks, expecting the young braves or Girard at any moment to rush upon him and wreak their revenge. At the end of the second day, too exhausted to go further, he stopped by a pond to make camp. As he wearily began to attend to the equally exhausted horses, he heard a voice, "God's blood, finding you setting up to welcome those savages coming to skin you alive 'tis enough to make Job swear!"

"The horses can barely walk, and I fell out of the saddle twice," Julian protested.

"Blast! Matters not if the horses be needing to ride you. The Shawnee are still hopping mad and are aiming to clean out all settlements within fifty miles. Being an old friend and still having a tender regard for me, Red Eagle allowed me to leave. Girard and White Bear are after leading raiding parties, and if either finds us—let's just say they is not me old friends. We'll cache the furs and supplies and sell the horses in the next settlement."

"Is there a settlement this far out?"

"Little Glasgow. Some addle-headed borderlanders decided 'twould be a good idea to settle down between four warring savage nations."

"Won't you warn them about the Shawnee?" Julian asked.

"And what sort of price would I be getting for the horses? Besides, if you was to be murdered tomorrow, would you want to be knowing it today?"

Little Glasgow consisted of six crude log cabins built in a hollow—the deep shade adding cold to starvation. A dozen naked and near-naked children sat in the dirt in front of the cabins, too hungry to play. A few stricken chickens wandered the yard feebly clucking. Bragg made a deal to leave the horses with a ragged gaunt woman holding a baby gnawing at her breast. Two other women shyly stood behind her, equally thin and shabby. Bragg promised that if he didn't come back in a year to redeem the horses, she could have them to pay for their board. Julian was near certain that the starving families would butcher and eat the horses as soon as they were out of sight.

The deal agreed upon, the woman then asked, "Have you news of Millard Barnes, my husband? He be a tall man with a reddish beard. Left four weeks ago with traders who needed a guide to Shawnee land, and he is not come back. Anne's husband, Bertram, went also."

"The leader of the group be having a face like a tomahawk?" Bragg asked.

"You could say that," she replied. "In truth he didn't

sit well with me, although, in truth, I shouldn't be so uncharitable."

"Your husbands left you alone to fend off the wild beasts and the savages?" Bragg queried.

The woman blushed. "Including Mason's sons, there are five grown men hereabouts. A Scotsman who needed to pay an urgent debt sold us this parcel with his cabin for two pounds. 'Twas a chance to own something. We always worked other people's land. You're saying you saw Millard."

"I wasn't catching the names of those that was with Uriah, but your Millard will be coming back anon, and you'll be wondering what all the fuss and worry was about."

The woman shook her head. "From your lips to the Lord's providence."

As they rode away, leading a single packhorse loaded with lead, powder, salt, tea, pemmican, two kegs of whiskey and several bottles of rum, Bragg commented, "Those folks be hardly worth robbing, so they might not be worth murdering."

"Why did you not tell them the Shawnee are on the warpath?" Julian accused angrily.

"One of these days I'll be whipping you properly for failing to show your master due respect. If you be having one of your qualms of conscience, go back yourself and inform the good wife that her Millard had a lance run through his body from asshole to gullet. And don't be thinking I'll entertain their company. How far do you think we'd travel with a baby and those starving brats? Who'd get the task of strangling the babe when we're having to keep quiet? Her best chance, lad, be the Shawnee. They may adopt her and the brats. If not, they will kill them quickly—White Bear and Girard not taking to torturing women and children."

Julian shuddered at the thought of what awaited the poor woman. "Do you possess any true allegiances, master?"

"Arrah now, boy, is that an accusation or a question now? Since you ask, I be giving my allegiance first to whatever will help me survive to the end of the day. Second, I give allegiance to whichever side pays me best. Third, I am a man owing nothing to no man, so I give my allegiance to whatever I damn well please, and what I damn well please is to make me own domain so mumping ragamuffins like you wed their heathen princesses, beget savage brats, and reign like lords."

The rest of the day, Julian reflected on recent events. When he bedded down at their fireless camp, he finally spoke: "Well, I thank you master for looking out for me when you didn't have to."

"It distresses me to lose property until I get fair use out of it. Also…" Bragg grumbled, then paused as if unwilling to finish the sentence. "Also, there would be hell to pay explaining to Molly Brant why I was letting you perish. I could never step in Pennsylvania or New York again without her sending one of her numerous kin with the express order of bringing her me scalp. Nay, Molly is one savage not to be crossed, sure."

"She's just a girl and she's not a savage."

"Molly be more a woman than girl and very much a savage. I would not be living so long without having acquired the knack of judging character. She'd be plotting me death if I became careless with your life. I saw it in her eyes when she commanded me to take care of you. Don't fool yourself that you won her heart, lad. The wench will marry Johnson and chase away his other mistresses. But she is deciding you must live, and I must be obliging her, come hell or hurricanes."

Five days later, they encountered a group of uproariously drunk traders. After uncorking a bottle of rum and offering it to the leader—a fantastically bearded dwarfish man—Bragg introduced himself.

"I'm Rutledge," the leader replied after taking a long swig. It soon became obvious from the winks and nods between the traders that they were aware of the bounties, however Bragg pretended not to notice.

"Now be keeping your trap shut," Bragg whispered as he passed the bottle under Julian's nose, taking a sip, then complaining loudly about encountering a raiding party of Ottawas. "They was after lifting our scalps when old Julie here shot three of the savages, persuading the rest that our hair be not sold for less than two kegs of blood."

For the rest of the day, Bragg entertained the traders with wild stories of battles and beautiful squaws and terrible punishments. "I was nearly marrying her except her ugly cousin got jealous mad and plucked out an eye…" The traders seemed to be biding their time. Although Bragg frequently lifted the bottle to his mouth before passing it on, Julian didn't observe the swallowing motion in his throat.

MANKITA

IN THE LATE afternoon, Julian, Bragg, and the traders passed through the gates of a Lenape village called Mankita, or Great Water, because it was situated at the narrow end of a long lake. The palisades were ten feet high and well-made. Three longhouses, several dozen wigwams, various sweat huts and a fifty-foot square council house crowded into the protected space. Refugees from other tribes—Miami, Caughnawaga, Mohican and even Pequot—fleeing wars and disease, lived within the compound along with the Lenape. The braves were taking their ease as befits the time of day, smoking pipes and conversing while the squaws roasted game or stirred iron pots that hung over fires. A dozen yards inside the gate, a half-bent hooded figure blocked the party of traders. The hood dropped revealing an ancient squaw's wrinkled face.

"Will you allow us to pass, Mohegan Woman?" Bragg asked in English, then repeated in her language.

The squaw smiled showing a half dozen teeth scattered about her gums and held out a hand.

Bragg sighed and reached into his shirt and pulled out

a long ribbon which she immediately seized. "You are a true she-wolf, Mohegan Woman. Always hungry, always asking for more and giving naught in return."

The smile deepened and the old woman's lips disappeared.

"Why do you give her a gift," Julian asked after the woman turned to Rutledge with an outstretched hand, "if she never gives you anything back?"

"Why cross yourself after prayer? Why show a leg to a gentleman? Why doff your hat to a lady? 'Tis just something you do because 'tis done. A trader in this village must give a gift to the Mohegan Woman even before paying his respect to the sachems."

The Mohegan women still blocked them, mimed an exchange of goods taking place, and then uttered in thick English, "Business in morning."

"Damn," Rutledge said. "Dealing is always brisker after they quaff a few."

While Julian attended to the horses, Bragg wandered off with a keg of whiskey under his arm in search of acquaintances. When Julian returned to the wigwams set aside for visitors, he discovered that Rutledge and his friends had broken into a keg of their rum and were now on the way to becoming stupidly drunk. They informed the world that would listen, in other words, themselves, that they were heartily sick of their life, of savage wheedling, of the French, of mosquitoes, of diseased squaws, of risking their necks for a pittance. In their excess of self-pity, they decided to finish consoling themselves with what remained of their whiskey and then, on the morrow, make their way, sober as Presbyterians, back to civilization. Julian left this maudlin assembly, hauling his and Bragg's blankets to an empty wigwam.

After accommodating himself in the wigwam, he toured the village. Mankita was the most prosperous village they had visited yet with four sweat houses—two for men, two for women—solidly constructed dwellings, a swarm of fat dogs, a stack of firewood higher than the palisades, dozens of scaffolds of drying fish, venison, squash, and pumpkins. Yet Julian felt uneasy. The traders were losing what little self-control they possessed, and some of the braves were eyeing warily the wigwam from where their raucous drunken laughter was erupting. Later that evening, Bragg appeared in the company of a plumpish squaw who couldn't stop cackling. The pair began undressing as soon as they had ducked inside the wigwam. Although Bragg could have sexual intercourse with the whole village watching, Julian had no appetite for their grunts and squeals so settled himself outside.

Julian woke up inside the wigwam. He had no memory of crawling back. He poked his head into the cold gray morning hovering at its entrance to look for Bragg.

"What..." he started to say as a hand grabbed a hunk of his hair and pulled him all the way out. He managed to glimpse a fierce tattooed face with a dangling nose ring and pendulous silver braided earlobes, before a kick to the stomach knocked the wind out of him. As Julian doubled up, rough hands stripped, dragged, and tied him to a pole erected in the ashes of the previous night's fire. Julian danced in the hot ashes, eventually kicking enough away to make the spot endurable. He saw several bands of braves leave and realized that a pursuit was underway.

That didn't mean Julian was ignored. Those that remained—children, squaws, and a few old braves—amused themselves by inflicting small torments on him. Compared to the Mohawk or Shawnee, the Lenape weren't particularly cruel, but they still had an extensive repertoire of tortures. Julian endured pricks, pinches, stinging ants up his nose, hot embers placed under his feet, testicle squeezing, chopping at his toes and ankles with small knives and tomahawks. A young brave, disconsolate at being left out of the pursuit, brandished a knife and pulled back Julian's hair as if preparing to scalp him. He ended by painfully shaving Julian's left eyebrow, which elicited much laughter from the children. The Mohegan Woman also visited him, shrew-like, witchlike, and chortling as she ran her hand down his side and leg. The braves returned midafternoon with eight bloody scalps and two gloomy captives. Julian forced himself to examine the scalps—there was no wild black-gray mop with hawk bells.

The last brave to return was the one who had dragged Julian out of the wigwam. Stopping in front of the post, the brave regarded him like a cat might regard a mouse caught in-between its paws. A black margin painted around his lips and the orbits of his eyes seemed to enlarge them. A bristling ridge ran down the center of his otherwise shaved head. His sole article of clothing was a breechcloth, which revealed a well-formed body crisscrossed by tattoos.

"No, you will not discover the scalp of Bragg in our harvest," the brave said with the cultivated tones of a gentleman.

"You speak English?" Julian asked, relieved and astonished.

"I am Long Arrow, the war sachem," The Lenape brave answered. "I speak French and English. My father sent me to a missionary school in Quebec where the priests attempted to make me into one of them, but I would not become the servant of a God that permitted enemies to nail him to a tree. On crossing the Saint Lawrence on my return home, an English captain kidnapped me and transported me to London where I was sold to a man who charged a tuppence for those desiring to view human novelties and oddities. He hung a sign on me that read, 'Savage Mohawk,' and I was exhibited for the amusement of the public who wanted to hear my savage war cries and see me tear a wig off a bald woman. For some, I represented the unspoiled man, and not a few ladies were willing to be serviced by me. A man with skin like a snake was also one of the novelties. He was born into a noble family who abandoned him because he was so repulsive. He befriended me and taught me to speak your tongue."

"Master Bragg escaped?" Julian asked, shivering and too concerned about life and limb to be interested in the story.

"Mr. Bragg is too clever by half." Long Arrow bared his blackened teeth. "The traders, of course, were plotting to collect the bounties, however when Master Bragg proposed to steal our furs if they manned the canoes, the drunken rabble saw an opportunity to double their takings. They didn't suspect that as soon as he threw the furs into the canoe, he himself would raise the alarm. They nearly escaped having taken the best canoe. Bragg fled west on horseback. One warrior, Seksu, pursued. Unfortunately for you, Bragg killed Seksu, so we are obliged to compensate his widow with your slow death and scalp."

"I had nothing to do with this killing and stealing," Julian protested.

"Since there's a bounty on you, I assume you have murdered or thieved elsewhere. Besides, the squaws and children were hoping for entertainment tonight, and I'm not certain that our other two captives will entirely satisfy them."

"Can't you explain I'm innocent of any crime against you? We English didn't kill you when we captured you. I'm sure you met kind and merciful people in our country."

"Do you imagine your London taught me to love the English?" Long Arrow sneered. "Bah, I know your people inside out. You're a vile dirty dishonest white-livered whoring nation of men whose bodies crawl with vermin and who trod on their own shit and hang children for stealing combs. Your God was so ashamed of his son that he sent him to suffer for other men's crimes. Your king is no better than an old woman with dried teats. Your women carry foul pestilence in their bodies. I assure you I'm the last man to show you mercy or pity."

Soon after Long Arrow left, a figure approached Julian wearing a bearskin and a wooden mask, half red and half black. This apparition performed a frenzied dance around him, shaking a tortoiseshell rattle until reaching a feverish pitch, then pressed his mask close until it touched Julian's face. It uttered words that Julian didn't comprehend, but seemed to promise great suffering. The frightening figure eventually retreated, leaving Julian thoroughly unnerved.

As soon as the sun had set, the drums and dancing began in the sandy area next to the pole so Julian was able to watch. One captive trader, stripped naked, and hands bound behind him, was kicked and pushed into the space left open by the onlookers—the several hundred men, women, and children from the village. Julian recalled that his name was Peregrine Smith. Peregrine was a large man, well-proportioned with broad shoulders, black hair laced with gray, and a scarred body showing he was no stranger to brawling with sharp-edged weapons. Peregrine gazed about wildly as Long Arrow approached holding a skinning knife and a torch.

"Cut and burn a man who isn't able to defend himself and you call yourself a warrior," Peregrine cried out defiantly.

Long Arrow paused, looked at Peregrine appraisingly, and slowly smiled. He handed the torch to a brave in exchange for another knife. He went behind Peregrine, cut his bonds and gave him the second knife. "When I apprehended you," Long Arrow said. "You were running away as quickly as your legs could carry you, which is what you English call cowardice. Yet I will treat you as a guest and honor your request. We will begin equally armed, then we can see whether you will die with courage or begging like a coward."

They faced off. The trader's reach overlapped Long Arrow's by the span of a hand so it appeared that the war sachem had misjudged the contest. Peregrine growled, "I'll cut out my own tongue ere you see me beg."

Then he lunged. Long Arrow stepped to the side, so the trader's blade slashed the air. Keeping just beyond his range, Long Arrow crouched low as if coiling to spring. Peregrine circled to his right, away from war sachem's blade, then backed up, assumed the same crouching posture as Long Arrow, and continued circling. Suddenly, Long Arrow flipped the knife into his left hand and struck, slicing the trader's right arm making him drop the knife. He placed his foot on the blade while Peregrine stood watching his blood spill onto the dirt.

"You're still my guest," Long Arrow declared, putting his right arm behind him, and lifting his foot off the blade. Peregrine dove, snatched the weapon and rose to his feet shakily holding the knife in his left hand, blood now covering his torso and legs. Long Arrow whistled an English alehouse tune and danced a jig while Peregrine bent low snarling. Changing his step, Long Arrow kicked dirt into Peregrine's eyes, whirled, slipped behind him and opened a gash in the trader's thigh. Blood welled out of the wound, and the trader dropped to his knees.

Long Arrow shook his head as if he were sorrowed by the spectacle and repeated, "You're still my guest," then knelt in front of Peregrine, within easy reach of the blade. Peregrine thrust straight, but as the arm straightened the tip of Long Arrow's weapon entered at Peregrine's wrist and dug in, stopping the thrust when the blade hit the elbow bone. Long Arrow rose, spoke a few words in Lenape, then translated for Julian's sake. "I ordered my braves to pour hot embers into his open wounds. Do not avert your eyes or I'll slice them out." The squaws and children were given that chore while the braves danced. Peregrine screamed for a long time and then finally begged them to kill him.

The second trader was given to the squaws and children as their plaything. Though his howls indicated that he was still alive, he wasn't recognizably human by the time they finished carving him. Afterward, Long Arrow approached Julian carrying the knife still stained with Peregrine's blood. Julian shut his eyes. The knife pricked the inside of a nostril, caressed an ear, and the base of his testicles. Long Arrow then gave a speech, which seemed to compare his genitals to his foot and which made everybody laugh. Long Arrow made another facetious remark as he twisted Julian's hair in his fingers and the laughter grew. He then whispered, "We have had enough entertainment for tonight, my lad. Remember well what you saw. Worse awaits you. In the morning, you will run the gauntlet, only I promise you won't be permitted to die until the evening of the third day when we take out your bowels a little at a time and burn them before your eyes."

Julian was then untied, stretched out, and staked down. The braves, squaws, and their children retired to the longhouses and wigwams, and he was left shivering in the cold wet darkness. Wild imaginings of his coming ordeal crowded out all other thoughts. Julian made the decision to force his tormentors to kill him quickly. Once his bonds were cut so he could run the gauntlet, he would attack and wouldn't stop until they beat him to death. His end would be bloody and quick and unsatisfactory for his persecutors. Near dawn, the skies let loose a torrent. Julian shivered so violently that his wrists and ankles bled where the rawhide cords bit into them.

GAUNTLET

Morning came with a feeble light and a cold mist hanging in the air like a ragged shroud. Julian was ignored while the squaws busied themselves cooking breakfast. Children raced around the village screaming and laughing. Braves lounged in front of wigwams in perfect ease, wrapped in their blankets and matchcoats, smoking, sharpening lances and knives, or playing with the children. Finally, Long Arrow loomed over Julian and released him from the stakes, saying, "Good morning. I hope you slept well."

The people were now streaming out of the village, joking and laughing, carrying clubs, birch switches, broken lances, rocks, unstrung bows, rawhide cords to use as whips, hoes, even a shard of glass, and the stock of a broken musket. Julian was led through the milling crowd to the starting point a quarter mile beyond the village gate. As he passed through the crowd, stumbling on his numb feet, some could not resist a poke or a blow. Soon all the villagers from toddlers to an ancient blind man had lined up in a double-file, their weapons raised.

They stopped before the narrow corridor created by

the armed villagers. Laying a hand on Julian's shoulder, Long Arrow said, "I am aware you are planning to force us to hasten your death. That is a waste of effort. Remember, I claim the privilege of choosing your last hour."

With that, Long Arrow pushed Julian forward and jabbed him in the buttocks with a lance. Julian yelped, lurched between the rows of battering, scourging, and stabbing implements and fell on his face much to the glee of the villagers. Immediately, the blows, prods, and pokes viciously rained on his back, buttocks, and legs. Julian was attempting to get up when a warrior gave him a kick in the stomach and he doubled up and fell again, vomit streaming from his mouth. He had not yet progressed thirty feet. Laughter and cheers rang in his ears while he was flayed and pummeled mercilessly. Blood in his eyes blurred the path before him as he struggled into a crouching position and charged, then immediately slipped and skidded face-first in the mud. Four young men with clubs assailed him now with such fury that Julian imagined his body being beaten into separate parts. He tried willing himself to die. He would have cried or begged but for the mud in his nose and mouth. He could only writhe and squirm forward on his belly.

Abruptly, the blows and laughter stopped. A stronger man would have regretted the cessation because Long Arrow had obviously halted the punishment in order to preserve Julian until the chosen hour. Julian waited for the war sachem's taunts, and when he heard nothing, lifted his head and surveyed the hostile faces of his tormentors, expecting the onslaught to resume. He then saw the back of a short broad figure standing in front of him with an upraised hand. Black hair fell thick and uncombed over a robe of iridescent wild-turkey feathers. All those in the two lines of the gauntlet had lowered their weapons. The figure spoke—the high wheedling voice of a woman of indeterminate age. The squaw took a step forward motioning to Julian to follow. He scrambled to his feet and limped behind her. For the full quarter mile, he grimly followed the short square woman, trying his best to control his uneven gait, feeling the glares almost as if they were blows.

Near the end of the gauntlet, a young squaw holding a war club blocked their path. Her blackened face indicated grief, and Julian knew this must be Seksu's widow. His protector halted. The club trembled and slowly lowered as seemingly the widow was disarmed by the squaw's stare alone. A brave grabbed the club, shouting, face contorting with rage. Julian's protector replied, voice menacing. The brave made to swing the club. The squaw turned slightly and rammed her shoulder into the brave, pushing him out of the way. Julian continued following until they only had to pass Long Arrow who leaned on his lance at the end of the gauntlet.

Long Arrow's face darkened as the squaw argued with him. His answer was a snarl and the point of the lance at her throat. Unintimidated, she pushed it aside. Then, she turned and circled Julian in a series of lurches as if inspecting him to see if he were worth the dispute. His first impression was that she was comely, possessing fine features, lips rather full, skin with a childlike smoothness. But that was the left side of her face. When she stood in front of him, Julian stared uncomprehendingly at the other half, which belonged to a demon. Burn scars roughened and loosened the skin, her right eyelid drooped leaving only a slit for a bloodshot eye. Spittle ran from the right corner of her mouth. Her right ear was inverted and swollen to twice the normal size. Her right shoulder rose into a hump, but her right leg was shortened, which accounted for her lopsided gait. Yet, she obviously commanded enough respect to challenge Long Arrow. She turned towards the war sachem again. It was a contest between stone and fire. Long Arrow gave a furious yell that echoed in the hills and directed his lance again as if to run both of them through. The woman remained obdurate.

Finally, Long Arrow shoved the lance into the ground and addressed Julian as if he had never been angry: "My sister insists on adopting you as a husband, English Rat. I tell her it's impossible for, obviously, she never had a husband that she needs to replace and you cannot hunt and provide for her like a husband should, yet beyond all reason, she contends that you will become her husband. I tell her to take you as a slave. She says I will kill you if you are only a slave and then find someone else to replace you, which is true, so she desires you as her husband. I tell her that her clan never will accept an English Rat, and I never will accept you as a Lenape. She says she doesn't care what sort of rat her husband is. My sister saved your life for the nonce, English Rat. I suggest you study ways to please her, for she is changeable as the wind and will cast you off as easily as she has lifted you up."

"What does your sister expect of me?" Julian caught the good eye of his savior, which if one good eye could be said to be beautiful, it was.

"I suspect she wants you to bed her, beyond that, I

am not able to fathom my sister's strange notions." Long Arrow gazed pityingly down at Julian.

"What's her name?"

Long Arrow translated and the strange half-mutilated face looked directly at Julian and replied in a husky voice, "Lady Gertrude."

"Yes, that is an example of her strangeness. My sister spent a year at a French convent school and the only thing she acquired there was an English name. God knows why. She didn't learn a word of French, much less the priests' foolish catechism."

The people had already begun to wander back to their village sullenly carrying their implements of torment while this conversation took place. Long Arrow followed. Lady Gertrude took Julian by the hand and led him through the gates, past the scaffolding with drying meats, past the council house, past the post and the dirt darkened with the blood of the traders, past the sweathouses and past the refuse pits. They came to the Mohegan Woman tending a cooking fire in front of an isolated wigwam.

The old woman didn't look up when Lady Gertrude lifted the buckskin flap and they went inside. Lady Gertrude made him lie down on a latticework plank that lined the wall of the wigwam. While Julian gazed up at the dried corn, dried squashes, dried pumpkins, and dried strips of venison that hung from a dozen different leather cords, she examined his injuries. Muttering and tisking, she turned him over, chuckled at the wound in his buttocks, slapped on a bear-grease salve brought in by the Mohegan Woman, turned him over again and grunted approvingly when his penis partially responded to her caress. Lady

Gertrude pulled off her robe and then the single remaining garment—a buckskin dress.

Julian resisted the desire to turn his head away. The deformation continued down the entire length of her body: the right side—with its hump, flat pendulous breast, and withered leg—welded to a well-proportioned left half. Julian tried to fix his eyes on the comely part as she continued her inspection, running her fingers through his hair, pinching the muscles in his arms and chest, fondling his genitals again as if assessing their quality. She lifted up his crooked foot and eyed it from various angles. She twisted it and seemed surprised when he cried out. The Mohegan Woman brought in a bowl of cornmeal sweetened with maple syrup. As quickly as he finished, another bowl was placed before him. Lady Gertrude watched in fascination as if she had never seen a man eat before. Julian then closed his eyes, very aware that Lady Gertrude hadn't stopped staring at him. He didn't believe sleep would come as fast as it did.

Julian was awakened that afternoon by Lady Gertrude stroking his penis. Being a young man, this eventually had the desired effect. Lady Gertrude grimaced, then gave a small pleasure groan as she straddled him. He closed his eyes, but she grabbed his hand and bit it until he reopened them. This was Julian's first time with a woman, and he awkwardly didn't know what to do with his hands while the lower half thrusted and bucked involuntarily. Afterward, he lay somewhat stunned by the experience. The activity felt more natural the second time a half hour later when he was on top, although the Mohegan Woman had to shoo away children peeking in at the entrance. Lady

Gertrude turned her face so he could only view the comely half when her pleasure reached its climax.

After another nap, Lady Gertrude painted his face and entire body with outlandish red, white, and black stripes then, chanting in a loud voice, led him naked through the village and outside the palisades, although the people seemed to be at pains to ignore them. They skirted the fields of squash and corn, traversed a copse of elms, and halted at the shore of the lake. The ruffled waters provided a troubled mirror to the blue sky. Lady Gertrude gave him a belt of blue and white wampum, then took it back. She divested herself of her white tunic and blouse. He again noticed how her misshapen half struggled with the comely half for dominance. Clumsily pulling him into the water, she rubbed the paint off him with sand while chanting.

Julian was aware that this was the ceremony of washing the foreign blood out of him, however the whole tribe usually attended such rites of purification to demonstrate approbation and acceptance. A couple of children giggled behind a tree, but by the time Julian emerged from the water, they had fled. Taking their place was Long Arrow along with two other braves, armed with tomahawks and knives. Unfortunately, Julian would soon become familiar with those braves: Lostboy whose dark blond hair and name showed his origin as a captive, and Chinkwe, dead Seksu's son, who was not much older than Julian.

Lady Gertrude tried to brush past her brother leading Julian by the hand, but Long Arrow halted Julian with a knife to his throat. Long Arrow addressed his sister in Lenape then Julian in English, "You will never be a Lenape, no matter how hard my sister scrubs you. I despise English rats. I like not your diseased white skin; I like not your smell of shit and fear; I like not your pale hair; I like not the dirty hairy faces of the drunken traders. I even hate the squawking words of your language when they leave my mouth. So, I am exacting a payment from you as punishment for pretending to be one of us."

Lostboy and Chinkwe grabbed Julian's arms. "I think I make you… how would the English put it… ah, yes, equivalent to my sister. Choose what you want to lose— eye, nose or both ears. Choose, please, so you can join my sister in being mocked."

A child's voice interrupted them as the Mohegan Woman entered the clearing, leading a small boy by his hand. Long Arrow, Lostboy, and Chinkwe froze as she sat down and pulled the child onto her lap. The child snuggled in as The Mohegan Woman sang softly to him and guided his hand tracing circles in the dirt with a small stone knife. Long Arrow called to the boy who started to struggle in an effort to come to him, but the Mohegan Woman restrained the wriggling child. A young squaw burst out of the woods screaming. The child stretched out his arms. Still, the Mohegan Woman held the child firmly with one withered bent arm while the bony hand of the other arm cupped the small hand with the knife. Lady Gertrude pulled Julian forward, Long Arrow's blade grazing his neck, drawing blood.

Long Arrow called out, "My sister and the witch cannot protect you forever, English Rat, and for every day you live, I'll add an hour to your suffering."

Julian found a breechcloth, a buckskin jacket, and leggings waiting for him at the wigwam. He worried about the Mohegan Woman facing off three warriors, but soon the old woman reappeared. She quickly went about preparing the meal of roasted venison cut into chunks and dipped into bear fat sweetened by maple syrup. Lady Gertrude positioned herself so Julian only saw the attractive half of her face and glanced at him shyly from time to time. She said several words to Julian, but seeing his blank look of incomprehension, shrugged her shoulders in frustration. The Mohegan Woman left, returning minutes later accompanied by a squaw with chestnut hair, pale skin, and hazel eyes.

After listening to Lady Gertrude, the squaw explained to Julian in English. "My name is New Spring. I am the wife of Ahas Lenu or Crow Man—my husband chose his name for the clever bird who brought fire to our people. Lady Gertrude wants you to know that she will not let her brother harm you. Sleep on a feather and dream of singing birds and running rivers. She also says I am not as evil as my ugly side nor as good as my comely half. I wish to be a woman to you, just that, as much as you are able to see me that way. If you are unable, instead of turning you over to my brother, I shall help you escape. I desire you make the effort to be with me; however, I do not force you."

"I am indebted to Lady Gertrude and will be assiduous in fulfilling my role as her husband," Julian replied, hoping that New Spring didn't make him sound so pompous, and aware that Lady Gertrude was afraid to look at him. When she finally did, he smiled with an effort, which could have only made the impression of insincerity worse. Desperate to change the subject, he asked New Spring about herself.

"I was born Mary Landers in the Wyoming Valley in Pennsylvania. When I was twelve, I was captured." Her gaze became distant and her mouth formed a thin line.

"Didn't your family search for you?" Julian asked, then realized how foolish the question was.

"They couldn't," Mary whispered and hesitated. "I made a life here. I think my mother and father would want that for me. I have four children. That would please them. A woman who lost two sons when traders murdered them adopted me. She was good to me and I became what I am now, a Lenape squaw. Everybody was so kind when I came here. They were certain I'd be happy as a Lenape. My husband is a kind man. I am happy as a Lenape. You will see that you will be happy too."

That night, after reviewing his options, Julian resolved to make the effort. He doubted he could be happy, but he would be alive.

TWO WINTERS

THUS, PASSED THE first day of Julian's life as a Lenape, only a little different from the succeeding ones. Julian had picked up a few dozen words of Lenape at the Moravian mission and the Mohegan Woman had a few dozen words of English, so communication of sorts was established when New Spring was absent. New Spring did visit frequently, usually with her husband Ahas Lenu and her children who were fascinated by this man who came from the same nation as their mother. Mary took pains to say a sentence in English, then in Lenape thus amplifying Julian's vocabulary. Early on, when Julian tried through New Spring's to thank Lady Gertrude for rescuing him, her reply surprised him.

"You owe your life to Misinghalikun, not me. I wanted you, but if Misinghalikun failed to give me hope and courage, I would not have dared to step into the gauntlet."

"Who's Misinghalikun?" Julian asked.

"The masked being." Lady Gertrude had taken to putting her hand over the deformed side of her face when speaking to him. "Traders believe he is the devil because in his bearskin and wooden mask he frightens them, but he really comes to bless us. The man who wears the mask takes on the thoughts of the god. He blessed you, which means the *manito*, the spirit, blessed you. There was much talk about it. Why would Misinghalikun bless a man about to suffer a terrible death? Golden Hawk who wore the skin and mask said he didn't know why. He did what Misinghalikun wanted him to do."

"Then I will thank Golden Hawk,"

"No, you must only thank Misinghalikun," New Spring insisted.

Because she was reticent about her history or anything that made her seem odder than she already was, it took Julian awhile to piece together Lady Gertrude's story. She was born misshapen. The Lenape believe such deformity comes from evil spirits. Her mother, who belonged to the Turtle Clan, set her out on a mountain to be devoured by wild animals. After two days, nobody mentioned her as is the Lenape custom with people who die.

On a cold morning a week later, however, the deformed child was found squalling in front of the council house. Marks of an eagle's talons were found on her body. It was taken to be a miracle. There was much discussion about what to do with this child apparently sent back to them by divine intervention. The Mohegan Woman claimed that she had seen the Thunderbird delivering her. Yet the child didn't belong to the clan of the feathered creatures, so many asked why a bird would rescue her. In any event, the Mohegan woman was ignored because belief in the

Thunderbird was a silly superstition. Thunder everybody knew lived in a cave.

The people of the clan of the furred creatures believed that the Mohegan Woman had secretly rescued her. They wanted to put the baby on the mountain again and keep an eye on the Mohegan Woman to see if the eagle was certain this little monster should live or, to really test the *manito's* will, lay her at the entrance of a bear cave. The clan of the feathered creatures and the clan of the wolf argued that the Great Spirit doesn't like to be doubted. They won out and the baby wasn't put to the test again.

The child's mother still refused to suckle her so the Mohegan Woman fed the baby for six months, thoroughly chewing the food before putting it in her mouth. The Mohegan Woman named her Thunderbird's Gift. Not believing that the Great Spirit would favor such a monster, the children made her the target of their cruel tricks and called her Toad-That-Must-Be-Stepped-On. Lady Gertrude fought her taunters—spitting, scratching, trying to make the cruelties not worth it in the process making herself hated as well as despised. When she was twelve, the fourteen-year-old Long Arrow kidnapped her, tied her to a tree, piled wood around her, and set it on fire. The flames burned through the cords so she was able to escape—although the misshapen half of her now carried burn scars. It was said that the Mohegan Woman screamed louder than Lady Gertrude. She even tried to murder Long Arrow, a scar which he still carries on his neck.

Something had to be done so Lady Gertrude was given to the priest Son-of-gray-wolf when he next visited their village. Son-of-gray-wolf had walked everywhere in the world and seen everything so might know someone foolish enough to take in the wounded little monster. The priest carried her to a convent in Quebec. It was there the misshapen child received her first experience of kindness aside from the Mohegan Woman. The nuns let her choose a different name, and after due consideration and to the mystification of everybody, she chose Lady Gertrude. She loved the nuns, however that didn't make her want to take the vow. Lady Gertrude saw no sense in a god who didn't send his son to earth as a Lenape. She resisted learning the catechism and even the French language and no amount of punishment or kindness could alter her intentions. The Mohegan Woman had followed her and lived in a wigwam outside the convent. She acquired a small silver cross, which was said to be the only item she refused to trade. Despite good treatment, Lady Gertrude longed to return to her village. She believed she was Thunderbird's gift and had a purpose to fulfill. After three years in the convent, Lady Gertrude left with the Mohegan Woman, braving a fierce winter storm that would deter pursuers.

The villagers weren't pleased when Lady Gertrude and the Mohegan Woman reappeared yet were a little afraid of this monster that the gods kept pushing on them. They shunned her. When she sat down by a fire, they'd turn their backs. When she spoke, it was as if her words carried no sound. Some wanted to burn her and the Mohegan Woman for witchcraft. An old intemperate brave, Badger Eyes, accused them of casting evil spells every time a brave, squaw, or child suffered misfortune, and slowly through repetition, the accusations gained currency.

When most of the warriors had gone off on a raid, a

hundred Ottawa braves laid siege to the village. Despite the formidable palisades, the remaining boys and old men couldn't defend the village for long against a force of experienced warriors. Badger Eyes claimed that it was Lady Gertrude and the Mohegan Woman who had brought this curse on the village. He spoke long making his case, he spoke bitterly, he spoke to their fears, and there is no viciousness to match that borne of fear.

"If she is the Thunderbird's gift, then we will give the gift to our enemies who may appreciate it," Badger Eyes reasoned.

They stripped Lady Gertrude, shaved her head, and painted her ludicrous colors.

"She will carry her curse to them like white men carry their diseases to us," Badger Eyes assured them.

They bound Lady Gertrude's hands behind her, then tied around her waist a long cord with the other end attached to the neck of a strangled dog. They pushed her outside the palisades. The Mohegan Woman followed, wailing. They laughed the empty cruel laughter of those who are about to die as she staggered dragging the dog towards the Ottawa braves, then disappeared as the curious warriors gathered around her.

Badger Eyes spent the following hours delightedly detailing the torments the war party was visiting on Lady Gertrude. Later that afternoon, to the villagers' amazement and dismay, the priest Son-of-gray-wolf emerged from the forest, followed by Lady Gertrude dressed in the robe of iridescent turkey feathers and the Mohegan Woman also wearing fine new clothes. The three of them approached the palisades. Standing before the gate, Son-of-gray-wolf demanded that they be allowed to enter so they could talk peace. Badger Eyes shot at him, but the gun misfired, which surprised nobody because this priest had special protection from his god. The gate was opened. The three walked in. The whole village crowded around them. Peace terms weren't discussed but rather dictated.

"This beautiful child," Son-of-gray-wolf gestured towards Lady Gertrude who kept her head modestly down, "pleaded for your lives, although you mocked her and humiliated her. Because the Ottawa people are baptized into the true faith, I interceded with them on her behalf and your behalf, and they agreed to not burn your village, kill the men, and enslave the women and children. This is a gift of my God to you, a village of unbelievers except for a few. But my God exacts a price. You will treat Lady Gertrude and the good Mohegan Woman with kindness and respect. Truly I say unto you, as long as she prospers, so will your village prosper. If you fail in this regard, your village will come into dark times."

Son-of-gray-wolf's god wasn't quite finished. Within a fortnight Badger Eyes suffered a paralyzing seizure. As his starving body shrunk because he couldn't take in food, his eyes grew into black orbs of hatred. No one dared taunt Lady Gertrude and the Mohegan Woman after that. The pair of them set up their own wigwam and insisted on their own section of the fields. Lady Gertrude, protected by the aura of the priest, took advantage of his reputation for special magic and sold potions and philters. The Mohegan Woman had a knack for bartering and with a few trades could transform a handful of beads begged from a trader into a smoked side of venison.

Lady Gertrude's moods ranged from shy and compliant to angry and dissatisfied. One morning, instead of making love, she growled to Julian, "You are not a brave and you are not a squaw, but something in-between and useless."

She pulled Julian outside, and marched him through the village, extracting an old man named Winged Feet from a wigwam along the way. Julian first believed she wanted Winged Feet for protection because he carried a bow and a quiver of arrows, but the wizened man bundled in two blankets against the fall chill didn't appear very formidable. They halted just outside the palisades. Facing Julian, Winged Feet fitted an arrow to the bow, drew back the string, his skinny arms doubling with the flexing of his muscles, and aimed straight at Julian's heart. Julian was certain that his futile life was about to end. Winged Feet swiveled and shot the arrow into a post. He did the same with three other arrows, then offered the bow to Julian.

"You won't share my bed until you put three arrows into that tree." Lady Gertrude pointed to a pine thirty yards away.

Julian met her eyes and nodded. He took the bow— two long strips of cedar glued together and bound with sinews at the tips and in the middle—then imitating Winged Feet, nocked an arrow, drew back the string of sinew, his arm quivering with the effort. The first arrow struck the dirt. Lady Gertrude snorted in disgust. The second arrow made a wobbly arc falling short of the pine.

"I can do this," Julian muttered to himself, drew back the string and, making an effort to control the shaking, let go. Like magic, the arrow appeared in the pine vibrating buried an inch. There was an emphatic exchange between Lady Gertrude and Winged Feet.

At this point, Chinkwe approached with his friends, carrying a small stuffed hide for a ball game. An arrogant, preening, mocking youth, Chinkwe saw Julian's existence as an affront to his honor. He observed Julian's next three misses adding caustic commentary. Chinkwe then asked his little brother for his half-size bow. Holding the small bow with trembling hands, he caricatured Julian's efforts by shooting the half-sized arrow a wobbly few feet. His cohorts laughed wildly. Chinkwe then made a great show of presenting the small bow to Julian as a gift.

As much to avoid Lady Gertrude's reproachful looks as for the pleasure of exercise, every morning Julian delved into the forest until he found a secluded spot to practice. He had ten arrows in his quiver that he would shoot no less than two hundred times. Although he could barely lift his arms afterward, he found the practice—the building tension of drawing back the string and the sudden release—deeply satisfying. He shot several rabbits, which were skinned but not eaten, a turkey, a squirrel, and several raccoons. The Mohegan Woman took extra special care in preparing the dishes of his kills.

Lady Gertrude also insisted that Julian accompanied the Mohegan Woman to the fields to help with the harvesting of the beans and squash. When he complained that doing woman's work made him an object of mockery, Lady Gertrude clutched both of his hands to her chest and forced him to look her full in the face and called out for New Spring to come and translate: "You talk to me about mockery? I know nothing else. You must learn to listen, my English Rat, listen until you understand. Be glad that they are mocking you. Long Arrow is mocking you. Lostboy is mocking you. When they stop mocking, maybe you will have learned enough to deal with the harm they intend to do to you."

So Julian listened to their chatter and tried to join in. His mispronunciations and confusions became a major source of entertainment for the village. "Do you know what foolish thing the English Rat said today?" was a constant refrain. Others, however, began to treat him kindly. An old man called Many Tongues early on tried out his aberrant form of English on Julian. Dancing Turkey, a middle-aged squaw with a longing gaze, seemed quite enamored of Julian.

Long Arrow still continued to devise ways to show Julian his hostility. After a raid on a small Palatine settlement, the war sachem entered Lady Gertrude's wigwam with a flushed shivering girl, her blond hair fanning out in wild tufts, blue eyes shining with panic. Her scratched and bloodied legs showed she had been walking for days. Long Arrow bowed to Julian, his sister, and the Mohegan Woman who were eating their breakfast.

"English Rat, I bring one of your own kind. I know what you English find pleasing in a woman. White smooth skin. Dainty features. Round bottoms. Here, she's yours. A gift of peace between us. Pretty as a flower. Drink the heady wine and eat the sweet fruit of her body. Look." He ripped open the shift which was her only garment. The girl stared down, weeping as the shift fell off. "Yes, ravishing a young virgin is a great diversion among you English. Don't be ungrateful. Don't refuse this gift of peace. Or, perhaps, if she were like my sister would she be more to your taste? Let's see." He passed his knife over the girl's face. "Shall I begin with an eye?"

Suddenly, the Mohegan Woman lunged forward, piercing the young girl's thin chest with the knife used to skin squirrels and possums. There was a look of surprise and possibly of gratitude on the young woman's face as she collapsed. Long Arrow drew out his tomahawk and cocked his arm to strike the old woman. The Mohegan Woman squared off, crouching with the bloody knife, hissing, circling around him. Long Arrow burst out laughing. "Little black snake would die happy defending this monster who it rescued from the mountain. No, old woman, I need to make you suffer like all who challenge me."

"I'll eat your heart first," the Mohegan Woman declared, lifting the dripping blade. Long Arrow shrugged and left. The Mohegan Woman dragged the corpse of the girl outside of the wigwam, and soon a group of children were using her to practice scalping.

"The girl was pretty like I can never be," Gertrude said as she took off her outer garments for bed and then looking down as if she were ashamed. "Would you have taken her?"

"I don't know," Julian replied. "I truly don't because taking her would save her life. What would you have done, if I had accepted her?"

"I also truly don't know, my English Rat. Letting Long Arrow kill you would do nothing to heal my broken heart."

A month afterward, as an elaboration of the same joke, Long Arrow presented to Lady Gertrude a beautiful

Cherokee youth he had captured. "I come to make a trade. This young man is strong and honorable and can fulfill the duties of a husband better than the English Rat who has failed to get you with child. He will keep you warm for the rest of your winters. He does not care about your deformity. He will sire strong children. I don't want my blood mingling with the blood of the English Rat who I will kill sooner or later out of disgust. This fine warrior I'll lift up as a brother."

The Mohegan Woman rose from the fire she was tending and picked up the knife she used to scrape hair from deer hides. Long Arrow drew out his tomahawk and leveled his gaze at her. She cackled at this obvious threat, then made a show of carefully examining the Cherokee brave, making comments like, "He has large ears. He must be a wolf in disguise." "His skin is soft like a woman's." She squeezed his testicles. The young man gave a yelp of pain. "He squeals like a girl. He will not be able to sire strong children so I will take him as my husband because I'm too old to bear children."

"And as dry and tough as smoked venison gristle," Long Arrow snarled. "He's mine to give."

Grinning at Long Arrow, the Mohegan Woman responded, "And he'll be Lady Gertrude's to give, and she won't deny me such a gift. Don't worry, if he proves able to penetrate my gristle, then I'll pass him on to your daughter when she is of age."

Long Arrow shook his head and said to the Cherokee: "my sister won't adopt you, so nobody here has use for you. Tonight, you will sing your death song."

One morning several days after the autumn harvest, Julian was crossing a stubbly field with his bow when he saw a half-grown bear cub amble out of the woods. A group of women and children were working nearby, pulling out the dry dead stalks and burning them in a bonfire, the ash later to be used as fertilizer. He saw Sparrow Hawk, the three-year-old son of the warrior Little Heron, toddle after the cub, perhaps considering it the right size for a playmate. Sparrow Hawk's mother screamed at the same time the its mother emerged from the woods—a brown monster, fur bristling—charging to protect her cub. A swipe of her great paw knocked the child forty feet, but when Sparrow Hawk landed facedown, he was still between the cub and its mother. Racing forward, Julian shot three arrows in quick succession, all hitting their mark in the neck and side and haunch of the bear, none having the least effect. Ignoring the dozen snarling nipping dogs, the huge she-bear advanced on Sparrow Hawk who had risen to his feet bloodied, dazed, and crying.

The creature reared up on its hind legs as Julian interposed himself between her and Sparrow Hawk. A swipe from her great paw knocked the bow out of his hands, leaving Julian grasping only a thin arrow to defend himself. He stumbled backward, ending up on his rear next to the terrified child, shakily raising up the arrow in a futile gesture of defense as the large shadow of the beast fell over him. To get at him, the bear had to disable several dogs which it did with easy swipes of its giant paws.

Suddenly, the Mohegan Woman, who had seized a large burning branch from the fire, lunged in front of the beast. Pushing the torch at the bear's paws and snout, she became the aggressor. The she-bear towered over her, roaring. Still, the Mohegan Woman pressed forward. Julian grabbed Sparrow Hawk with one arm, retrieved the bow with the other hand and rolled to the side. Not quite trusting his aim, he helplessly watched along with everybody else this absurd contest between the small wizened woman and the massive raging creature.

Julian felt a rush of air as Long Arrow charged past him with a lance. The lance struck the bear in its side—the muscled boneless belly—with such force that it went completely through the roaring beast, up to where Long Arrow's hands grasped it. The bear tried to turn and attack her new enemy. The Mohegan Woman closed in, distracting the bear by thrusting the torch into its eyes. Long Arrow yanked sideways on the lance, breaking the straight cedar and began to devil the creature with its jagged end. Little Heron, who had also run up, discharged a musket at point-blank range at the bear, blowing off its lower jaw. As the infuriated creature swiped blindly with its great paws, other braves shoved in lances, and the animal died in a bloody rage. While the braves danced around the expiring animal, Julian retrieved his arrows from the carcass and, although shaken, walked off into the forest to practice.

Lady Gertrude violently shook him awake a few mornings later. Julian tried to bat away her hands as he gained consciousness.

"Today is your great day, English Rat," she exclaimed, covering the deformed half of her face while she grinned. "Today, you learn how to swim."

"Why do I want to swim?" Julian protested.

"You cannot run like a brave. You cannot ride a horse like a brave, even if Long Arrow allowed you your fat horse. You cannot paddle the canoe faster than the Mohegan Woman. You eat like three braves, and you will get fat unless you do more than shoot arrows at trees and squirrels. When you go into the water, swing your arms and kick your legs like you see the boys do."

Julian sullenly followed her out to the lake. The air had a steely chill to it, the water was ruffled and gray.

"What if I drown?" Julian asked after he had paddled the canoe out into the middle of the lake.

Lady Gertrude caressed his cheek and looked him full in the face. "I will be very sad and Long Arrow will be very happy."

Remembering Bragg's admonition to face danger directly, Julian heaved a sigh, stood, temporarily rocking the canoe, and jumped. The shock of the cold water knocked the breath out of him. After thrashing and swallowing three or four huge icy gulps, Julian began to cry out in desperation. Lady Gertrude watched impassively.

This went on for several minutes, then another part of his brain took command and said: *Die bravely, at least.* Willing himself to stop gasping and crying, Julian found enough presence of mind to lay in the water. He started kicking and hitting the water with his fists as if he were fighting it. To his surprise, he made progress forward. Still, it seemed more likely that he'd swallow the lake than swim across it. A dozen yards of effort later, Julian discovered that with open hands, he could make better progress. Panting from the cold and exhaustion, his feet finally touched the muddy bottom. He began to wade towards the shore. Unfortunately, before he reached it Lady Gertrude blocked him with the canoe.

"I'm tired," he pleaded.

The left side of her face hardened into disdain; the right contorted horribly. "That's because you're fat."

Shivering, he climbed into the canoe, and she paddled again to the middle of the lake. Four more times, she made him swim to the shore. "I want my brave strong so other women desire him and envy me," she said after Julian struggled to the shore for the last time.

Julian started to protest that he wasn't a brave, then realized he would either be that or the "English Rat."

The next morning, Lady Gertrude made him row to the other side of the lake and explained. "We do this every day until the lake is frozen."

When thin ice crusted the edges of the lake, Julian asked whether he would swim that day. Lady Gertrude eyed him maliciously with her good eye. "Are you afraid of the cold, English Rat?"

"Freezing is a stupid way to die," Julian asserted.

"You won't die." She then gleefully slathered bear grease over his entire body, led him naked except for breechcloth through the village to the lake, then sitting on a blanket smoking her pipe, she watched him wade in, breaking the thin crusts of ice, and shivering, begin his first strokes.

Finally, after a brutal freeze, the ice became so thick that Julian, slathered in bear grease and wearing only his breechcloth, walked across the lake and back. He now believed he could finally enjoy the smoky ease of the winter months. He was anxious to join his new friends.

Ahas Lenu who belonged to the Feathered Creatures Clan invited Julian to his wigwam almost every evening to share a pipe with two braves of the same clan—Little Heron and David Gray Thrush, both whom Julian came to love.

"Let me tell you about your enemy Long Arrow," Little Heron said on the first evening Julian spent with them. Little Heron's eyes always appeared to be smiling in his small triangular face. He was a well-respected brave, judged a better tactician than Long Arrow, once luring a band of Ottawa raiders into a trap by walking with buffalo hooves strapped to his feet. However, he was never considered as a possible war sachem because he also possessed the reputation of being too light in the head and soft in the heart. As a young man, Little Heron had fallen in love with a captive English girl. When she was exchanged, he followed her to New York. He slept on her porch throughout a winter and did other foolish things to prove his love. She eventually rejected him. Like many men who had engaged in public folly, Little Heron didn't take the opinions of others very seriously. The open affection he now showed his plain wife bordered on scandalous.

"Long Arrow swears he will kill me." Julian tried to sound unafraid.

Little Heron wasn't fooled. "Long Arrow neither forgives nor forgets, brother. He is respected as war sachem, yet he is not loved. You are loved."

"Little Heron should be war sachem," David Gray Thrush claimed. Having a judicial temperament, resonant voice, and natural gravitas, David Gray Thrush would eventually become the next sachem. In argument before the present sachem, a brave of advanced years and increasingly shaky understanding, David Gray Thrush usually carried the point.

Little Heron shook his head. "That I cannot be. Although I have taken three lives in battle, I never felt the pleasure others do when they scalp an enemy lying at their feet. Long Arrow glories in the kill. So that you learn about Long Arrow and always be careful where he is concerned I will tell you his story:

"When Long Arrow returned from England, he still showed the broken spirit of a captive. He did not talk much. Younger men shoved him aside. Nothing was expected of him. A squaw in the village, Laughing Moon, was also once a captive. A vicious trader, Antonio Larkspur, kidnapped her and imprisoned her in a cave. Larkspur was especially feared because after disarming his enemies, he used his giant hands to twist their necks until they broke. Antonio was a great friend of the Seneca. He hunted with them, raided with them. He took a Senecan wife who he spent his winters with. He murdered and raped many, but few dared go after him for they didn't want to make enemies of the numerous Seneca tribe."

David Gray Thrush poured rum into a wooden bowl and offered it to Julian. "Drink," he said. "This is a story that requires strong spirits."

Little Heron went on: "After a month, Laughing Moon escaped from the cave where Antonio had imprisoned her. Naked and bruised, she walked for ten days back to the village. Laughing Moon was changed. She never smiled. She never looked a man in the eye, her shame was so great. After Long Arrow heard her story the first winter of his return, he went into the sweathouse where men from his clan beat his body with birch to purge the English pollution from his blood. Then he disappeared. Many many days passed. It was believed he died or went east because he no longer possessed the courage and honor to remain a Lenape.

"We thought it best to forget the once promising youth. But in the spring, Long Arrow returned, striding into the village with the proud bearing of a war sachem, carrying a canvas sack. He went up to Laughing Moon's wigwam, called out her name, and when she appeared, drew out of the sack Antonio Larkspur's head. Laughing Moon smiled for the first time since she had escaped."

Little Heron grasped Julian's shoulder and pressed hard to make his point. "If you don't understand your enemy, your enemy will prevail. Long Arrow had tracked Antonio to a Senecan village near Lake Chautauqua. He pretended to be a wandering Mohegan who traded this for that. He spoke English and French so there was no reason to doubt what he claimed to be. Also he carried with him a keg of rum. Long Arrow made friends with Antonio Larkspur and was allowed to sleep in the same compartment of the longhouse because he was generous with his rum. He waited until Antonio and his wife were in a drunken stupor and the others in the longhouse were asleep. He acted swiftly, so the sound Antonio made when Long Arrow slit his throat was no different from what a sleeping man makes. Long Arrow made sure the flow of blood when he severed the head did not disturb Antonio's wife. Then he crept out of the longhouse with his bloody trophy.

"The Senecan braves pursued him for forty days and nights but, in the end, gave up. Long Arrow laughed at them saying he enjoyed leading them in circles and was sorry that the game was over."

Long Arrow didn't come up often in their evening talks. These new friends appreciated a well-told story, a jest, and each other's company. They imparted their knowledge to Julian—told him stories about their spirits or *manitos*—the comet, corn mother, the tornado, and the snow boy. When Julian expressed skepticism, Little Heron claimed Julian would understand the truth of what he called myths when he could hear the earth's heartbeat.

During the deepest part of the winter, his friends showed him how to build a hut over the ice, cut a hole, and fish. Once Little Heron acquired three bottles of rum, and the four of them crowded into the hut, got hilariously drunk while pulling in a dozen fat walleyes. As they helped each other laughing, slipping, and stumbling across the ice with their burdens of freezing fish, Julian realized these were his friends, his countrymen, his people, and he would fight and die for them.

Early that spring, Julian discovered he had an audience at his archery practice. Ahas Lenu, Little Heron, and David Gray Thrush were seated on a fallen tree and watching with interest as he nocked arrows and buried them into a pine thirty yards away. After placing three arrows within an inch of each other, Little Heron approached and said to him, "Come, brother."

Julian followed his three friends deep into the forest. Stopping at a little ridge above a deer trail, Little Heron explained, "You make too much noise to stalk an animal, so you stand here and shoot at whatever passes you."

While Julian waited, the sun described a quarter of the sky. He was beginning to suspect that his friends were playing a practical joke on him. Then he heard the pattering of hooves and a moment later spied a buck bounding down the trail. He nocked an arrow, and as the brown blur passed aimed, shot, and missed. Quickly nocking another one, he drew, let loose and saw the shaft fall miserably short. Foolishly, he nocked and drew a third time, then released as the buck leaped a stand of brush, and was amazed to see the arrow hurtling through the air further than he had ever shot an arrow before and pierce the beautiful animal's neck. Ahas Lenu, Little Heron, and David Blue Thrush came down the trail grinning.

"We give you a new name," Ahas Lenu declared. "We call you now Gets-it-right-the-third-time." Then they skinned and quartered the buck and carried it back to Mankita singing.

Often Julian would wake early in the morning and gaze at Lady Gertrude while she slept on her disfigured side. She seemed truly pretty. Then an eye would open clear and intelligent, and the corner of her mouth would lift in a half-smile. She knew he was admiring her. Only reluctantly would she raise her head, revealing her full face. Once, she said as he involuntarily flinched, "I would give half the years of my life to be wholly beautiful to you." Still, she now took care to plait her hair or roll it into a bun and hold it in place with a bone comb. On the normal half of her face, she put vermilion on her cheek, eyelid, and ear like the other squaws. They engaged in gentle teasing. She kept on coming up with reasons why she saved him, "I saved you for your pretty buttocks." "I saved you because I never saw anyone make my brother so mad." "I didn't save you because I wanted an argument." "I saved you because you're a beautiful liar."

"I don't lie," Julian protested.

"You lie to yourself that you love me. I like that lie."

As the second winter and Julian's seventeenth year came and went, Long Arrow seemed to have settled into indifference, although Little Heron and David Gray Thrush warned otherwise. Julian could now swim across the lake with ease. He hunted regularly with his friends and became adept at waiting unobserved for the quarry. He was welcomed at most campfires for his good humor, his storytelling, and his kindness. The people eagerly listened to his stories—about his life in London, the crossing of the Atlantic, his adventures with Bragg, or what happened the other day when the dogs cornered a badger, or even his retelling of their own tales. He participated in the planting and the harvest. He helped the squaws carry their heavy loads of firewood. He wrestled with the children, awkwardly joined in the ball games, sang their songs at the festivities. He brought in small game—raccoons, porcupine, turkey, and even a few geese—while his friends were on longer hunting trips.

When Julian groused to his friends that Lady Gertrude complained too much about his smell, they appeared to be listening sympathetically. But then, suddenly, Little Heron seized him while Ahas Lenu and David Gray Thrush stripped him, and tied his hands. They dragged him to the sweathouse. After an hour forced to endure scalding steam, his friends attacked him again, scrubbing him with sand and whipping him with birches. They pulled him outside, doused him with icy water, then pushed him back in for another round. Julian shook and swore every oath Bragg had taught him. The second time they dragged him out, Ahas Lenu wrapped an arm around his neck, while Little Heron shaved his scalp with a sharpened mussel shell, dipping his fingers in ash to help his grip on Julian's hair. Soon, all that remained on Julian's head was a bristly ridge running down the center ending in a lock that hung six inches down his back.

With Little Heron and Ahas Lenu dancing in their wake, David Gray Thrush led Julian naked through the village proclaiming in stentorian tones for all to come out and follow them. Julian was afraid he was going to be subjected to another gauntlet until he grasped what his friends were saying. "Come and meet our new brother. Come and meet our new brother."

Half of the village poured out of their wigwams and followed them down to the lake.

"I wash the white blood out of you," David Gray Thrush announced as he bore holes in Julian's earlobes with sharpened bone and would have done the same to his septum had Julian not violently refused, shaking his head. Ahas Lenu recruited New Spring and several other pretty squaws to pull him into the lake. As they pushed him beneath the water chanting the song of welcome into their tribe, over a hundred Lenape villagers stood on the shore laughing and yelling encouragement. Julian imagined a throbbing deep under his feet like a giant heart beating and realized he was now a Lenape, and the happiness reached deep into his soul.

Then he saw Lady Gertrude standing apart high on the bank, weeping uncontrollably.

THE LONGHOUSE OF THE DEAD

THERE WAS ALWAYS great anticipation before the autumnal celebration wherein the Lenape thanked the gods in minute detail for the bounty of their life, and those of the tribe with visionary dreams would recount them so all could glimpse the future. The council house was swept clean and purified with hickory smoke before the festivities took place. For eleven days, the oblong deer-hide drums were pounded by two drummers at each end of the house; pleasing tobacco smoke was blown into the faces of the clan tokens; savory dishes were served while grateful acknowledgment was expressed to every entity that comprised life and livelihood from beaver to the blades of grass to the spirits in the mountains, springs, and lakes.

During this thanksgiving, a tortoiseshell rattle was passed around, and if the brave holding the rattle had an important vision or dream to impart, he would stand and walk to each of the twelve posts in the council house and proclaim it. On the penultimate day, the eleventh, it was the turn of the women to relate their visions and dreams. Lady Gertrude never failed to contribute. Her far-flung imaginative narrations such as flying through space seated on the cusp of the moon, or being carried into the underworld on the back of a giant ant, or commanding King George's armies against men made out of ice were considered the most entertaining.

The whole village crowded into the council house on that eleventh day. From the smiles, the small attentions, the eagerness to talk with him, Julian believed that most were happy that he was now Lenape. Sated and dizzy from the thick cloud of tobacco smoke, he could barely focus his gaze on Lady Gertrude when she rose to speak. Everyone fell silent. The speaker was always granted absolute attention. The visionary dream was customarily delivered at a slow pace accompanied by the beating of the oblong drum. Lady Gertrude, however, started by violently shaking the tortoiseshell rattle. This continued for an uncomfortable length of time giving the impression she would never stop until she did.

Julian sensed the tension rising in the council house. Unusually, instead of going to each post to proclaim a portion of her vision, Lady Gertrude lurched to the center of the lodge where the pole is said to attach earth to heaven. She turned slowly, meeting the gaze of everyone present. She stood for such a long time silent while the drums beat that Julian began to doubt whether she was going to speak at all. Abruptly, Lady Gertrude heaved a long sigh and held up the rattle covering the disfigured side of her face. Again, with her one clear black eye, she scanned the faces in the lodge, the drums still beating. With her deformity covered, it wasn't hard to imagine her as an attractive woman. She began to speak in a raspy old-womanish voice.

"In my dream I found the ladder to the twelfth heaven. Trembling with fear, I climbed it." Lady Gertrude made the motion of going up the ladder with her burn-scarred right arm for a very long time. "When I arrived, the Great Spirit, Kisheleunkong, met me and said in greeting, 'Welcome, my lovely child.'

"'You do me too much honor, Lord,' I told him, looking around. 'This world is indeed beautiful, yet where are the others?'

"Kisheleunkong smiled at me and replied, 'I have prepared a place for you in my house where you will find those that came before. Our fire is warm, our bellies are full, and we have many stories of brave warriors and beautiful squaws.' He took my hand and led me inside a longhouse. It was very dark and I could not see the end of the passageway. I walked for most of a day with Kisheleunkong, passing by many people sleeping, but I could not make out who they were. Finally, the faces became clear—Meadow Lark rose up and showed me the smooth skin on her cheeks where once there had been smallpox pits. Great Stork bared his chest and I could see that his wound had healed without a scar."

There was an uncomfortable shifting in the council house. It was forbidden to speak aloud the names of the dead. With raised voice, Lady Gertrude continued announcing those who greeted her, always adding the special attribute or distinguishing mark of each. Julian heard stifled sobs and murmurs of anger as the names brought back old injustices and griefs.

"We walked until I came to an empty part of the longhouse. Kisheleunkong gave me a mirror and told me to look at myself for I was no longer like this." She switched the rattle to the other side of her face briefly showing her deformity, then switched back. "I was wholly a beautiful woman. Kisheleunkong told me to take my seat. I asked if I could sit closer to Meadow Lark and Great Stork. He said that I could not. He gave me a bowl of sweet hominy then a drink of pure water from the skull of a Frenchman. The water cooled my throat and lifted my spirits.

"Kisheleunkong left. I thought I would be alone and began to weep. Soon Kisheleunkong came back with Little Heron who sat beside me. Little Heron said, 'I am glad to see that you are well, Lady Gertrude.'" Little Heron had a slight stutter which she imitated. "I offered him a drink from the skull of the Frenchman. He took it and said, ''Tis good.'

"Soon, Kisheleunkong came with Lostboy." She mimed Lostboy's arrogant stride. "Lostboy said, 'I am glad to see you are well, Lady Gertrude,' and gave me a broken arrow. I offered him a drink from the skull. He took it and said, ''Tis good.'"

For several hours Lady Gertrude spoke, giving names of those who were going to join her in the house of death, imitating their voice or miming their gestures. Julian guessed that she listed more than forty of Mankita's three hundred souls.

Finally Lady Gertrude finished saying, "Then Shy Quail came and took a child out of her belly. 'His name is Gone-to-heaven,' Shy Quail said. She took a drink from the skull and offered it to Gone-to-Heaven who drank from it as if it were a breast. ''Tis good,' she said."

Shy Quail, Little Heron's wife, was sitting across

from Julian, her pregnancy just beginning to show. This effectively gave those named in Lady Gertrude's vision the length of time they would live. Abruptly, Lady Gertrude dropped her rattle and sat down.

Long Arrow rose, a breach of etiquette on the day reserved for women and declared, "I apologize for my sister. We all know her head is filled with foolish notions, and what she claims to have dreamed can be of no importance." He sat down. No one else stood to recount their dream. When the people of the village filed out on the twelfth and last day and lifted their hands to the east chanting their prayers twelve times, there was grimness in the air rather than the usual exhausted cheer.

Later, when Julian tried to visit Ahas Lenu, David Gray Thrush blocked him at the entrance of the wigwam. "We no longer desire your company."

"Was it Lady Gertrude's dream?" Julian asked.

"We are tired of your company," David Gray Thrush insisted. "Go peacefully. Do not ask questions."

"Did you really have that dream?" Julian questioned Lady Gertrude as they settled down to sleep.

She covered the comely side of her face and replied, "Have you known me to lie?"

Over the course of a fortnight, most of those named found excuses to visit Lady Gertrude. They pretended to be interested in potions, but they all managed to slip in the question whether she had actually dreamed what she had related in the council house. Lady Gertrude invariably responded, "I recounted what I dreamed, yet as you know, my dream is the raving of a foolish woman." This answer satisfied few.

As autumn was lengthened out by an Indian summer, Lady Gertrude inexplicably began to waste away—the distorted half of her face aging, bones pushing against her skin. She talked little, the Mohegan Woman not at all. Julian's friends continued shunning him along with the rest of the village. Children were reprimanded when they approached him. The only relief from this isolation was the brief appearance of Grayson. He stepped into the wigwam one evening and, without a word, started to open his satchel. The Mohegan Woman stopped him saying, "Your God doesn't give enough wine for me to be happy with him."

Grayson's lips formed his cast-iron smile. "Belief in him is his wine, and there's more than enough. Now Mohegan Woman, allow me to confess you and Lady Gertrude."

"No, Son-of-gray-wolf, I do not believe in him today, but I will give you food for your journey." When she took down several large pieces of dried venison off the racks, Grayson raised a hand stopping her and opened a small pouch. The Mohegan Woman filled Grayson's pouch from her basket of powdered cornmeal. Grayson closed the pouch, made the sign of the cross, muttering a few words in Latin. He acknowledged Julian with a nod and then offered, "Come away with me."

"These are my people." Julian asserted angrily.

"As the English were once," Grayson replied, glancing at Lady Gertrude. "I will pray for her body and your soul."

Lady Gertrude's strange debilitation slowly turned into a fever. The last time she had become sick, the children led by Chinkwe took it upon themselves to torment her. After tying up the Mohegan Woman and shutting her in the sweat lodge, they had invaded the wigwam, tickled or poked Lady Gertrude even as she vomited and voided her bowels. The Mohegan Woman freed herself by gnawing through the rawhide bonds with her seven teeth and went after the children with her little stone knife.

This time they entangled the Mohegan Woman in a fishing net, dragged her to a thick pole and tied the ends of the net to it. Then they invaded the wigwam, apparently not taking into account that Julian might defend Lady Gertrude. He was trying to administer a sip of water to his trembling grimacing patient when they pushed him aside and started flailing her with birch branches and thorn bushes. Grabbing an unstrung hickory bow, Julian went on the attack, whipping and jabbing. The smaller boys fled. Julian grabbed Chinkwe by his scalp lock with one hand and began to force him to the ground as he scourged him with the bow. Chinkwe shook himself free. Julian tripped him as he lunged outside and began to lash Chinkwe again when he tried to regain his feet.

Whack, whack, whack—the sounds summoned the whole village to the scene. Lostboy let loose a tomahawk which sailed past Julian probably because he was afraid of hitting Chinkwe, then charged with a raised scalping knife. Julian caught the arm with the blade as it descended. They stood struggling for a long moment, each of Julian's hands locked on Lostboy's wrists. Gradually, Lostboy was overpowering him. He was considered the strongest man in the village, able to carry alone a ten-foot palisade pole.

Julian, surprisingly, seemed nearly as strong. He almost

didn't recognize the muscled arm resisting the downward pressure of Lostboy's muscled arm. Contorting his face into a horrible grimace, Lostboy opened his mouth and twisted it towards Julian's nose with the intention of biting it off, a favorite way of humiliating an enemy. Chinkwe whipped Julian with the discarded bow as Lostboy's snapping teeth grazed Julian's averted cheek. Behind him, Julian heard a scream, and out of the corner of his eye saw Chinkwe clutch a slashed neck. The Mohegan Woman who had escaped was on her knees behind Lostboy, reaching up with a small stone knife into his breechcloth, twisting her hand to get underneath the leather flap. Lostboy stiffened, turned red, and relaxed his arm. He dropped the knife. Julian let go and took a step back. Suddenly, Lostboy dove for the knife, but Long Arrow, who had been observing the fight, kicked it away. "Patience," he hissed. "Not too long now. Patience."

Lostboy stood, nodded, and gave Julian a blood curdling-grin, saying in thick barely comprehendible English, "Patience name of mother."

When Julian tried to reenter the wigwam, the Mohegan Woman—no more than wizened skin wrapped around a skeleton—blocked him.

"You leave now." The Mohegan Woman twisted her face into a snarl.

"You can't stop me."

The Mohegan Woman brandished the stone knife tipped with blood. "You think not?"

"I want to help her." The ache in his heart was not what Julian ever expected to feel for Lady Gertrude.

"No, English Rat, you will not see her die."

Suddenly, Lady Gertrude appeared just inside the entrance, naked and shuddering. "My English Rat," she whispered, sinking to her knees. "Take him away, Mohegan Woman. Take him." The Mohegan Woman grabbed for his arm, but Julian slipped past her.

"Lie down, dear," Julian begged.

Lady Gertrude began to sink down, obeying. Then, with a final burst of energy, she leaped on him like a mountain lion with bare claws, yet before she could hurt him, she fell back, groaning. "I have no more strength. Go, my dear English Rat. Follow the Mohegan Woman. Do not see me die. I will be so much uglier in death. Go. That is my wish. No words. Just go."

The Mohegan Woman pushed and prodded Julian, who seemed to have lost his will, out of the village. They skirted the shore of the lake until they came to two large stones. The Mohegan Woman fell to her knees and began to dig in the sandy soil like a dog, indicating that Julian do the same. He wearily complied. Soon they were uncovering a canoe stocked with a bow and arrows, furs, pemmican, and a small purse filled with shillings.

"Leave now," the Mohegan Woman commanded. "Long Arrow will want his sister to hear your screams before she dies. Leave, English Rat."

"Why must I go?" Julian asked as anger put life back into him. "I have friends here. I can shoot an arrow as straight as any brave. Little Heron is teaching me how to track. I will prove myself as a hunter and warrior. I will prove myself to Long Arrow. I will pay for the harm I've done to Chinkwe in furs or in rum. I am a Lenape."

"Yes, you are a Lenape, English Rat, and you are a fool.

You have no friends except for me. Do you remember Lady Gertrude's vision?"

"Of course, I do."

"Did she name you?" The Mohegan Woman hissed.

"No, I wasn't named, but surely you don't believe…" Julian hesitated, not quite knowing what the Mohegan Woman might or might not believe.

"You weren't named. You weren't going to die. You must understand, English Rat, how we think. If you then die first, that means the poison of the dream is undone, and Lady Gertrude's vision becomes only the foolishness of a crazy woman like Long Arrow said. We will kill you in the hope that the ones Lady Gertrude named will live."

"Why did she tell about her dream if it meant I would be killed?"

The Mohegan Woman was silent.

"What will happen to you, Mohegan Woman?"

"To me?" Her obsidian eyes regarded him from their narrow slits. "There is a child of six winters with the face of an angel but who does not sit up. His mother has lost hope and will leave him on a mountain to die. I will steal the child with the face of an angel and raise him to be a strong man."

"Won't Long Arrow take out his revenge on you for helping me?" Julian asked.

"Long Arrow may do many terrible things, yet he will never shed the blood of his mother's mother." She grinned. "Nay, he will never kill me."

PURSUED

As JULIAN PADDLED down the length of the lake and entered the river that it fed, the warm autumnal evening gradually gave way to an early morning chill. First light found him on the gray ribbon of water that snaked between hills so thickly wooded that a raiding party could observe him undetected within a few feet of the riverbank. Would Long Arrow pursue? There was no reason to go after him—he wasn't a slave, the goods in his canoe hadn't been stolen. Yet an indigestible certainty churned in Julian's stomach that Long Arrow and Lostboy would not give up this last opportunity for revenge. Around midday, Julian discerned a lone canoe a quarter mile behind him. At a bend in the river, he paddled to the shore, pulled the canoe into the high grass, and taking bow, tomahawk, and knife, hid behind the tangled branches of a clump of sycamores.

Julian's heart rose with hope when he made out David Gray Thrush, Little Heron, and Ahas Lenu propelling the canoe with their keen strokes. David Gray Thrush boomed out his name, "Gets-it-right-the-third time," again and again, the echoes disturbing the peace of the river valley. When his friends paddled around the bend and no longer saw Julian's canoe, they stopped mid-river.

Little Heron called out: "Why do you flee from us, brother? We have always been your friends. We are your family, your nation. You love us and we love you. Long Arrow has no wish for vengeance, now that Lady Gertrude is dead. Come back. Mourn with us the death of your wife, and after your heart has healed choose another squaw who will gladden your days and warm your nights."

Although he had shunned Julian along with the others, Little Heron would not have been offended by Lady Gertrude's dream. He had always taken his mortality lightly. He liked saying, "When the Great Spirit is tired of his present company, he will take me because I will make Him laugh." Little Heron was also infamous for his ruses—although being of a benign temperament, this talent showed itself mostly in practical jokes.

Reasoning that if Little Heron were telling the truth, he was saved, and if he were lying, it made little difference because he couldn't out-paddle three strong braves, Julian called out, "I am here, brother." The canoe swiveled towards his voice. Standing up, Julian now noticed a musket, a bow, and several tomahawks in the canoe. "We will talk, Little Heron. Come ashore without your weapons."

"Agreed, but you must also meet me unarmed."

A few minutes later, Julian laid his tomahawk, knife, and bow down as Little Heron stepped out of the canoe with a wary smile. Julian then threw down the quiver in such a way as to make the arrows scatter in front of him and asked, "You don't believe Lady Gertrude's dream?"

"If I am to die because of a squaw's dream, then I am to die. I've always protected my brothers. I've always protected you, and that I would not change even with death clawing at my throat." Little Heron approached holding out his hand as if to shake his.

Julian returned his friend's smile and let out his pent-up breath. Little Heron spoke in part the truth: he unfailingly protected those he loved. Then, seeing tears in Little Heron's eyes, Julian realized with sinking despair that the truth cut both ways. His friend's greatest love was for Mankita and his people. Although he loved Julian, Little Heron like the rest of the village was afraid of Lady Gertrude's dream. If possible, he would undo the poison of the dream by killing him. He would do so for the sake of the lives of his wife, Shy Quail, and their son she carried.

Julian struggled to keep his calm. "Yes, brother, I'm deeply grateful for your friendship." How was Little Heron going to attack? Julian pulled away from the proffered hand and crouched. "The question I ask myself, brother, is do you love me enough to distrust Lady Gertrude's dream even though it condemns to death your wife and child?"

Little Heron shook his head ever so slightly, shrieked a war cry, reached back into his queue and drew out a thin iron spit woven into the hair. At the same moment Julian fell to his knees and grasped one of the arrows he had spilled. In a swift overhand motion Little Heron brought the spit down towards Julian's neck, but the arrow encountered flesh first, piercing underneath the ribs. The shaft of the arrow throbbed as it entered Little Heron's beating heart. The spit made a long gash in Julian's back, not penetrating very deeply. Quickly, Julian recovered the bow and the other arrows as Ahas Lenu and David Gray Thrush charged out of the canoe, both firing muskets. Missing, they knelt to reload.

"Brothers, do not move." Julian stepped forward with a nocked arrow, feeling brutish, bloodthirsty, and proud. Ahas Lenu and David Gray Thrush stood frozen at his mercy. Julian could easily fire two arrows before they finished reloading.

His friends then slowly rose, tomahawks in hand, prepared to die fighting.

Julian shook his head. "Go, brothers. I wish you no harm. Take Little Heron," Julian said suppressing a sob and backed away until he was behind the sycamores. David Gray Thrush and Ahas Lenu carried Little Heron's body to the canoe and paddled beyond the range of Julian's arrows, joined now by five more canoes each with six braves outfitted for war.

As the canoes approached, Julian grimly assessed his chances of escape. His pursuers were faster on land and water, better armed, better shots, and outnumbered him. Then he remembered Little Heron describing a fight with a young Mingo warrior, "I had the advantage. He had to battle two—his own fear and me."

"And didn't you also battle your fear?" Julian asked.

"No, I made friends with my fear long before, so I don't ask too much of him and he doesn't ask too much of me."

Julian needed their fears to take his side.

"Good afternoon, English Rat," Long Arrow called

from the largest canoe. "Lostboy and I made a wager as to who will take your scalp first." Julian spotted two canoes break away and head towards a landing on the shore near him. "Too bad, you weren't there to comfort your lovely maiden in her last moments. I told Chinkwe to not be so cruel…"

Aware that Long Arrow was trying to distract him to give the others time to pin him down, Julian ran a short distance to a steep hidden bank on the next bend in the river. Hanging the bow over his shoulders, he dove in, swam across, and surged knee-deep through a sedge-y patch to the other shore. Thrashing forward into the dry underbrush, he found an animal trail leading into a stand of birches on a small promontory. When he glanced back at the river, he saw several braves standing on the opposite shore and three canoes cautiously nosing along the riverbanks.

Julian might as well dig his own grave as to flee into the vast forest. He was too slow and too easy to track. He needed to make them afraid and have their fear work on his side. Unseen still, Julian nocked his bow. "Do unto others as they would do unto you," he muttered, rewording the golden rule, then stepped out from behind the tree and quickly shot three arrows at a passing canoe, scoring a hit in a cheek and another in the arm of the two paddlers. The braves quickly spilled out of the boat and struggled towards the shore.

From the middle of the river, Long Arrow raised his musket and wisely lowered it, the distance being too great for accuracy. Then picking up a bow, in less time than a single breath, he shot three arrows. One whizzed by

Julian's head, another grazed his ankle starting a trickle of blood. Belatedly, Julian fell flat.

Long Arrow called out: "Did it ever occur to you, English Rat, why I'm called Long Arrow? Here I show myself." He thrust out his bare chest. "I will not move. Let's see how far you can shoot."

Julian drew the string as far back as the length of his arms would allow and let an arrow fly. It sliced into the water five yards short of the canoe. Long Arrow raised and nocked his bow with the fourth arrow, laughing when Julian dove back into the cover of the trees.

Julian jogged clumsily along a trail that roughly paralleled the river and at the same time was shielded from it by the thickly forested banks—panic winding him as much as the exertion. Every time he rested a few seconds, his sweat chilled him and a sense of futility sapped his strength. The jaws of the trap were closing. Six Indians were debarking downriver, another canoe headed upriver. Long Arrow positioned himself midway in the river, bow in hand, to guard against his crossing. Given the job to flush him out, Lostboy and his five companions ducked into the cover of the trees directly below Julian.

So much for unnerving his pursuers.

He was to die. Julian wasn't sure his grief for Lady Gertrude and Little Heron left him any real desire to live. Still, he would sell his life dear. Long Arrow and Lostboy had wagered for his scalp. Neither would win because his life would cost them theirs. His advantage lay in that they would be unaware he had accepted his fate on those terms.

Julian hobbled up a game trail leading to the ridge's summit, cursing as his bad foot kept slipping on loose stones.

He situated himself behind a lightning-scarred oak stump and waited. Although this position was untenable, he had a clear view of twenty yards of the trail that his pursuers would use, which would allow him the opportunity for one good shot at Lostboy. Before Julian could settle himself, the brave leading the party cautiously crept into view. Lostboy followed a moment later. Julian rose from behind the stump, quickly drew and released. The arrow streaked past Lostboy's head causing him and his four companions to drop flat behind the cover of a large bush. "I wonder," Julian said to himself. With a half-drawn bow, he arced the course of the arrow slightly so it landed in their midst. The five of them fired their muskets and retreated a half dozen yards back into the trees. Julian flattened himself and waited.

The noose was tightening. The approaching parties of braves signaled each other with birdcalls from three directions. Unless Julian moved, he would die in this spot. He decided to not make it so easy for them. Rising shakily, Julian awkwardly ran along the ridge for a dozen yards, then slid down the steepest part of the slope lunging from tree to tree, praying that he could go faster downhill through the undergrowth than Lostboy's group could run across and intercept him. Reaching a meadow, Julian thrashed through the high grass, awkwardly doubled up. He heard a musket misfire. Then a hot bullet whizzed under his ear followed by the sound of another discharge. He dove behind a rock, looked back, nocking an arrow, just in time to see an Indian vaulting on him. The arrowhead was already touching the Indian's chest when Julian released the string, and the shaft burrowed an inch into his assailant's collar bone making him drop his tomahawk.

Julian started off again, his bad foot twisting with each step, zigzagging through a copse of sycamores so dense that his pursuers wouldn't get a clear shot. Lostboy's party could have chased him down, but possibly his marksmanship with a bow intimidated them—a small victory of fear over their minds on his way to inevitable death.

Julian reached the rocky beach. Relieved to see Long Arrow no longer guarding the river, he plunged ahead into the marshy shallows. As musket balls made tiny splashes around him, he dove into a deeper current still holding his bow and swam to the cover of a half-submerged tree.

Lostboy and a second warrior sprinted onto the beach, launched their canoe, and paddled furiously towards Julian. The wet bow string slipped in Julian's hand, and he lost an arrow as Lostboy raised the musket. The ball exploded the bark on the tree spraying his neck and face with wet splinters. Julian ran his fingers along the string to get rid of the excess water. His next arrow hit the paddler where the neck joined the shoulder, making him drop the paddle into the water and fall forward, rocking the canoe violently. While the paddler struggled to pull the arrow out of his neck and Lostboy reloaded the musket, the canoe spun slowly. Two other warriors arrived on the riverbank.

"God, give me his life," Julian prayed profanely and swam desperately towards the canoe as Lostboy lifted the musket and aimed. The wet powder ignited with an insipid puff of smoke. Lostboy threw down the musket and drew out a tomahawk. Eyes glinting, he bent his arm back as if to throw, Julian dove as deep as he could. Nothing happened. Lostboy would be waiting for him to surface, gasping for air, to finish him off.

Julian touched the muddy bottom, his lungs aching. His life was worth exactly one breath of air. He looked up and spotted the floating cedar wood paddle on the other side of the canoe. Shooting to the surface, Julian grabbed the paddle as a shield. The flying tomahawk immediately split the paddle in two and gashed his shoulder.

A second later, the large murderous warrior leaped on top of him, slashing with a knife. Julian dove to avoid the frenzied cuts and thrusts, then as Lostboy followed, he turned and grasped the slashing arm with both of his hands. Lostboy caught hold of Julian's scalp lock. Kicking and kneeing each other, they rose towards the surface. Lostboy broke through first and exerted all of his strength to keep Julian from getting air. Julian arched his neck and, as he felt the hair tearing from his head, slowly pulled Lostboy's hand with the blade toward his mouth. He bit down viciously on the wrist. He gnawed and tore, his teeth sinking through flesh and muscle to the bone. The knife dropped away. He continued to tear, shaking his head violently like a wolf ripping at the carcass of a kill. Failing to pull his scalp off, Lostboy pummeled Julian with his fist and gouged at his eyes.

Eyes squeezed shut, Julian kept shredding muscle and tendon with his teeth. Suddenly, blood gushed into his mouth. He had pierced an artery. Letting go, he watched Lostboy helplessly try to stanch the copious flow from his mangled wrist. Julian burst to the surface, gasping and thrashing. Struggling in a huge red stain, Lostboy drifted away. Julian slid onto the canoe. He pushed off the groaning brave who had failed to extract the arrow from his neck. The wounded man joined Lostboy who lay on his back in the water, spinning slowly, emptying blood into the water. Bending forward, Julian paddled as if the river was on fire toward the opposite shore.

A musket ball pierced the stern of the canoe, cutting a groove in Julian's thigh and exiting near the bow. Before a second volley was released, Julian beached the canoe and was crashing through the undergrowth. Slowing to a walk on reaching the cover of the trees, Julian continued pushing deep into the forest. He carried a bow, three arrows, and a tomahawk he had taken from the wounded brave. Although whenever he paused and strained his ears, Julian heard nothing, he knew the warriors of Mankita would never stop pursuing him—for revenge and the honor of the tribe. If Lostboy and the paddler died, that would make three less warriors, three less hunters, three less husbands and fathers and cause an immense grief in the village.

The sun sank behind the wooded hills. A huge shadow washed over the forest, and night dropped from the sky like an unraveling black curtain. Julian walked despite his wounds now crudely scabbed over and the yearning exhausting aches engulfing the heart and all the fibers of his body, walked through the dense blackness of the forest and under the shimmering stars in the meadow clearings, walked because he had no other plan and his legs seemed not to know how to do anything else.

Near morning he became aware of an unnatural hush surrounding him, an increasing tension as if the whole forest was holding its breath. His pursuers were close. Julian crouched behind a tree which he knew by smell as mulberry. Even if he had possessed the strength, escape was futile and beside the point.

It was Long Arrow's turn to die now. One clear shot—that was all Julian needed and just possible in the setting quarter moon. A little patience, a little luck, a steady eye and arm and it would be done. Light footsteps of an invisible pursuer passed through the grass a few yards in front of him, then halted. Julian nocked the bow and rose slowly. He saw the lone figure barely silhouetted against a white rock, not fifteen yards away. This was the moment, but before Julian could release the arrow, the figure fell back into a pool of darkness underneath the shadows of a half-dozen trees.

"I smell you, English Rat?" Long Arrow directed his voice at the mulberry tree. "I instructed my men to return to their canoes so it is just you and me now. I have a bow, tomahawk, and knife. You have the same I believe. I stand between you and the Mingo village. If you make it past me into the village, then I will desist from the pursuit. If you fail, I will endeavor to capture you alive so I can surrender you to Lostboy's widow to give her the satisfaction of avenging his death."

Although the Mingo village lay nearby, on principle Long Arrow wouldn't tell the truth to a foe—an enemy didn't deserve truth to his way of thinking. Replacing the bow with a tomahawk and crouching, Julian waited.

"Your stink is stronger, English Rat," Long Arrow said, shifting toward him although still in the shadows.

There was a slight rustling in the dead leaves behind Julian. How many braves were coming? He had to make his move soon. No alternative it seemed but to rush the shadow.

At the moment Julian charged, Long Arrow cried behind him, "Here I am, English Rat."

Julian spun around. His sudden unanticipated movement had caused Long Arrow's tomahawk to miss. Julian hurled his tomahawk as Long Arrow burst out of the shadows like a striking snake. The blade glanced off his hip. Long Arrow gasped, stumbled, and rose again, raising a war cry to summon the others.

Julian found himself clumsily fleeing through the tangling darkness, branches whipping in his face, vines catching at his clothes. He was uncertain how long he ran—a few minutes? An hour? Wildly panting, he arrived at the fields that surrounded the Mingo village.

The corn and squash had been harvested so what remained was a stubbled field with thirty yards of exposure in the yellow quarter moon. A brave, likely a Mingo, was standing on the edge of the field, staring at him. Catching his breath, Julian opened his mouth to call for help.

"Behind you," the brave yelled.

Julian turned. A dozen indistinct forms emerged from the forest and surrounded him.

"Capture you or kill you with my own hands? That is the question, " Long Arrow said as he lurched forward using a war club as support, the hip wound more severe than Julian thought. Long Arrow's other hand gripped a nearly invisible blade. "Hard to decide, English Rat, but the temptation to become the instrument of your death I fear is too great."

Julian heard Bragg's voice counseling, "Always look

danger in the eye when you can't show it your heel," as he lunged toward the club knocking it away. Unbalanced, Long Arrow's knife sliced air. Julian caught the wrist on the second stroke. They fell, tumbling together.

Long Arrow ended up on top, his left forearm pushing his right hand with the blade slowly against Julian's resisting grip. Suddenly, Long Arrow wrenched both his arms back, freeing them. Before the coup de gras was delivered, Julian jabbed Long Arrow in the eyes, then bucked and twisted free. Rising first, he kicked Long Arrow in the ribs with his bad foot and fell on him, pinioning the hand with the knife. They rolled onto their sides, then still locked in each other's murderous embrace, staggered to their feet. Blood flowed down Julian's arms and legs although he had no memory of being cut.

The circle around them tightened, the warriors ready to intervene when Long Arrow gave the word. Time slowed to almost a stop as they stood frozen in their struggle. Julian inched his teeth toward Long Arrow's nose ring. Biting down on the thin silver, he shook and jerked his head. Long Arrow yelped. This was Julian's split second of opportunity to avenge his own death in advance.

"Your life for mine," Julian whispered hoarsely as he spat out the ring and butt his head full force into the stomach of Long Arrow. Julian fell on top of the warrior as he collapsed, straddled him, and pinned both arms with his knees and added the extra pressure of his left hand to Long Arrow's knife-wielding right hand. Digging his free thumb and forefinger deep into Long Arrow's throat, he pinched the windpipe and yanked. Digging deeper with his fingers, he yanked again, then again. It was like trying to dislodge the root of a young tree out of the ground. Now incapable of defending himself, Long Arrow sputtered and his tongue bulged out of his mouth. A dozen strong arms suddenly gripped Julian, lifted him up and threw him back. He stumbled barely keeping his feet.

This was it. He had no weapon. Julian gave a brief prayer for a swift death. A figure stood in front of him—a large warrior with a tomahawk. Deciding to meet death with open eyes. Julian stared defiantly. Nothing happened. In the back of his mind it now registered that the brave had warned him in English. And the voice had been familiar. There, in the early light, he discerned in front of him the sober face of Nickus Brant. The other braves—Lenape, Mingo, and three grave Mohawks—kept a respectful distance. Long Arrow was on all fours gagging like a dog who had swallowed a bone.

Nickus Brant's smile seemed out of place on that gloomy fall morning. "Molly always insists I bring her back a gift whenever I travel. I think this time I bring her back something that may amuse her for more than over the course of an afternoon."

PART II—1754

FAMOUS BEAUTY

"Did you not see the famous beauty at Goram's farm?" Hugh Kean asked, stirring the embers in the fireplace and directing a broad malicious grin at Julian. Hugh then winked at his brother, called John Thunder by those who wanted to stay on his good side, which was nearly all humanity. John Thunder held up a lighted twig to the long pointed nail of his forefinger. Millie, their sister, had taken off her shift again, which she called a dress, and stood in the center of the small cabin naked. She would remain there until Julian took notice, then would harrumph disdainfully and put on her other shift or her brother's shirt. The father, a taciturn ancient, sat in the corner, his empty gaze suggesting an empty mind. He emanated the strong yeasty smell of fermentation because he slept in the shack across the way that housed the still. Every once in a while, his gaze would narrow and he'd give one of his rare orders in a hawking voice. His sons and daughter always jumped to obey.

"I'm afraid I'm not familiar with Goram's farm." Julian dealt often with the Keans. They weren't much as farmers.

Millie tended a poor vegetable garden that might provide a sorry squash or a dwarfish ear of corn to the family meal. Hugh and John were fair shots, but few creatures with marketable fur remained in the neighborhood, so their marksmanship was used to occasionally supply squirrels or possums for a stew. The Keans, however, excelled at two profitable enterprises, producing whiskey and fattening hogs with the leavings of their still.

Millie pranced in front of the meager fire, smiled toothsomely at Julian, then ran out of the cabin. The brothers ignored her. John Thunder reignited the stick and carefully let the flame lick the long sharpened nail of his middle finger. The Indians called Kean's whiskey lightning-and-thunder water, and Julian purchased a fair amount for trade. Julian had qualms about selling whiskey and rum, unfortunately no trader could pursue business without these basic mediums of exchange. If he oversold a village, he always made sure to put distance between himself and the festivities.

"It lies a little ways down the road past Firelock Creek. If you want to see John's wife to be, Julie Boy, you might take yourself a peek." Hugh gave another leering wink while John Thunder applied the flame to a third sharpened fingernail. A professional brawler, John was as vicious a man as Julian had ever encountered in the frontier which drew vicious men out of settled areas like a magnet attracts iron filings. John challenged just about every newcomer to a fight, including Julian each time he visited. Hugh took wagers on the outcome and collected the winnings. If the person was foolhardy enough to accept the challenge, he was fortunate to only lose an ear. John had been known to bite off noses, gouge out eyes, and rip off testicles, so Julian wisely ignored his challenges. If John Thunder became overbearing, Millie might prance between them stark naked.

This visit the father halted the bullying with the words, "Lay off, John. Won't do us no good if you rip off the balls of our best customer."

John had grunted and Hugh had slapped Julian's back saying, "Pap's partial to you. Something is up with the savages, and they're buying all our whiskey. We'd be out except pap insisted we save some for you."

"Did you make arrangements with the father of this famous beauty?" Julian couldn't imagine any father allowing the vicious foul beast near his daughter.

"Corinne don't have no father, leastwise not hereabouts. She's bound by indenture."

"Is anybody in these parts wealthy enough to afford a bondservant?" Julian asked.

"Wealthy? Nay, Goram's not what you call wealthy." Hugh grinned. When the conversation concerned subjects that had nothing to do with brawling, he usually spoke for his brother. "Three years back, Goram set to clearing fifty acres with his three sons and this Frenchy girl, which he purchased from Shawnee savages."

"Then Goram will sell the indenture of this famous beauty to your brother?" Julian involuntarily shivered at the idea of the sale.

"Old Goram don't have no say in the matter for Old Goram is soon to be the late lamented Old Goram," Hugh replied mysteriously.

"He's sick?"

Hugh rocked back and forth, obviously relishing what he was about to relate. "Well, let me tell you what will happen. Old Goram comes hither inquiring about a parcel of land in the next valley for his eldest to farm. He wants our advice on how to treat with the savages being we deal with them all the time. Pap kenned John had an eye for the famous beauty, so didn't he lead Old Goram on. Didn't Pap give Goram a belt of wampum we got off a brave which he shot sneaking off a keg? The brave belonged to that nasty pack of Creeks that hunted in the valley—and Pap figured if old Goram went to their village and showed them the belt, the savage's kith and kin might insist on him answering questions he don't know how to answer."

"That was a mean trick," Julian commented. Uriah had visited this Creek village five years before, taking a half dozen scalps, and that undeserved cruelty had poisoned them in their dealings with settlers and traders. Since Uriah's raid, lone travelers passing through their territory occasionally disappeared without a trace. Although Julian had acquaintances in the village through Blue Dove, his Creek wife who had died a year and a half back, he avoided the suspicious surly tribe. A farmer and his son arriving there with a stolen belt of wampum asking for land wouldn't fare well.

Hugh blew out a small explosive exhalation. "How come whenever one do a clever thing, other folk call it 'mean?'"

"Does the famous beauty want to marry you?" Julian directed the question at John Thunder who was testing his hardened nails by scratching grooves in the wooden floor planks.

"Why would that signify?" Hugh raised his eyebrows in mock surprise. "It don't matter to John what the wench wants. I don't care. Millie might, but she got no say in this business."

"The girl still will be under contract to Goram's sons," Julian observed.

"Really Julie Boy, you're pretty thick in the head today. Goram took his eldest, so he's done for too. John Thunder will pick a fight with one of the other two brothers, and we all ken how that will end. And what can the last son do against the three of us?"

Julian had come to hate his troublesome voice of conscience that urged him to take the trail leading to the Creek village and exercise whatever slight influence he possessed to help the father and son. That yapping voice, which did not allow him to sleep peacefully or eat with pleasure until he obeyed, would be his death one day. The voice reminded Julian that anyone who survived on the frontier owed his life to the intercession of friends and strangers, and he was obligated to do what had been done for him countless times.

In Julian's case, the intercession had started with Molly. On his return to Fort Johnson with Nickus, Julian had paused at the looking glass in the anteroom, expecting the reflection to show the same scrawny ragged kid with chilblains. Blue-gray eyes now questioned the apparition staring back. Sandy hair and the initial scrapings of a beard framed an open face. He stood a foot taller; his shoulders were broad and well-muscled from swimming and practice with the bow. He was certain that his mother wouldn't recognize him.

Then a taunting voice behind him had exclaimed, "Beggar boy became a man."

Julian turned surprised at what he saw. "And you've become a beautiful woman."

Molly appeared to blush. She had attained the sort of beauty that derived its force from an overall magnetism rather than perfection of feature or body. Her mouth still hovered between a smirk and a beguiling smile. Her eyes could glint mischievously, soften into amber butter making adversaries surrender, or harden into little stones making them tremble. She had become Johnson's only mistress, a virtuous state of affairs that the great man hadn't experienced since his arrival in the new world.

At Molly's insistence, Johnson cleared up Julian's involvement in the deaths of the marines, then advanced him goods so he could try his hand at trading.

"If you come across Bragg, tell him come hither if he dare and petition me for the balance of your indenture," Johnson said on parting.

"Sir, I hardly doubt that he will do that, given he is wanted for piracy and murder."

Johnson shook his head. "I hardly doubt that he could resist the temptation, but from what I hear, he's living with the Lakota, trying to persuade those savages who don't know him well yet to proclaim him a king."

Julian's mother, now Mrs. Skylar, had sent twelve letters, six of which Molly had answered. She confessed without shame to letting her imagination have full rein. Given that he wasn't dead, he supposed her inventions were close enough to the truth. Julian did pen a long letter full of sincere love and, because of the impossibility of making his mother understand the chasm separating their worlds, with as many inventions as Molly's letters.

Molly saw him off with another wheel of cheese and the words, "Don't you dare lose your scalp, beggar boy. 'Twill bode ill for my reign as princess."

After happening on a beached bateau with several hundredweights of fur and four traders dead from typhoid, Julian was able to pay off his debt to Johnson. Although Croghan and Johnson offered him employment in their trading enterprises, Julian preferred to remain independent. Partly to avoid running into any of the Lenape from Mankita, Julian drifted into the Carolinas and Georgia trading for whitetail deer hides with the Cherokees and Chickasaws.

Julian supposed this life suited him. He developed a reputation for honest dealing. Not only had he friends in many villages, there were also people he had come to truly love. One couple in a Cheraw village, Rachel and Henry Silverfish, had gotten into their heads that he was their son. Perhaps, not literally, yet they always welcomed him as if he were. They fed him the best food; they gave him little gifts they had chosen especially for him; they made sure he slept in their wigwam on the softest furs. Their sole child, a daughter, lived in another village.

Henry was considered a man with no real attainments—he had never scalped an enemy, he wasn't skilled at hunting or trapping, he wasn't an orator and was too shy to express himself in the councils. Rachel was perhaps a little simple. Her constant smile seemed to be a way to cover her lack of understanding. They both adored Julian, who found it endearing that they would treat him in such a way and good-humoredly went along with their indulgences.

Then Julian visited their village two days after a disreputable band of traders had decided to occupy the place. This band consisted of the sort of men who took up trading because they would have been hanged in a profession that required them to stay near settled areas. Half the village was raging drunk when Julian rode in, the other half hiding from these scoundrels who used the threat of militia and seizure of land to commit their outrages with impunity. Two of their number had decided to amuse themselves by making Henry into their horse. While Rachel sobbed uncontrollably, they forced the old Indian on all fours, saddled him, and at the moment Julian rode in, were trying to force the bit into Henry's mouth.

Julian had never thought of himself as a brawler, yet without actually considering what he was doing, he leaped from his horse, grabbed a burning log out of the fire and hit the trader trying to mount Henry square in the face, the second blow to the second trader in the chest disintegrated the log. One sat dazed; the other frantically brushed the embers out of his hair. When Julian went for the second burning log, both scrambled away cursing. He threw the log, which exploded on the ground between them.

Afterward, while Rachel rubbed bear grease on his hands, he stared wonderingly at his skin. Aside from a large blister on each palm, they were hardly burned.

The story of a mad man who could put his hands into fire and throw burning spears and the tale of his escape from Mankita wherein he killed twenty braves established Julian's reputation as a formidable warrior. In the tradition of frontier tall tales, these stories weren't fully believed, but, after that episode, no trader abused an Indian in his presence.

Then there was Rebecca and Resurrection Peter. Rebecca ended up marrying Albert after Meg died of smallpox and now spoke English with a German accent. Julian became a substitute in part for the family she had lost. She was teary when he arrived and teary when he left and in-between those times did everything possible to persuade him to stay. Two or three times a year, Julian spent several weeks at the maroon village—hunting and fishing and conversing with Peter, playing with his children, trying to digest all the food that Harriet placed before him. After Blue Dove had died, the Creek girl who gave Julian the name Pale Otter and took most of his heart with her, Julian simply refused to move from the site of her grave. He had loved Blue Dove overmuch so the land had taken her. He wanted to force the land to take him.

Hearing of his distress, Peter traveled fifty miles and dragged Julian numb and starving away. Peter and Harriet nursed him until he recovered from the nearly fatal grief. They made no demands. Their children—playing with them, listening to their concerns, holding them—better than all of the consoling words conveyed a sense of hope and future. Julian's grief at Blue Dove's death softened with time: in a strange way, he came to value the grief because it proved the depth of his love.

Peter had moved the village twice since their first meeting, each time losing slightly more followers than he gained. "I 'spect I seeing t'other ocean afore I dying," Peter said after the last move west. Julian also made Peter into a business partner, storing his furs and merchandise with him, giving him a percentage of his transactions. Peter never asked for money or questioned his take. "I trusting you, Pale Otter. Your conscience better bargainer with your purse than your poor brother."

Julian carried on his packhorse three kegs of Keans' whiskey along with a variety of other trading goods. On passing by Goram's farm—a tidy clay-daubed and birchbark-shingled log cabin at the edge of a field studded with dozens of tree stumps—he glimpsed at a distance what must have been the famous beauty. She stood in a cloud of feathers, cap and petticoat askew, holding a struggling goose with a bag around its head. She seemed to be either apologizing to or swearing at the bird in French as she plucked it and failed to notice him. Although the circumstances didn't show her off at an advantage, Julian could discern her honey-colored hair and, even at a distance, her fretful blue eyes. Just beyond the cabin, he came upon two rawboned young men, on either side of a stump, arguing.

"'Tisn't right you helping her, Isaac." The brown-haired boy leaned on the handle of an ax and wagged his finger at his brother accusingly.

"A thousand pities, Matthew, Corinne needed help, which you weren't about to give." Isaac, the blond version of the same elongated physique, faced his brother defiantly, feet apart, hands on hips.

"By your reckoning, she always needs help. What is so hard about gathering broomweed? I needed help too pulling a stump out of the ground."

"You became hot to pull the stump out of the ground when I said I wanted to help her pick broomweed."

"Ever since you woke up one day and discovered that Corinne was a girl, you been conjuring up ways to keep your ugly gob in her line of sight." Matthew tittered at his own wit.

"And what's so bloody wrong with helping her? You're just put out because she likes me better."

"Corinne likes me just fine because I'm the one who works around here."

"So, you say…"

Julian saluted the boys, and they looked up, startled. "I hear your father went to visit the Creeks three valleys over to see about some land."

"That's right. He and Joshua, my sane brother, figured on purchasing a parcel from them," Isaac answered.

"Has he ever treated with those Creeks before?"

"Our pa knows dealing with savages," Isaac said. "Didn't he get our Corinne from the Shawnee for a mule and a keg of whiskey?"

"You talk like we own Corinne," Matthew accused Isaac. "She is indentured for seven years. In four years, she is free of you."

"Also, of you and…"

Julian tipped his hat and left the boys as he found them, arguing about the famous beauty.

When Julian walked into the scattering of rude cabins and wigwams which with a ruined palisade and a half-collapsed council house comprised the Creek village, he could sense the hostility simmering beneath the placid masks of the squaws and braves. If it were a simple matter to kill him, they would have probably done it. But they were aware that he had two powerful protectors—William Johnson through the influence of Molly Brant and, closer at hand, Resurrection Peter who had also let it be known that he considered Julian his brother.

The Gorams, father and son, were tied naked to posts in the open area next to the council house. The boy, smaller and darker than his brothers, hung his head and wept. The father sat erect, staring straight ahead, his eyes icy gray pools in his granite face. Both were covered head to foot with bruises and cuts, showing that they had run the gauntlet.

"Come to join your brothers, Pale Otter?" A portly Creek heading a delegation of a dozen warriors asked in English. His wide grin and frock coat ill-suited his ritually scarred cheeks.

"Yes, Yaholo," Julian replied in a bantering tone. "I want my brothers to join me, so perhaps we do a little business."

"Wait until tomorrow, and then you won't have to trade for them," A buzzard-face brave called Broken Tooth interjected in the Creek language.

"No, that is not true. The old man's skin is worth a keg of whiskey." Yaholo slapped Julian on the back, a gesture he had adopted from a trader he once traveled with. "I think I make a shield out of his hide to stop bullets. Squaws were clubbing and mashing the boy into cornmeal, so the old man went back and finished the gauntlet carrying his son on his shoulders. We see how many gauntlets the old man run before he breaks."

"That is unwise, Yaholo," Julian said. "When the governor sends soldiers, your people will be running a gauntlet from here to the Cherokee River."

"The governor pays Uriah for the scalps of our squaws and children. We piss and shit on the governor," Broken Tooth declared, the words "piss" and "shit" rendered in English.

"There's no bounty on Creek scalps. Uriah sold them elsewhere." Julian shifted the conversation. "The old man and his son did not kill Falling Star. The wampum belt was given to him by the Keans because they wanted you to kill them."

"How did the Keans get Falling Star's wampum?" Yaholo poked Julian with his tomahawk to emphasize the point.

"Falling Star couldn't live without whiskey—you know that's why he stole the wampum belt. When the Keans wouldn't accept it in trade, he tried to steal a keg and was shot."

"Then we kill those whoreson dogs after we kill you, the old man, and his son. The governor will be too busy to send soldiers because we just received this." Yaholo drew out from a satchel a black wampum belt, which was an invitation to join other tribes in war.

"If there is to be fighting, then you'll need new muskets and lead and powder, Yaholo," Julian observed.

"Which I will get when I kill you," Yaholo replied, grinning.

"You are a sachem of great sagacity," Julian declared. "And know the nations that join a war the soonest, lose the most when it turns bad."

"We miss out on the plunder if we join late. Only one thing in your favor, Pale Otter: we don't want to offend our friend, Resurrection Peter, so if you give us a good deal, we might not kill you." Yaholo beckoned Julian into an oversized wigwam that now served as their lodge. The negotiations took most of the night costing Julian his keg of whiskey and three muskets. The two horses the Gorams had rode were also forfeit. All this time, the father and son were kept tied to the posts, suffering the cold and small torments visited on them by the children and squaws.

"I hope you don't think us ungrateful if I ask what advantage you gained by ransoming us," Goram said to Julian when they were released in the morning.

Julian studied the grave sincere face. "Backwoods courtesy. Do a man a favor and eventually it passes around and comes back to you."

Goram shook his head skeptically. "That may be, but we are still in your debt and will make up your losses."

"As you wish," Julian said.

"As I wish, good sir." Goram nodded. "Next harvest I'll sell my beets for cash. I pay you then."

Goram's son, Joshua, was given the horse because of his injuries. Goram tried walking but after a few miles his injuries began to tell and he kept slipping back. Julian took the remaining supplies off the second horse, buried them next to a split pine, and urged him to mount.

"Our debt to you increases," Goram said as he accommodated himself on the horse with a grimace.

"Nay," Julian protested. "I'll pass back this way in a few days. I have caches all over the country. One more won't make much difference."

When they arrived at the cabin, Goram and Julian lifted Joshua off the horse, carried him through the door and laid him down on a corn-husk mattress near the hearth.

The famous beauty suddenly burst in, rushed to the mattress and knelt.

"Joshua, Joshua, what they did to you? *Quelle horreur*! I told you not go to those people. You not believe me when I say I know the good savage and the bad savage?" Joshua couldn't look the girl in the eye. Isaac and Matthew stood in the doorway bewildered by the scene. "What 'appened," Corinne asked again, the French accent thickening in her excitement.

"We had a misunderstanding with the Creeks, Corinne, which Mister Julian here helped clear up," Goram said, straightening his shoulders with an effort.

Corinne gave Julian a quick glance. She would have been perfectly beautiful with her honey-gold hair falling out of a laced-fringed cap and summer-sky blue eyes, except for a rash on her cheek, a habit of cocking her head to her right side like one does when pondering a question, and a nose a little overly up-tilted as if in search of scents.

"They ran the gauntlet," Julian explained, staring at Corinne and wondering why she wasn't unfamiliar.

Muttering, "*Non, non, non*," and then other gentle words in French, Corinne slipped off Joshua's clothes to examine his injuries. He lay there naked and groaning as she carefully checked him for broken bones. She looked up. "Father, you have hurt too?"

"Naught this old body isn't used to," Goram replied.

Corinne stated her disbelief with a snort and a brief frown, then began to order Matthew and Isaac to bring this and that. They obeyed stumbling over each other. Feeling in the way, Julian left the confused scene. With the evening coming on fast, he set up camp outside. He supped on pemmican and walnuts. Having accidentally left the two books he owned—the Bible and Gulliver's Travels—with his supplies, Julian had only his thoughts to distract him. For a moment, they were enough. An hour later, the main object of his musings emerged from the cabin and knelt down by his fire,

She gazed at the flames quiet at first, then said, "I must ask the pardon, Mister Julian. We are the bad hosts. You save life of Joshua and father and we not offer to you the crust of bread."

"Joshua needed tending more than I needed crusts." Julian gazed at her trying to sort out her familiarity. "You call Goram father?"

"I have that honor to call him father. *Mon père française* is dead so now I have my father *anglaise*." She smiled then grimaced as she leaned forward. "Your foot, let me see."

Julian was taken aback. "Why do you want to see my foot?"

"You think I not know who you are. You walk all day on the clubbed foot, so she hurt you, *non*?"

"My foot is not clubbed. A carriage in London ran over it," he explained for the ten-thousandth time.

"You are the boy with the bad foot who kill thirty Lenape braves with the bow."

Julian laughed. "So, 'tis thirty now. Last I heard 'twas twenty. If I live to my dotage, 'twill be a hundred with a slingshot. Nay, the truth is I killed three—one a friend, who I still grieve. My scalp would be decorating a lodge had not Chief Brant rescued me."

"The spirit of the village, you kill. Many from Mankita come to Chinoota."

"Did Long Arrow go to your village?" Julian asked, his thoughts scrambling because Chinoota was one of the few Indian towns he avoided visiting.

She shook her head. "Long Arrow go to the Ohio country. Thy foot, *monsieur*." She demanded, smiling, and bent forward more, the firelight reflected in her great unyielding eyes. She was obviously no stranger in dealing with male stubbornness so he complied and slipped off his boot. From a pocket somewhere in the folds of her dress, she produced a small pot with a minty smell. Corinne frowned, wrinkled her nose, and then with her tongue just protruding between her lips began to rub the tingling lotion into his foot. As pleasurable as the warmth spreading through his foot was watching her lovely face concentrate on massaging the skin. Suddenly, it came to him who she was.

"You were the girl at Chinoota by the river," Julian blurted out.

The firelight didn't entirely hide the blush. She continued rubbing. "*Mais oui*, I am girl by the river who talk to you, Shawnee captive until father took pity and bought me for a mule, a hundred pounds of dried venison, and a keg of rum. I cannot tell what the old fool was thinking. He had no French, no Shawnee. I had no English, and his words were like the barking dog to me."

Julian vividly recalled clearly her great eyes in the twilight and the basket of roots and berries. "I asked you to go with me—so foolish. You didn't have my words but you seemed to understand them. I did not understand your reply."

"What else would the young man say to the girl by the river?" Corinne shrugged her shoulders, and he felt her smile through the darkness. "I have not the memory of what I said. Later, I hear of a boy's escape from the village of the Lenape, and I know 'twas the boy who ask me to go away with him."

"Only you couldn't go with me for…" Julian sought the right words to impart the delicate fact.

Corinne shook her head and rubbed an eye. "*Non*, the Shawnee slave with the Shawnee baby in her belly could not. White Bear, the brave who kill my father and brother want me for the second wife. I am willing to bury my father and brother in my head and become the Shawnee squaw. So many girls forget. Two English sisters in Chinoota hide when the traders come because they like being Shawnee. They have Shawnee husbands who are so kind to them. But White Bear has the jealous wife, Bright Flower, who swear the oath I never become the Shawnee, swear the oath to make me suffer all the days I live with Shawnee. Brave warrior White Bear afraid of little squaw

Bright Flower." Contempt edged into her voice, then she gulped and sighed.

"I become the slave. When Bright Flower cut off my toe after I run away," Corinne pointed to where her small toe would be underneath her wooden shoe, "White Bear tell Bright Flower she can punish me, only not make scar on me. When I birthed Eagle Heart, Bright Flower take him because she only birth the dead daughter. Ten days I hold Eagle Heart to give him the breast. Then another squaw lose the baby, and Bright Flower say the squaw who lose the baby now give Eagle Heart the breast. White Bear, weary of Bright Flower jealous words, sell me to Father Goram during the hungry winter. I am afraid of my new master. I become the slave? I become the harlot? Non, I become a daughter and sister. Calling him father is the honor I owe him." Corinne shifted so she was leaning on her side.

"It seems Isaac wants you as a wife, not a sister," Julian commented.

"If Isaac is the only son, I wed him with joy in the heart. But the others will hate the brother I marry. I will be the sister only. I marry no one and so remain sister until I die."

"John Kean also fancies your hand in marriage."

She pushed out her bottom lip frowning. "I marry his pig first. If I am forced to marry Mr. Thunder, better he never sleep for I will cut his throat when he sleep. Only father will not sell my bond to Mr. Thunder."

Julian contemplated the fire, then glanced at Corinne and thought that if he were one of the brothers, he'd also fight over her.

"You trade with Chinoota?" Corinne looked away as if afraid of the answer.

"No. I fear that some of the braves believe I owe them my scalp, although I've met Shawnee who say as an honest trader I would be welcomed."

"Bring me word of my son if you visit Chinoota."

Julian couldn't resist the plea in her voice. "I will visit Chinoota and bring you news of Eagle Heart."

"I thank you, Mr. Julian," Corinne said, half choking on the words.

"Does Goram know about Eagle Heart?" Julian asked hesitatingly.

"I cannot say. I not tell father. White Bear not tell because he believe the English want the untouched woman. Bright Flower say the English fools not to desire the fertile squaw. Father never ask question about my life with the Shawnee, yet he understand what must the girl slave suffer. He is kind and gentle to me like I am the hurt child. He understand, but his sons... of the bad world, they have no knowledge."

"I'll keep your secret."

"I am grateful to you for saving father and Joshua." She laid a hand on his shoulder, then abruptly stood and left.

The next day, Julian retrieved the supplies he had cached, and returned late afternoon. Corinne burst out of the cabin when he rode into the clearing and with much more animation than necessary invited him to supper.

Goram occupied the head of the oaken trestle table, Corinne nominally the other end, but she was rarely in her chair. Always springing to her feet at the slightest pretext, she even passed a jug of cider by picking it up and carrying it. Julian sat beside Joshua whose dark complexion and middling size set him apart from his lanky father and brothers. He was still shaken and weak from the beating he had received in the gauntlet and shrunk into himself even further by hunching his shoulders and lowering his head. Isaac and Matthew shared a bench on the other side. They were a sober family of men—their conversation concerned weather and crops and the strange case of a neighboring Dutch family that had completely disappeared—no corpses, no sign of robbery or violence.

Mentioning the black wampum belt, Julian commented, "Means war only if other tribes accept it."

Goram nodded and advised his sons to keep their firearms close while they worked in the fields.

The conversation soon passed on to more pleasant topics. Corinne regarded the Goram men not only with great affection but also as objects to get as much fun out of as possible. She deviled them and catered to their needs by turns. She coaxed smiles out of their grave faces and even occasionally a laugh. She paid special attention to Joshua, resting her hands on his shoulders and assuring him that he would soon feel better soon. Isaac and Matthew stared jealously at Joshua.

"You run the gauntlet, and the savages, they beat you the black and blue, then I treat you the same way," Corinne said, responding to their scowls.

"Father ran the gauntlet also. He's not in a bad way," Isaac contended.

Goram sat ramrod straight in his chair.

Corinne gave her Gallic snort of disdain. "Father, he is made out of the hickory wood. I tell you the squaws and the children in their hands and arms feel more hurt when they strike father than he feel on his back."

"What is Joshua made out of, then?" Isaac asked.

Corinne shot Isaac a hard look. "The flesh and the bones like both of you. You fare no better than Joshua."

"Corinne, did you ever see a prisoner run the gauntlet when you were with the savages?" Matthew asked.

"Strong men, I see die weeping in the gauntlet."

"Father isn't made out of hickory. He is made out of flesh and bones like us," Isaac asserted.

"He's made out of harder stuff than me," Joshua whispered.

"Stop speculating on my physical constitution," Goram interjected irritably. "God gave me the hide of an alligator to compensate for dull wits. Corinne, sit down. Why don't you ever keep in your place?"

"Because taking care of four stubborn men gives me too much work to sit." Corinne gave Goram a mocking frown.

"Sit down please afore I lash you to the chair," Goram insisted.

Corinne stuck out her tongue at him and squirmed into her seat.

Goram reddened. "If you was a son Corinne, then the gauntlet would be preferable to how I would scorch your backside."

"I am less than the son. I am the servant and must do your bidding." Corinne appeared to be offering her pink smooth cheek for him to slap.

"I never raised a hand to a woman, but if I ever change my mind, you'll be the first to know." Goram turned to Julian. "Forgive this impudent French scullery wench. Corinne pretends to be of frivolous temperament, yet we are as well cared for as any homestead in the valley, even the ones chock-full of womenfolk. For that, we are obliged to her. When Corinne came to us, she hadn't a word of English and only knew savage and French ways of doing things. But she learned words like a thirsty man at a well, and she only had to be showed once how to do a thing. She is a blessing to us. So we abide Corinne's Frenchified ways and her refusal to stay seated more than the space of an 'amen.' Come winter, I'll lash her down and teach her to read. I didn't learn until I was twenty-six, and she is quicker than I ever was."

Joshua began to slump. Corinne sprang to her feet, helped him get to his feet and supported him as he walked unsteadily to the cornhusk mattress. "There now, *mon petite frère*," she whispered. "You must rest now. *Mon petite frère*. Tomorrow, you feel better."

"Do I have to be beaten nearly to death for you to cast an eye on me?" Joshua muttered sleepily and wearily.

"*Non, non.* You and Matthew and Isaac, I always carry close in the heart." She tucked him in like a child, and then returned to the table. "If you abide my Frenchified ways, I not see why the King George cannot tolerate the King Louie."

"If you tried to forbid us to go into half the house, we might not be so tolerant," Goram answered.

"Which side do you think the Shawnee will take?" Matthew asked.

"I was the slave, not the sachem. The Shawnee love not the English like Johnson's Mohawks love the English or the Ottawas love the French. They feel the insult when the Mohawk pretend to speak for them. The Shawnee love themselves and will support the giver of the best prices or the winner of the last battle."

A political discussion followed between Goram and Corinne while Isaac and Matthew seethed and exchanged jealous glares. Corinne pointedly ignored both of them except when one disparaged the other, which would guarantee that the recipient of the slight received a smile or a caress from her. Gradually, their posture stiffened and the expression on their faces froze into mutual animosity.

"You think to laugh would hurt your faces. You are sober as Presbyterians on the cold Sunday morning," Corinne commented.

"I raised my sons sober," Goram replied gravely, "so they wouldn't starve. Work is sober. Prayer is sober. But we laugh just as much as the next family."

"No one has laughed in a year except moi," Corinne declared.

"We laugh at you," Goram said.

"You mock my Frenchified and my Shawnee ways, only you not laugh when I laugh."

"That's because you laugh too much and you mock everything and everybody," Matthew said.

Goram added, "If we laughed when you laughed then all we would do is laughing. No work, no sleep, no eating, only laughing."

Corinne's face darkened momentarily. "I cannot

breathe if I not laugh so I laugh and breathe and work." She stood up.

The evening ended on this unsatisfactory note.

Julian tried to persuade himself that he wasn't smitten while at the same time he kept finding excuses to delay his departure. He had seen plenty of men addled by a hopeless affection and was disappointed in himself. Corinne would soon choose one of Goram's sons—probably Isaac because he and Corinne couldn't say two words to each other without setting off sparks. Julian also had a nagging feeling of disloyalty to Blue Dove who he had believed was placed on earth to be his life companion. Pretty in a way that you would never tire of, funny in her ability to mimic people and animals, passionate in her surrender, her death had seemed to hollow out the part of him that could love. And, of course, her death seemed to prove Bragg's point that the jealous land wouldn't allow any rivals in matters of the heart. Since losing Blue Dove, Julian hadn't allowed himself feelings that might go anywhere near his heart.

Corinne did appear to harbor a certain affection for him, including him in the mild teasing she directed at Goram and his sons. She softened the "j" into a cat's purr when she called him Julian, her voice sometimes rising at the last syllable. Corinne would also search out Julian to explain herself or ask questions—how this made her happy, why she was worried about one of the brothers, what Indian nation had the most beautiful women—conversation too frivolous for the Goram breed of man. Her accent was always more pronounced then, dropping her h's and lengthening her i's as in, "I so am 'appee today."

"They're jealous, you know," Julian commented once after she described a wrestling match between Isaac and Matthew, which they had claimed was about who should clean the hogsty but really was about her.

"A new family with the three sisters more pretty than me, all untouched unlike me, make the homestead a mile away." She wriggled her nose as if trying to find it a comfortable place on her face, then frowned. "I not pretend I am the untouched woman with the husband. The brothers 'tis not possible they understand. They believe I am the angel of chastity. The father, I think 'tis possible he can."

On the fourth day, Corinne came down with a fever. The Gorams didn't show much concern. This fever apparently recurred several times a year and would pass with rest. After dreaming he smelled smoke, Julian woke with the conviction Corinne urgently needed his help. Afraid for her, he crept to the cabin door and whispered her name. He was about to call out to her when he suddenly realized that he couldn't continue nibbling at the forbidden fruit. He crawled back to his blanket and dreamed achingly of Blue Dove.

CHOICE

"Mastair… Julian, mastair… Julian," Corinne shook
him awake, panic making her English difficult to understand. It was late morning, at least for a farming family.
"Julee, father, 'e eez to fight John Thunder who challenge
Isaac. Father tie up Isaac, Matthew, and Joshua and sez 'e
go in 'is place. 'E forbade me untie them. Please, will you
'elp 'im."

Julian saddled his horse and started off at a gallop. He
had no idea how to dissuade the old man. It was an impossible fight. John Thunder was half his age. The injuries
from the gauntlet were still fresh. The best plan seemed to
do to Goram what Goram did to his sons—wrestle him
down, bind his hands and feet and, if necessary, take his
place. At least, he had the advantage of youth, of hearing
John Thunder boast about his tactics, and he fancied himself nearly as strong, although he couldn't dance around
with his twisted foot.

He caught up with Goram just as the old man was
entering the clearing where the Kean's cabins stood. John
Thunder filled the doorway then stepped out, stretching

his thickly muscled arms. Millie, naked, ran inside. Hugh emerged from the shed where they stored the whiskey with a jug in each hand.

"I hear tell the savages had some sport with you," Hugh commented, anticipatory delight spreading across his face as he set down the jugs and made himself comfortable on the porch.

"I'm here to fight in the stead of my son," Goram stated.

By this time, Julian had interposed his horse between them. He addressed Goram, "John will rip you apart. Let me take him on."

Goram stepped in front of the horse. "Back off. What sort of man would I be to let you fight for my son?"

Hugh chuckled. "The old man's right, and pap won't be so pleased if John walloped our best customer. Besides, John will just be finishing what the Creeks begun."

Goram grimaced as if remembering the pain of the gauntlet. "Where do we box?"

Hugh rubbed his hands together. "Box, you say? Well, you may call it that. We box right here. Mind you, John don't think the fight is done till you lose something significant to you like a nose, eye, ear, or your balls, so even if you say you're licked, you're obliged to stand there and let John choose what he will take from you. If you run away before the fight is over, when we catch you, he takes two parts from you."

Goram stood stiffly. "I hear you like to wager. Three Dutch pounds you get if you win. If I win, I want you never to molest my sons or Corinne again."

"Three Dutch pounds and one little pretty French wench. Come to think of it, you can keep your pounds.

When we feed your balls to the pigs, you might want to hold on to your currency to buy another pair." Hugh shook his head. "You're a brave old man, but you're as stupid as a pile of fresh horseshit."

Julian dismounted and tethered his horse, still intent on intervening before much harm could be done. John and Goram stepped into the clearing in front of the cabin. The father tottered out of the fermentation shed and sat on the stoop. Millie returned dressed in one of the long blouses of her brothers. John Thunder roared with pleasure, then stripped off his shirt revealing chest and shoulders thickly knotted with muscles. Goram stared for a moment, hesitated as if he wanted to change his mind and then began to take off his coat.

Hugh yelled, "On the count of three the contest begins. Three!"

John lunged forward swiping at Goram with his sharpened nails. Arms still in coat sleeves, Goram stepped to the side and John Thunder missed. Before he was able to free his hands, the giant charged again, roaring. Goram dropped to his knees and John tripped over him. Then with John kneeling on the ground, Goram wrapped the coat around John's head as he disengaged his hands and in less than a second landed three blows on the blinded face. John threw the coat down and roared again.

"You're a cunning old fart. I give you that." He then whooped with delight, "Nothing makes life so glad like a good tussle."

John Thunder circled around Goram, reaching out with sharpened nails, like a cat pawing at a dangling watch, then approached directly with the same pawing motion, backing the old farmer slowly toward the wall of the cabin. Hugh placed himself to the side preventing an avenue of escape. Julian prepared to intervene as the space for Goram to maneuver diminished. Suddenly, Goram went on the attack landing four blows to the stomach that actually staggered the giant. The nails grazed Goram's shoulder, tearing his linen shirt off him. Julian hadn't gotten a good look at Goram in the Indian village. Now, as the shirt fell to the dirt, he saw a leanly muscled physique quite the opposite of John Thunder's knots and bunches. The Keans seemed surprised also.

"It appears you is no stranger to bruising your knuckles," Hugh said.

Goram smiled coldly. "This young dog here only picks fights with boys he's sure to lick. He is too much a coward to challenge a man that were his match."

John Thunder, now quite red in the face and panting heavily, began the process of trying to corner Goram again. "This ain't finished till I take your tongue and your balls, old man."

"Trying to scare me with words? Words are just breath and breath is naught, lest…" Goram suddenly lowered his head and rammed John Thunder in the stomach knocking him on his rear end. "You don't have it."

John Thunder got up, his huge chest heaving. Goram bared his teeth in a sneer as he let the giant recover. Then John rushed, clawing viciously like a badger or an enraged bear. Several streaks of blood sprung up on Goram's chest. Goram countered and John reflexively held his arms up to face. Goram's blows were a quick blur and Julian was uncertain whether the farmer had landed any until he saw blood dripping from Thunder's lips and nose. John wiped his arm across his face. His eyes widened when he saw the blood on his forearm. Goram attacked again, a dozen blows landing with dizzying speed.

And so, the fight went on. Julian could not tell how long John Thunder suffered the beating before he staggered to his knees. It seemed like hours, however probably didn't last more than ten minutes. Thunder showed his mettle by refusing to go all the way down, even though eventually he stopped trying to claw Goram because not only was it futile but it opened him up for effective counterattack.

All the while, Goram also tore into him with insults, calling John a fool, a coward, a jackanapes, an asshole, a whoreson dog. When Goram began to tire, he took more time delivering the punishment. Still, Thunder didn't fall. "You'll see me in bloody hell afore you see me go down. I am a rock. I will die standing," Thunder proclaimed through his bloody lips and broken nose.

"'Tis not my intention to kill you. I'm just making sure you never forget your match with a real man."

Thunder tried to trick Goram once, inviting a closer approach by pretending to stagger. Goram read the move and when Thunder lashed out ducked and caught him in the belly—his soft spot—with a large bony fist. Millie wept uncontrollably as her brother sank to his knees once again. Hugh stood gaping, too astounded to speak. Old Kean chuckled, appearing to enjoy the display.

Thunder rose, staggered, slipped to his knees, raised himself, rushed Goram swinging blindly, hit the wall of the cabin, turned around stunned, opened his bloody mouth with several new gaps and screamed, "I'm not down yet!"

In the next encounter, Goram kicked him behind the knee causing John Thunder to fall on his rear. "I'm not down yet! I'm getting up." He rolled onto his side and got up, dug his claws into his own face. "You can't keep me down, no you can't."

"You're punished enough for my purposes," Goram declared.

"I'm still holding my ground. You leave, I win," John Thunder shouted through his bloodied mouth.

"Do you want me to cripple you?"

"You can never make me stay down." John beat his chest.

Goram addressed Old Kean: "I can cripple him so he won't ever walk right again, or if you say he lost, I can walk away. As of now, 'twill be several fortnights ere he'll be of use to anybody."

The old man spat out a hunk of tobacco. "A few fortnights? For twenty-four years, he's not been good for nothing except riling neighbors. Seems to me gimping him be plain justice."

Goram turned toward Thunder who, sheathed in blood and sweat, swayed in the effort to keep on his feet. "You lost because I say you lost. You dare molest my sons or Corinne again, you won't get a chance to fight me. I'll kill you and I'll kill your pigs, and I'll destroy your still, and I'll burn down your cabin." Goram turned toward Hugh and the father. "Keep him away from me lest you want to suffer my wrath."

"Gimp him, I told you. 'Twould give me pleasure," Old Kean cried out.

Goram mounted the horse.

"I said gimp him," the old man shouted. "Gimp him, gimp him," he continued as Goram rode away followed by Julian.

Goram didn't wait until Julian asked the question he obviously was going to ask. Heaving a sigh, he said, "I was born into a family of day laborers. That meant we'd work like slaves eight months a year and starve and freeze like beggars four. At the age of sixteen, at least I think I was sixteen, not having letters at that time and as ignorant as the beasts of the field, I decided I might do better and ran away to London. I guess I wanted to work on the docks or become a sailor or anything but a tool of other men's fortunes. It didn't enter my noggin there were thousands of dull clods like me with the same wish.

"Four pence and a growling stomach was all I possessed when I came upon this giant man in the middle of the crowd claiming he could knock anybody down standing face to face with him in less than a minute. If you was on your feet at the end of that time, you won four pence. If you wasn't, you lost four pence. I saw two burly roughs accept his challenge. He felled them as easily as swatting a fly. Then I took him up even though he was half a head taller and half a shoulder broader than me. I didn't know nothing about fighting, only I knew eight pennies was more than four pennies, and I was strong. He landed a dozen blows, handling me as badly as I handled John Thunder, but I stood my ground and returned to him a measure of what he was giving me. The minute ran out and I still stood trading blows. Finally, I knocked him to the dirt and told him I wanted his four pence. He started to laugh. 'Four pence? You want four pence, you say. Come with me boy, and I'll make you so rich as Croesus.'

"I never heard of Croesus, but I knew he must have more money than me so I went with him. Barry was his name. Barry taught me the art of pugilism. He entered me into bare-knuckle competitions. I won most. For two years, I fought once a week, and the rest of the time I trained. I was so quick that my nose was never broke, my ears never turned inside out like cauliflowers. Barry and I made a lot of money. I ate my fill at every meal. I slept warm and dry. I owned four suits of clothes. I afforded the whores with smooth skin and sweet voices.

"Likely, I would have stayed a pugilist until somebody better beat my brains out, but then two events changed my life—no it was three events. I broke the neck of a country boy in a match, a boy new come into London like I once did, which greatly weighed on my conscience. Barry was nabbed by a press gang, and I met Evelyn. Really, I met her father first. He came to the inn where I stayed and was as sorry a sight I ever beheld in a man. He related to me how his daughter was took advantage of by this wealthy swain. Well, the swain made promises only a silly girl couldn't see through. When she discovered that she was with child, instead of telling her parents, she ran off to London to confront her seducer and hold him to his promises. The swain's manservant laughed in her face when she appeared at the door, telling her his master was already engaged to a young lady of quality, and he didn't like harlots on his doorstep, but since she looked hungry and mangy, if she went around back, the cook might portion her an old heel of bread to eat.

"Learning of his daughter's predicament, the father followed her. He also attempted to interview the young swain, which ended with two footmen tweaking his nose and kicking him down the street. Still desiring an audience with this so-called gentleman, he offered to hire me to protect him and Evelyn from the scoundrel's lackeys while they talked. After I agreed, I met his daughter who was now staying with her father at an inn. I would not call Evelyn a great beauty, nay, yet she had this smile and these eyes you could spend a life with.

"I asked the father to allow me to manage the affair. I found out where the rascal liked to tipple with his friends. Like many young highborns, he thought it vulgar to pay his gambling and merchant debts. I also offered my services to several of his creditors to collect on those debts. A famous pugilist gets better attention than a humble tradesman. I went to the tavern where he was amusing himself, batted aside his companions, a few of which I was collecting for, told him I was there to help him settle his debts and dragged him off kicking and shouting. He sputtered and protested, threatened me with the law and the Royal Navy. I bundled him into another tavern where Evelyn and her father waited. I knew his type well. Take away the braggadocio and his title and he's merely a tissue of a man, a name dressed in fancy clothes and naught else. On seeing Evelyn, the swain climbed on his high horse and proclaimed that he certainly wasn't the first to plow her field and accused her of trying to saddle him with another man's brat.

"Evelyn kept her poise throughout these vile insults and accusations and then asked, 'Does it bother you that you're such a coward?'

"After laughing at her and saying, 'You welcomed my cock so lustily as any East End whore," he stood to leave.

"I told him the interview wasn't over until he either agreed to marry Evelyn or paid the debts of his creditors which I represented in full. He tried to draw a dagger. I only struck him once, and he toppled to the floor. I emptied the money out of his pockets, pulled the rings off his fingers and stripped him of everything of value, including his boots and silk waistcoat. The tavern owner, a friend, wrote the items down and gave him a receipt. I warned him as he ran away that the next time he crossed my path, I'd strip him to his drawers and sell his clothes to pay off more of his debts.

"And do you know what Evelyn said after all this?" Goram shook his head in amazement. "She said, 'He'll never marry me now.' I told her he never was intending to marry her anyway. 'Well, what am I to do,' she cried, looking about as foolish as a woman can.

"'I'll marry you,' I said not thinking about what I was saying.

"She replied tartly, 'I can't marry you. You're stupid and ugly.' Those were her words.

"'And you're with another man's child,' her father reminded her. 'And I don't think he's stupid despite his station.'

"Evelyn looked at me hard for the first time and said, 'He's a man who earns his living beating the brains out of other men. Eventually, somebody will beat his brains out, and then what will I do?'

"I told her 'twas true I was ignorant and beneath her. 'That is the fault of birth,' I said. 'For my first sixteen years I labored in the fields with my father and brothers so I know as much about working a farm as any man, and I can boast a savings of three hundred pounds from my winnings, which is more than some have who claim to be gentlemen.'

"Evelyn wasn't finished challenging me. Glaring, she went on, 'So when I thrust into your arms another man's brat, will you hit me for being unfaithful?'

"I told her that I'd never lay a hand on her, but since she was so opposed to my offer, I didn't see why we was discussing the matter. She and her father then left. I had put it into my head to forget them when two days later they appeared at my rooms.

"Evelyn blushed and said, 'I changed my mind. You'll do if your proposal stands.'

"I wasn't too sure so I asked, 'Why are you altered in your opinion, especially since you consider me slow of reasoning and not so pretty as the swain who got you with child?'

"'Us sinful folk always cast the first stones,' she said. 'Forgive my unkindness. I promise you will never regret marrying me.' Then she laughed and took my hand. 'Don't look so glum. I'm a silly girl, but I will make a good wife to a good man.'

"That was the thing about Evelyn. In whatever place she found herself, she made the best of it. We married quickly, then left England to start a life away from wagging tongues. She was right: I never regretted marrying her. She got used to my ugly gob, and I could farm as well as any man, and after teaching me my letters, she came to realize I had wit enough."

When they arrived at the cabin, Goram put on a new shirt, sat down at the table and asked for a tumbler of cider. Matthew, Joshua, and Isaac also seated themselves. "Why are my sons untied?" he asked.

"*C'est moi*," Corinne declared. "When they swear they not follow you."

"So you sent Julian to drag me back instead of them."

Corinne's defiant smile answered that he didn't forbid her to do that.

"What happened at the Keans?" Isaac asked.

"John Thunder and I have come to an agreement that he stays away," Goram answered grimly.

"John Thunder isn't the type to listen to reason," Matthew said.

"With some men you have to reason harder than with others," Goram replied, then taking a great gulp of the cider announced, "I've had enough of this poisonous rivalry between my sons. I don't blame you, Corinne. 'Tis my sons' foolishness that sowed this dissension. Each is trying to prove himself the better man. You are good, Corinne, only when you show favor to one, t'other two hate him. A family must work together. For that reason, I am asking you to make a choice. T'others will reconcile themselves to your decision. Within a day's walk, there are a dozen fine women they can court. So, who takes your fancy? Isaac, Joshua, or Matthew?"

Corinne flushed. "I love all three... as brothers. Do not ask me the choice. I'm so sorry for the trouble I make. I scar the face so they not think me pretty." She seemed to exaggerate her habit of tilting her head to the side.

Goram frowned. "You shan't suffer for what's not your

fault. You are as much a blessing to our family as any woman could be."

"But I no want to marry nobody."

"My three fools may accept your resolution for a while, but by and by, they'll start scheming to change your mind," Goram insisted.

"Just keep me as I am. We live together for three years, we make the same life for always, *non*? I become the sister who never marry, *non*?" She wiped her forearm across her eyes.

"If you marry one, you are a sister for the others. You may think about it a fortnight, but you must choose at the end of the time." Goram struck the table with his fist indicating the finality of his decision.

Corinne stood, shoulders squared, eyes hardening. "If I must choose, then I do not need to think. I choose you."

Goram's stare locked with hers. "I'm not part of the offer."

"I choose you, I say. Your sons, they find the wives elsewhere and not make jealousy for each other."

"I said choose one of my sons." Goram raised his voice.

"You are the stubborn father with the stubborn sons— stubborn in the love, the hate, and the jealousy. The one I marry, the others will hate, but they will not hate you. I can be with the family I love the rest of my life and give you more the stubborn sons and daughters."

Goram spent a small eternity in deep thought. "Nay, Corinne. 'Tis not that I'm blind to your beauty. When I brought you here, the thought occurred to me to make you into my wife. But you were frightened and so young, I thought it better to treat you as a daughter."

"Your way of thinking you can change," she begged.

He slowly reached out his hand and caressed her hair. "No, dearest. I want you to give me grandchildren, not children."

Corinne shook her head violently. "Well, if you are forcing me, then I choose him." She pointed to Julian who didn't quite comprehend the turn this family quarrel had taken.

Goram riveted his gray eyes on Julian in disbelief then looked at his sons. "Corinne, here is three good men who will love and support you all the days of your life."

"You force me to choose, so I choose." She kept her trembling finger aimed at Julian.

"What sort of husband is that gypsy with a clubbed foot going to make? He'll drag you all over the frontier then trade you back to the savages for a parcel of furs," Joshua said, his dark skin mottling with anger.

"And he'll owe us four years remaining on your indenture," Isaac added. "He don't have a penny to his name."

"My indenture, you will buy, Master Julian?" Julian could feel Corinne's eyes searching to meet his.

"Forty pounds," Joshua insisted, obviously reaching for a figure beyond Julian's means.

"I pay the forty pounds," Julian replied slowly, certain that the exorbitant sum was buying trouble, yet not certain what exactly the trouble was.

"Joshua and I owe him our lives." Goram's voice had harshened into that of an old man. He glanced around as if searching for a way out of the dilemma.

"The club foot will not have her for nothing!" Joshua was unnervingly staring at the musket by the door.

"We don't have to sell her bond, so we won't." Matthew pounded his fist on the table.

Goram raised his hand. A tense silence followed. "If Corinne wishes to leave us and he willing to pay, then I won't keep her against her will."

"Choose me, father, so I stay." Corinne rubbed both eyes, not quite catching all her tears.

"Corinne, you won't find better men than my sons. I cannot say this Julian is bad, but he has no family, no land, no roots. He spends his time with savages who made you suffer. He'll bring more suffering into your life. My sons I vouch for."

"I vouch for them too," Corinne said wildly. "With all the heart, I vouch, only I will not choose one over the others."

"But you would marry me over my sons?"

"Do you no understand that is the choice of the heart?" Corinne pleaded. "I own so great an affection for you as for any man who ever live."

"And Julian here, is he also a choice of your heart?" Isaac asked bitterly

"Julian, he is not a cruel man. I will be his servant and obey him."

"And if he commands you to bed him, will you do that? Will you?" Matthew said, his voice lowering, his hands flexing and closing into fists repeatedly.

"The woman you want to marry, she do worse," Corinne whispered.

"Do you expect me to believe that?" Isaac said.

"I am the slave of the Shawnee. What do you think that means?" Corinne blushed. "I am the mother of a

Shawnee boy. Proud sons of Goram, you still desire the mother of the savage child?"

A struggle to not comprehend what she was saying registered on the faces of Goram's sons.

"Any son who thinks that matters leave the table," Goram announced.

None did, although they all bent their heads in concentrated stubbornness.

The force of Goram's large fist shook the table. "Julian is departing on the morrow. If you won't marry my sons, Corinne, then go with him and be damned."

Julian didn't expect Corinne to hold to her decision. Although he had lost part of his heart to her, she had chosen in anger, and he doubted whether she could share his vagabond life. Isaac would likely win her hand in the end, a boy teetering on the edge of manhood, full of intensity and good intentions, capable of arresting Corinne's gaze a little longer than the other brothers, and capable, Julian believed, of considering her Shawnee son as having less consequence. Hence, he was surprised to be awakened in the early morning by her hand on his shoulder, "Will you bring me to my Eagle Heart?"

Julian groggily sat up. "I can do that, only for what purpose? The Shawnee won't give him up. They might enslave you again."

"I then become the slave for my Eagle Heart. Maybe Bright Flower is dead. Maybe White Bear, he will want me as the wife. Maybe not. I am French, then I am Shawnee, then I am English. No matter to me what I am. The only matter is I am allowed to stay. If I am allowed to stay, I do all in my power to make you the most favored trader."

"Choose Isaac. You prefer him."

"Beautiful Isaac, he is just the boy. A boy cannot protect me in the world where men like John Thunder live." Corinne made a tearing gesture with her hands. "Master Goram beat John Thunder bad, non?"

"True, Goram could have crippled him for life, I warrant he even could have killed him."

"But he did not. Goram is so gentle and so strong. His sons, they are good men, hardworking men." Corinne shook her head. "At times I weep because to be good and hardworking, 'tis not enough. You need…" She rubbed her eyes, "You must have the strength… here." She folded her hands over her heart. "Goram is strong. Beautiful Isaac is good and hardworking, yet he has not the strength… here."

Worried now, yet also relieved that Corinne wouldn't become someone whose loss he would grieve, Julian no longer slept.

CHINOOTA

THEY LEFT AFTER Julian counted out the outrageous payment of thirty pounds—the difference compensating for what he paid to ransom Goram and Joshua—and placed it on the rock because Goram refused to touch the money. The chill, the dead gray sky reflected the mood of the father, his sons, and Corinne. She refused to mount the horse at first. "I walk fast. The horse, I not ride."

Julian didn't want to argue just yet. Corinne managed to keep up for a few miles, then she doubled up and vomited. "I can take you back to the Gorams," Julian offered, watching her shake and hold herself, then wash off her face with water from a stagnant pond. "I wager the money is still on the rock."

Corinne lifted her head showing her teary bloodshot eyes. "You break the promise to take me to Chinoota?"

"I keep promises if I can, but you must ride, not walk."

She mounted, grimacing as she awkwardly draped her legs over the left side of the horse. Managing a smile, she patted the horse's neck. "You the gentle horse, I the gentle master."

"We leave the horses at the Moravian mission, then travel by canoe to Chinoota," Julian said. "'Tisn't more than a three-day trip."

After riding half the morning in silence, Corinne suddenly announced, "You may treat me as the wife until we come to Chinoota."

"Only if you treat me as a husband," Julian replied, somewhat taken aback. Her voice was heavy with obligation, not desire.

"I obey you in everything until Chinoota," Corinne replied solemnly.

"In what I've observed, few wives obey husbands in everything."

"I know not how to be the wife, then," she whispered, refusing to look him in the eye.

They were silent again which lasted until nightfall.

Julian didn't take advantage of her offer, not because of a strenuous sense of virtue or lack of desire, but because with her lowered head and silent fits of weeping, he would be pouring salt into an open wound. He asked Corinne again if she wanted to return, and she responded by vigorously shaking her head and muttering, "*Non, non, non.* I to see Eagle Heart."

When they stopped to make camp, she refused to allow him to lift a finger. She hobbled the horses, made the fire, put on the pot for tea. He noticed that she never sat properly but always knelt or lay on her side. As the evening sky unrolled its carpet of stars, Corinne whispered, "You have not the desire for me?"

"Hugh Kean was right to call you a famous beauty, but I won't bed a woman who isn't well disposed towards me."

"Why is that the matter? I am to be the Shawnee's harlot if they accept me. You pay too so much money for me. How can I no give you what you want?"

Julian thought of the various Indian women he had shared a blanket with, some beauties, although only Blue Dove matched Corinne. Most had had a sense of fun that was completely absent from Corinne's submission out of obligation. The French girl of smiles and laughter had vanished. "I did not think I bought your bond for that."

Corinne frowned. "You are to sell me, then?"

"We are traveling to Chinoota so you will be with your son. If the Shawnee do not take you in, then I return you to the Gorams. I will get out of the way, and you can puzzle out your differences."

"You are the liar. You bought me to have me. Thank you, Julian," She pronounced his name with her endearing softening of the consonants. "I dream about Eagle Heart every day. What he is doing now? Is he learning to hunt? Is he sleeping? What is he eating? Is he dreaming of the woman with hair of the honey-gold?"

Julian's uncomfortable abstinence might have continued into the third night had not a branch caught the fabric of Corinne's dress, making a tear in the bodice. He caught a glimpse of a perfect breast before turning his head. Corinne dismounted and changed while muttering in French and English something about extra chores. That night, with all of his senses keyed to her softly breathing presence three feet away, Julian couldn't sleep. Gazing at her face in the low firelight, he thought Goram a complete fool.

"I need a wife now if you're still willing," he whispered as soon as her eyes flickered open in the morning.

Corinne nodded unsurprised. She somberly got up, slipped off her dress and shift, her naked body—beautiful warm roundnesses of breasts and buttocks—shivering in the dawn coolness. She knelt down, then lay next to him. When he first kissed her lips, they tightened, then softened just enough to return the kiss. She was obedient, docile, and unresponsive. The act was wordless. She groaned several times as she received him stiffly. Julian regretted that he had given in to his desire. When he finished, Corinne rose, walked over to a nearby creek, and bathed herself in the cold water. Returning, she put on her dress and started the morning chores. Julian was glad that either the Shawnee or the Gorams would take her off his hands soon.

After half a day of easy canoeing with the current, they arrived at Chinoota. Girard, his face painted red and black, accompanied them the last mile leading several other canoes of warriors, making Julian feel like a boar nipped at the hooves by hounds. Having exhausted the local firewood supply where the old village stood, the tribe moved the palisades, the wigwams, the timbers of the council house five miles down the same river. Chinoota still prospered—the seventy wigwams were surrounded by extensive fields. The Shawnee were nominally pro-British or at least neutral, yet they would have also received the same black wampum belt as the Creeks. They had sufficient reasons to join a war. Settlers were closing in. Disputes would have already occurred. Girard and White Bear weren't the sort of men to change their opinions. When they saw their advantage, they would pick up the war hatchet and cut a wide swath of carnage across the frontier. Julian hoped they hadn't decided quite yet.

Landing on the incline in front of the gate, Julian stepped ashore and helped Corinne out of the canoe. Scalps hung on the palisades, some of the fresher ones blond. Julian remembered the Dutch family that had disappeared. They were soon surrounded when braves from the village and squaws and children from the fields joined Girard's warriors who had disembarked at the same time. White Bear met them at the gate. Corinne started talking to him hesitantly, then more hurriedly in a pleading tone. White Bear suddenly struck Corinne, knocking her to the ground, and bloodying her lip. She lay on her side looking down, weeping.

"Where's Hilda?" Julian called out as he stepped in front of Corinne. "Where is she?"

David Gray Thrush emerged from the crowd. He was diminished, hollowed-out, no longer having the presence that marked him as a future sachem. "Hilda is dead. I translate for you, English Rat, if you haven't forgot your Lenape."

"I remember my Lenape. I am happy you are well," Julian replied.

David Gray Thrush nodded and pointed to the scalps. "White Bear says those belonged to a French family. He says he adds now the scalp of Torn Feather."

"Those scalps belonged to a Dutch family. There are no French families hereabouts. Torn Feather is my servant.

I am English so she is English. To harm her is to make war on England." Julian and White Bear measured each other.

White Bear replied, speaking slowly and not hiding his contempt while David Gray Thrush translated, "We do not know whether you are telling the truth, but we ask ourselves, why do you let your servant beg to become our slave?"

"'Tis her wish to be near her son. Torn Feather is the mother of Eagle Heart. 'Tis my wish to help her."

"Torn Feather comes to steal the boy." White Bear pushed Julian out of the way and stood over Corinne as he spoke, preventing her from getting up. David Gray Thrush kept by his side. "Before she became big with child, she escaped two times. Second time I cut off her small toe." White Bear made a sawing motion. "I told her I cut off all her toes, if she escapes again. She pretends to be Shawnee, but when we are not looking, she will steal Eagle Heart."

Sensing that arguing further courted disaster, Julian said, "Let Corinne at least see her son; afterward, we go."

Julian then bent down, lifted Corinne to her feet and away from White Bear. White Bear took a step forward and made to strike her again. Girard sidled besides White Bear, and David Gray Thrush unsheathed his knife. Keeping hold of her waist, Julian pulled Corinne toward the river, the crowd grudgingly letting them pass.

"Julian, I wish to stay," Corinne cried, trying to shake free, stopping their progress. "I wish to make the life here like before."

"No life nor son here for you, slave," White Bear sneered in thick English. With unaccountable scorn, the squaws started to heap insults on Corinne.

A squaw with eyes that were angry black dots and who pecked at the air with her sharp features elbowed herself forward. David Gray Thrush translated her screeches: "The slave, Torn Feather, has no son here. We gave her a child to watch over. She fell asleep, and the river swollen by rains took him away so the child of her womb belongs to us."

"I am the Shawnee," Corinne cried. "You cannot deny I am."

"You are slave. Shawnees aren't slaves," Girard responded, rubbing his thumb along the blade of his knife.

A sturdy little boy with flaxen hair slipped between the adults. Looking at Corinne, he gave a child's shrill version of an Indian war whoop and ran away giggling. Corinne stared after the vanishing boy, then asked White Bear, "You love him?"

White Bear gave a bare nod. "He is my son. You have now seen the child of your womb. Go."

Girard blocked their retreat, his whole posture showing imminent violence. Julian challenged him, "You know who I am. You know I never harmed you or any Shawnee. You know the esteem that William Johnson and the Six Nations hold me in. The Shawnee are a great people like the people of the Six Nations, and as a great nation you must treat the friend of another great nation with respect."

Girard spat. "Chief Brant and William Johnson call us women. We owe them no favors. The only reason I am not nailing your scalp to the post is because you are the brother of Resurrection Peter, who is the brother of the great sachem, Mist-on-the-hills. Do not come here again. That is expecting too much forbearance."

David Gray Thrush added, "My wish is that you die

ten deaths, English Rat, if it were in my power. Ten long deaths for the death of Little Heron."

As they paddled up the river, Corinne recounted the incident of the drowned child: "They give me the little boy, Yellow Cloud, to watch. I close the eyes because I am so tired. When I open the eyes again, he is running away from me. I tell him stop and he say he will not obey the slave. I am heavy with child and cannot catch him. He run into the river. I run into the river. The river, he carries us away. I grab Yellow Cloud, but he bites me saying he is not going to obey the slave. I do not drown." Her shoulders heaved with a dry sob, then she said, "Take me back to Goram. I am certain they have not touched the money. If I must choose, the choice is Joshua."

"Why Joshua?"

Corinne's smile seemed more directed inward than outward. "He is like me. He is not the Goram's son and I am not the Goram's daughter, yet we both are the first to stand with him."

"How did you know Joshua wasn't Goram's son?" Julian asked.

"I live with the family three years. In him, I no see no thing like the father, no little thing except the kindness. I marry him so I no see every night in the bed the face like the face of the man I truly love." She then added, "I am not the wife to you tonight."

Julian didn't really consider her wooden surrender to him as wife-like. "As you wish. I am sorry that my flesh was weak and I…" Julian didn't believe the words existed to finish the sentence. "I will say nothing about what happened. I need to pick up my furs and packhorses before we return. They are being kept by a friend."

In truth, Julian had become fed up with the backcountry. He yearned for a warm inn, a responsive woman, the company of people with experiences different from his, and to be far away from the wilderness populated by dangerous creatures—animals and men.

"Who is this friend you trust with the furs and horses?" Corinne asked.

"Resurrection Peter."

"The escaped slave outlaw?"

"That outlaw saved our lives at Chinoota."

THE CONTAGION OF WAR

PETER HAD MOVED forty miles beyond the settlements and was already scouting out other sites further west. His boast that he always kept his people safe was still true however not uttered with the same confidence. Julian wasn't allowed to approach the village alone, rather he would camp in a field where Peter would meet him and escort him after making sure no unwanted stranger was near. When they made camp in the field, Corinne's only question was "How long?"

Julian answered, "Never more than three days."

"If you sell me to the friend, I kill myself," She said with a deadened tone.

"You have no reason to doubt my word, Corinne," Julian replied angrily.

"Why do I think the bad thing can happen?"

On dutifully finishing her chores, Corinne would wander off to lay by a stream making it clear she didn't want company. Having the leisure to observe her, Julian realized what was odd about Corinne's behavior. She always avoided sitting. She either stood, knelt, or lay on her side which she had done for the entire canoe trip to Chinoota. From time to time, she would inhale sharply with a yip and her eyes would go blank. The second day, early in the morning, Julian came upon her crying, rubbing her thigh, and he realized she was in great pain. That evening, after she saw to the horses, made the fire, heated the water, and started to cook a stew of rabbit and beans, he asked, "What's the matter with your legs, Corinne?"

"There is nothing wrong with the legs." Her gaze was prickly.

"Why don't you ever sit down?"

"'Tis not my way."

"Why isn't it your way?" Julian insisted.

A red wave suffused her face. "The questions you ask, a man must not ask the woman." She muttered something about more firewood and left.

When she returned with her load, Julian said, "'Tis plain to the dullest eye you are in pain."

"Woman born to suffer the pain," she answered coldly.

"Not pain that keeps you from sitting."

"Six nights ago, when you see my body, you see the ugliness in her? Any scars or blemish except I have no small toe? I show you her again, so you have the certainty." Her disdain for his desire was unmistakable.

Julian's temper surged. "Damn you! Either sit like I'm sitting or explain why you can't."

She stared at him defiantly, then shuddered. "No person can cure what is the wrong with me. I no want talk of it."

"Tell me, then I will stop asking you," Julian promised.

"So you understand what the poor bargain you make

when you buy me? You see Bright Flower, the wife of White Bear. She hate me from the first day and beat me always. She cut off the toe not White Bear. After that, White Bear command Bright Flower not to make the scar on me again. She can punish me but leave no mark. My skin is too beautiful for the scars, he say. The compliment, it gives Bright Flower the jealous rage. White Bear, he is away hunting. She take the small bones the squaws use for the stitching. She split them down the middle so they are like the needle, then she break them so they are the size of this." Corinne held out her little finger. "Bright Flower tie me down and then deep into me, she push the little needles. She keep me tied down for six days so the skin heal over them and White Bear see no scar. She put them in…" Corinne's blush intensified, "in places so I feel the pain when he take me. When I sit like you sit, the pain make so much, all I can do is not scream."

"How many?"

"Seven, but two come out."

"And Goram never knew?"

"Only you, and you can do nothing for it, so what is the use?" She shrugged her shoulders although there were tears in her eyes.

"When we…"

"*Mais oui*, good master. When you bed me, the five needles, I feel them burn like poison fire inside me, but you not hear me cry, non?"

"Oh, God, I'm so sorry."

"What use is the sorry? 'Tis what I am." She looked away indicating the conversation was over.

Julian wanted to shout, 'No, 'tisn't,' but that wasn't

true. The pain would be part of her as long as the needles remained buried. The jealous squaw who pecked the air had determined that Corinne would suffer the rest of her life. Julian determined to also leave a mark on this woman who now was trembling with the effort not to cry in front of him—a mark that she could never deny. There was no cure except extracting the needles. No surgeon or doctor that he had ever met or heard of possessed such skill.

However, one man whose strange odyssey gave him special knowledge of the human body might.

Peter arrived the following day with Jeremy, his youngest son, trailing the packhorses. Two of his three daughters had died, one from smallpox, the other from a snakebite; however, those tragedies were long enough ago that the grief had retreated to two deep lines etched in his forehead. Peter grinned broadly when he saw Corinne and tipped his cap. "Julian little slow at introductions. I Peter, ma'am."

"I am Corinne, sir," Corinne responded shyly.

"I taking extra lead and powder, Julian. We settle accounts next time you swing through."

"I have further business I want to propose to you." Julian took Peter off to the side and explained Corinne's plight.

"Poor lass," Peter said softly, then blew air out in a half whistle and continued, "I no saying Billiam can do it. Hell finding them splinters and hundred hells digging them out … I no saying. Come back with us. Billiam needing to look at the poor lass."

"Do you give me the choice?" Corinne asked when

Julian explained that they were going to Peter's village. Julian did not give the real reason because he sensed the less said to Corinne in her present contrary mood, the better.

"I promise you'll be back at Goram's farm within a fortnight."

"No promise," she said bitterly. "My father, he promise always to protect me. White Bear, he promise I become the wife. Goram, he promise that I always have a home."

When they arrived at the village, Peter immediately consulted Mussulman Billiam. After a quarter hour, Billiam emerged with Owl Woman and took Corinne by the hand saying in his uneven voice, "We looking for them needles, Miss."

Julian had expected resistance, but not quite the explosion that followed. Corinne tore her arm away from Billiam and screamed. "*Non, non, non.* No hand touch me. *Aucune personne! Aucune personne!*" She ran to the horse and tried to mount it, but the sudden movement apparently agitated the needles and she bent double, pressing her hands to the top of her thighs. "Eez the lie. I no feel hurt. I have no needles in me. 'Eez the lie, the lie. I want Julian think me the damaged property. *Ecoutez-moi! Je ments!*"

Owl Woman took her hand and firmly pulled her toward the wigwam. Corinne thrashed and struggled, but the old bent squaw was more than a match and dragged her inside. When Julian tried to follow, Corinne spat at him. "*Allez-vous*, Go away, you serpent. You vile snake. Seeing you makes me want to scratch out the eyes."

Julian waited with Peter outside the wigwam listening to Corinne, losing the contest, subsiding into sobs and heavy breathing. Then began an endless pleading repetition of "Mon Dieu, Mon Dieu, Mon Dieu," as Billiam and the Owl woman examined her. Every once in a while, Corinne emitted a gasping scream, and Billiam would reply in French with what sounded like comforting words. Several hours later Owl Woman emerged, exhausted and shaking her head.

"Can Billiam take out the needles?" Julian asked.

Owl Woman knelt on the ground and drew a figure in the dirt. "Billiam need this. Wide net. Strong so not break."

"Can Billiam get out the needles?" Julian repeated the question.

Owl woman's flecks of obsidian between the heavy folds of her eyelids regarded him. "Billiam ken three needles. After he cut much blood. We work here." Owl woman pointed to open space where Ivan had been tied to the post, "in the light of the sun."

"What's the net for?" Julian indicated the figure in the dirt.

"Billiam bind girl so she cannot move. Need plenty whiskey." Owl Woman cast a significant glance at the keg on a packhorse. Julian unstrapped the keg and handed it to her.

Peter turned to Owl Woman. "Tell Billiam go gentle."

"Nay, I tell Billiam make fingers fast like lightning."

While inside the wigwam Owl Woman plied Corinne with whiskey, Mussulman Billiam sat outside sharpening his knives, critically examining his tweezers and forceps and directing the construction of the frame. Detesting whiskey, Corinne's cries were almost as loud as during her examination. When all was ready, Owl Woman led out the swaying Corinne wrapped in a blanket. Billiam ordered the square cleared except for Harriet who was given the job of keeping the curious away. Julian and Peter retreated to Peter's wigwam.

First they heard Corinne's voice rising, "*Non, non, non, non. Mon Dieu, mon Dieu, mon Dieu.*" Then a blood-chilling scream stopped Julian's heart, followed by, "*Aleckhallee. Aleckhallee.*"

"That Shawnee for 'get away, you devil,'" Peter commented. "Poor lass, poor poor lass." The wild screams continued slowing time to a crawl, then subsided into hoarse coughing punctuated by whimpers.

A half hour later, Billiam entered the wigwam blood-smeared and grinning with three small bloody bone needles on his open palm. "These the little devils. T'other two not so much. Took a while knowing where to dig. I suss out them needles pressing her skin this way and that. When she curse God for living I near. When she curse me to hell I not. When I finding where the little devil lies, I cut the skin just so," He held up his forefinger and thumb showing a half inch gap, "dig quickly in and yank the little devil out. One time only I digging in wrong place and getting mess of screaming and mess of blood."

Julian didn't visit Corinne until the following noon. She was lying on her stomach. On a spot between her thigh and buttock, there was a small spot covered with a cobweb bandage. When Julian pulled the blanket over her, Corinne shuddered and turned her face away.

"Why you not kill me? The *démone Africaine* and the old witch, they stretch me, pinch and knead over and over again like I am the lump of dough to find where most the hurt. Only the hurt is everywhere terriblement."

"Well, 'tis over," Julian observed, "And 'tis a good thing the needles will give you no more trouble."

"You no understand. Better have the death than such pain. I dream yesternight the *démone Africaine* is taking out ten more needles. I so afraid I soil myself. You no understand."

Over the next four days, Julian paid Corinne brief visits. Her anger toward Billiam, Owl Woman, and Peter receded gradually. She seemed to hold Julian solely responsible and refused to speak to him.

"Well, I can't force you to converse, but you will listen to me," Julian told her on the fifth day. "I will escort you back to Goram like I promised when you are able to travel. I do not expect you to forgive me. I don't ask it; however, to tell the truth, by God, I'd ask Billiam to do it again." He then went on, ignoring the sneer on her face. "Marry Isaac. He is the most like his father."

"Now you tell me which brother I to marry." Corinne managed a hoarse laugh. "Non, we forgive each other is no possible. I am not the good servant..." She hesitated, "or the wife to you. To see Eagle Heart, I tell any lie, commit any sin—the murder, renounce the faith, deceive the good man into buying my bond because I am pretty. Yes, I return to Goram. Which one I choose is no matter. I do not think I forever hate you." She nodded, then closed her eyes.

Julian stated his intention to Peter of taking Corinne

back to Goram's farm and then returning to Charleston to enjoy the pleasures of a proper bed, tavern food, and women who simplified love into simple commercial transactions.

"Brother, come inside with me," Peter said. Once in the cabin, Peter showed Julian a black wampum belt. "I receiving this yesterday. In your shoes, I not going to Goram's farm. War spreading like wildfire from west. French and English and all tribes soon clawing at each other's throats."

"Why would that signify? Corinne is not a soldier. If she takes a part, 'twill be the English because she loves the Goram family."

"No matter which side she choosing, brother. War in the towns a grand parade of soldiers with huzzahs and women waving scarves. War in the frontier a spark on dry tinder and a conflagration nary a soul escapes. A band of Choctaws massacre three families in valley near Augusta. The other families take their revenge on a trader and his Choctaw wife and two sons. The settlers waiting in their blockhouse for the Choctaws to even accounts, which they doing anon. And into this boiling cauldron coming Uriah prowling around with two score bloody rascals, and he smelling war like a wolf smelling blood. Corinne not safe. One side murdering the French maid, t'other side scalping the English bondservant."

Julian shut his eyes hard and crossed his arms, feeling the sense of loss in his gut. "I knew the trader. Greg Thompson, and his wife—she called herself Mary— were friends."

Peter grimaced as if he briefly experienced Julian's

pain then went on: "When they seeing black wampum belts making rounds, young braves dreaming warrior dreams of enemies dead in bloody heaps at their feet, then dreaming on their return home to brandish fresh scalps on their spears to pretty wide-eyed squaws, and old men shaking heads for they having no stories matching the young braves' deeds. Soon, whole frontier burning and bloody battlefield."

"Which side will you be on, brother?" Julian asked.

"French winning, I free man, only this war nobody winning."

When Julian informed Corinne about the outbreak of war, she glowered at him suspiciously. "Why they think the war makes the difference to me? I care not about the King George. I care not about the King Louie. I only care about my family. I love them same if they are the French or the Shawnee or the Spanish or the African or the Tartar. If they are to have trouble, then I want to have the trouble with them." Corinne laughed. "I not know which frowning-face brother I wed, but he must understand I marry him for all."

They waited another week. Corinne tried to sneak away once, but Billiam caught her and bound her to the bed. Julian untied her and said to the eyes spitting hatred, "I won't block you, if you can point in the direction of Goram's farm. If you can't, then as long as you are my bondservant, I will not allow you to get yourself killed through your own mulish stupidity. Remember, I own you until Goram hands me back the money." Julian intended to only take one packhorse with just enough provisions to reach Goram's farm, but on consideration, he loaded a second with what little remained of his trading goods including a keg of whiskey, a keg of rum, and six hatchets.

Peter returned a quarter part of the lead and powder saying, "Care, brother, good men and bad sharpening knives."

Corinne started out on foot, defiantly rejecting a horse in her unwillingness to admit that the operation had done her any good. After a hundred yards, Julian blocked her way with a saddled horse. "I do not want this trip to last longer than necessary."

Corinne formed her features into a stubborn glowering expression showing that she was about to refuse.

"But since you take so much pleasure in my company, we both walk at a leisurely pace."

"Your company does not please me because I never please you." Her features relaxed and she mounted the horse.

"You cannot know what pleases me or not," Julian declared, noticing with satisfaction that she settled herself easily onto the saddle.

"Peter tell me of Blue Dove. He see the joy in your eyes when you are with her. I see the trouble in your eyes when I am with you. How many days to my family?"

"Four days," Julian said.

"Four days in your company." Corinne shook her head in resignation. "Four days I pretend not to hate you."

From that moment on, Corinne apparently decided to return to her more natural talkative self. She told the story of her childhood. She grew up in a small hamlet of six families on the west shore of the Mississippi. Her father was a voyageur and coureur des bois like the other men. Her mother was one of the young women brought to New Orleans on the cargo ship *Baleine*. Although she never left the gray walls of the orphanage of the Hospital General at La Salpetrière until the age of 17, Corinne's mother adapted quickly to her new half-savage life.

They dressed like Indians, grew beans and squash like Indians, and sometimes painted their faces like Indians. For Corinne, it was an Eden—she could not imagine a better life. Her mother died of a fever when her father was away, so at the age of twelve, Corinne took over the care of her little brother. "I have the pride to do work of the older women—the spinning, stitching, cleaning, washing, cooking, the tanning hides, growing the beans and the squash in the garden. They called me Madame Corinne because I work like the married woman."

Even when her father came home sick, she didn't mind caring for him. The other families supplied whatever her family lacked knowing her family would do the same. Plenty and hunger were shared among them all, so there was never despair. That beautiful life ended when she woke one midnight to find White Bear holding a knife to her throat. She still carried the small scar. White Bear picked her up and threw her down from the upper loft to the floor below where her father and brother lay scalped. Still alive, her brother was crying and holding his hand to his head as if trying to find what wasn't there.

It was late autumn, and she was forced marched barefoot ten days over frozen ground. She thought she would lose her toes—but they rubbed bear grease and mint into her feet morning and night so her toes survived the frostbite. Corinne knew the best course was for her to be adopted into the tribe. "I hope to become the Shawnee like the other captives. I put my father and brother into the little box and hide the box away from my heart. My father was the voyageur and would have the understanding if I become the Shawnee squaw, have Shawnee babies and forget my French words, but Bright Flower only accept me as the slave."

The middle of the second day, Corinne unexpectedly asked, "Tell me about Blue Dove."

As Julian told his story, he saw Blue Dove, small and slight like most Creek women, her round pretty face quick to smile, her hair so thick that he could barely hold it bunched in his two hands, and her eyes which seemed to be an observer apart from her person except when they softened. She was the last thing Julian expected to find in New Babel whose people were now more beaten, degraded, and hopeless than when he had first visited the village four years before. Bragg had once explained: "You see, lad, we all limp along on our pride like a crutch. You knock away that crutch. You steal or kill what a man loves, then you offer him rum. That be the plight of the savages of New Babel." Any man, trader, savage, or simply a soul too brutish for civilization, could do what he pleased in New Babel without fear of reprisal as long as he brought rum or whiskey. The women of New Babel were resigned to rape.

Julian had set up camp in the vicinity of the village and was just starting his meal of slightly rancid pemmican when he heard the thud of blunt metal on flesh and bone, saw stars, and realized just before he blacked out that he had been brained. After a moment of unconsciousness, he opened his eyes a sliver expecting to see a knife coming toward his scalp. Instead, he spied a teenage girl and two young boys scavenging his saddlebags and the packs for food. When the girl stepped close, he grabbed her ankle, tripping her. Immediately the two boys, no more than five and seven, were on him, pummeling him with all of their might, while the girl fought back furiously, snapping at him with her teeth and raking him with her nails. Not before considerable scratching and a few bites was he able to subdue her and tie her to a tree. The boys redoubled their fury in the effort to rescue their sister. The skirmish ended with Julian tying them to another tree.

After all three were secured, the problem remained of their wailing and sobbing, which showed no sign of abating. Julian thought chewing might shut them up—so like a bird putting food into the open mouths of nestlings, he began to break off small chunks of pemmican and feed them. "One for you, one for you, and one for you," he said as he popped the bear fat and cranberry mixture into their mouths. After a few mouthfuls, the girl saw the humor in the situation and began to giggle. The giggle was infectious. By the end of the evening, he had untied them all, Blue Dove was holding a compress to the large lump on his head, and they were still laughing. Blue Dove had bits and pieces of several Indian languages plus two or three score of English words so communication was odd but not impossible.

She explained that she always left the village with her two brothers and hid in the woods whenever traders arrived. The traders usually only stayed a day or two, however this group had lengthened out the time. She and her brothers became very hungry and so had attacked him. Julian returned with Blue Dove and her brothers to the village. When he bade them farewell, she put a hand on his shoulder. It would have been easier to break apart iron shackles than that light restraining touch. Three nights later they became lovers. Blue Dove's uncle, a man of stern resolve who had moved beyond the Alleghenies, arrived soon afterward and took his nephews away. Blue Dove remained Julian's companion for two years. They traded all the way to the Mississippi, wintering with her uncle and brothers. Harriet and Blue Dove became fast friends, and just before she died, Julian was planning to introduce her to Molly and William Johnson and ask for the settled situation of managing a trading post.

When he finished the story, Corinne asked, "Is the love worth the grief?"

"Yes," Julian said, blinking. "'Tis."

Corinne shook her head. "For you. For me I do not know."

Late afternoon on the second day, Corinne and Julian came upon a frightened group of traders fleeing east. The traders had been doing business at a Mingo village when an army of braves arrived led by French officers.

"Five hundred from a dozen different nations swarmed over us like angry wasps," complained a flat-faced man with a gray beard who had taken on the role of a leader.

The war party confiscated the traders' furs and all their goods of exchange from powder and lead to peacock feathers and ribbons. The French captain promised to kill the traders quickly if he saw them again—he assured them as a favor, so the Indians wouldn't kill them their special way.

Corinne asked if they had passed by the valley with Goram's farm.

The leader rubbed his beard as he regarded Corinne, "You're French, Miss, no hiding it from the way you talk. I heard tell of a French girl servant in a pretty little vale who ran away just before the Choctaw attacked. Some thereabouts think the two events be not unconnected. I heard tell of petitioning the governor to put a bounty on that French girl's head."

"Corinne went away with me, and I'm no spy nor traitor," Julian stated, hand now hovering close to his primed pistol.

The trader held out his hand palm down in a calming gesture. "I didn't say you were and I didn't say she was, I just said what I heard tell of. However, I'd say the notion that this little French girl betrayed them to the savages is lodged pretty strongly in people's heads, some of them not too particular about which eye they get for the one they lost."

Deaf to the warning, Corinne asked, "Henry Goram and his sons, they suffer in the raid?"

The trader considered: "Isn't Goram's place just north of the Keans' still? The settlers in that part of the valley fought off the savages only losing a few horses and a twelve-year-old boy who were scalped when he was getting water out of a well, so I suppose this Henry Goram and two of his sons be alright."

"I hope the scalped boy is not poor Lowell." Corinne heaved a sigh. "I take care of Lowell and the sister when the mother have the measles."

Early the following morning, twelve miles from the valley, they encountered a group of thirty odd men, women and children on foot and loaded into three wagons traveling in the opposite direction. Many carried the blank exhausted expression of people whom no further horror could surprise. The leader, the only one mounted, steadied his pistol when he saw Corinne, saying, "So you return, little Frenchy, to see the bloody handiwork of your damned nation."

Julian interposed. "How could she have a part in the raid?"

"Whether she did or not, her kin did, and it would feel awfully satisfying to murder a person of French extraction." He spat out black tobacco cud which splattered on Corinne's horse as well as the ground.

"Where's Goram, Mister Tanner?" Corinne inquired, ignoring the pistol aimed at her forehead.

"Where's Goram? Where's Goram? She asks." Tanner laughed, nearly hysterical. "Ask his sons, why don't you? I leave you to their mercy or not."

Trailing the last wagon with hunched shoulders and lolling head half blackened by gunpowder, Isaac was difficult to recognize. A young woman accompanying Isaac, also with a blackened face, grabbed him and turned him in the right direction when he began to stray off the path.

Corinne called out, "Isaac! Isaac!"

He stared dumbly at her, then shaking his head questioned, "You? Why you?"

Matthew suddenly sat up in the wagon. His heavily bandaged left forearm ended in a stump. A young girl with a slash underneath her eye tried to make him lay down again.

"What happened?" Julian asked, turning to him.

"I blocked a tomahawk," Matthew said, swaying with exhaustion. "'Twas either my hand or my head. A miracle I didn't bleed out."

"And father?" Corinne made a hesitant gesture to touch him but was stopped by his companion's protective glare.

"Father's dead," he said, his weary eyes focusing on Corinne. "He told us he'd stop them. Joshua shot the savage who took my hand off, then went back to help father."

"You see him die?" Corinne asked, her tone disbelieving.

"Nobody survived except maybe those who got to the blockhouse. Ernst Frank and his family dead, the Travers family, the Clyburn family. I saw the smoke from the burning cabins. Sarah…" He looked at the woman tending him. "Sarah has nobody now."

"Father, he is not so easy to kill. I go to him and bring him back to you," Corinne declared.

"Maybe if he made it to the blockhouse. No… Impossible." Matthew glanced pleadingly at Julian. "Tell her nobody survived. Corinne, I know you had nothing to do with what happened in our valley but many think otherwise."

"Then I bury the body," Corinne whispered bitterly as the band of survivors passed on.

"You might as well throw yourself into his grave also," Julian said.

"*Mais oui*, I might as well," she answered and spurred her horse forward.

After a few minutes of fruitless reasoning, Julian concluded that short of tying her up, Corinne wasn't going to be deterred from visiting the farmstead. He tried a different tack, "We don't need to act foolishly in this."

"I no want your company. They no are your family; they are my family."

Julian grabbed her reins, stopping the horse and looked her in the eye. "And you're my bonded servant, so you must deal with my company whether it pleases you or not."

"I stab you to death in the sleep." She made a slashing movement with her hand across her throat.

"I trust you won't, and I know you need my help, so allow me to help you. If Goram managed to escape getting scalped, you won't further his cause by losing your scalp. The raiding party likely moved on, but we should approach by the backways."

Before they could turn off the main road, John Thunder, Hugh Kean, and four other men appeared doubled mounted on three horses. The strong smell of gunpowder, the blackened faces, the bloody rags around arms and heads, the wildness in their eyes indicated a recent engagement that hadn't come off well.

Hugh saluted them. "You're heading the wrong way to collect her bounty."

John Thunder kept his gaze down, his face white and his left hand, wrapped in a brown dirty cloth, might have been missing a few fingers.

"Seen Goram?" Julian asked.

"What's left of him," Hugh replied grimly. "We went by his place to recruit the old bugger to help us save the blockhouse. The savages got to him afore they got to the blockhouse which was a heap of ashes and charred bones when we found it. At least, the old hound gave them a prodigious good fight like he gave John because they ate his heart. They just don't give that compliment to any man, only to them buggers who impress them favorably."

"Did you bury him?" Julian asked.

"Bury him? We was running too hard to squat and take a shit much less have leisure for such niceties. Out of twenty, we're now six and only two in fighting fettle. More than two hundred people lived in these valleys and to my reckoning, less than two score escaped." Hugh raised a pistol at Corinne. "Now, lend us the French whore so we can get a little of our own back. We'll return her when we're done so you can collect the bounty."

Corinne stared at the raised pistol, daring Hugh to fire.

"I've never knew Keans to return anything," Julian said evenly. "Corinne had nothing to do with the raids."

Hugh spat. "She's French, and the French riled up the savages. I don't need no other reason. One hundred and fifty butchered and she's here in front of us sitting pretty."

"Shame to escape the savages, then be shot by your own side," Julian said, drawing out his pistol. The others dully looked at the impasse. "Then again with the savages in the area do you want to draw attention to yourselves just now?"

"Pap's dead, Millie's dead, the still is broken, the pigs slaughtered. Don't know how much I care at the moment. But in consideration of my men and that I am heartily sick of spilling blood, as long as you keep in that direction, I'll let the savages do my work."

Keeping a hand on Corinne's tensed arm, Julian surveyed the cabin from the cover of a stand of trees fifty yards away. Three slaughtered cows, a disemboweled dog and goat littered the yard.

"Stay here. I go in first," Julian said.

"Non, 'tis my family, 'tis for me to bury them." Corinne tried to jerk her arm free.

"I understand you have to bury the bodies," Julian said, tightening his grip. "But I want to make Goram and Joshua decent for your last view of them."

Corinne closed her eyes and rocked forward onto her knees. Julian let go. On approaching the cabin, the swarming flies lifted off the slaughtered animals, circled and settled again. Julian discovered Joshua leaning against the wall in the back of the cabin, staring dead-eyed and scalped. Inside, Goram's body lay stretched out on the table, the open chest cavity verifying what Hugh had claimed. Julian dug a grave for both behind the house, laid the corpses down, covering their heads with rags and Goram's chest with a horse blanket. He hadn't noticed Corinne standing behind him until he turned. He wasn't sure how much she had seen.

"I guess now we say a prayer," he said.

Corinne stared incredulously at him. "My prayer is goddamn you God." She stalked away, but then stopped and returned to the graveside. "Father no want I say the blasphemy over the grave." She bowed her head. "No man deserve the death less or thy mercy more. No man, Lord. Amen."

Then she screamed. Three braves in warpath regalia rounded the corner of the house, holding their knives ready for a fresh kill. Bloody scalps hung from their belts. His other weapons laying two yards away, Julian raised the spade and met the gaze of Night Fox. Corinne started for them, fully intending to attack with her bare hands—as certain a death as could be had. To stop her, Julian whacked her in the rear with the spade, knocking her down. Night Fox laughed, the other braves joining in, then said, "I owe you no more lives, Pale Otter."

Julian held the spade chest high as if it were a spear. Night Fox and his companions moved forward purposely and now stood over Corinne. One reached for her hair.

Hearing movement behind him, Julian assumed more braves had arrived to participate in the slaughter. Then he heard a soft voice say in Lenape, "Enough bloodletting for this day, Night Fox." Grayson slipped in front of him, bent down and helped Corinne up. "I'm overjoyed to see you, child. I thought I would have to bury the French girl of this valley and say a prayer over her grave." Grayson turned again toward the braves who seemed indecisive. "Only the strongest and bravest warriors are capable of mercy." He spoke now with the air of command. "Go, and take the scalps, plunder the farms, burn the houses in the next valley, and damn your souls to hell, but here, now, you take no more life."

Night Fox sneered as he raised his tomahawk, "You think I cannot split your head, Son-of-gray-wolf, and become the famous man who defeat your magic."

Grayson replied calmly and firmly, "Another day, you can, Night Fox, but not this day."

"And what will you give me to save your scalps?"

"I will pray for your soul's salvation, Night Fox, and

the souls of your companions. For twenty years, I traveled the length and breadth of this country from the great bay in the north to the Floridas. I never carried more provision than what would last me three days. My only weapons are a knife and fishing line. I never went hungry, never was mauled by wild beast, never captured by enemies. My prayers protected and sustained me. You will need my powerful prayers when your enemy stands over you with his lance at your heart."

"I could scalp you." Night Fox swiped the weapon over Grayson's head. The priest stood serene, unflinching, palms out. The expression on Night Fox's face passed back and forth between anger and fear. Anger finally seemed to gain the upper hand and he gave a bloodcurdling whoop and raised the tomahawk for the kill, his eyes bulging with rage. His arm shook violently as if an invisible hand was holding it back. "Damn your God and his magic, Son-of-gray-wolf. You must pray for me every day for the rest of your life," Fox muttered lowering his tomahawk

Grayson nodded.

The braves left for the next valley with murder in their eyes, and Julian felt certain that they would not show mercy again any time soon.

When Corinne stood up, Grayson took the sacramental cloth out of his satchel and gently wiped her face as if she were a small child. "You must go to New France, my daughter. Pale Otter will guide you. I pay him with prayers for his heretical soul."

"I'll need more than prayer," Julian said, his voice still shaky.

Grayson replaced the sacramental cloth back in his

satchel. "Many of the true faith are caught up in this brutish business. I must see what I can do for them." He turned and started down the same path as the braves.

After finishing burying the bodies, Julian asked Corinne, "Have you family in New France?"

"An uncle in New Orleans who is the merchant," Corinne replied dully. "I meet him once when my mother is alive. He boast that when he see the two pretty *jumelles*—sisters who are the twin—with the other women who come from France in the *Baleine*, he think he must marry the one and his brother must marry the other. The sister of my mother, she is also dead. He will welcome me. Do not bother for your bondservant now, Julian. I find the way. My uncle, he is the honorable man and will pay you for my indenture."

"He won't be able to pay me if you're scalped along the way. I will guide you to a French trading post on the Cumberland River whither you can take a boat to Kaskaskia and on to New Orleans."

Corinne narrowed her eyes. "The French is your enemy so much as the English is mine now."

"They are not putting a bounty on my head. The French esteem gallantry, and as for savages, if you request hospitality afore they raise their tomahawks, they customarily grant it to you."

Corinne remained quiet for the first mile, then suddenly blurted out, "I hope Father Goram spoke true when he say the fortune, she sometime have the pity for the fool."

For the remainder of the afternoon, Corinne kept silent, the features of her usually expressive face hard and grief-stricken. They turned westward following a trading path, riding through meadows and forests of oak, elm, and hickory. The country became rougher as they headed toward a series of ridges, discernible as blue silhouettes layered against deeper and mistier blue silhouettes. Wild strawberries stained the legs of their horses. Flocks of wild turkeys scattered at their approach. A foraging black bear ambled across their path, spooking the horses. On top of a flattened hillock, they found the ruins of a vast village, sticks and rotten posts showing what remained of hundreds of abodes. Julian hoped to avoid the Cherokee who now dominated the area. Although among the more even-tempered of Indian nations, you could not anticipate the sympathies of any tribe when the outrages and bloodletting of war started.

Corinne insisted on doing all the chores that evening. They supped on dried meat and parched corn at their fireless camp. While Corinne was still busying herself with brushing down the horses and uttering French endearments to them, Julian fell asleep.

Near midnight, Julian was roused by strangled whelps. He first thought it was a catamount. The creature was known for its strange mournful cries, but then he discerned in the thin moonlight Corinne huddled on a fallen tree a few yards away, shaking as she tried to stifle her sobs, either from pride or consideration of his sleep. He had never heard such desolation. Julian debated whether to comfort her grief. Finally, feeling if he didn't do something, his own heart would rupture, he arose and, wrapped in his blanket, sat on the fallen tree two feet away from her. She continued struggling to hold in her cries, neither acknowledging him nor requesting him to leave. Moving closer, he covered her shoulders with the blanket. He held her. She began to push him away, then fell against him, her chest heaving but still muffling her cries.

When he woke in the morning, Corinne was curled up beside him. He dimly remembered holding her for a very long time until the sobs subsided out of exhaustion. Corinne blushed when she opened her eyes, then got up and went about her chores in her normal efficient manner, the intimate warmth of the previous night dissipating quickly.

That day they only engaged in the conversation necessary to ford the dozen or so streams and navigate the difficult trails snaking up the ridges and descending into narrow vales. Corinne seemed less distant, and when a pitch-black cloud rumbled across the sky spewing bolts of lightning and a bone-soaking deluge, she nestled close to him while they sheltered dismounted with their skittery horses underneath an oak.

That night, after finishing the camp chores, Corinne blushed and whispered, "If you hold me, I promise I no cry." She didn't keep her word at first, pushing her head into his shoulder so hard as if she wanted to burrow through him and convulsing. But the tempest passed, and she fitted herself into the space between his bent knees and out-flung arms. He awoke to the minty smell of her hair; and underneath his hand, the skin of her arm lay smooth and cool. The shared warmth had made the night's passage more than agreeable. The fourth night she announced, trying to bend her mouth into a smile, "I know this is difficult for the man to hold the woman and do nothing. I am the wife to you tonight."

"I won't oblige you." Julian had vowed to himself to never cause her pain again.

"No, Julian, I want this for you. Just hold me after like yesternight."

Although Corinne wasn't wooden, she was initially awkward in her attempt to please him. Gradually, she softened and relaxed and then suddenly she was pulling him into the world of measureless pleasure. When Corinne curled into her now customary position, her back nestled against his chest, her legs drawn up, her head resting on the crook of his arm, she whispered, "I no hurt now. At first, I am so young with White Bear, and then the needles Bright Flower put in me take away the pleasure, and I want the death, but now I no hurt. Not at all. Men also make noises like they are hurt, yet you seem to need it."

"It makes us feel very good." He kissed her on the back of her head.

"I will let you have my body, but I no want to be the wife or squaw, Julian. You are the good man like Father Goram, yet do you not see, the good people I love are taken away from me. Mother, father, brother, son, Goram, his sons. And I have not the twenty-one years, and I only ever want is the happiness where I am. And you, dear Julian, care not whether to live or die. You make foolish errands like guiding the sad French girl into the country of the enemy. So, I wish you to go away." She contradicted herself by snuggling closer. "I give you the pleasure? I do not understand how men get so much pleasure out of the…" She searched for the word, "coupling."

Corinne stoically endured the long days of travel through a broken country of steep forested slopes, endless ridges, cascades that sometimes appeared to burst streaming out of solid rock into the jagged ravines. Still recovering from the Billiam's surgery, Julian could see the battle of willpower against fatigue play out on Corinne's features as she refused to rest unless he did. Like Julian, she renewed her strength from their nights, although she always rose first, mercilessly letting the icy morning violate their warm cocoon. Turning north toward the Cumberland River, they entered an area claimed by a dozen different Indian nations, not to mention the French and English. As in the Cherokee country, Julian steered clear of the villages, not being certain whether a particular tribe was favoring the English or French that day. Julian didn't blame them. To choose the losing side guaranteed loss of land and invited annihilation.

Despite precautions, one evening a band of a dozen Mingos swarmed into their camp, proprietarily rifling through their supplies, then sitting by the fire grinning and keeping the long knives and tomahawks in their laps. Fortunately, Glad Face, a Mingo half-brother of Molly, recognized Julian. Glad Face informed him that the English had been run off of the Cumberland River and the Shawnee and Lenape had now joined the French cause to not miss out on the plunder.

"Only Mohawk for the English is Molly and Nickus," he confided, giving them an appraising stare. "Safer go by the River of the Cherokee. The Cherokee did not pass on the black wampum."

Accordingly, the following day Julian and Corinne turned south.

Several days later a small army of Miamis headed by a French captain appeared at the far edge of a meadow. Flight would have been fatal, so they rode forward and were enveloped by several hundred bare-chested warriors, jostling them, muttering low taunting threats, brandishing tomahawks and lances festooned with scalps. Corinne shook off a brave trying to take off her cap and caress her hair. A dozen more hands reached for her, but then the captain, a tall rangy bald man with thick eyebrows and an unmistakable air of command, interposed with a sharp order. The braves sullenly backed off.

After a brief exchange in French, the captain asked in passable English, "And this man who is he? Do not lie. Is he not the English?"

"He is the husband," Corinne replied.

"Why are you not fighting for *les Anglais*?" The captain addressed Julian, a distrustful smile creasing his weathered face.

"I can't fight for either cause without killing my kin or her kin, which I don't aim to do," Julian said, returning a smile which he hoped conveyed sincerity.

The captain scratched his chin, seeming to be contemplating their fate. "The trading posts on the Cherokee, which your wife said is *votre destination*, are abandoned."

Julian held onto his smile, despite several braves being close enough to tomahawk him before he could draw a weapon. "That may be. Still, with the Lenape and Shawnee on the warpath, the river is the best way to get to Kaskaskia."

"The river, she is dangerous now," The captain

responded. "Many leagues flooded and *les sauvages*, all are on the path of war."

"My wife isn't strong enough to travel over land, so we take our chances."

The captain shrugged. "The chances are poor either way you go. Your story I believe for now, only if I find you east of here, I will think you are warning the settlements, and your scalp I let *mes amis* take."

They continued several more days southwesterly on a trading path nearly overgrown from disuse, hoping to intercept the River of the Cherokee near a Chickawsee village where the eastern-most French trading post was rumored to lie. The Chickasaw sometimes fought the French, sometimes were allied with them; however, regretfully, they had never been well-disposed toward the English.

RIVER OF THE CHEROKEE

On a bluff above the river roughly in the place where the post was rumored to be, Julian and Corinne came upon a village of about thirty wigwams. They observed only three braves on entering the village, raising Julian's suspicion that the male part of the population were off raiding English settlements. When Corinne asked in French the gathering squaws, children, and old men to take them to the trading post, they replied in a language that wasn't Chickawsee, nor Cherokee, nor Creek. This lingual impasse continued until an old woman dressed in a blue velvet jacket and lace cap thrust herself forward and explained in broken French that they were the great Natchez people.

Corinne slowly reiterated her request to guide them to the trading post. The old squaw began to smile as if dimly comprehending a joke. She told Corinne and Julian that she would indeed take them to the trading post, but as Julian was obviously English, she wouldn't advise it. The head trader was a fierce giant who kept up his strength by boiling and eating an enemy every new moon. And his

354 | JAMES SHORT

greatest enemies were the English. The English weren't
aware of his existence because no Englishman had ever
set eyes on him and lived to tell. The trader resided in a
wigwam made out of the skins of bears he had strangled
with his hands. He could become invisible. He was probably over by that tree listening to them right now.

Despite this warning, Corinne encouraged her with a
length of ribbon, which occasioned a toothless grin, and
the old squaw motioned to them to follow.

Julian had expected to find a small blockhouse perhaps manned by a dozen French soldiers and surrounded
by a palisade. There would be a few wigwams nearby with
the Indian wives of the soldiers and the usual hangers-
on, who made their living toting, or tracking, or trading
whatever fell into their hands, or begging when those
options were exhausted. Therefore, he didn't realize that
they had arrived when the squaw stopped in front of a
bateau upended over a trench just above the high mark
of the riverbank.

"Danton!" She screeched.

Julian looked around to see whom she was calling.

"Danton! Danton! Danton!" She pounded on the
upended bateau.

The back of a gray head poked out into the trench
from underneath the boat, then swiveled to look up.

"Danton!" The squaw gazed down maliciously and
triumphantly. The terrible Frenchman pulled himself out
of the opening and slowly straightened himself in stages
in the manner of an old man. He was indeed tall, but
nowhere near a giant. He wore a dirty woolen cap, a bear
claw necklace around his wrinkled skinny neck, and a

breechcloth which didn't quite satisfy modesty. His legs were remarkably short and spindly for his height. His face was singularly lacking in ferocity. Rheumy eyes gazed at them through an alcoholic mist; a nose that started out from its bridge valiantly ended up drooping down to the level of his mouth; and one bottom tooth poked out from between his lips.

While the squaw was berating him, Corinne stepped forward, and his face lighted up at this unexpected vision of beauty. He made the gesture of sweeping off a cap out of respect to her loveliness, which would have been a grand gesture if he had been wearing a plumed headdress. The squaw pushed herself in front of Corinne to pursue her diatribe. Danton's eyes hardened into arrowhead points, and he roared an order making her retreat, squealing protests. His gaze softened again as it refastened on Corinne.

The conversation between Danton and Corinne was accompanied by much gesturing and pointing and punctuated by several "*Mais ouis*." Corinne paused to explain, "Danton is the voyageur. My father who is also the famous voyageur is the old friend. He say he will bring me in the bateau to Kaskaskia."

"You trust him?" Julian asked.

"What Englishman know meaning of trust?" Danton growled in a thick accent, then continued with his emphatic stream of French words.

Corinne translated: "Danton say the old voyageur and the young woman are asking too much the favor of God to make the trip alone, so you must come." She shook her head. "Julian, you take me here. That is more favor than I deserve. Return to your people."

In his annoyance, Danton raised his voice and appeared to be boxing the air with his gestures. Corinne shook her head weakly. "Danton say to return the way you come here is to run the gauntlet of the hundred leagues. Where the River of the Cherokee meet the Ohio, you are closer to the Nation of the Seneca who not always hate the English and might help you."

Danton spent the next few days waterproofing and repairing the bateau and its sails. He then went from wigwam to wigwam, bullying supplies out of the villagers. Anything not necessary, including the horses, was traded for dried beans, parched corn, dried pumpkin and squash, a hundred squares of pemmican wrapped in cornhusks, strips of dried venison, salted tongue, two salted bear paws, sixty arrows, several spare tomahawks and knives, fishing lines and hooks, five pipes with more tobacco than a man could smoke in a year. Danton kept the cask of rum, the cask of Kean whiskey and added a dozen bottles of French brandy that he had extracted from a secret cache in the woods.

They were delayed an afternoon by the arrival of two Choctaw braves, tall young men with long noses and a Gallic glint in their eyes somewhat at odds with their flattened foreheads, dirty leggings, and torn shirts which most Indians wouldn't deign to wear. Danton greeted them joyfully, exclaiming, *"Mes fils du Choctaw!"*—my Choctaw sons.

His sons' arrival caused a commotion in the village because the Natchez were the Choctaw's enemies. Several boys and old men appeared in warrior attire on the bluff shouting insults. Danton's sons gleefully returned the compliments calling them, "Maggots on the corpses of their ancestors, high and mighty no more." Danton explained that the Natchez once had six towns as large as New Orleans and fielded five thousand warriors. War and disease had whittled down the great nation to two small villages and a hundred braves.

After a few hours of trading insults, the five of them gathered around the fire and shared two bottles of brandy and a keg of rum. Corinne did not drink saying, "My wits, I need more when the men lose theirs." The conversation went deep into the night. After the first bottle, Danton was weeping because as Corinne explained he received the news that a grandson and granddaughter had died from smallpox. When Danton dried his tears, he asked about the river.

A Choctaw son pointed at Julian with a tomahawk from which hung a scalp and uttered in heavily accented hostile English, "You only English on Cherokee river." Then he buried the tomahawk in the ground. "This your end."

Later that evening, Bragg came up as a topic.

Corinne translated. "Two years ago, your master pass through their village. The French put a bounty on him also. Master Bragg say he is tired of the bounties, and he travel west until he find the country where the people know not what is the bounty."

Julian mentioned Long Arrow. Danton's sons had never heard of him.

Danton launched the boat at first light, his sons having disappeared earlier. As the bateau glided into the water and its sail filled, the vessel assumed a grace unattainable on land. The hull was thirty feet long with a single mast, two sets of oars, two paddles, and a long pole for pushing. The front part of the bow was covered, providing a place to keep supplies dry. It was more stable than a canoe and swifter than one in a brisk breeze.

Handling the tiller, Danton's gaze sharpened and his bearing became more like that of a man who knew his craft. Quite a talker, he jawed for hours, alternately moistening his throat by taking a swig from a bottle of French brandy, then drying it out by puffing away on his pipe. This uninterrupted chatter was wearying Corinne who occasionally tried unsuccessfully to interject her own words.

When she dozed off, Danton directed his monologue mostly in French at Julian who attempted to nod pleasantly in response, but soon felt his eyelids dragged down by an irresistible weight. In midafternoon, Danton rubbed his stomach, attached a bit of pemmican to a hook on a line, trailed it behind the boat and within minutes pulled in a long-nosed fish the length of his forearm. They tied the boat to a tree on the bank, and after Danton and Julian had scouted the area for signs of Indians, they roasted the fish on the small beach and finished off a bottle of brandy in celebration of the first day. Then, they all fell fast asleep.

The next morning, just as the shimmering river bent around a spit of sand, they heard a reedy voice calling, "Holp, holp, holp."

They didn't see the source of the plea until a small boy dressed in a nightshirt ran out to the end of the spit of land, sobbing and waving. Danton and Julian exchanged glances. This was the favorite ruse along the river. As soon as they landed, a hundred braves would rush out of the dense woods and slaughter them. They both shook their heads. Corinne put a hand on Julian's arm. "This not the trap."

Danton pointed to a brown wisp above the trees and inhaled. "*Les sauvages* burn human flesh."

"This not the trap," Corinne insisted.

"Drop me on t'other side of the bend," Julian whispered. "I'll work my way back. If you hear my pistol discharge, move on. I'm caught. Wait for me until dark. If I'm not returned by then, move on."

"Put me ashore," Corinne pleaded. "I first to die, if I make the mistake."

"Nay, I go alone," Julian disengaged her hand. "'Tis better you stay with Danton. You understand each other, which can mean life or death if you need to act quickly."

Julian scrambled up a slippery bank in the shadow of two large oaks, then fought noisily through the dense undergrowth for several hundred feet. In addition to a musket, Julian carried his bow. He wanted to draw blood, at least, get some compensation for the sacrifice of his life, if he fell into a trap. The sun was hot, the air sticky, and despite plastering on bear grease with fish gall, a cloud of midges swarmed over him, searching out every centimeter of naked skin.

The terrain flattened and the brush thinned, more or less, as Julian traced three sides of a square, traveling a mile inland, a mile parallel to the river and a mile toward the spit of land where the boy had stood. Every so often, he'd stop, quiet his breathing and strain his ears to listen, not for footsteps but rather trying to discern areas of silence in the surrounding forest that might indicate the presence of the raiding party. In the mud next to a small creek, he came across a dozen footprints heading toward the river. He explored up and down the creek searching for prints going in the opposite direction but found none. He was tempted to abandon the project as a lost cause and regretted the actions of the wise man and coward were often indistinguishable. He then thought about the boy and the look of distress on Corinne's face. He couldn't be a coward in front of her even if that meant acting the fool and losing his life.

The blackened shell of a cabin stood in the clearing just beyond a stand of beeches. The homestead was recent—fewer than a dozen trees had been felled, a dozen more rimmed, and a crude fence outlined a hope of a garden next to the smoking ruin. Julian became aware of a hewing squeaking noise. Nocking an arrow, he bent low and circled toward the front of the cabin. The scalped naked bodies of a man and a woman hung upside down from the branch of a black walnut tree over a heap of smoldering logs. The noise came from the rope rubbing into the thick branch as the bodies swung. There was absolutely no wind. The boy was a decoy, and he needed to get away fast.

Suddenly, both bodies dropped. Julian froze, his fingers holding the string with the nocked arrow tensing, all senses on alert. Then the old voyageur emerged from behind the tree and dragged the bodies off the blackened logs. Danton caught the small boy who ran forward to see what was happening and carried him away. Julian waved, called out, and took over the job of dragging the half-burnt bodies to a grave Danton had dug and burying them. He worked quickly, wanting to leave this damned place as soon as possible.

When finished, he discovered Danton, the boy, and Corinne unaccountably idling on a flat rock, dangling their feet in a small eddy. Julian was working up his outrage at their lack of urgency despite great danger when a bundle in Corinne's lap squalled. Bending down, she dipped her bonnet in the river and let a small greedy pink face suck it.

"The little boy and his sister hide there." Corinne directed Julian with her gaze to a large hollowed out log. "Danton say the savages come yesternight."

The boy pulled on Danton's shirt. "Papa and mama, help them?"

Danton attempted to gather the boy into his lap. "*Ils sont morte.*"

Rubbing small fists into his eyes, the child squirmed and tried to pull away. "Help them!"

"The mother and father cannot come with us," Corinne said, brushing his hair back. "They are dead, *mon chéri.*"

Danton picked up the boy and held him while he furiously pounded his shoulder sobbing, "Help them, help them."

The baby, a girl, wasn't yet weaned, so they had to figure out how to feed her. Danton caught a fat reddish bass, cooked and carefully deboned the fish, then mashed the flesh with water to make a gruel. Corinne mixed corn-meal and flour with a little water, made a fire and baked small, hard cakes which she turned into a paste by adding more water. The baby was too hungry to reject the fish gruel and cornmeal paste. While his sister ate, the boy whose name turned out to be Johnny gnawed on a piece of pemmican, mucus and tears streaming down his face.

Although the trip down the River of the Cherokee continued, the presence of the children made everything different. Progress, of course, was slowed considerably. They were constantly pulling over to the shore to prepare gruel for Andrea—the name Corinne had christened the baby—or wash her soiled clothes. Danton protested a delay once, and the defiant tilt of Corinne's head and her hailstorm of irritated French made him hold up his hands and say, "*Je me rends.*" And then in his guttural English, he whispered to Julian, "I glad I only have savage daughters."

Against her will, Corinne had fallen in love with Andrea. She put Andrea to sleep with lullabies. She engaged in absurd antics just to make Andrea laugh or smile, which was always answered by her own radiant smile. Whereas before she was quick to point out the beauties and novelties on the riverbank, she now only had eyes for that pink yawning or burping or sniffling or yowling face. Fear too was present in Corinne's loving gaze as she rocked the baby slowly in her arms. Her expression touched Julian to the quick—he also was very intimate with the fear of loss.

When Julian made the mistake of suggesting that Johnny and Andrea might have relatives elsewhere who could take them in, Corinne's expression darkened and she replied with the angry certainty of faith, "*Non*, you cannot say that. They are alone. Danton say only the scapegallows settle in the dangerous country." Danton's Gallic shrug indicated sympathy with Julian.

Danton had really no right to admonish Corinne for the delays. He was in his way as smitten as she was. The old voyageur had taken Johnny into his heart, holding the little boy on his lap, their four hands on the tiller, steering, while subjecting him to his unending monologue in French. They also fished together, Johnny's small hands pulling in the line behind Danton's huge knuckly fists. Beginning with words about steering the boat and fishing, Johnny's vocabulary in French grew, and soon Corinne had to gently correct him when he mixed languages.

Johnny was prone to nightmares—the terrifying images of the raid took life again in his dreams—so Danton slept near him and whenever the boy began to thrash and cry out, the old voyageur would tenderly reach out and wake him murmuring, "I am here. *Je suis ici, mon chouchou.*"

One afternoon Danton pointed to a brave and squaw paddling a canoe toward them and proclaimed with pride and pleasure, "*Mon fil et ma fille Muskogee.*" Then, suddenly, he paled and after a sharp intake of breath, he shouted to Corinne who thrust Johnny into Julian's arms.

"No see…." Corinne did not have time to finish the sentence.

A sliver of ice ran down Julian's spine as he pushed Johnny under the bow with the command, "Don't speak."

Danton's Muskogee son was holding up two scalps, one dark blond like Johnny's hair, the other red not unlike

Andrea's red fuzz. Corinne whispered a translation of the exchange, "The brave says he has the gift of English scalps for his father to decorate the boat. Danton says he is sorry but he will not display the scalps he not take with his own knife. Danton's daughter ask why her father is traveling with the English enemy. Danton say you are the prisoner that he will give up to the captain at Kaskaskia. His daughter say there is more value to the English scalp than the English prisoner. The Iroquois League is now with the French and soon all English will be dead."

Danton talked and bartered a little more, and his son and daughter were soon laughing, however they gave Julian a forbidding stare as they paddled off. The frontier also being a wilderness of rumors, Julian doubted what Danton's Muskogee son and daughter had said was entirely true, yet he couldn't shake the feeling of being a blindfolded man walking along the edge of a precipice.

As the boat glided smoothly down the river, so glided the days, Danton always steering with Johnny on his lap, Corinne fussing over Andrea, Julian scanning the shore, the unnatural serenity adding to his feeling of unease. Despite claiming that he was glad he had never sired a French daughter, Danton had taken to calling Corinne, "*Ma fille*"—and sometimes scolded her in unmistakable parental tones. Julian occasionally took the tiller, giving his eyes a respite from trying to see through the forest and his imagination a rest from populating its banks with hidden hostile warriors.

Looking out for enemies was easier than wrestling with the growing ache in his heart now that his time with

Corinne was drawing to a close. Corinne still slept by his side. Twice, to his surprise, she initiated making love with soft caresses, a very surreptitious activity with two children and an old man sleeping a yard away. So, Julian concluded he wasn't the only one struggling with desire. Afterward, when Corinne curled up close to him, Julian sensed in the darkness the smile on her face. After the second lovemaking, she whispered, "Dear Julian, forgive me, my heart, I must take back."

For the thousandth time, he remembered Bragg's admonition: do not love anything overmuch for the land like "a jealous mistress will deny you whatever you love out of pure spite." And for the ten-thousandth time he remembered Blue Dove. Corinne kept her distance the following night, pretending that Andrea needed comforting.

Soon after meeting Danton's *fils du nation du Yuchi* with their very odd language, they beached the bateau on an island, the canebrake being too dense on the riverbank shore. While Corinne made cornmeal paste and Julian closed his eyes, surrendering to afternoon drowsiness, Danton waded out with Johnny into the shallow waters.

Suddenly, a scream roused him. Julian sprang up to his feet and saw Corinne pointing at what appeared to be a floating log.

Danton hoisted Johnny onto his shoulders as the alligator propelled itself forward, surging half out of the water, huge jaw gaping, water and vapor gushing out of its nostrils, making a horrible roar.

Tripping backward, Danton fended the creature off making a series of short stabs at the snout with his long dirk while Johnny clutched his gray queue for dear life.

The creature's upper jaw kept opening perpendicular to the lower then shutting with the sound of heavy planks clanking against each other.

An arrow would bounce off the tough hide, so Julian loaded the musket, took aim, and shot. When the bullet skipped off just as an arrow would, Julian grabbed a long oar and started to run. On his knees now, Danton could not reach higher with his blade than the top of the creature's red gaping maw.

Charging, Julian shoved the oar into the alligator's gullet and pushed with all his strength while Danton scrambled back. The creature thrashed, violently knocking Julian to and fro as he drove the oar deeper. Finally, the oar snapped in two, but by this time, Corinne had sloshed through the water with the reloaded musket and standing over the creature regurgitating the stub of wood, shot it point-blank in the head.

Out of the corner of his eye, Julian spotted two smaller caimans heading toward the spot on the shore where Corinne had left Andrea. Corinne also saw the caimans and shrieked, "*Mon Dieu, non!*" Julian sprinted faster than he believed possible with his twisted foot, reached the beach at the same time as the first caiman, dove onto the serrated back as it throttled toward Andrea, and wrapping his arms and legs around it, hooked its stubby limbs.

The other caiman slid back, attracted by the bloody smell of its dying cousin. Julian hugged the leathery tornado with all of his strength as they rolled around between the water and the pebbly beach a dozen times, the enraged creature twisting and snapping. For a precious instant, they were stalemated, Julian on his back holding the caiman belly-up, his arms locked with the caiman's forelegs, his legs violently knocked back and forth by the tail whipping between them, his head straining to avoid the beast as it tried to turn and snap. Julian felt his grip loosening as the violently twisting back and forth continued, the open jaw angling toward his head. Then, suddenly, it went limp. Danton loomed over them, blade dripping scarlet in his hand, which he plunged into the exposed white belly of the caiman again for good measure.

"Good eating," Danton commented.

Staring at Julian madly, Corinne squeezed Andrea tightly, who had been completely unaware of her close call. "Her, I no lose."

Andrea burped, then cried because of the pressure of the embrace.

Corinne repeated, "Her, I no lose. *Je suis…*" her voice trailed off. "I am so… *elle est…* safe. *Comment…* How… I not want…" Corinne shook her head. "You are hurt?"

Gasping for breath, Julian said, "Well, I hope not to have to wrestle for my dinner every night."

She managed a smile but the strange look remained in her eyes.

The river broadened, turned northward away from marshes and canebrakes. Danton's progeny continued to hinder their progress—Julian had counted twenty-three thus far—sometimes just exchanging a few pleasantries and gifts from a canoe, other times insisting on a meal that lasted deep into the evening. Johnny didn't show fear of the visitors as long as Danton held him.

Although Corinne maintained physical distance from

Julian, he would often catch her gazing at him. When he did, she'd invariably ask an inconsequential question like, "The rain, you think we have in the morning?" as if that was the purpose of her gaze. She would always begin the night sleeping beyond his reach, but often he'd awake with her curled up in her accustomed position next to him. Despite the frequent family reunions, Danton seemed increasingly wary and peered at the banks with a searching intense stare as if he wanted his eyes to pierce the dark green wall of foliage. His progeny were becoming more admonishing than cheerful. Danton was more peremptory. Often, a son paddled away angrily after apparently receiving an unsatisfactory explanation for Julian's presence.

"Why does he not betray me?" Julian asked Corinne after one such episode.

"Danton say we are his new children who need the care. Danton die before he betray the children who need the care."

Storms were usually brief afternoon affairs, although occasionally the roiling waters would necessitate that they beach the bateau, unstep the mast, and huddle underneath the canvas sail as protection from the downpour. Danton could smell a storm brewing, demonstrating this useful talent even on cloudless days.

Once, when the sky was merely a drizzly pearl gray, and Julian believed that the weather wouldn't worsen beyond an uncomfortable dampness, Danton sniffed, sneezed, and lost his composure. He steered the bateau for the shore, ordered Julian and Corinne to empty the boat, pull it into the woods, and upend it over their stores. As they lay flat in a depression covered by the sail, the wind rose, first humming, then screeching, and then roaring. A strange apparition—a huge white column of whirling mist connecting water with sky—appeared coiling down the river. Suddenly, a band of lightning shot down parallel to the column, then another and another.

"Waterspout?" Julian cried.

"Merde!" Danton responded, and the deluge struck with a thousand lances of lightning, earthshaking rolls of thunder, a wind from the vents of hell, and more rain that seemed possible for the sky to hold. Johnny buried his head in Danton's shoulders, holding his hands over his ears. Andrea sobbed buried beneath Corinne's cloak. The waterspout passed within minutes, but behind it, the river ran higher.

Later that day, a delegation of Danton's Kickapoo sons, their elongated dangling earlobes wrapped in silver wire, their faces bright vermillion, their chests tattooed with wolves, flowers, and crescent moons, met them mid-river and insisted on feting their father. They wanted to exclude Julian, but suspecting a ruse, Danton insisted he join them, claiming that Julian, Corinne, and the two children were also his family. After repairing to the council house and sharing a four-foot pipe sheathed in speckled snakeskin, the feasting and talking began. Gleefully, the braves conveyed more bad news about the war. An entire British army had been scalped after a great battle. Not only were settlers abandoning their farms but also towns were emptying as everyone filled up the boats going back across the great water.

As for Julian, where could he find refuge if his people

were gone? All the nations along the river knew he was traveling with Danton, and as soon as they passed a village where Danton had no family, his scalp would be added to the thousand others. Out of affection for their father, they offered to guide Julian to an English-speaking Tuscarora Indian who would be happy to take him to the last English ship.

"Do not give them the trust," Corinne whispered in Julian's ear.

Danton's gifts to his vermillion-faced sons of a keg of whiskey and all that remained of his dear tobacco could be taken as a payment of ransom. They set off in a drenching downpour several hours before dawn.

Two nights later, Julian woke up with a start. Corinne, Danton, and the children were missing. Glancing toward the river, he was reassured by the mast of the bateau gently rocking back and forth in the weak moonlight. Then he heard a singsong chant coming from a lone voice deep in the woods. Gathering up his tomahawk and knife, Julian headed toward the voice, and soon discerned a glow flickering through the dark silhouettes of the trees. A dozen more steps brought him to a clearing where Corinne sat cross-legged with Johnny and Andrea on her lap in front of two candles on a fallen tree, all three mesmerized by the robed Grayson who was intoning the Latin phrases of a mass. Danton, who stood just inside the shadows, caught his eye. Julian sidled up to him.

"My father priest. No trust them buggers," Danton whispered in thick English.

When the ceremony finished, Grayson approached Danton, extended a hand and said, "*D'accord.*"

"*D'accord,*" Danton grumbled. "Damn you, Priest Son-of-gray-wolf, I give you what you want—*d'accord.*"

Grayson carefully put the implements for mass back into his satchel. He kissed Corinne and the children on their foreheads. His icy gaze briefly skimmed over Julian, then in his silent way, he vanished into the pathless forest.

OLD ENEMIES

AS THE PEACEFUL beautiful days followed one after another, a dreadful certainty grew in Julian that they were being watched. Danton, apparently of the same opinion, scrutinized the banks as they floated along with barely a ripple. They scouted the campsites thoroughly and forbade campfires. He and Julian had an unspoken agreement that one of them should always be awake during the night.

Julian was unsure whether he hadn't gone to sleep out of turn when the crow's caw woke him. Drowsiness depriving him of voice, he observed as in a paralyzing nightmare the dark shape of a brave raising a palely glinting knife over him. A sudden blast from the recumbent shadow of Danton made the Indian stagger backward. Julian rolled over, grabbing his bow, just in time to see another figure skirting into the dark margin of the woods. He shot an arrow at the same time the thud of a misfiring came from the cover of the trees.

A low hoarse laugh pierced the darkness, and a familiar voice rang out: "You would not have missed five years ago, English Rat. But do not worry. You are safe now. I am alone, and my powder is wet. I invite you to come after me, so we can stalk each other through the night. You nearly succeeded in killing me once. Come, finish the job. If you refuse my offer, I return tomorrow with fifty braves, and between sunrise and sunset we will run you to the ground and murder you. Come, bring your bow, tomahawk, and knife. We've carried each other's scars too long, English Rat. Let's end this with your death or mine."

"Only a fool agrees to fight on his enemy's terms, Long Arrow," Julian replied, trying to fix the location of the voice. "When you lure me away, your braves will attack the camp."

Andrea began to whimper. Long Arrow addressed her: "Dear English child, Long Arrow promises you'll shed no tears anon."

"Yes, brave savage Long Arrow strangles babies," Julian shouted.

"You call me savage? You, an Englishman. I saw a boy of eight hanged in London for stealing a comb. Having little weight, the boy wriggled choking to death for an afternoon to the amusement of the crowd. That is savagery! Ah, I hear the woman trying to load the gun. She's not very adept at it. My dear lady, 'tis near impossible to aim at a voice. The old voyageur knows that is so because he is sitting patiently with his reloaded pistol. Old voyageur, tell English Rat that his best chance is to kill me before I bring my warriors to seal the warrants of your deaths. Come, pursue me. Fortune was always kind to you, English Rat, why distrust her now?"

A moment of silence was followed by the sound of the powder poured into the barrel then the ball inserted.

Julian let loose an arrow in the direction of the sound and lurched sideways into the nearby dark undergrowth. Corinne grabbed the two children and dragged them behind the boat. Danton ran into the undergrowth at the other end of the clearing.

"You're losing your best chance, English Rat, to live through tomorrow," he called out again. Chinkwe sleeps at my camp. He will pursue you into the far reaches of Hades for your scalp. But if you prevail, then he never will know how close he came to avenging his father; and you can live out the remainder of your days peacefully."

"When have you told the truth to an enemy, Long Arrow?" Julian shouted.

"You must pray I am telling the truth, otherwise you have no hope."

Corinne yelled in French to Danton who replied. Long Arrow began to taunt them in French.

Corinne shouted to Julian. "Julian, no listen to him. You cannot run. He can. You make the sound when you walk in the forest. He make the silence. He hunt us after he kill you. We all die if you die."

Julian backed away.

Suddenly, Danton fired into the darkness and then yelled at Long Arrow. Corinne translated. "Danton say that the three braves are clumsy and make too much noise to hide. Danton say that the one swimming using the log as cover is already the dead man." Danton reloaded his pistol and shot into a form rising wraithlike out of the water. Both Danton and Julian dashed back toward the boat. A musket ball tickled the hair on the back of his neck. Lifting the children inside, they slid the boat into the water and were off. Three musket balls whistled over them in the darkness.

"I am bringing vengeance and death to you tomorrow, English Rat," Long Arrow shouted joyfully. "Death for you and those unfortunates you love."

Bending low at the tiller, Danton angrily muttered his response translated by Corinne, claiming that he knew the river better than his mother's face and he could out-sail any damn savage paddling any damn canoe. He went on to explain that because the river was running high, he could pass through the rapids blindfolded. Beyond, they would find the river flooding the low countryside and creating a shallow lake with a maze of hundreds of islands.

When the four canoes came into view in the late afternoon, Julian had just shipped the oars, having rowed with a few breaks near fourteen hours. "Vengeance is nipping at your heels," Long Arrow yelled from a few hundred yards away.

Julian wearily picked up the oars again. Danton shouted, "*Non!*"

"Surrender?" Julian questioned angrily. The canoes were fast gaining.

"*Merde!*" Danton replied, then issued instructions in French.

Corinne shoved Johnny and Andrea under the bow, tossed Julian a rope, ordering "To the mast," then secured herself with another line to an oarlock.

The boat violently plunged forward, informing Julian as his feet slipped from underneath him that they had entered the rapids. Corinne thrust an oar in his direction, which he grabbed and, following her mimed gestures, edged forward until he was sprawled on the bow.

Bucking and squirreling, they were propelled forward. Breathing in as much water as air, Julian tried to fend the boat off the rocks with the oar, his failures resulting in reverberating cracks that threatened to shiver the hull. Slipping on her knees, Corinne bailed with an empty rum keg. Once, the bow dipped at such a steep angle that for a harrowing moment they seemed to be heading straight toward the bottom. The hull then struck a hard surface twice. The tip of the boat lifted and surged out of the water. Glancing back, Julian saw Corinne fishing Johnny and Andrea from the swamped bow compartment and Danton clasping the tiller, his eyes wide, a grin showing all of his teeth and the gaps between.

"*C'est fini!*" Danton yelled above the roar.

Julian raised sail after the rapids, giving the boat a sudden spurt despite the foot of water in the hull, which Corinne was hurriedly bailing. Andrea and Johnny were pushed back into the half-flooded bow compartment. Two of Long Arrow's canoes successfully navigated the rapids, and two others were being carried via a narrow portage path around the dangerous passage. Muskets were useless after the dousing so Long Arrow tested the distance with his bow, the arrow falling a dozen yards short.

Although sail power propelled the bateau faster than paddle could a canoe, the gap closed every time they tacked. A second arrow sliced into the water six yards away, the next three feet. At this desperate juncture, Danton suddenly lurched forward, severed the main halyard with his knife, and before the canvas had completely come down over Julian, leaped back to the tiller.

They were in the rapids again—this set longer and wilder. Julian stuffed the sail into the storage area covering Johnny who was holding onto the shrieking Andrea, then returned to his sprawled position on the bow to mitigate the violent buffeting between the rocks. Corinne continued bailing furiously, her eyes wild, her hair flying in all directions like a goddess of the wind and sea. Danton wrestled the boat holding the tiller in tight embrace to his chest, his face that of a deliriously happy madman.

They struck a rock square on, then slid over, landing sideways. The boat turned so it was going backward, then spun and hit another rock sideways, and again they found themselves bucking through the current backward. Julian tried to steer, dipping the oar into the water, bracing it against his body. The boat heeled until water rushed in over the gunwales.

Danton yelled desperately in French. Corinne screamed, "Head down!" At that moment, the boat rocketed over a falls, crashed ten-feet below into the turbulent froth, and momentarily was sucked sideways toward the cataract, but then straightened and shot forwards. Scrambling, Danton knotted the ends of the halyard together and reattached and raised the sail.

With the wind at their backs, the run was quick and easy for the first mile. Their pursuers hadn't dared navigate the cataract of the rapids. Julian joined Corinne to finish bailing, then inspected the boat for damage. The soggy wood had bent rather than split and he discovered only two small leaks. Johnny emerged from the bow compartment clamping Andrea around the middle, frightened and curious.

As Danton had predicted, the river widened, stretching over the entire landscape. An unearthly forbidding silence had taken hold of this world. A light breeze wafted them between islands that had once been hillocks, where a trapped deer or bear or baleful wolf could sometimes be glimpsed. Teetering momentarily on the dark horizon, the sun sank. As the light faded to a pale-yellow streak in the western sky, they moored the boat in a shallow cove of an islet. The air cooled rapidly. Huddling together in the hull for warmth beneath the sail and soggy bearskins, they soon were overcome by utter exhaustion.

The dense morning fog hugging the flooded countryside made it impossible to discern the bow from the stern. Nevertheless, Danton, whispering his orders, cast off, trusting the current to carry them forward. Julian leaned over the bow and signaled with his hand which way to turn whenever the branches of a half-submerged tree loomed out of the thick gray curtain, and, if necessary, fended the boat off the obstacle with the oar. Standing at the mast, Corinne relayed with her hands directions to Danton. Johnny held Andrea beneath the bearskin and rocked back and forth to comfort her. At times, there was so little sensation of motion that to reassure himself, Julian would pick a thread off his shirt, drop it into the water and watch it slowly drift toward the stern. Near midmorning, the fog began to thin in spots, the gray hinting at blue, and an orb glowing dully in the eastern sky would show itself briefly. However, before the eyes became accustomed to the weak sunlight, they'd slide again into gray blindness. In one of these clearing patches, Danton suddenly raised his forefinger to his lips. Four canoes lay among the trees of an island. Smoke rose from a fire a dozen yards inland.

As they ghosted by the camp, Andrea chose that moment to demand breakfast, her wail splitting the silence. Immediately, Long Arrow, Chinkwe, and twenty other braves ran onto the beach and began to shove the canoes into the water. Julian nocked his bow. Corinne buried Andrea beneath her blouse, giving her a breast that contained nothing but nevertheless distracting the infant. Just then, a thick fog bank swallowed them. Corinne resolved the problem of no milk by putting the corn paste on her breast. Still, it was only a matter of time before the sun burned away their foggy shroud.

Julian held his breath and prayed the boat would not become entangled in any submerged tree as they drifted. The sound of the braves paddling receded as each canoe set off into the gray wall in a different direction, although apparently not in theirs. Andrea continued to softly whimper, but perhaps could not be heard over the sounds of dripping water, birds hopping from branch to branch, and animals rustling in the undergrowth of the islets. It was easy to imagine no other human souls existed on earth.

Two thuds suddenly shook the bateau as they glided beneath the low-hanging branches of a half-submerged tree next to a temporary island. Turning around, Julian was confronted by a brave stepping toward him with a hatchet raised. Danton grappled with the second intruder. Glimpsing the bateau and figuring that it was going to pass near the small island, the braves had landed their canoe on the far side, ran across, and climbed onto the overhanging branches.

Two others, who had just missed the boat, were trying to pull themselves up the gunwales. Corinne, swearing in a torrent of French, whacked one in the face with a paddle and poked the other in the eyes.

Julian leaned in, blocked the descending arm, then caught the brave's wrist before he could swing again. The brave tried to pass the hatchet to the other hand, but Julian intercepted it. They swayed back and forth locked in their struggle, four hands grappling for the same weapon.

When the brave angled his mouth in order to bring his teeth into play, Julian recognized the contorted features of Chinkwe. "Get away!" Julian screamed as Johnny crawled onto the bow. Johnny ignored him and with a small knife Danton used for scaling fish began to stab at Chinkwe's ankles and feet.

Chinkwe lost his balance and Julian pushed him overboard. Corinne again smacked the face of an intrepid bloody brave placing a foot into the boat. Julian recovered his bow, nocked an arrow and shot through the eye the Indian trying to bite off Danton's nose. Danton dumped him overboard, exclaiming, "I salute you, Englishman!"

Julian raced to the stern and shot several arrows at the braves who were swimming toward the island. Blood swirled to the surface of the water where a brave dove to avoid Julian's arrows. Johnny stood on the bow, waving his bloody knife challenging anyone else to board while Corinne screamed at him to hide. Danton steered towards a thick gray bank, the current running faster now and collided with the canoe just emerging from the fog holding Long Arrow. Nobody had time to react except for Long Arrow whose tomahawk hit the mast.

As the canoe turned over, a brave grabbed the bateau's gunwales. Julian tore the tomahawk out of the mast and in a single movement slammed it down on the brave's hand. A cry went out and the hands slid off leaving two severed fingers.

The idea of hiding in the gray banks turned out illusory as a stiffening breeze whirled the fog away. Julian suddenly felt naked. Danton shouted at Corinne who took the tiller while he jumped forward and hoisted the sail. Close behind them, three canoes emerged from three narrow channels between the islets. Danton muttered something.

"He says, pray for more wind," Corinne yelled.

The following hours were a contest between wind power and muscle power. Sail was faster, but the wind was variable, and they had to tack several times to take full advantage of it. Difficulties arose whenever an island or a bend in the river blocked the air current. Julian would then pick up the oars and standing to gain deep enough purchase row like the devil towards a rippling patch of water. Paddling in a straight line at their disciplined even tempo, Long Arrow's braves would close the gap. Just before the boat reached a spot where the sail could do the work, Long Arrow and another brave would fire and load their muskets as fast as they could, but the distance was a challenge to the best marksman. When the sail took over the work again, Julian would rest the musket on the gunwales to steady the aim, but never had a decent shot.

The three canoes drew together. Men were transferred between the various canoes, and the one filled with the wounded braves set out for shore. Danton swore and Corinne translated. "This Long Arrow is the subtle savage. The wind no lose the strength like the arms lose the strength. Four paddle while four rest so they not far away when the wind die, then they have us by the …" Corinne paused mulling over the translation. "…throats."

"What's to be done?" Julian asked, envisioning a bloody twilight battle.

"Disparu." Danton laughed, his tangled hair, staring eyes, wide open mouth with rotting teeth making him seem like a freshly awakened river god. "Disappear," Corinne translated. "If God is merciful, he allow us to disappear."

After a freshening breeze had left the canoes a half mile back, Danton made a low guttural sound. Julian didn't realize that he was being asked a question until the mutter became louder and Corinne said, "Danton asks how far the bad foot can walk?"

"It walks just as far as my good foot," Julian replied.

"We walk the six leagues," Corinne translated what followed. "We carry the children, and we do not stop."

When a bend in the river put the canoes out of sight and blocked the wind, Danton instructed Corinne to unfasten the halyard and let down the sail. With the remaining momentum, Danton steered into a cove half obscured by an islet. Before they stopped, he was knocking out the wooden blocks that stepped the mast. Balancing Johnny and Andrea on her shoulders, Corinne waded through the water to the bank, then returned for what was left of the parched corn and pemmican. Chest deep in water, Julian and Danton tilted the boat until it flooded and sank, then they followed Corinne. The operation took only a few minutes. From the cover of dense undergrowth, with Corinne's four fingers stuffed into Andrea's gumming mouth, they observed the canoes glide by, Long Arrow carefully scanning the river and its banks. Julian felt his face burn as Long Arrow's eyes passed over the spot where they were hidden, but he did not spy them. When the canoes had disappeared behind an island, they set off.

REFUGE

HACKING WITH HIS long knife through dense undergrowth, the old voyageur led them up the slope. There was no real trail. Danton said as long as they were climbing, they were heading in the right direction, however progress was difficult, and sometimes the brush was so thick that it forced long detours. Corinne modified one of Julian's shirts into a sling to carry Andrea on her back. Julian and Danton took turns toting Johnny in a makeshift knapsack.

It was pitch-black when they reached the top of the bluff. Danton paused to study the stars, came to a decision, and they set off again following the bluff which paralleled the river. Although the going was easier, Danton only allowed brief stops. Corinne stumbled several times. Julian took Andrea who had been whimpering for the last hour. A few minutes later, Corinne reclaimed the baby. "Andrea, I carry her now," she whispered. "I have the rest I need."

Near dawn, Danton pointed down at the river and muttered his disapproval. A dozen canoes were now exploring the coves and inlets. "They find the boat soon and follow," Corinne translated. "Two leagues to the trading post. There, we are safe. They cannot attack the trading post without making the enemies of the French and the tribes who trade with the French. The young braves travel fast so we cannot rest."

Later that afternoon, they arrived scraped, dirty, and exhausted at the post, which consisted of a forty-foot square palisade and a blockhouse nestled in the river valley and surrounded by a scattering of wigwams and small houses with thatched roofs and chimneys. A few weedy gardens and irregular plots of corn and squash separated the dwellings.

The commander of the fort, a jowly irritable man with a pockmarked face, lacked the usual Gallic hospitality. He informed them that they could take any empty wigwam, but protested that he wouldn't interfere if Long Arrow demanded them. "I have eight soldiers. What can eight soldiers do against a hundred braves?"

Danton looked down his long nose at the commander and shook his head pityingly as if to say, "You are no Frenchman."

Julian was too tired to care. He experienced a momentary sensation of being back on the bateau as he laid down on the hard ground, then complete unconsciousness. During the following hours he had a vague sense of Corinne leaving his side and returning as she ministered to the needs of Andrea and Johnny. Once, she rubbed an ointment of bear grease and mint into his foot. He heard Danton arguing with the commander, whose voice had taken on a whiny quailing tone.

When he finally awoke, Corinne laid a plate of beans

and corn before him. "Danton says Long Arrow will not attack the post."

"Then, we are safe?" Julian asked with unaccountable difficulty.

She wiped her eyes, then abruptly stood and left. Julian finished the meal and went out to survey the surroundings. The post, which hosted a heterogeneous mix of peoples, was situated on a tributary of the Cherokee River. Consequently, several residents were occupying their morning fishing. Many good-naturedly greeted Julian with "*Bon jour, bon jour*" and a few heavily accented "good mornings" as they went unhurriedly about their tasks. Children scampered everywhere—their varying skin colors proving the fecundity of the intermarriage between European and native. Squaws prepared meals over outdoor fires. Braves lounged in front of their humble wigwams like kings, smoking and lazily gazing at their wives, mothers, and sisters working. A good portion of the refuse piles consisted of fish bones. Dogs ran around scavenging and begging. A family bathed naked in a pond. Three hunters slipped into the forest following three low-slung hounds. The only activity these people seemed to do with any enterprise was gossiping, as much with shrugs, nods, and raising of eyebrows as with words. Julian gathered that his party, the new arrivals, were the current topic of discussion.

Corinne appeared at his side. "I live in the village like this. Ten months of the year we are happy, two we are hungry and cold. My father call me his princess and brings me always the first new strawberries. My mother always singing." Corinne hummed then half-sang a few French words. "'Tis called 'By Moonlight.' The man asks the friend to let him in, and when he will not, the daughter does. So funny."

"Could you live here?" Julian asked.

"This is too much danger for you. Commander Anton wants to put you in the chains for you are the English. Danton says he will call all his sons together to burn the fort to the ground if Anton puts you in the chains. Anton is afraid of Danton but has the pride so he say after you rest the three days to recover the strength, then you leave. Anton make the promise to give you the guide to escort you to the Seneca nation."

"And what will happen to you?" Julian's voice showed the beginning of the ache in his heart.

"A boat goes down to Kaskaskia in five days and from Kaskaskia many boats go to New Orleans. On his honor, Anton make the promise I am delivered to the uncle's house with not a hair harmed on the head." Corinne smiled weakly.

"This is how we planned it." Julian searched her face, sensing she had more to say. The last few days on the river he had tried to ignore how beautiful she was, but now that he had to part from her, he could no longer fool himself that once again he had loved too much.

"*Oui*, just so." Corinne drew in a deep breath. "I tell the lie when I say I no remember the words I speak to you by the river at Chinoota. I only speak French and Shawnee, and I know you are the English so that is foolish to want you to understand. I am so afraid because the terrible things they do to the captives. I am so afraid because I am always the slave until Bright Flower find the way to kill me. I speak then what is in the heart. I ask you to come back, come back for me, come back after my son is born and take us both away. This is the silly thing to say. This is silly to think you understand me, and I know this never happen. Later, the good man Goram buy me. My heart still weeps for him, and I feel," she put her hands around her throat briefly. "I think no finer life than the wife to that good man. To care for him and his sons, I am willing to burn in the hell like the priest tell me, but I no have interest in the God who no understand. They are my family. Then you come. I am afraid you come for me, to take me away from the family I love. But you rescue the father and Joshua. I am so thankful, but I am still afraid you take me away."

"You were the one who decided to go with me." Corinne had started to weep and Julian longed to kiss her wet sniffling face.

"*Mais oui.* If Goram, heart of my heart, want not to choose me, then I want to see my son, Eagle Heart. I think if I go, the kind man Goram miss me so much and come for me again to marry me. And you know what is the captive. And you know I have the child, Eagle Heart. I no have to hide what I am from you. You know not the other secret: lying with a man is so too much painful. When you learn the secret you decide is better I suffer the hell for the day than the purgatory for the life." She shuddered.

"More than the pain is the shame. I hate you greater than the Shawnee White Bear who kill the father and brother. I hate you greater than Bright Flower who make me the slave. To see you is to taste bile. Still, you not leave me. I have not the surprise when Goram and Joshua die. *Mais oui*, everybody I love die. And there is talk of a bounty on me? On me?" She shook her head wonderingly. "You collect the bounty? *Non*, instead you treat me with the kindness. And all the while we talk like people who keep no secrets from each other. You risk your life to make me happy. And then... then... the terrible thing happen: I become happy with you—just being near you. Terrible for I am so afraid you die like everyone I love." She gulped and then continued, "If you can, if you can have the happiness with me, I ask you again, come back. You understand now. The war is over soon. The men who decide the war change their minds tomorrow. Come back, if you think I make you happy. I wait."

Julian looked down realizing his two hands completely covered hers, then with difficulty met her eyes. "Two armies, two angry kings, a score of savage nations on the warpath separate us. This war might last ten years. I might die on my way back and never be found. No, dearest, do not wait for me."

"You saying you cannot be happy with me." She withdrew her hands, turned but didn't walk away.

He touched her shoulder, then gently turned her around to face him. He folded her into his arms realizing again how she fit perfectly. "I love you." He felt his whole chest might burst with the sobs he was containing.

"Then come back, my Julian," Corinne insisted.

"I don't want you to suffer another loss." Julian regretted again that wisdom sounded so much like cowardice.

"That is why you must come back. The God must do this one thing for me who always try to do good. For all of the people I love and He took away from me, I want you." She glanced over her shoulder at Johnny holding Andrea in his lap by the pond. "Besides, if you not have the notice, we are now a family."

"I promise to try," Julian slowly released her, "if you promise to not wait. Marry well, and I'll do my best to keep myself alive. When the war is over, I'll visit you and your family in New Orleans if your husband allows."

"I kill him if he makes the little frown at you." She gently kissed him and whispered, "*Je t'aime.* Only you. *Je t'aime.*" She pushed him away. "Now, English trader who will not stay, go quickly."

Julian left the following morning after purchasing a horse for six Spanish dollars. He refused the guide, who being part or full Indian, might see more advantage in currying to Long Arrow's favor rather than helping an enemy of the Great King. With three weeks of hard travel, Julian could reach the Moravian mission. Rebecca would provide sanctuary, replenish his supplies, and give him the sympathy of a sister to a loved brother.

From there he'd go to Peter's village to pick up his furs then back to Charleston to wait out the war. He tried to distract his imagination with the warm solid pleasures of Charleston—the good company and strong ale of a tavern, perhaps the featherbed of a widow who last year had taken a liking to him. Warm solid pleasures which he feared would count for little. Bragg was right. Love the jealous land but nothing else overmuch. The frontier does not allow you to hold onto anything dear for long.

Corinne had learned that and so had been afraid to love him. She had failed. He had failed. Even at their first dim meeting by the river, they both had attempted to overcome the impossibility of being together. Julian could still hear the lift in her voice when she said "Julian"—as if she was declaring, "je t'aime" with the same breath. At least one wouldn't have to grieve over the other's grave. Better to ally your hopes and affections to mad dreams like Bragg.

Deep in these thoughts, Julian didn't notice the quieting of the woods before it was too late. He pulled up as a large band of horsemen suddenly galloped out of the forest and surrounded him.

"You don't appear pleased to see yer old friend." Uriah rode up, his long face grinning, showing the dirty black stubs of teeth. Long scraggly hair hid the severed ear. His eyes still had their intelligent malicious gleam. As always, he kept the freshest scalp tied to a ring on the end of his knife, believing it brought him good luck like his boots made from the skin of an Ottawa sachem or the tiny human skull he wore on his necklace. His forty or so companions, many wearing mementos of their butchery, watched and hopefully fiddled with their knives and tomahawks. "We was aiming to scalp you, only then I says to myself just in time, well, isn't that Julian Pale Otter."

"I'm surprised to see you this far out," Julian said. He had crossed paths with Uriah a dozen times over the past five years. The meetings were tense, but Uriah, aware that Julian was under Molly Brant and Resurrection Peter's protection, always stated on parting, "Give my regards to Mister Johnson. Report to him how I am advancing the cause of the English nation." That was a lie, of course. Uriah didn't particularly care whom he scalped—French, Indian, or English—for both sides paid. He often traded scalps to intermediaries who, in turn, traded them to Indians allied with the French who collected the bounties. This couldn't be proven because he was thorough in his slaughter. Although not particular about his victims, Uriah was useful in spreading panic and chaos wherever he did his business.

Studying Julian, Uriah reached out a hand and yanked a lock of his hair—a particularly terrifying gesture for those familiar with his reputation. "Surprised, you say. That's also what struck me. What possible explanation could Julian Pale Otter have for business in these parts?"

"My business is leaving these parts as fast as I can, Uriah."

"Well, we're after the contrary. A little French trading post ripe for the picking lies yonder. For our love of King George and the English cause we figured on paying them a visit. Want to come along and share in the spoils?"

"You know me, Uriah. With my crooked foot, I'd just be in the way. I probably get myself killed, and then you'd scalp me to add to your bounty." Julian was careful to appear unafraid.

"Just so. Why let the hair on a dead body go to waste? But we'd give you a Christian burial, which is more than most traders get out here."

"I thank you for your thoughtfulness, but the sooner I'm out of this god-forsaken country, the better I'll feel." When Julian tried to spur his horse on, Uriah blocked him.

"You still is not answering my question. What are you doing so near a French post in the first place?"

"Courting," Julian replied. "And I'm not telling you

who and where she is for I prefer my Injun wife with a full head of hair."

Uriah shook his head. "Is that so? I'll suss her out just to take a peek after we finish with the post. Blue Dove were the prettiest savage I ever laid my eyes on. I don't understand why you left her with her scalp after she had no use for it. That's just the way I think, which some find odd. I imagine your new squaw is also a looker. Still, you're passing up a profitable opportunity. Upwards of a hundred and fifty bounties, not to mention whatever they have on their persons and in their homes and storehouses."

SURRENDER

ON SEEING JULIAN approach on foot, the women working in the fields started their shrill ululations. Children ran yelling through the village spreading the news. The whoops and shouts of the strong voices of the braves echoed off the hills and summoned all within hearing. By the time Julian reached the gate, Long Arrow and Chinkwe stood in front of it with a dozen warriors, blocking his entrance. Several hundred Indians crowded and pushed Julian from the back and sides. Julian noticed a notch in Long Arrow's septum where he had pulled out the nose ring and the dozen puncture wounds in Chinkwe's foot. A brave with a heavily wrapped hand clumsily loaded and primed a musket.

"I need your help, Long Arrow," Julian said, putting down his tomahawk and rifle. The crowd fell quiet.

"And why would I help you, English Rat?" Long Arrow's face registered no expression.

Julian replied in Lenape. "You want revenge. I'm surrendering myself so you can have it on me, but I am asking a price."

Long Arrow smirked. "Why would I pay this price when 'tisn't necessary to do so?"

"Because I deliver another enemy into your hands. Uriah, the man who trades in scalps, will attack the French trading post. I want you to send your warriors to protect the post."

"This has the stink of a trap," Chinkwe protested, raising his war club, but Long Arrow stayed his arm.

"Why would I use myself to bait the trap?" Julian replied, holding out his palms. "I know well what you will do to me. I do not hate myself so much as to submit to your tortures if there was another way to stop Uriah."

"You cannot imagine what we will do to you," Long Arrow promised. "A dozen here from Mankita have scores to settle with you."

"I expect no mercy. Will you send your warriors to stop Uriah?"

Long Arrow drew out his knife and examined it as if he were looking for flaws in the metal. "Why do you hate Uriah so? He is English. He is a fine warrior for your king. You could fill our council house to the roof with the scalps he has harvested." Long Arrow regarded Julian curiously. "I know the answer. 'Tis to save the woman and the children. But the woman and children are not yours."

"Will you send the warriors?" Julian clenched his fists.

"I think I cut your throat first." Long Arrow spat on the blade and wiped it on Julian's cheek.

Julian grabbed his wrist. "Do to me what you will after you stop Uriah."

Long Arrow pulled his arm away. "I am not war sachem here. We will call a council."

"There's not enough time for a council," Julian insisted.

"War is a serious business and requires deliberation, but maybe when I tell the young braves about Uriah, they will be eager to get underway. You are now a traitor, English Rat. When I was in England, I saw a traitor executed. Hanged, taken down while still alive, drawn, his entrails taken out and burned before his eyes. We could not have done it better. Maybe, I'll give you English justice."

"Please, send your warriors," Julian begged.

"As you wish, English Rat, in due time," Long Arrow replied in English.

The meeting was brief, the fierce words reverberating well beyond the council house. Afterward, Long Arrow explained to Julian as he was trussed to a horse: "Some braves said we shouldn't trust you, English Rat. But I, your sworn enemy, told them that I never knew you to lie or deceive. I told them if you deceive us, the woman, the children, and the old man will die before your eyes in the most painful way possible."

When Long Arrow arrived with his eighty warriors, Uriah's raiding party had set fire to all the houses and wigwams and were now scattered throughout the smoky devastation busily scalping both the living who were screaming and the dead. From the palisades came a few blasts of gunfire, but the besieged were obviously conserving their powder. Uriah's raiders could deal with those inside at their leisure by waiting for the night, then smoking the defenders out and cutting them down. Profit couldn't be made from a burned scalp.

Hands bound and tied to the reins, Julian accompanied Long Arrow's party. While Long Arrow studied the scene, Julian forced himself to scan the dead for Corinne, Johnny, Andrea, and Danton, although he doubted that he could recognize them in the mangled state of most of the corpses. Expecting the worst, he at first missed Danton who, very much alive, was barricaded with a pistol and a cutlass behind a small beached pirogue outside the palisades. The corpses of two of Uriah's men were sprawled in front of him. The attackers carefully stayed out of his line of fire. Downriver a small party was crossing and would soon be able to attack Danton from the cover of the other shore.

Long Arrow gave a grunt of satisfaction. "English Rat, I am grateful to you. This is truly a magnificent day." His whoop was followed by eighty others that echoed throughout the small river valley. The band of warriors fired their muskets first, then lowering their lances, they swept down into the carnage of the battlefield.

Most of Uriah's men didn't realize what was happening. They looked up from their bloody tasks amazed to discover a lance piercing them or the tomahawk crashing through their skulls. Only Uriah and a few others had the presence of mind to fight back. They were soon dispatched except for Uriah who stood in a pool of blood, grinning and swinging his cutlass like a demon. Long Arrow stopped a brave who had leveled a reloaded musket. It would be an undeserved mercy to kill him outright.

Uriah's long deadly arms precluded an easy capture. After first directing his warriors to surround Uriah holding clubs and flaming torches, Long Arrow rolled a smoldering log into the circle, then another and another. Uriah rushed his tormentors swinging his cutlass but they beat him back with a hundred blows from their clubs. He threw down the cutlass and tried to pick up the burning logs and heave them, but he could not hold on with his blistering and blackening arms and hands. Screaming, he would drop the log, pick it up again and drop it again. In the choking smoke, the screams turned into hoarse barks. Skillfully, Long Arrow directed the braves to roll away logs that were burning too hot and even throw pails of water on the fire to prolong Uriah's torment.

When Uriah lay finally writhing in the embers, the flesh on his cheek, chest, and legs having peeled away to the bone, Long Arrow told his warriors to clear a path through the ashes. He strode forward, pulled aside his breechcloth and urinated on Uriah, then grabbed a clump of his hair, lifted and turned his head to make sure his victim got a good look at his tormentor out of the one eye that wasn't burned, and with slow deliberation hacked away at the top of the skull to take that with the scalp.

Corinne stumbled out of the fort with Johnny and Andrea. When she saw Julian, she sprinted towards him. Long Arrow, still holding the bloody top of Uriah's head, stepped in front of her. He pointed to Julian's tied hands. "He is mine."

Julian ached to hold her, but merely said, "I came back."

She hurled herself at Long Arrow's feet and pointed to herself. "*Moi aussi.*"

"No, lady," Long Arrow said, pushing her away. "Not you. I keep my word."

Corinne fell to her knees hugging the children and whispering, "*Moi aussi! Moi aussi!*"

PIT OF FEAR

JULIAN WAS TIED to a post in front of the council house. Rewarded by the grateful Commander Anton with ten kegs of brandy and all the scalps of the enemy, the victorious warriors had started their celebration. Several French traders had tagged along to participate in the festivity and to entertain themselves with the torture of Julian along with four of Uriah's men who had the misfortune to be captured. Two of the captives were being sported with now—their echoing screams showing the progress of the erasure of their humanity.

Julian had hoped the noble gesture of sacrificing his life for those he loved would lessen his dread, however as he listened to the shrieks of Uriah's men, he lost heart. Only fools didn't realize the virtues of cowardice. The courageous conquered the world, but the children of cowards populated it. Soon, Long Arrow would demand payment in full in the currency of pain. Julian would be turned into a mindless howling creature that would, if it could, sacrifice his immortal soul for a moment of relief. Better and stronger men than him died thus.

Julian tried to bring to mind the face of Blue Dove. If there were a just god, he would join her. But he couldn't hold on to her image. He yearned for Corinne and hated her for the life she would have because of his sacrifice. He yearned futilely, yet felt pride that he had saved her. The pride, however, seemed a small thing compared to the bitter regret for the pain he would soon suffer.

Then he heard Lady Gertrude's voice: "Look at my face honestly, English Rat. Don't turn away." Julian saw clearly her visage, half angel and half demon. "My face is life, English Rat," the image comforted and kissed him. "I will help you bear this trial." Was her face wholly beautiful now as she sat in the heavenly longhouse drinking out of the Frenchman's skull with her people? Julian regretted not looking enough at the comely half of her face.

Julian then recalled an odd conversation with Bragg who stated that he suspected that when you died you were united with your last thought forever. "That's where I think our Heavenly Lord gets us," he mused one night before a campfire. "Good people think of a choir of angels or God's glorious light. As for me, I think me last thought will probably be that the venison smelled a little wormy or, God's blood, me toenail hurts. To tell the truth, I'd prefer me final thought be 'Darling, let's do it again.'" Julian did not hold much hope that his final thought would be pleasant.

"See, he is still alive," a quiet voice interrupted these ruminations.

"Aye," a brasher voice replied. "And I'd wager he's planning what his last thought will be."

Julian opened his eyes. Grayson and Bragg stood

before him. Grayson, as usual, seemed a mist in a man's form about to vanish. Bragg was stouter, grayer, and with a more sardonic cast of face. Seven solemn Indians with tall feathered crests running down the middle of their shaved heads stood behind Bragg.

"You? How did you get here?" Julian asked.

Grayson took the question as addressed to him. "Why do people always ask me how I go from one place to another? I travel the same way as everyone else does: on my two feet." Then the priest, looking shifty and shy at the same time, inquired, "Master Julian, I don't suppose in the hour of your death you'd accept the true church of the Holy Father?"

Julian shook his head.

"Well, I fear you haven't time enough left in your life for me to persuade you of your errors. I have many children of the living God to bury at the post." Grayson made the sign of a cross and walked out of the gate, not even a dog noticing his departure.

Long Arrow now strode forward with a dozen braves and started to cut the cords. "English Rat, 'tis your turn."

"Just be waiting a minute now, Mr. Long Arrow," Bragg said, waving a paper. "He be me property. I have the contract of his indenture here. You cannot be taking away me property."

With narrowed eyes, Long Arrow looked on Bragg. "Ah, only he made a deal. He gave his word that if we saved the French post, we could take his life in whatever manner we please."

Bragg heaved up his chest to make himself look bigger. "He had no right to offer you a deal for what is not belonging to him. His body don't. Nor do the words which coming out of the mouth of his body belong to him. I was paying good money for him: body, mouth, word, and all."

Long Arrow's features relaxed. He shook his head, amused. "Out of respect to the delegation of the Lakota that accompany you, a courageous nation with whom we are anxious to make an acquaintance, we're not including you in the entertainment. Be satisfied with that."

"What is you having against me?" Bragg infused his voice with outrage. "When you catched t'other traders, you got all your furs back. I wasn't stealing a rat's tail from you. I even left me servant who if you was treating well would have rendered good service to your village even unto this day. I want to present me case to the council."

"You forget Seksu died at your hand. We are not calling a council meeting because you think you own this man. Come, English Rat." Long Arrow finished cutting the rawhide strips. "Payment is due."

Long Arrow led him to a clearing where the tribe had their outdoor feasts and entertainments. They had not yet removed the bodies of Uriah's men—three corpses missing various parts, and a blackened body still issuing moans. Bragg accompanied Julian and in his usual stentorian manner made his case to the gathered tribe. "You know me, your parents know me and even some of your grandparents remember when I first came among you…" What followed was a long history of his acquaintance with the Lenape, with the Mingo, with the Ottawa. The gathered tribe, averse to interrupting a speaker, listened politely. Julian couldn't see the purpose to this speech except to delay the inevitable. Guests or no guests, they weren't going to leave out the main event of the evening.

Finally, interrupting, Long Arrow addressed the crowd. "'Tis true that the noble Lakota warriors are our guests, but does a guest tell his host what to do? 'Tis also true that Bragg has traded with us a long time and as a result of our long acquaintance we all know that this Bragg carries an extra bladder filled with words." A titter ran through the hundreds assembled. "I owe the English Rat a death. For more than two winters we treated him as one of us. He ate the game we killed and the corn we harvested. He was kept warm by our fires. He was protected by our warriors. He shared a blanket with my sister. In return, he stole from us and killed our braves. Where is Chinkwe's father? Where is Flowers-by-the-spring's brother? He deserves many times over this death." Long Arrow turned to Bragg and smiling said, "I will concede this to show our goodwill: since you own the body, you can have it after we are done. That way you cannot claim we denied your request."

There were more titters. Long Arrow's reply served Bragg right for his long-winded speech.

Master Bragg called out in a strange tongue and his seven warriors gathered around him. He conferred with them, then addressed the people. "I deal not in hairpieces, and I deal not in hides, so his body is having no value for me. Death will own him, and I cannot be bargaining with death. I will lose the silver I paid for him. Yet, I am now claiming me right to draw the first blood, for he has been a most wayward servant, and I don't want you depriving me of the last opportunity to punish him. When you see his blood on my knife, he is yours to use as you please."

This compromise was agreed upon, in part to no longer delay the night's entertainment.

Four Lakota warriors surrounded Julian. Bragg whispered, "Be giving them a pleasing show, lad," and then grabbed his ear and sliced off its lobe. "That don't count," he called out grinning. "I did it too fast to get blood on me knife."

Laughter rippled through the gathering. The Lakota warriors raised their clubs. One struck Julian on the shoulder. As Julian retreated, another brave hit him in the stomach. Covering his face, this batting back and forth went on for a while. The blows were hard, but not so hard as to make him stumble. The audience appreciated the warriors' restraint so as not to exhaust Julian too early. Bragg then produced a hatchet, and the Lakota braves withdrew. Bragg made a swipe at Julian, barely missing him.

"Run, you little toad," Bragg snarled and began to chase Julian around and around. It looked comical because of Julian's bad foot and Bragg's great belly made the awkward flight and lumbering pursuit absurd. The audience was delighted with the show. Although Julian did move fast despite his choppy stride, Bragg could have easily cornered and butchered him. It occurred to Julian that maybe Bragg was going to do him the favor of a swift death. So be it. Better to end it all now. As he slowed, Bragg lunged and tackled him. Pressing his lips to his wounded ear, he whispered, "They be needing more laughing, lad, more after laughing, then we can be washing ourselves of them."

Julian couldn't make sense of Bragg's words. He seemed to be conveying a plan, but no plan could save him. Bragg began to caricature a war dance complete with rhythmic chanting, punctuated by blood-curdling yells and clumsy slices at the air with his hatchet. The laughter grew. Julian, not quite sure why he should give the pleasure of mockery to people gathered to see him suffer, began to quake as if with fear. At the same time, he stretched his mind to figure out Bragg's communication. "Wash up? Why talk about washing up?" It was like putting together a puzzle while running a race. Julian then noticed how odd it was that the Lakota Indians were standing in the crowd facing him in a double file three deep.

Bragg grabbed a torch and yelled, "I am setting you on fire, so I be taking yer life without drawing blood. What think you of that? Burn you so badly you be needing to cool off." He briefly singed Julian's back. Julian screamed and began to run, Bragg chasing him swinging the flaming torch wildly. "Be a mite thirsty. I'll quench it with fire. Fire! fire! Be making you into a human torch you dull-witted gallumpus."

The onlookers were convulsed with the hilarity of the scene. Bragg did another war dance and chant, and he truly looked like a demon with his sweaty reddened face and wild hair. "Save yourself!" He yelled and swung the torch.

Unexpectedly, at the height of the craziness of it all, the impossible happened: Julian understood.

Julian veered towards the Lakota warriors, then slipped between the double file pursued by Bragg. There was still an air of jollity as he raced in the direction of the river, pursued by Bragg waving the torch and doing an Indian war dance, flanked on both sides by the Lakota warriors and, a dozen paces behind them, followed by the people of the village.

"Big canoe," Bragg yelled. Julian leaped into a dugout canoe obviously larger than the others. Bragg tumbled in. The now seven Lakota warriors pushed off and jumped on. For a moment, perhaps a third of the village was still laughing, a third staring dumbfounded, and a third running back for their weapons. A minute later other canoes were launched, but a few yards into the stream, they foundered and began to sink.

"By the time they patch the holes, we be ten miles up the river," Bragg said, breathing hard and offering Julian a fistful of cobweb for his ear.

"I thank you kindly for saving my life." Julian held the cobweb to his ear, amazed to be still alive.

Bragg slapped his back. "No need, boy. I am always insisting on debts to meself paid. You are owing me nine years still, and I aim to get every single day out of you."

"You put your life at risk in order to make me work to the end of my indenture?" Julian asked, incredulous. "I thank you, sir, yet my gratitude won't extend so far as being your servant for nine years. You abandoned me in the first place. I can pay you for those years, then twice over for my life."

"Bah, as a matter of fact, you can't. Under law, you owe me one month for every week you were away. Nine years, four hundred fifty weeks means four hundred fifty months, which would be thirty-eight years dropped on top of the nine. That is quite a valuable term of labor. I think, by then, I'll have squeezed every ounce of good work out of your poor carcass."

"I didn't run away," Julian said. "You abandoned me to certain death."

"Not so certain that I didn't have to rescue you a second time from certain death, so in regards to that, we're square."

"No court in the colonies will enforce my indenture," Julian argued.

Bragg chuckled. "Heard of me lately doing business in the colonies, much less attending to the blather in courts? Nay, lad, I be just fiddling with you. 'Tis not me intention for you to be hanging like a millstone around me neck, planning your escape. Nay, I am selling you to a buyer."

"A buyer? I'm not worth anything to anybody except to Long Arrow."

"Arrah now, 'tisn't true." Bragg's eyes gleamed with self-satisfaction. "I struck a hard bargain. I told the cock-eyed priest that I'd save you from your own foolery of somehow making every savage on this river after your scalp if he promised to build a church in me new country. Every country is needing a church."

"Grayson bought me?" The conversation was making less and less sense.

Bragg wasn't finished with the jest. "I wouldn't be saying that. He was the middleman so to speak. He fetched me because your real buyer offered to confess his sins if I was saving you. Strange notion the priest has of a trade. But I also happen to owe a long outstanding debt to your buyer, which he agreed to cancel."

"That could only be Danton. What is your debt to Danton?" Julian asked.

"You may be familiar with the name—Jacques Dugard."

"I'm familiar with the name, of course. You're Jacques Dugard."

"Am I?" Bragg replied. "Am I not denying it to you and everyone else making that foolish accusation? I'm Irish—you hear not the Irish chords in me voice—yet your perplexity is not altogether unwarranted. This notorious pirate Dugard did loan me a ship and a crew and his name a while back, and he is wanting you in payment the cause being this French wench, which he says is like a daughter to him, can't live without this bloody damn lame Englishman, which be you."

At this point, they paddled around a bend and came to a cove where Johnny and Andrea sat splashing in a few inches of water. Danton stood behind the children with his arm around Corinne.

"As I promised you Jacques," Bragg called out to Danton. "Me debt to you is paid in full."

Danton held up his hand. Corinne waded towards the canoe, her face shining with tears.

The slim figure of the priest emerged from the forest to collect his payment.

If you have enjoyed this book, please
take the time to write a review:
https://www.amazon.com/review/create-
review/?channel=reviews-product&asi
n=B08ZJMLNWJ&ie=UTF8&

For free stuff including:

CHAPTER MINUS ONE: HOW THE SCHOLAR
STEPHEN ASHER COURTED THE HARLOT KATE

and

THE STORY OF THE PIRATES BARTHOLOMEW
BRAGG, JACQUES DUGARD AND
THE GOVERNOR'S DAUGHTER
(This is password protected because it contains
a spoiler. The password is free stuff.)

Visit my website: www.jamesshort.me
and go to MY FICTION PAGE

Twitter:
James Short
@JAMESSH35099520

Made in the USA
Middletown, DE
26 November 2022

15997205R00235